TAKE AND GIVE

AMANDA G. STEVENS

TAKE AND GIVE

HAVEN SEEKERS BOOK THREE

TAKE AND GIVE
Published by David C Cook
4050 Lee Vance View
Colorado Springs, CO 80918 U.S.A.

David C Cook Distribution Canada
55 Woodslee Avenue, Paris, Ontario, Canada N3L 3E5

David C Cook U.K., Kingsway Communications
Eastbourne, East Sussex BN23 6NT, England

ISBN 978-1-4347-0866-3
eISBN 978-1-4347-0805-2

The Team: John Blase, Renada Thompson, Karen Athen, Susan Murdock
Cover Design: Nick Lee
Cover Photo: Shutterstock

Printed in the United States of America
First Edition 2015

1 2 3 4 5 6 7 8 9 10

07152015

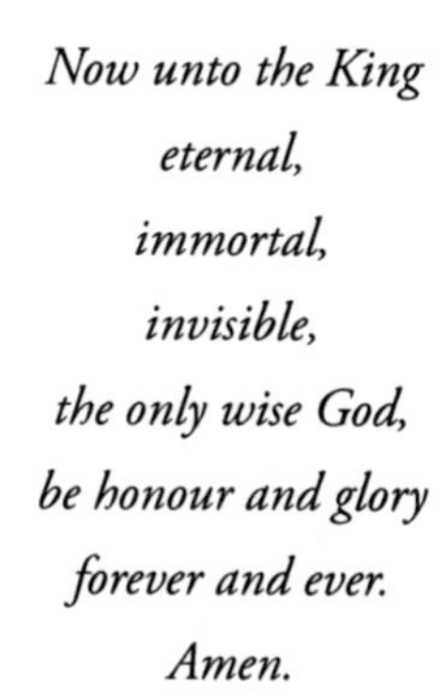

Now unto the King

eternal,

immortal,

invisible,

the only wise God,

be honour and glory

forever and ever.

Amen.

1 Timothy 1:17, King James Version

[. . .]

Whereas the behemoth of federal power has forgotten the responsibility that it carries to protect the liberties and autonomy of every citizen;

Whereas a corrupt federal government, drunk on control, has invaded our state, our police, and our people's last refuge of liberty—the freedom of thought in their own minds;

[. . .]

Whereas these actions constitute a direct attack on the sovereignty of our state and of our people;

Therefore, let it be known that we, the State of Texas, hereby reject the power of the Federal State and will henceforth no longer be subject to the authority of the United States of America;

Therefore, let it be known that we, the State of Texas, hereby reestablish our independence as the Sovereign State of the Republic of Texas.

[excerpts, Republic of Texas, Declaration of Sovereignty]

1

The footsteps behind her made no attempt at stealth. Lee picked up her pace across the parking garage. *Don't look back. Get to your car.* Her left hand renewed its grip on her purse, her right on the slim Mace dispenser.

"Can you help me?"

The voice behind her was male and, of course, sounded desperate. She lengthened her strides. His kept pace. Her pulse pounded in her head. If she ran, would he chase? Would he grab her hair, her jacket, yank her head back …?

She raised her right arm to level the Mace and pivoted to face her pursuer.

The man halted and raised one hand in the universal sign of surrender. He held a girl, six or seven years old, perched on his arm. Both her hands pressed a blood-soaked towel to her forehead, and the collar of her white polo bore a stain.

"Please," the man said.

Lee lowered her arm but kept the Mace in hand. A quick glance around the garage revealed no one else, but he could have a partner lying in wait somewhere. Except that the blood on the towel was real. The girl was bleeding.

Untrimmed hair screened the man's green eyes. "You're a nurse? I saw your scrubs and I thought … I mean, I hoped …"

She exhaled the last of the adrenaline and slid the Mace back into her purse. "The emergency entrance isn't far."

He shook his head. "We can't go to the hospital."

"If you don't have insurance, there are—"

"No, it's not that, it's—"

"Dad? My hand's getting tired." No whine in that small, high voice. Not even a plea, simply a statement of fact. The girl glanced from her father to Lee with wide brown eyes.

"May I take a look?" Lee motioned to the girl, and she lowered the towel.

Blood filled the inch-long laceration over her right eyebrow. In the second Lee stepped closer, a drop trickled toward the girl's eye. She swiped it away.

"How long ago did this happen?" Lee set her thumb and forefinger on either side of the gash. It was gaping.

"About an hour ago." The wobble in the man's voice echoed off their concrete surroundings. "I tried to take care of it, but it keeps on bleeding."

"She needs stitches."

His pallor grew sharper than his daughter's. If they had insurance, then what …? Certainty bloomed in Lee's mind, one sluggish petal at a time. She should have realized immediately.

"The paperwork would be problematic," she said.

The man took a step back, then another. As if an added foot of distance would save him, should Lee choose to take out her cell phone and call the Constabulary.

"You're a Christian."

His daughter's hand slipped on the towel. He pressed his free hand to her head. "Her mother could take her in and sign the paperwork, but she's not home, and … I can't."

Interesting marriage they must have. Raised in such a home, the girl had probably heard the tales of Jesus Christ alongside those of some other religion. Or had her parents agreed that faith was a forbidden topic? Not that it mattered.

"All right," she said.

"You can help? I thought maybe a nurse would have … I don't know, bandages? In your car, for emergencies?"

The conversation couldn't continue here. Lee wasn't the only nurse getting off shift right now. The girl shivered and leaned against her father's shoulder, a heat-seeking reflex against the October chill. He must have forgotten her jacket.

Lee stripped off her own jacket and draped it around the girl. "I can help you, but there are stipulations."

The man nodded. "I brought three hundred dollars. Cash."

"I can't do the procedure here. You'll have to come with me and not ask questions."

His mouth drew down, and he shifted his daughter's weight to his other arm. "Follow you, you mean?"

"No."

Sam would have to drive them all. They could blindfold the man to protect their route. Still … he'd see too much. Figuring out Lee's "person of interest" status wouldn't be difficult.

Too much risk.

But so was driving them in her car.

"I'll drive," she said. "You'll be blindfolded."

"Blindfolded?"

Seconds ticked down to a detonation, the moment someone who knew her—or even someone who didn't—exited that elevator and noticed them, the parent of a bleeding child arguing with a woman in scrubs. They would be memorable.

"It's necessary."

"I don't even know you, and you want me to leave my car here and—"

"You know I'm a medical professional who hasn't called the Constabulary, even though you confessed to a philosophical misdemeanor. You'll be returned to your car."

"I …"

"Make a decision," she said.

Tears flooded his eyes. *Please remain calm.*

His free hand swiped at his face. "Okay, we'll come with you. God answered my prayer, so I won't question His answer."

She was the answer to no one's prayers. But debating the point would be counterproductive, so she led the man to her car. She unlocked her car and motioned them both into the backseat.

"Sit on the floor."

Now she needed a blindfold. She grabbed a spare scrub top from her trunk and folded it into a long strip, tucking in the short sleeves.

On the far side of the garage, an elevator chimed and opened. Lee ducked her head into the car and held out the scrub top. He tied it over his eyes.

She always parked in the security camera's blind spot, not that it constituted hiding. Agent Mayweather could and likely did send a Constabulary car through the garage once a day to note her presence. Until now, her tiny parking rebellion had been futile.

The man's voice came up from the floor behind her as she backed out of the parking space. "My name's Gary. My daughter is Piper."

"I can't tell you my name."

"I understand that. And I'm thankful it was you who came out of that elevator."

Lee swiped her ID card at the exit and pulled out into traffic. Oh. Sam. She dug her phone from her purse and sent a text.

Off hook tonight, ttyl.

She had never canceled his driving her to the clinic before. Hopefully, he would understand and not show up at their meeting place a block from the hospital. The only part of her text he'd be familiar with was *ttyl*, their code for "no trouble."

Quiet infused the car. Lee drove west to the highway, then north. "Piper, how old are you?"

"Seven."

"How are you feeling?"

"My head hurts."

"Are you dizzy?"

"No."

Excellent sign. Lee eased her grip on the wheel. "How did you hurt your head?"

An extra second of silence. Unusual. Children her age enjoyed recounting drama.

"We were at the park, and she fell off the monkey bars," Gary said.

Lee glanced reflexively in the rearview mirror, which showed her only an empty backseat. Something in his voice made her wish she could see his face.

"Would it be okay for me to call you a name?" Piper's voice lowered. "I mean, a pretend name, since it's not okay to know your real name."

"Of course."

"Okay. Nurse Rebecca."

"Fine."

"Did I guess right?"

Ah, a strategy. And so subtle. Lee's mouth twitched. "No."

"Then … Nurse Taylor."

"Piper," Gary said.

"It's fine." Lee dipped a nod, though they couldn't see her. "If you guess correctly, you'll have earned the knowledge."

"So you'll tell me? If I'm right?"

"I will."

Piper lobbed names for the rest of the thirty-five-minute drive, which would have been twenty-five minutes without Lee's backtracking to avoid a tail. Not that she ever sensed one, but with a passenger in the car who would, if questioned, admit to his Christian faith—normal caution wasn't enough. Piper's voice remained coherent, so the blood loss wasn't becoming dangerous, and worse injuries than hers frequently waited longer in the ER waiting room.

When random name guesses failed her, Piper tried alphabetical order. Amy. Brittany. Cassie. Dora. Emily. At L, Lee tensed, but Piper said "Laura."

Lee pulled onto Indian Trail as Piper guessed "Wendy." The car's right front tire bumped over an eroded hole in the dirt road. Too many of them to evade. Piper didn't yelp, though, simply said, "Ow."

Lee pulled up the gravel driveway then behind the dilapidated house—dilapidated from the outside, anyway. She parked in the pole barn alongside Violet's little blue Ford, though behind the house might have been hidden enough.

"Gary, I'll ask you to keep the blindfold on for another minute."

"Whatever you want."

Lee rounded the car to help both of them. When she lifted Piper, a drop of blood ran down the girl's face from under the saturated towel. Lee set her on her feet.

"Still not dizzy?"

"No, but it hurts, though."

The simplest way to guide Gary to the back door was to set his hand on her arm. She tried to picture him as a patient, blind and feeble. The image eased the stiffness from her back as he lightly held her elbow. They made their way over the uneven lawn with Piper a few steps ahead of them.

Lee opened the door, motioned Piper inside, brought Gary in, and shut it again. Warmth wrapped around her.

"All right, Gary," she said.

He pulled the scrub top down so that it hung around his neck. His eyes roamed every visible corner, and a breath of satisfaction seeped into Lee. No one who drove past the rundown, vacant home would speculate it housed a black-market medical practice. The interior layout betrayed itself as a house, but with the three white-sheeted beds and the counter against the far wall bearing rows of instruments, it must look like a field hospital. Normally, *walk-in clinic* described it better. Lee would replace the carpets with tile, maybe remodel in other ways as well, if she could risk hiring a … contractor.

Thought trails always betrayed her. She truncated this one and motioned Piper toward the nearest patient bed. "Sit, please. I'll be right back."

Gary nodded, continuing to absorb his surroundings. His mouth still crimped with worry for his child but now interest widened his eyes.

Please refrain from touching anything.

Lee hurried down the hallway, toward the kitchen-turned-pharmacy and the sound of running water. "Violet?"

"Hey, back here. Belinda brought me over a little early. She had some weaving class or something. I'm going to change the Cidex, and I think we need to order some—"

"I have a patient."

Violet's blonde head turned from the sink. "Mr. Donnelly? He's early."

"She's seven years old, gaping forehead wound. I need to stitch her."

"But how did Sam know about her?" Violet's gaze darted over Lee's shoulder. "Wait a minute."

"Sam hadn't arrived yet."

"You didn't drive your car, *your* actual car."

"There wasn't an alternative."

"You brought a patient? In your car?"

"Violet."

"You know this kid?"

"No."

Violet slammed off the faucet. "Good grief, Lee."

Lee unslung her purse from her shoulder and set it on the counter. She grabbed her keys and found the one for the cabinet locks. Being robbed by a roving junkie was hardly likely out here, where corn and soybean fields spread out on the other side of the dirt road. No sense in taking chances, though.

She took a packaged PC needle and suture thread from the lower shelf, a syringe from the upper. "If you'd like to assist me, you can draw up the Lidocaine and epinephrine."

Violet blinked, reached for the towel. "If?"

Lee gathered the items and returned to her patient. Her tone had been too barbed. But Violet had no right to question Lee's decisions.

"I think it's bleeding a little less," Gary said as Lee entered the living-room-turned-treatment-room. He held the towel to Piper's head, and she braced her chin with one hand.

From over Lee's shoulder, Violet's voice came with a smile. "Hi, I'm the medical assistant."

Piper's wilting posture straightened, and her eyes brightened. "Hi. What's your name?"

"Um …"

"No guessing this time," Gary said.

Violet handed Lee the syringe. "Lidocaine and epinephrine."

Her hand closed around the tool of her trade. She would make this child well. "Thank you."

A shudder ran down Piper's body. Gary's hand shifted on the towel, and he met Lee's eyes over the top of Piper's head. "Needles scare her a little, but she's pretty brave about it."

Lee nodded. "I'm sure she is."

"And I tell her, needles are even less scary when you're older."

Not for everyone.

This memory was a fist that knocked the breath from her chest. He was there. Standing right in front of her. Callused hands and brown eyes, shoulders straining T-shirt seams, unflinching in the face of anything except needles. Knocking on her door and dripping blood through her hallway to the bathroom first-aid kit.

"No hospital. Just tape it up."

Lee blinked, and the room refocused. Gary's smile was beginning to flatten into uncertainty. Only a moment could have passed.

"That is often the case," Lee said.

"I hope so." Piper gave a long sigh.

Lee's fingers had spasmed around the syringe. She willed them to loosen and removed the towel from Piper's head. She funneled her thoughts, focused them. Procedure. Simple interrupted sutures.

Piper cried at the local injection, but she didn't fight or scream. Lee irrigated the wound with saline and opened the PC needle, already threaded. She'd used several of these in the last week or so, more than usual. She'd have to add them to the supply order.

As always, suturing calmed her. The care in each stitch, the resistance and then give in the skin, the needle pushing through and pulled out.

Violet gauzed away the blood and smiled at Piper. "So, what's your favorite subject in school?"

"Reading. And science."

"Yeah? I like science, too. Especially the ocean."

Piper's eyes followed Violet's hands as they gauzed more blood, but she didn't fidget. Soon Lee was tying off the last stitch then stepping back from her work.

"The scarring should be minimal."

"It's all done?" Piper's voice quavered.

"It is, and you were brave. Keep it dry, all right?"

"I promise."

The rattle of a doorknob froze all of them. Who …?

That was a key in the lock. Sam. His deep voice drifted down the hallway, toward the treatment room. A slow drip of steel infused Lee's spine. She would not debate with him. If she did, she would win.

Violet set the bloody gauze on the metal instrument tray that rested beside Piper on the bed. "Be right back."

Lee covered the stitches with a thin gauze pad and stepped back to face Gary. "I'll return you to your car now."

"How much do I owe you?"

"We'll discuss that on the way."

Gary hoisted his daughter into his arms. "Thank you. So much."

"One final thing. Wait here a moment." She didn't have time for a clash with Sam, and he'd paused in the kitchen. But Piper had earned a sucker, and she needed sugar.

Halfway down the hall, Lee sidestepped to let Violet pass with their next patient.

"Look, Lee, I made it."

Ray Donnelly's voice didn't carry far. Lee attempted a smile for him. "I see. Are you staying off that foot?"

"Sort of. I'm trying to do better." He bobbed his head, and his gray ponytail dipped above his collar. "I'd say I'm definitely doing better. And no walking barefoot, like you said."

"Good. Go have a seat."

"I bet the ulcer's smaller today."

"That depends on how much you've walked on it."

"Not as much as before you found it. I swear, I never felt a thing."

"Go in and have a seat. I'll be there shortly."

"Okay. Thanks, Lee."

"Ray, I need you to stop that."

"Stop—? Oh!" His cheeks flushed. "Sorry, I never remember. About your name, I mean."

"Please try."

He nodded and hobbled down the hall—yes, he was walking on his foot. She sighed. Unfortunate that his three-centimeter diabetic ulcer had startled an "Oh my gosh, Lee" from Violet six weeks ago.

Lee entered the kitchen and tugged open the sucker drawer. Sam leaned his lanky frame against the counter, and his legs stretched halfway across the room, an image of nonchalance. Hardly.

"Hello, Sam." She chose a mystery-flavored sucker and shut the drawer. "I see you interpreted my text."

"Refined sugar? That's not for you, and it's not for Ray Donnelly."

Lee faced him and folded her arms. "It is for my patient."

His dark eyes sparked. "So not only did you drive yourself here, you brought a patient with you. A new patient?"

"That's correct."

Sam crossed his arms and drummed his long fingers against them. "Do we need to review our roles here?"

"She's seven years old, and she was bleeding from a head wound. Did you expect me to call you and make her father wait in a cold parking garage while you determined he wasn't a Constabulary agent?"

"That'd be a yes." Sam pushed away from the counter and strode halfway across the kitchen. His finger, lighter brown in the underside creases and cuticles, poked toward her face. "You call me, and you wait."

"Sam, the Constabulary aren't injuring children and sending them out to—"

"That is not the point. Would you be okay with it if I started setting bones and handing out antibiotics?"

The sucker stick dug into the tips of her fingers. "If waiting endangers a patient's life, then—"

"Would it have endangered hers?" He jabbed his finger down the hall. "And that doesn't even cover all of it. Where's your car?"

"In the barn."

"So you drove up the driveway like you own the place."

"I do own the—"

He kicked his heel against the cupboard door behind him. "Oh, and we really want the Constabulary putting that one together, don't we."

She held back the flinch. Sam didn't get angry, not with her. She worked to level her voice. "I'm also capable of spotting a tail, even if they were changing cars, and I drove past Indian Trail the first time and doubled back to it. No one followed me."

"You can't know that. Not as long as there's an open case file on you, and last I checked—meaning two days ago—"

"You need to trust me, Sam."

"Do not go there right now." He scrubbed a hand over his coarse black hair. When had gray begun to pepper it?

Lee held his glare. "I'll debride Ray's ulcer while you take Piper and her father back to their car. He approached me as I was leaving work."

"Don't go thinking we're done with this topic."

"I won't apologize for choosing to treat someone who needed my help."

"I don't care about an apology. I want your word you won't do this again."

His ire didn't conceal the concern nested between his eyes. As if her decision might be based on something other than her patient's well-being. Sam didn't understand the identity that blazed every day at the core of her. Nurse. Fusion of duty and concern. She left the kitchen and returned to her patient.

2

Every week, the small-group classroom emptied the same way. A trickle of students here, there, several stopping at Austin's chair to ask questions or remark on the discussion of the evening. Extra questions normally didn't bother him, but tonight ... High school kids could be so clueless.

"So, about sin." Vinnie braced his hands on his hips an inch above the top of his black jeans. "It's, like, an actual thing?"

"Self-Imposed Negation." Austin gathered his textbook and Bible and stood.

"So it's not a thing, then. It's all in our heads."

"To an extent, sure." Austin stepped toward the door, but Vinnie didn't move. Okay, then. Austin faced him and recited the curriculum's foundation. "Sin's the part of your mind that weighs you down, Vin. The part that keeps you from your potential because it refuses to believe in your potential. So yeah, it's based on your perception of yourself, not your real self. But it affects you in real ways."

Vinnie blinked. "Uh-huh."

"That make sense?"

"Think so."

"Good." Austin tested another step forward, and this time Vinnie fell in beside him.

On his way to the back of the room, Austin straightened a few upholstered chairs that had been pushed forward or pulled back as people joined the group circle. He never used the whiteboard on the far wall, so no cleaning was needed. At the folding table near the door, his coleader Tamara was bagging up the leftover brownies.

"Are you taking them all home?" Vinnie said with a gesture.

"Not if you'd like some." She flashed a smile, not at Vinnie but at Austin.

"Great." Vinnie grabbed two baggies and headed out the door.

Tamara's dark hair dipped around her shoulders, smooth and soft. She propped one heeled shoe behind her, pressed to the wall, raising the hem of her jean skirt.

"It's a tough topic, sin," she said.

"It can be."

"Know why I wore this skirt?"

Pretty obvious. Austin raised an eyebrow.

"It's my coffee shop skirt."

Sure it was.

"Whenever I wear it, I get asked to join a guy for coffee."

Austin blinked. Not like Tamara hadn't dropped hints before, but ... "Good luck."

When he sidled past her to the door, she curled a hand around his arm. Her perfume was a mix of citrus and vanilla. Austin freed himself and stepped back.

"Tamara—"

"I heard you and Rick discussing degree programs last Sunday. It's totally my goal to go for a Master's, as soon as I graduate, and you mentioned you're working on philosophy."

"Yeah, I just got accepted into U of M for the fall."

"Focusing on philosophical crime and rehabilitation?"

She didn't get those details from accidentally overhearing. Maybe her interest was more serious than he thought. Not that he cared. If Rick tried once more to set him up on a blind date, Austin would slug him.

"It's been four months since you went out with that Violet chick. Come on, man, move on."

Tamara's hazel eyes sparkled from under thick black lashes. "I'm so fascinated by that stuff. How the illegal religious texts can still be around. What makes people so … I don't know, addicted to them. And how do we help them?"

"You guys are perfect for each other." Rick hadn't been kidding. Well, talking at Elysium couldn't hurt anything, didn't mean Austin had to ask her out to coffee or anywhere else. His grip on his books relaxed. Before he could respond, a skinny blue-haired girl scurried into the room.

"Hi, Tamara, hi, Austin. I left my purse under my chair."

"No problem," Austin said, but the girl had already grabbed her purse and scampered away again.

"When it comes to cyan hair, tolerance is *not* a virtue." Tamara's wink held more than humor.

Austin cleared his throat. "You didn't tell her that, I hope."

"Only as a joke."

Right.

Tamara ran her thumb and finger along the seal of a bag of brownies. "I'm an up-front person."

"I noticed."

"So, can I tell you something? I usually don't bare all before the first date …"

Uhh. Okay. Now she was just being silly. Silly and attractive.

She didn't seem to notice his brain had melted. "… but given your degree, I think you'll, well, appreciate this. More so than my parents, for sure."

Um. Wait.

"I told them last week, and they weren't thrilled. Anyway, I'm hoping to get recruited after college. You know, into … the Constabulary."

The thrumming of Austin's body went still, like a guitar string pinned to the neck midnote. Too much. She'd tipped over the edge of believability.

Rick. Had to be Rick. Somehow, at some point, Austin had given himself away. And Rick wanted to confirm his suspicions—probably wanted to wring Austin's neck—but couldn't the guy come to him and ask? Man to man. *Dude, do you work for the Constabulary?* Not so hard. Austin wouldn't have denied it.

Instead, Rick tried to set him up with a sexy spy. *Coward.* Austin ran his thumb along the spine of his Bible to avoid making a fist.

"Of course, my folks are like a lot of people their age." Tamara opened the bag she'd just sealed and took out a broken corner of brownie. Nervous eater? Nervous liar. "They accept the Constabulary's existence and all. I think they even understand society's need for it. But their own daughter making that her life's pursuit … kind of botches their plans."

He forced himself to nod. Tamara offered him the bag of brownies, and he forced himself to take one out, chew it, and swallow. To wrap his mind in an old green coat that kept him warm the winter he turned six, the winter Esther was born. He closed his eyes for the briefest space of time—*one Mississippi*—and buttoned the coat around him. The coat of calm.

Tamara's prattle had stopped, replaced by the low drone of voices in the room next to theirs, a meeting of some kind that must have adjourned.

"I said too much," she said quietly.

"Not at all."

Tamara dropped the bag, and brownie crumbs showered the floor. "Oops. Um." She crouched in her tiny skirt.

A spy move. One of those intentional spills to redirect conversation. *Rick, I'm going to*—If she burst into tears right now, she was a plant for sure. But she didn't. In fact, the bright pink seeping from her cheeks down her neck … Could a person fake that?

"Tamara."

Her eyes shot up to his.

"What did Rick tell you?"

"Rick?"

"About me."

The blush deepened. "Oh, nothing."

Austin shoved the nearest chair, and it tilted too far. He barely caught it. Well, better than shoving her while she stood back up in her heels. He shouldn't blame her, didn't. If Rick's Sunday morning messages were any indication, the man could have talked her into this with a single well-uttered sentence.

One phone call, and Austin's boss would approve an audit on Rick's precious Elysium Fellowship of Believers. The guy would lose half his members. Forget revenge for a second—Austin should have audited them a year ago, anyway. Two thousand people attending the same church? Talk about common ground for revolution, even if they did submit to Constabulary monitoring.

"I'm sorry." Tamara set the bag on the folding table. "You're right, we talked about you. If you'll sit down, I'll tell you everything we said."

"Sure you will."

"Austin, I—I really wanted to go out. With you." She twisted the hem of her skirt with one hand, and it crept further up her leg.

"And you're trying to distract me now? I'm a guy, not an animal."

Her hand jerked then smoothed the skirt back down. "Rick told me you'd never ask me out."

"No kidding." Austin sank into a chair, and Tamara sat next to him.

Her face puckered, but she didn't cry. "Here's what Rick said. That you're a great guy, which I knew already. That you're smart, which I knew. And that the right things matter to you, and that you'd be a great conversationalist."

He wanted a lie to lurk in her eyes, but … no. If she was spying for Rick, she didn't know she was.

"And … he said …" She pinched her skirt hem, but this time, the gesture looked unconscious.

He said he doesn't trust me? Needs more information about me? Thinks I might be keeping official tabs on his church? The irony pulled his lips into a smirk. Rick would never believe Austin attended and worked at Elysium on his own time.

"He said you'd only take me out once, if that, because of the other girl."

Oh.

"He wasn't trying to gossip or anything."

Gossip. That's what she thought this was about. A sigh fell out of him.

"So I know there won't be … you know. Happily ever after." Her mouth quirked in self-deprecation. "I admire your teaching at Elysium. The way you see things. And I told Rick one date would be fine with me, and he said, 'You won't know unless you ask.'"

It was a sincere crush, or it was carefully constructed flattery. Either way, Austin held the badge and the gun and the upper hand. Something Rick needed to know. Austin buried the lingering impulse to find him and bounce his head off a wall.

"I'm sorry, Austin. I promise he didn't tell me what happened with you and … her."

"He doesn't know." No one did or needed to.

"You could tell me about her, if you felt like it. Or we could talk favorite philosophers. Or we could … not go at all." She ducked her head and swiveled her legs away from him, prepared to stand and walk away.

"Just a minute."

She waited.

The door to their room was open, but they were at the end of the hallway. No one would walk by now that small-group sessions had let out and most people were headed home. Austin pulled his wallet from his pocket and flipped it open. The gold badge glinted under the fluorescent ceiling light.

Tamara's tiny gasp held surprise, not fear. The sigh that followed it held something else altogether. Fascination, maybe.

"No way." She stretched a finger toward it.

He pushed it toward her. "Here."

She cupped her hands around it as if cradling a treasure.

Look at that, Violet. Some girls appreciate what I do.

"Michigan Philosophical Constabulary," Tamara whispered. "I can't believe it."

A smile pushed onto his face, and he didn't push back. "Me, either, sometimes."

"Yeah, hey, wait a minute." Her saucer eyes jumped up to meet his. The rubbing of her skirt, the edge of tears had vanished. "How old are you?"

"Twenty-two." He could blunt it, doctor it. *Twenty-three next year.* Sure, in September. The calendar had entered October a week ago. Anyway, his age only made the whole crazy story more impressive.

"That's … that's unheard of. I didn't know it was possible."

Neither had he, when Special Agent Jason Mayweather recruited him last year, straight from his undergrad. *Summa cum laude* had major advantages.

"I can't believe it. You're only three years older than I am, and look where you are, what you can do, for society and—" A twinkle lit her eyes. "Are you … carrying?"

He laughed. "Always."

"Can I see it later?"

A pleasant heat traveled his body, and the way her teeth bit her lower lip, released it too slowly … She knew what she was doing. He didn't want to give Rick a concussion anymore.

"Please?" Tamara leaned toward him, pushing his wallet into his hand and tapping it with one manicured nail. The skin of her wrist smelled like vanilla and oranges.

"Nope." He slid his wallet back into his pocket and stood up.

"Come on. I've never seen one up close before."

Wow. He shook his head. "A firearm is not a status symbol."

"Sure it is."

"Or a toy."

"Hmm." Tamara flipped her hair over one shoulder. But then the playfulness abated, and she shook her head. "This is the most unbelievable … You thought Rick sent me here to find this out, didn't you?"

"You offered me a brownie and started lauding the virtues of the Constabulary."

"And naturally, I couldn't mean it." She pinned him with a glare.

"In my experience, no."

"Tragic."

Yeah, it kind of was. *Violet, I would've made you happy. I would've …* The memory sucker-punched the breath out of him. Appropriate. Could he ever make it right? He wouldn't know until he talked to her. And he couldn't talk to her until he found her.

He walked Tamara to her car, a flimsy thing that would probably blow right off a bridge in bad weather. He opened the door. She hugged her leather jacket, crossed her arms. Her body inched closer.

"Chilly out here," she said.

Austin nodded. "Tamara, listen. I'm … not interested in … that."

Her smile seemed to catch on something. "I get it."

"You don't."

"Whoever she is, she's still got you."

"Her name's Violet, and I haven't seen her in four months."

Tamara leaned against her SUV wannabe and crossed her arms. "Why?"

"Because …" No excuses. So his brain had blacked out. So his body had assumed Violet was a real threat, the kind that could pick you up off the floor while you were watching TV and toss you into the wall. None of that justified the irrevocable moment in time when he hit her in the face.

"How about you just tell me? In lieu of a first and last date."

"I hurt her." The words rusted over between them while Tamara watched him. His thumbs pressed into his burning eyes then lowered. "And she found out about my job."

"Maybe you should call her."

Like he hadn't tried forty-six times in the last four months. "She doesn't answer."

"Well, she can't fall off the face of the earth."

"She did."

A frown creased her face. "Huh?"

"Nobody has seen her. In four months." Not her parents, not her best friend, not her coworkers or anyone from the small group at church. Tamara was new, or she'd have met Violet, back in the other lifetime. The lifetime that started in February when he met Violet and ended on a humid night in June when he'd proved how no-good he really was. When she'd marched out his front door without looking back.

"Oh …" Tamara touched his shoulder. "What's being done to find her? Are the police looking?"

"Her parents haven't filed a missing persons report because they say they know where she is." With the Christian resistance.

"But—"

"I'm looking for her. With the … resources I have." When his boss wasn't paying attention. Agent Mayweather had explicitly ordered him to leave Violet's case alone, told him there was "no case."

The four-month-old fear never let go of him. Either Violet's mother was right, and she had remade her life, or she'd gone to the Christians for help and somehow threatened them, which made no sense if you knew Violet. But for some reason, the Christians hadn't let her come home.

How could Mayweather say this wasn't a case?

"I hope you find her." Tamara opened her car door. "And thanks."

"Thanks?"

"For, you know, being … honest, when you thought I wasn't. You've got me excited to believe in my own dreams again."

She leaned away from the car on tip-toes and set a kiss on his cheek. "In lieu of a first and last date."

3

Violet should be studying, yet the sound of the television drifted to Lee as she removed her shoes in the foyer. She headed toward the living room.

"Is that you?" Violet called.

"If it's not, we have a problem."

"Come quick, you have to see this."

Lee hurried to the living room, where Violet sat in one corner of the couch with her feet up on the coffee table, one sock blue and one yellow. Her GED study guide, highlighter, and flashcards littered the couch cushions.

Violet pointed at the TV. "The President had a press conference, and now they're interviewing all these people about what he said, but they keep replaying the speech, too. You won't believe it."

The news channel showed footage from outside a sprawling brick building that looked like a library. A crowd was gathered, painted poster board signs raised high and waving. *"Good Riddance, TX." "Lone Star Has Fallen."* Various other signs told Texas where to go and what to do to itself.

The news anchor was interviewing a young man in a pink hoodie. "It's great, you know? Those Texans were weighing down the economy anyway, and everybody knows it."

"What's he talking about?" Violet said.

Lee perched on the stuffed chair across from her. "He doesn't know."

The footage cut from one interview to the next, varying locations across the country, a recorded montage. Every person praised the decision of the federal government. Texas wasn't worth fighting or fighting for, everyone said. Letting them go allowed the rest of the states to concentrate on maintaining law and order, on fighting terrorism in their own backyards. Two of the interviewees wore gray Constabulary uniforms, and in one shot, half a gray squad car jutted into the screen from the far left, green lights flashing. Yellow crime scene tape fluttered in a strong wind that billowed dust. Nothing like a photo op.

Now the newscaster became a voice-over, as the footage shifted to a gray-haired man in a blue suit, stepping up to a podium. "If you're just joining us, the President has announced that the United States will recognize the New Republic of Texas as a sovereign nation and will respect the borders of said nation. This decision has been supported by a great majority of citizens, several of whom we were privileged to speak with today and, with their permission, we share their opinions with our viewers."

With their permission, of course. What hoodie-wearing college kid wouldn't enjoy seeing himself on national news?

"I don't get it," Violet said. "I thought they'd try to stop Texas. Remember two months ago when the media was all, 'the Christians could gather in Texas and amass weapons and attack us in the name of God, danger, danger'?"

"Something's changed." Lee shrugged.

"Don't you want to know what, though?"

The fate of Texas did not affect Lee. Her life would continue tomorrow unaltered, and her energy couldn't be spent on pointless anti-Constabulary curiosity. Michigan Christians and those aiding them were no less threatened because of this decision.

The news program transitioned to a new story. Some female celebrity's bar fight.

"Finally," Violet said. "They've been looping and looping it, but I wanted to make sure I didn't miss anything, if it changed. Sometimes they tweak little words and things."

"How long have you been watching this?"

"An hour or something. All the studying was making me stupid, so I turned on the news."

Lee raised her eyebrows. Interesting choice.

"I know, I know. Propaganda and stuff. But even if it's only half true, it makes me feel less … you know."

Caged away from the world, living out her senior year as a philosophical fugitive who couldn't even watch TV at night without shutting the blinds. Lee nodded.

"Lee, this could be good for everybody. Right?"

"For those who choose to flee, I suppose."

"If Texas had left sooner, would—?"

Lee stood. "You should return to studying."

Would he be alive? Not the question Violet would have asked, surely—only the one in Lee's head.

Violet picked up her highlighter and study book. "I'll work with the TV on, in case they say more."

"All right."

Lee crossed to her bookshelves and found an old favorite, a frontier nurse's autobiography. The details of medicine-sans-technology had proved helpful to her work, and the words of another nurse were often affirming. She curled up in a corner of the couch and slipped into the old words.

"Um, Lee, I don't know if you remember, but the, um, memorial … I'm going to Chuck and Belinda's tomorrow after dinner."

No reason to respond. Violet knew Lee wasn't going. Trust Belinda Vitale to decide an official night of remembrance was in order, four months after his—

Death. Stop stumbling on that word.

Lee sealed her thoughts against everything but her book. Pages later, Violet shut off the TV. More pages later, her voice broke in. "GED question of the night. Biology is the study of …?"

"Living organisms."

"Actually, the answer in the book is 'life.' My other multiple-choice options are plants, water, and death."

"Impressive."

"See why watching the news is better for my brain?"

Lee set the book aside and reached for the flashcards. "Should we try a quiz?"

"Do you know it's after midnight?"

Oh.

"You got home later than usual."

Time was difficult to track when she wasn't at work. It never had been, before.

"You went off to your place?" Violet whispered as if Lee were a deer in a thicket, poised to dart away.

Tension ached in her spine. "Yes."

Violet set the GED book on the coffee table and stood up. Her mouth lifted at the corners, and Lee focused there, couldn't look higher to the eyes that held warmth and sorrow. For Lee. "Hope it helped you. G'night."

Lee didn't move until Violet shut the guest room door. She pulled her knees to her chest and wrapped her arms around them. No harm in telling Violet what "place" she escaped to, yet Lee couldn't speak about her retreats to the local nursery, still open. She walked into the greenhouse like any other customer then stayed until they closed. Wandering the aisles, pea stone grinding under her shoes, flowers and foliage embracing her in color and scent. Letting her stop thinking, stop feeling. Letting her simply breathe.

While he didn't.

Nausea pummeled her. *No, Violet. It didn't help.*

Bile burned the back of her throat. She swallowed hard. She hadn't thrown up in several weeks. Regression wasn't allowed.

The Constabulary wouldn't give burial to a body whose death had to be concealed. They would most likely cremate it. She should stop wondering about something so irrelevant. He wasn't in that body anymore. He wasn't anywhere.

Or perhaps he was. Perhaps God had measured his sacrifices and considered them enough. Perhaps, as he'd always told her, his deeds weren't part of the process at all, and God had decided his fate based on his faith in Jesus Christ. Either way, he couldn't be denied a secure, painless eternity.

Lee pressed her chest against her thighs and closed her eyes as if these unconnected physical actions could calm her stomach. She rocked forward, back, forward, back, and still she had to throw up.

Control. Cope.

She retrieved her book from the floor and opened it. Read. An hour later, the nausea had passed, though she'd only turned the page four times. She put the book away and padded down the hall to Violet's room.

If Violet slept lightly, Lee could never have developed this futile habit. She let the hallway night light angle into the guest room and crept across the carpet. She opened the nightstand drawer and pulled out the worn leather book, closed the drawer, and returned to the living room.

Wind swept across the windows. She nestled into the throw blanket and pressed her back to the couch pillows. She opened the Bible and flipped through.

His handwriting was concentrated in certain books, most in the second section, called New Testament. Sometimes the margins contained his questions, sometimes his prayers, sometimes his gratitude for the refuge he found in a passage. No one had known him better than Lee, yet she'd failed to see that fear clawed at him some days. He never gave it a hold on his decisions, never even expressed it except that one night in the Vitales' kitchen, too tired to think. Too tired to hide weakness.

She found another book filled with handwriting. Romans. But this was the end of the book. Lee flipped back, a page at a time, absorbing the even block letters in black pen.

Saved so God will get more glory.

He won't let go.

In chapter 8, Lee's hand froze on the page. Her stomach tightened. His writing looked smaller here. *Not afraid. Help me.*

She read the entire chapter and wanted to burn the book. God knew His people were abused and killed. Yet He continued to claim that nothing could separate them from His love. The evidence didn't support the thesis.

She wouldn't read any more of this intolerable text, even the underlined portions. She'd read only the handwriting in the margins, and context could go hang itself. But she froze again at the third chapter, which was … highlighted.

He never used a highlighter, and this one was pink.

New handwriting. Green ink, painstaking cursive script. *This is what God does for me!*

Lee flipped backward for pages, chapters, books. Throughout the Gospels and Acts, the feminine writing left notes. Every few pages, new lines had been highlighted.

Something ice hot spurted through Lee's veins and throbbed from her chest all the way to her fingertips and toes. She snapped the Bible shut and charged to the guestroom and flipped on the light.

Violet rolled over and squinted up at her. "Hey …" She jolted up in bed. "Is it con-cops? Are they here? I'll go hide—"

"You had no right."

"What?"

Lee's hands shook. She opened the Bible to the first page of Romans, where the underlines lost to the highlighting. Only a single black-penned note: *What I believe, not what I do.* The green ink responded: *So good to know this!* The other side of the page bore a green flood. *Jesus cares about this stuff! Honor Him with my body for the rest of my life! No more unrighteousness!* The exclamation points were dotted with circles.

Violet stared at the book open across Lee's hands. A smile bloomed over her face. "You're reading the Bible?"

Lee snapped it shut.

Violet withdrew against the headboard. "Lee—"

"This book does not belong to you."

"Sure it does, he gave it to—"

"Don't touch it again."

Panic widened Violet's eyes. She jumped from the bed and stepped toward Lee, mouth drawn tight. "Give it back."

The leather spine pressed into Lee's palm. His book. Perfect lines, careful letters formed by his hand. He'd left bits of his heart in these pages, and Violet had scribbled on them. Lee pinned the Bible against her body.

"You can't take it." Violet's voice pitched with tears. "Please don't take it."

Lee pressed the Bible harder against her stomach. She would preserve it from the stain of further green ink. Or maybe she would rip out every page until nothing remained but an empty shell. A corpse of a book.

"Lee, I don't think he'd mind if I write in it. I think it would make him happy."

Irrelevant. *No, it's not.* Someone else had found faith in his God. In Jesus Christ. He would smile with the creases around his eyes. He would call Violet family.

Lee clutched the Bible and the numbness.

"Lee?"

Do what he would want. She offered the book to Violet on an open hand. "You're correct. It's no longer his."

"I'm sorry. I'm really, really sorry."

Do not be sorry.

"I hate the con-cops for what they did to Marcus."

They shot him and watched as he bled out, as he struggled to the last to stay awake, keep breathing, fight the pain. Lee had dreamed the scene so many times, it was like a memory.

"Listen, just because he gave it to me, it's not only mine. I mean, if you want …"

To read it. Violet surely prayed for her, for God to change her heart, which amounted to changing her mind. *I won't let You.* She had made the only possible logical choice about God, long before what He had done to Marcus. She tried to walk to the living room with smooth strides, but they shuffled.

Violet followed. "Lee."

"No." She turned and put up a hand. "No."

"Do you want—?"

"Go back to bed."

Lee waited until Violet trudged from the room, head ducked. Then she curled up on the couch, knees to her chin, small as possible. She tugged the blanket over herself.

"You are dead," she whispered.

"Yeah."

Marcus didn't speak. Not for a moment did she believe he had. But she knew the words he would say, how he would inflect each one. She inhaled and tried to smell him, his soap, clean sweat, the work he loved—wood and sawdust and drywall. She shut her eyes and tried to feel the room as it was when he filled it. Pacing her rug, trying to rub the knots of stress from his neck. Broad and strong and earnest.

"Your God did not save you."

"I'm okay. With all of it."

If she opened her mouth again, she might scream. *How dare You abandon him. How dare You require his death.* She tried to hear her name in his voice, the way he could speak a whole sentence, a whole paragraph, in only three letters. But silence pressed her down. The room throbbed, empty and cold. Lee curled tighter.

4

Agent Mayweather parked the car on a square of blacktop to the east of the detached garage. He shut off the ignition, and a glance from his laser-blue eyes was sufficient reminder, whether he intended that or not. *Impress the boss or else.* Austin didn't allow himself to fidget.

Mayweather shook a jingle from the keys. "Questions? You don't get to ask any once we're in there."

Yeah, why exactly are you taking the twenty-two-year-old rookie on this interview? Well, he'd rise to the privilege. "I've got it, sir. She's a voluntary witness, we're only here for her signed statement, straightforward and easy."

"Good summary."

Austin nearly said *thanks*, but that might not have been a literal compliment. Anyway, no use appearing overeager.

Mayweather got out of the car and pocketed the keys, and Austin waded after him through a lawn overgrown with more weeds than grass, now brown and wilted by frosty mornings. Something poked his knee, and he glanced down at a burr stuck to his suit pants. He peeled it off and flicked it away.

"Why not uniforms, sir?"

Mayweather hit the doorbell. "First, when it's just us, you call me Jason. Second, stand next to me, not behind me. Third, the uniform's for suspects. Not witnesses."

But last week, Agent Tisdale had been in uniform all day, in and out of the office, and he'd been interviewing both suspects and witnesses. Austin stepped up beside his boss, but a frown tightened his mouth.

Mayweather—could Austin really think of him as Jason?—tipped his head. "That's not how everyone does it. That's how I do it."

"Right. Sir. Jason."

The man grinned like a toothpaste commercial model. "Relax, Austin, seriously."

The door opened to a woman somewhere between Austin and Mayweather on the age scale. "Yes?"

Mayweather flashed his badge long enough for her to read it. Austin's badge nearly slipped from his fingers, but he dipped a quick catch that no one seemed to notice.

"I'm Agent Mayweather and this is Agent Delvecchio with the MPC. Reese Cabrera-Hill?"

"That's me."

"We're here for your written statement."

"Oh, right, of course." The woman waved them inside, and the bangles on her wrist clinked when she lowered her arm. Her plum sweater brightened her dark eyes and Latina complexion.

She gestured them to the small dining room left of the entryway. "May I offer you some coffeecake? Made from scratch this morning."

"I don't turn down refreshments," Mayweather said.

"Coffee?"

"Sure."

Austin squashed the surprise at both of them from his face. Didn't Reese Cabrera-Hill want the con-cops out of her house as quickly as possible? And didn't Mayweather want professionalism here?

"I'll grab some plates." Reese disappeared.

Mayweather pulled a folded paper from a pocket inside his trench coat, the witness statement, composed of blank lines and a question at the bottom. *Do you attest that this statement is true to the best of your knowledge and contains no hearsay or speculation?*

Or outright lies, Austin always wanted to scribble into the margin, though attesting a statement was true ought to preclude deceit.

After slinging his coat over a chair, Mayweather opened the paper and smoothed out the folds, not a nervous gesture but an absent one. Around the room, his glance ticked, as if he had a mental checklist. *Chairs. Table. Curio cabinet. Check, check, check.* Every item of furniture had been painted wine red. The lack of clutter here stood at odds with the overgrowing lawn.

In two trips, Reese brought three mugs of coffee, forks, creamer, and sugar. By the time they all sat down at the dining room table, Jason and Austin had been here for fifteen minutes and accomplished not a bit of Constabulary business.

"I've made three coffeecakes in two days." Reese took a bite and smiled. "Cinnamon was boring me, so this is chocolate. And not bad if I do say so."

Jason tried the cake and sipped his coffee and approved of both before handing her the witness statement.

"You should have this thing online, Agent Mayweather. Electronic signature and all that. Honestly, the Constabulary makes legislative progress almost every week. Tech progress couldn't hurt."

Between Austin's shoulders, inching up his neck, a finger seemed to tap. Maybe not a warning but a clue. Mayweather half smiled at his witness, and he lifted the slice of coffeecake right off the plate to take another bite, as if she hadn't provided forks.

"Psych reasons, probably," he said. "Nothing replaces the gravity of your signature in ink."

Had these two met before? Nothing sparked in the air between them, not like that, anyway, but … they didn't feel like strangers. And truly, Austin had no reason to be here. He ate coffeecake and listened.

Mayweather should have left him at his desk combing through phone records. This couldn't even be called a first interview. So much for proving something, or whatever he'd hoped to do when he latched onto this opportunity like a band roadie offered a chance at the front man's mic. Mayweather handed Reese a pen from inside his suit jacket, and she pursed her lips and scrawled on the lines of the witness form.

Maybe Mayweather was the one proving something. Austin forked a bite of coffeecake, little crumbles falling from the top onto his plate.

"You like it, Agent Delvecchio?" Reese's writing didn't pause.

"It's great."

"I agree. I think I'll make one for my cousin and his girlfriend this weekend. They're visiting from Kalamazoo." She wrote for another minute then signed the form, looping the pen back to make a whorl in the center of her last name not unlike the chocolate in the center of the coffeecake. She pushed the page over to Mayweather.

"Cross your *t*'s?" He stacked Austin's now empty plate on top of his own.

Reese bobbed her head, and her gold earrings glinted against her neck. "Don't think I missed anything."

"Take a quick look, Agent." Mayweather passed the form to Austin.

Okay, sure. Austin pressed the paper flat on the table.

Date of Incident: October 19

Two days ago.

Please recount the events in your own words: I was leaving class on 10/19, Monday night, and across the parking lot, I heard a girl crying. I went to make sure everything was okay. I came around the back of the row of cars and saw two girls from class, Aaliyah Johnson and Stephanie Eggers, sitting in a small white car. They didn't see me, and I stood there a minute, trying to decide if I should interrupt. Steph said, "I know this sounds stupid, but I'm not that scared of re-education. They've been in my neighborhood twice in the last month, and I know eventually they'll be on to me, so I'm ready for that. What I'm not ready for is my family to find out. They'll never speak to me again. I'm so scared of that, I can't witness to them."

Aaliyah proceeded to encourage Steph. She recited what sounded like Bible verses, and then she prayed for her to be protected from the Constabulary and for God to give her courage to tell her family "the truth about Jesus." She also closed her prayer by saying, "in Jesus' name."

I left without confronting Steph and Aaliyah. I called the Constabulary as soon as I had gotten back to my car and locked myself in. I didn't feel safe enough to wait for them to arrive, so I told the dispatcher I would provide a written statement at another time, and this was acceptable to her. She told me to do what was necessary to feel safe.

Reese's handwriting looked like a computer font, one of those swirly ones that showed up everywhere from greeting cards to bakery boxes. Austin pushed the paper back. "I do have one question."

Mayweather's eyebrows drew together.

"For Ms. Cabrera-Hill," Austin said, and Mayweather nodded.

Reese waved a dismissal. "Hill is fine."

Austin shrugged. "Ms. Hill, are you familiar with archaic Bible translations?"

Her hand jerked on the table and rattled her bracelets. "Of course not."

"Then are you sure the verses Aaliyah was quoting weren't from the Progressive United Version? I mean, they were probably inspirational verses about courage or something, right? Nothing controversial enough to be retranslated."

Both Reese's hands drew back into her lap, and she shifted to cross her legs under the table. "That's true, but it was obvious that both of them were Christians. People quoting the PUV have legal beliefs. These girls were crying about the Constabulary."

Obviously, she was right, and he hadn't needed her to make that point. He shrugged, more toward Mayweather than Reese. "Just clarifying."

"Which is part of the job." Mayweather's white teeth flashed at the witness, and he picked up the statement, skimmed it for less than a minute, then set it back down. "Speaking of clarification, how many people did you see giving spiritual comfort to Stephanie Eggers?"

Reese's nose crinkled, making her look closer to Austin's age. "Just Aaliyah. Which is what I wrote down."

"And you even signed it, so technically, I don't have to offer this to you, but are you very sure you don't want to amend it?"

"Why would I amend it?"

Austin's neck prickled again. Answering a question with a question. Avoidance.

"Because when we questioned Stephanie, she maintained she was alone in the parking lot, the prayer had been hers. Five hours later, her exact slip of the tongue was, 'I won't say anything to get *them* arrested.'"

Reese blinked. Before the silence could stretch, Mayweather leaned forward.

"Ms. Hill, was there someone else in that car?"

"No."

"Are you sure?"

"Yes."

"Was Nicholas Lowe in that car?"

She jolted in her chair and put both feet to the floor. She leaned forward to meet Mayweather's stare. "Absolutely not. Where are you getting this nonsense?"

"Well, I'm trying to figure out a motive for you to leave someone out of your story, and 'we were engaged once' is a good motive."

"I haven't seen Nicholas Lowe in ten years. This is ludicrous."

It was. But the air was thickening as if with fumes, gasoline waiting for a match. Surely Mayweather would back off now.

"I'm thinking based on your 'legislative progress' comment earlier that you do pay attention to national news, Ms. Hill. I'm sure you know you're legally required to report Christians and people harboring Christians."

"I turn in Christians wherever I find them, sir. Case in point, the witness statement I just filled out for you."

"Maybe. Or maybe there's someone you need to come clean about here."

"Or maybe I should call my lawyer."

This was crazy. She was a friendly witness, and Mayweather was turning her more hostile with every word he said. Austin's hand flattened on the table, half-stretched toward her.

"Hey." The word fell from his mouth before he could consider how his boss might react to being interrupted. By the rookie.

He was so screwed.

Might as well follow through and save this woman some lawyer fees and the Constabulary some embarrassment. "Listen, ma'am, that's not necessary. No one is threatening you here, okay?"

"Oh, yeah?" She cocked an eyebrow at Mayweather, who had gone still and expressionless.

Crap. Austin's face flooded with heat. "Yeah. But if the suspect's telling us something different than you are, we've got to get to the bottom of it, obviously. So … how many people were in the car?"

"Two."

"Okay."

Not a blink, nothing forced in her eye contact, not a twitch in her body. No reason existed to think this woman was lying. Austin slid a glance to Mayweather that he hoped conveyed, *Your call, boss. Now that I've essentially contradicted you in front of a witness.*

But the man's expression smoothed, and a smile slid over his face. "Well, Ms. Hill, at this point, my only reason to doubt you is the pronoun use of a distraught girl five hours into her interview. Certainly possible that she misspoke. But as Agent Delvecchio said originally, clarification is part of our job."

Reese's shoulders lowered, giving away how tight they'd been a moment before. She glanced down at the piece of paper that lay between them.

"Thanks for the coffeecake." Mayweather stood and folded the statement, then tucked it into his suit and pulled on his coat.

"Thank you for taste-testing." She managed a tiny smile.

"And thanks for making the effort to help preserve your society from crime, especially from criminals with a propensity for violence."

"I'm happy to do my part, Agent Mayweather."

The Twilight Zone took over as Reese Cabrera-Hill walked Austin and Mayweather to her front door. She smiled as they stepped onto the porch, not a relieved smile but an easy one. The door closed behind them, and Austin followed Mayweather back to the car and tried to steel his ego.

"You're fired." The words would hang in the air any second now. He might not be the one to type out Austin's termination letter, but he could make it happen. He left the driveway and stopped at the first traffic light before speaking.

"You have thoughts on your first interview?"

"Thoughts?" Ouch. Austin's voice wasn't supposed to bite like that.

"Yeah, lay them on me, kid."

He faced the passenger window. No sense in letting Mayweather see the flush of … well, that was just it. Austin was either ashamed and disappointed in himself or he was furious with his boss for conducting an interview with such stupid aggression. Might help to know which.

"Austin."

"Sir, I spoke out of turn, and I apologize."

"But?"

Austin risked a glance at Mayweather's profile. "But, sir, I was concerned that her reaction would become counterproductive, so I tried to …"

Mayweather's face cracked into a grin.

Like a single plucked guitar note, understanding twanged through Austin's mind. "Did you set all that up, sir? To see what I'd do?"

"Sure thing."

"Did you bring me on this interview with the sole purpose of testing my reaction to … that in there?"

"If this was a test, how do you think you did?"

"I have no idea, honestly, sir—"

"Jason."

Still Jason? Okay, that was good. Austin let his body relax against the seat. He'd been coiled up inside for the last fifteen minutes. He sighed.

"Come on, kid. You've got a brain in that skull. Tell me if you passed my test."

"Well, either you wanted me to keep quiet—which means I failed with flying colors—or you wanted me to speak up. Which means I … did okay."

"Why would I want you to keep quiet?"

"Because you're the boss."

"Right, I am, but you're not my robot pet. In case that fact escaped you before now."

Quiet eased over them while Austin turned the scenario over in his head. "So, I think you're saying I didn't fail. Because I said something."

"That's the small piece. Here's the big one. You didn't just speak up, Austin, you defused the situation when I agitated it. You keyed in to my bad cop—yeah, you assumed it was real, but you don't know me well enough yet to assume anything else. What matters is, you took on the good cop role. You balanced me. Got it?"

Oh. Yeah. He'd done exactly that. "It wasn't deliberate."

"Nope, it was instinctive. Which is worlds better."

Warmth seeped into Austin's chest. A few miles rolled away under the tires, and his hand itched for the radio knob. All this quiet pinged around the car, empty and irritating. He wanted music. Ideally, he wanted his guitar, chords strummed from his own fingers, but he'd have accepted *Billboard's* Top 40 station by the time Jason fractured the silence again.

"You figure out the rest yet?"

There was more? Austin angled a glance at his boss and found the man smiling again. "Give me a minute, sir."

Jason nodded and flicked the blinker. They'd arrive back at the Constabulary office in a few minutes.

As they pulled into a parking space, Austin snapped his fingers. "You *do* know her."

"Good work." Jason shut off the car.

"Is she … I mean …"

Jason's laugh always had an odd wheeze under it, something animalistic that sounded nothing like his voice when he talked. He hopped out of the car, and Austin followed.

"You know I'm married."

Sure, but that didn't stop some people.

"Happily, may I add. Three boys. Reese and I go back about a year. She's a frequent informant. Sometimes I think she's got genetically enhanced hearing or some crazy crap, the things she overhears, the number of Christians she's helped us catch. Used to wonder if she wasn't fabricating this stuff for attention, but we've never failed to get a confession out of the people she calls in."

"Is this test thing … you know, regulation?"

Jason cut a glance at him and shook his head.

"But you do this to all your rookies?"

"Nope."

Their shoes gathered recent raindrops from the grass island that stretched from the parking lot to the sidewalk. They ambled shoulder to shoulder, sort of like partners, which was a silly, glamorous thought. They weren't detectives on some TV show. Plus, Jason Mayweather didn't do partners. Plus, Austin glowed green, test passed or not. In fact …

"Did Reese know why you brought me?" Kind of humiliating, if she did.

"Don't worry, hotshot, you impressed her." Jason smirked. "Platonically."

The time it took to hit the sidewalk and reach the office door was the time it took Austin to rally his nerve and bet everything on his A+.

"Jason?"

"Hmm?" The man missed the taut thread in Austin's voice. He put out a hand to open the door.

"Wait, I want—I need—to ask you something."

Jason's hand lowered to his side. "Shoot."

"Violet DuBay."

One eyebrow lifted, and the man's slim frame rocked back on his heels. "Go on."

"I know we've discussed her in the past. I know the case is listed as cold, and you don't believe there's a case."

"Sometimes girls that age go missing on purpose."

"Violet didn't."

Jason leaned against the glass door, his eyes never wavering from Austin's, but an odd distance shuttered them. *He knows something.*

"I want to do an interview, an official one, where I walk in and announce that I'm a con-cop and they have to answer my questions."

"Her parents?"

Austin shook his head. "Her parents do not know or care where she is. I want to talk to the Hansens."

Jason pushed away from the door. "Nope."

What? Why? Austin's pulse stuttered. He couldn't accept a no. Not about this. "I only want to talk to them. And you know I won't antagonize anyone. I just proved that to you."

Jason tugged open the door and headed inside. The heat bundled around them as Austin followed him down a Spartan corridor under fluorescent lights. He had to convince Jason before they reached the man's office, where he could shut a physical door on Austin as well as a metaphorical one.

"Please, sir."

"You proved to me that you've got good instincts when you're dealing with strangers."

Oh. Jason's strides were on a mission, and Austin lengthened his. "Knowing Violet doesn't change anything."

Jason spun to face him. A glare eclipsed the calm. "Knowing her changes *everything*, kid."

Agent Tisdale approached, coming from the office. With a glance at Jason, Tisdale sidestepped both of them, and one of his Hulk-sized shoulders brushed the white wall. Jason didn't return his acknowledging nod.

Austin dug his heels into the carpet. "Sir, I don't want to lose anyone, whether it's a suspect or a missing person or whoever. I want to be better than that."

The professional calm melted from Jason's face like wax. His arms crossed over his chest, and whatever partnership might have stretched between them shattered against the flint in his eyes.

Oh crap.

"I, um, I wasn't talking about …" *About the escape of a suspect on your watch.* Or so went the rumors from some morons on the squad. "About anything in particular."

The next moment, maybe two, blurred. Then Austin stood with his back pressed to the cold wall, and Jason stood inches from him. No need for Jason to poke a finger in his face. The tone of his voice accomplished that.

"You do not lie to me, Agent Delvecchio. Ever."

"I'm not."

"Own it. Own your inappropriate, hardly subtle comment."

Get out of my face. His pulse ratcheted up while Jason waited for a response. While Jason loomed in his space and looked ready to grab him by the shoulders and shake the words out of him. *Don't do that.* Or he was going to hit a Constabulary agent while standing in the administrative office. No. He wouldn't hit Jason. He wouldn't freak out. This was his boss, a good man. Jason didn't throw kids into walls.

Austin licked his lips. Had to answer him. Only way to make him back off.

"I wasn't deliberately referencing Marcus Brenner, Jason. But I get how it sounded. Sorry."

The moment refused to end. Jason didn't move. The cock of his head measured Austin's sincerity. Couldn't blame him. If Austin *had* made the allusion on purpose, it would be a low blow.

Okay, good. Focusing on thoughts besides the obvious one (*back-off-don't-grab-me-don't-push-me-don't-hit-me*) was bringing

Austin's heart rate down. Jason stepped back several feet and nodded. And continued down the hall.

He didn't seem to notice that Austin was following until they reached his office. He spoke without turning. "You stay away from Clay Hansen."

5

She should have known Belinda would expect her to eat. The woman incorporated food into everything. Around the dining room table, Belinda had set plates and silverware and cloth napkins, settings for four. The center held chips and two kinds of dip, fruit, and a berry pie, all of it dwarfed by the length of the table.

A gentle hand nudged Lee's shoulder, and Violet whispered from behind her. "I didn't know about the food, I promise."

She shouldn't have come here. She should leave. Now.

"Sit anywhere." Something, maybe their reason for meeting, softened Belinda's Southern twang. "Lee, I hope you like three-cheese dip. I made it this morning."

As Violet took the chair beside Lee, their glances met, and Violet's frown deepened. Lee arched her eyebrows: *You can stop with the unnecessary concern.* With a quick blush, Violet averted her eyes.

A slow breath, in and out, and Lee was ready. She could manage a few bites. She could endure the company for an hour or so; courtesy didn't require longer, and an hour should achieve her purpose in coming. Tonight she would sit in this chair carved by his hands and open her own hands and let his memory spill out of them like the first handful of dirt over a coffin. A coffin he wouldn't have. When this night was over, she would once again control herself, mind and body. She would deal with loss and move on, like everyone else who faced the death of someone who mattered. She could have moved on sooner if she'd done this sooner, dedicated one night to his memory so that it could fade.

She should have realized it was necessary. Wasn't that the purpose of a funeral, after all? Lee served herself a slice of the pie and ignored Violet's lingering look.

Across the table, Belinda's smile beamed. "There you go, sugar. Pie always helps my hurts."

Only the clinking of silverware kept silence at bay as Chuck piled his plate with a sampling of everything at the table, as Violet spooned herself a generous helping of cheese dip and scooped two handfuls of chips onto her plate. Belinda chose fruit, caramel dip, and a slice of pie.

Lee forked a bite, slightly more tart than sweet, chewed until she could keep it down, and swallowed. Look, she was perfectly able to do this.

"So, Pearl," Chuck said, using his wife's nickname. "You want to explain what we're doing tonight?"

As if any of them didn't understand their purpose here.

"First off, we decided to sit at this table because it's his. Marcus's. Made all this with his hands. And I guess that's the first thing I'd like to tell you about him—he made good furniture. None of his stuff's ever broken, or—or …"

Belinda's eyes glistened, and Chuck nodded to her as if accepting a baton in a relay race. "Lee and Violet, we thought, since it's a memorial, we should remember. So we're going to do that—talk a little about what we remember, about Marcus."

Lee's pulse quickened. Of course, they would want to talk about him. This aspect of the night was as predictable as the food. She should have anticipated it.

"So." Chuck finished off his bunch of grapes. "I'd like to say that we knew him almost two years. A friend of ours recommended his work, that's how we met him. And it was the best recommendation I've gotten. With his business, he was always fair, never did me false. Not in any way."

He nodded as if to emphasize his words, or signal that he was finished. As if his words summarized the whole of a man who not only built him furniture but also fought the Constabulary with him; ate his food and drank his coffee; showed up here with bloodshot eyes in the early morning hours, fugitives in need trailing behind him.

Chuck twirled the stem of his grapes and looked away, then back to them. "And I'd like to say that he was a good man. A frustrating, stubborn good man and my friend."

"That he was," Belinda said.

The silence had started to choke the room when Violet shifted in her chair and spoke.

"I barely knew … Marcus." Her voice hushed on his name, and her gaze found Lee's, then flitted to Belinda, then to Chuck. "But I can say a few things. And the first thing is that he cared a lot."

True. Violet couldn't know how much.

"And the second thing is, I wish I could thank him. For letting me go when he didn't want to and for giving me a Bible and … I owe him a lot."

Lee's heart hammered her ribs as Chuck and Belinda turned as one to her. She couldn't speak.

"You knew him best," Belinda said quietly.

Yes. She knew him. Had known him. Verb tense shouldn't faze her, not after four months, not after her mind had already moved him to past tense, yet every word they spoke ripped into her composure like bullets into flesh. She set her fork on her plate, and the *clank* was too loud. She flinched, and they saw it.

"Could you maybe tell us something, sugar, something we don't know? A story, maybe?"

A story. Of Marcus.

How he'd stood on Kirk's porch, twenty-three years old, eager to do his job until she stood on the other side of the screen door and wouldn't unlock it. He refused to leave when she slammed it in his face with a twenty-year-old's ire and fear. He ran around the house to the only open window and started yelling at her.

"I'm calling the police, Marcus Whoever-You-Claim-to-Be."

"Brenner. I'm supposed to be here, I'm the contractor—heck, put the phone down."

"Lee?"

A story of Marcus. The hurt in his brown eyes when she said she wouldn't date him if he were the last man on earth—he should've known she was lying, clichés weren't her style—and the fury that replaced it when she forced the truth into the air between them.

"It's not because of you."

"Why, then?"

"Marcus, I ... When I was eighteen years old, I was raped."

"Pearl, if she doesn't want to talk, then ..."

A story of Marcus. How he laughed at silent movies. How he devoured every dish she'd ever cooked for him and practically salivated over her beef stroganoff. How he grinned like a little boy when she threw a Frisbee so poorly it curved over like a boomerang. How his voice trembled over the phone when he needed help to fight the desire for whiskey. How he would have done anything to prevent the damage in her past and anything to protect her in the present. Her fortress, always giving, longing to hold her in his arms and staying with her though she couldn't even reach out and hold his hand.

His hand.

No. Violet's. Resting on Lee's wrist under the table, invisible to the others. "Lee."

"No." The word ruptured something deep. Beating. Rushing. The room blurred.

"You don't have to talk, sugar, it's fine. So it's my turn, then. I remember how Marcus loved my coffee. He'd drink it any old way, but hazelnut creamer was his favorite. Sometimes, with all that went on around here, I was … you know, just the old Southern woman in the housecoat, nothing much to offer in a fight. Until Marcus came in and asked for my coffee like it was the most important part of winning the day."

A story of Marcus, and another and another—Lee couldn't shield herself from the inner barrage, as if every word he'd ever spoken to her, every moment they'd shared in ten years tore through her all at once. Every time they'd wounded each other, every time they'd trusted each other, every time she'd wondered—could she learn to be touched if the hands belonged to him?

"I remember how Marcus—"

"No."

The room blinked back into focus. Three faces stared up at her. She'd pushed her chair back from the table and stood. Her hands balled at her sides, nails digging into her palms. Her pulse raced.

Violet stood too. "If we need to go …"

Which meant her emotions were visible. Lee breathed in. Calm. Cope. Seal the cracks inside, lock the vault. Whatever that beating, rushing was inside her, it spurted now like an artery. Lee backed away from the table.

"Yes," she said. "Violet, we need to go."

"But, sugar, you got here not thirty minutes—"

"Lee's probably right, Belinda. I've got studying to do. It's okay. Thanks for the food. Your cheese dip is awesome."

Blur again. Steps through the foyer, the front door, outside. The car. Keys. But her purse was ... Oh. Hooked over Violet's arm. Violet dug through it and clicked the remote.

"Passenger side, Lee."

"I'm capable of driving."

Violet huffed or laughed. "I know your panic-attack thing even when you hide it. I'm a better driver than you are right now, guaranteed."

"You shouldn't be seen driving my car." Though at the moment, her brain couldn't process why.

"I'm going to pray for an angel to follow us home with an invisibility shield. I don't think that's in the Bible, but God can do anything. Get in the car, come on."

Lee slid into the passenger seat. They drove for several minutes, but the night around them refused to focus. Lee's lungs refused to relax. She pressed her back into the seat and tilted her head up.

"You going to throw up?" Violet said quietly.

"I'll be ..." Her stomach turned. "Yes. Pull over. Please."

A little while later, they sat parked in an empty Kroger parking lot, several yards away from the former contents of Lee's stomach. She palmed the sweat from her forehead and let her arm drop to her side. Weakness trembled in her limbs, but breathing was easy again.

The quiet was easy as well, almost soft. She closed her eyes and allowed herself a minute of fortification. Her behavior required an explanation, though.

"I apologize."

After another minute, Violet shifted against the driver's seat, a brush of sound against the upholstery. "I pretty much expected this when you all of a sudden announced you were coming."

Lee slit an eye open. "It will not happen again."

Violet's thumb rubbed her wrist. "Are you serious? You can't promise me that, especially when I don't think you know why this is happening to you."

Something about her inflection ... ah. "You insinuate that *you* know why?"

"I—I think so."

"Please enlighten me." Ice encased the words because Violet was being absurd. Lee wasn't predictable, wasn't easily read.

"Um." Violet poked the key ring that hung from the key in the ignition, and it swung back and forth with a quiet jingle. "I've been doing some research online. About ... um ... losing people."

Lee sat straighter. She was not an invalid, psychologically or otherwise. She did not require assistance from an eighteen-year-old.

"About grief, Lee. I don't know *how* close you were. You and ... him. But I know you were close. I'm not stupid. And—look, you've been throwing up since the night he died. You've got to admit, that's extreme."

"I—"

"I know, not as often as you did at first, but still. You're not ... You don't talk about him, you go on with life like you never met him."

People dealt with loss differently. Violet's online research should have taught her that. Lee wasn't Belinda, didn't need to express herself in words or tears or anything else. Those she lost remained inside her forever. Marcus's memory was cradled close alongside … the other.

"Lee, the stuff I read … I think the grief's trying to come out of you, and you won't let it."

Absurd. She'd prove it, in fact. She got out of the car and locked her knees to keep them steady. Around the hood, through the headlights' twin beams, shivering from the chilly air and nothing else. She opened the driver's door, and Violet's upward look held desperation. *Not necessary.*

"I'll drive from here."

Violet let her and didn't speak again.

When they arrived home, Violet left her alone. Lee went to her room and grabbed underwear, heather gray sleep pants, and a size-large sweatshirt. A shower would pound away the tightness in her chest.

"Why?"

The word was out of her mouth before it registered in her thoughts. Who was she asking? The cosmos? No. The Source of the cosmos, Marcus's God. Marcus's Christ. The vise gripping her lungs clamped down hard, and her hands curled into the cotton pajamas.

"You can't possibly claim there is an acceptable reason."

The answer didn't matter, wouldn't right anything. She shouldn't need it, and didn't she have it already? He was dead because evil was allowed to exist and he chose to fight back.

"He did more than You do. And You have all the power."

The clothes fell from her hands.

She walked to the window sill and wrapped her hands around the geranium's clay pot. Hold on. Stay grounded. An all-out panic attack hovered at the edges of her vision along with the border of gray. She bowed over the flower, and its distinct smell eased her lungs. In. Out. Slowly.

Marcus was dead. He was dead, he was dead, he was—

"How could You stand by? You're disgusting. Your choices are disgusting."

Her surroundings blurred. She couldn't live with nothing but blisters of memory raked open, but she had to hold onto them, keep them this raw and vivid for the rest of her life, because these were the only memories she would ever have. Years would pass. She would turn thirty-one, then thirty-two, then thirty-three, and for that year they would be the same age, and then she'd be thirty-four. Older than Marcus. Someday, her hair would go gray. She would hunch over when she stood, and her limbs would creak when she walked. And Marcus would still be muscular and young, with arms that loved to work and legs that loved to run and a heartbeat that had been silenced.

Her nails dug into her palm. No longer wrapped around the pot, her hand was crushing one of the flowers. She opened her hand, and the bloom lay there, a few red petals torn away. Lee sank to the floor with the planter in her lap and dropped the petals into the soil. Cupped the smashed flower and snapped it off the stem. She plucked another petal, then another, then another, until the flower was bare green in her hand and the dirt in the planter was scattered with petals.

6

No way Jason could've been following him, not all the way from Elysium on a Sunday afternoon. But a hundred feet after Austin's turn into the Hansens' neighborhood, a rotating green light flashed in his rearview mirror. And yes, that was his boss behind the wheel of the gray SUV. Not a Constabulary vehicle, but Jason had slapped on one of those magnet things. Either he kept that handy in his car all the time, or he'd acquired it for his purposes today. One of those options should bother Austin more, if he could think.

He pulled to the side and put the car in park. What was the worst that could happen right now?

Do you really want to go there?

Jason stopped at his window and gestured, and Austin rolled down the window. "Sir, all I want to do is—"

"Get out."

"What?"

"Does Hansen know your car?"

Austin shook his head.

"Come on. We're going for a drive."

Boss or not, this guy needed a lesson in boundaries. Austin wasn't a teenager, and he wasn't on duty. "No, sir."

Jason crossed his arms and rocked back on his heels. "You go with me today, or you're out of a job tomorrow."

Not the time to test whether Jason could follow through with that. Austin stepped out of his car and hung his keys on a belt loop of his jeans. Frayed slim cuts to go with his red V-neck sweater and black bomber jacket that Violet liked to wear whenever they had gone to a concert together, which hadn't been often enough. He looked like a college kid, a civilian, nothing intimidating about him. And he'd proved he wouldn't barge in on Clay Hansen waving his badge around. No reason not to trust him with this.

Jason slid behind the wheel, and Austin opened the SUV's passenger door. He could handle himself. He was armed, after all.

"Where are we going?"

"Back to the office. Something I want you to see."

Fine. Austin slid into the seat and shut the door too hard. The clean upholstery smell mingled with the scent of cinnamon gum. "I know the terms of Hansen's deal, Jason. Unconditional amnesty."

"It's right there in your voice, kid."

"What?"

Jason pulled into traffic, and his right eyebrow twitched. "Disdain."

"Maybe you're projecting your experience with other agents." Or maybe not.

"You remember what I said about lying to me?"

Austin shifted against the passenger window as Jason made a left turn. Yeah, he was headed back to the admin building. He was also shooting Austin glances like darts.

"I'm not sure I agree with unconditional amnesty, no matter what the case. But especially not this case."

"Of course, not this case."

"Jason, if something happened to Reese Cabrera-Hill, if she vanished, would you pursue every option of finding her?"

Jason shrugged.

"You would, not only because she's an innocent person but because she's worked with you, worked for you to further your mission. Well, what about Violet? She put herself in harm's way for us, and then maybe real harm comes to her, and we wash our hands. That guy knows more than he wants to tell me, and I can't even have a street-clothes conversation with him."

By the time his rant dried up, his pulse was pounding a warning. Jason didn't respond for long minutes—not the longest of Austin's life, of course, but enough time for his heartbeat to level. Enough time to convince himself he'd be jobless tomorrow.

"That's why we're going back to the office," Jason said.

So you can hold your hand out for my badge and gun in official surroundings.

They didn't break the quiet for the rest of the drive.

Jason took the correct road, then drove past the building. Austin's frown was met with a shrug.

"You said we were going to—"

"Clarification. The property behind the office."

Austin pressed his lips together and watched out the passenger window. Jason turned left and then left again, a right angle that took them down a cracked residential street. They *were* behind Constabulary property—state property, one long row of skinny public housing projects. Had anyone ever lived here? One house appeared half-naked, tar paper exposed to the elements. The rest were finished with white siding, black shingles and black doors, empty copies of copies somehow both new and worn, run down not by careless occupants but by weather and time. Between the houses and the street sprawled one boundless front yard. The grass stood two feet tall, still mostly green and long since conquered by weeds and some pink wildflower.

Jason parked in front of the houses—no, in front of a particular house, as if they weren't all the same. Austin followed him up the driveway, stepping around knee-high nettle plants that sprouted from the cracks. *Where … what … why …?* Nothing made it out of his mouth, though, as he trailed Jason past the garage and around, behind the house. A long-lost metal lawn chair wedged the back door shut. The doorknob had been removed.

"Jason?"

Jason pushed the lawn chair aside and opened the door. Did he own this place? He glanced back at Austin, and light from the lowering sun brightened the blue of his eyes.

"Okay." Jason twitched a smile. "Come on in."

Even without electricity, the place was lit well by the many windows on this side of the main level. Austin shoved his hands into his jacket pockets; of course, the heat wasn't on either. They walked on ivory carpet through the living room, mostly pristine, but a few dirt smears betrayed a former trespasser. At the kitchen threshold, an odd stench hung in the air.

Austin followed further, to the door of a closet or something. A regular door with a regular doorknob … that locked from outside. A shudder gripped him.

"Okay," Jason said and unlocked the door.

The smell came from inside, heavy and rotten, and just as Austin's brain identified it—sweat, urine, human grime—his gaze cleared Jason's shoulder. The floor of this tiny room was the same pale tile as that of the kitchen and littered with empty foil wrappers. In one corner sat a deep plastic bucket. In the other slouched a man.

Back to the wall. Legs half-bent in front of him. Body sagged forward, chin on his chest. Without the wall behind him, he'd collapse to one side. So motionless he could be dead, except for the quiet, wheezing breaths. But as the fading light slanted into his prison, the man lifted his head. Not an empty gaze. The brown eyes, dull with pain and bright with fever, focused on Jason.

Jason stared back. "Kid, I'd love to watch you poke at Hansen, unearth that girl's hiding place … But see, I can't let you."

Austin tried to follow, tried to think past revulsion. What did this man have to do with …? Wait a minute.

"Marcus Brenner? Jason, this is Marcus Brenner?"

The man's gaze, emotionless but aware, traveled to Austin's.

Brown hair curled past the collar of the T-shirt that was probably red when clean. His beard was scruffy, his elbows and knees and wrists and jaw all too sharp. His khaki shorts gaped away from his waist.

"How long have you … had him?"

"I never *didn't* have him." Jason stepped further into the pantry. He turned his back on his prisoner because Brenner couldn't move, much less attack or escape. "Four months, he's been here. While all of them—including you, kid—thought I couldn't catch him. Other than Tisdale, who thinks I killed him."

Jason aimed the smirk down at Brenner, and the man met his eyes.

"Uh …" Stay calm. Don't challenge him. Live another day. The survival litany flooded him, the vivid color of memory including his own blood, but this wasn't his father. This was Jason.

"Which has actually turned out pretty convenient. Guy doesn't cross you when he thinks you're capable of murder."

Aren't you? Austin breathed in and leveled his voice. "What're you going to do with him?"

"Fair question."

The room wasn't meant to hold three people, but Austin stepped inside. No fear. Agree with him. His head pounded.

"I thought he'd be dead by now, but …" Jason paced one step away and met the wall, then pivoted back. "Guess that's not how it's going to go."

"But isn't this a risk? Why not put a bullet in his head?"

"Right, but … not yet."

Austin's stomach knotted. He forced a deep breath of the urine-choked air. *What are you going to do about this?* Nothing. Because he couldn't. Look at the man. Brenner was already dead.

"I've had this in the back of my head since we started working together more. Really, your hounding me about Hansen, that was the push I needed."

"I … Jason, I don't know if I'm following you."

"You need to know I get my guy."

"So you'll … hold him in here until he starves?"

"Oh."

Jason reached to his inside coat pocket, and every nerve in Austin's body jolted. *Gun*—No … granola bar in a foil wrapper. Jason tossed it on the ground at Brenner's feet.

"I make sure he gets one every day or two, when I can get over here. And water sometimes, though I didn't bring any today."

Jason wasn't this person. Jason was logical and noble in his goals for re-education, for Constabulary success. He followed the law.

Do something.

"Thank you for … trusting me, sir."

"Part of telling you was simple necessity. Hansen knows enough about the details to be dangerous. I can't have him thinking we're reneging on the deal. But really, you earned this information, kid." He tilted his head and turned to Brenner, who was still watching him. "See, Brenner, I give what's earned. You want all this to end, just say the word."

The silence stretched out while the two of them stared each other down. Fever glittered in Brenner's eyes, but he didn't blink.

"Come on, man," Jason whispered. "Say. It."

Whatever "it" was, Jason's hands had begun to tremble at his sides. Austin backed up to the doorway. "Jason, maybe he's too sick to talk."

"He can talk when he wants to. But I'll make it easy. Just nod, man. You're wrong about God. This room proves it. You're ready to give it all up. Nod, and I'll count it as the answer."

Brenner's inhale was slow, shallow, but deliberate. His voice rasped. "No."

Jason rammed the toe of his boot into the man's ribs.

Brenner's gasp broke into a cough, and he bent forward, one hand clenching the hem of his shorts.

Austin surged a step forward and froze. How many times had Jason done this over the last four months and *what are you going to do about it, Austin?* The room faded around him, but the sounds didn't. Jason kicked the man twice more while heat washed through Austin's limbs. He had to stop this, had to fight Jason, had to defend that man helpless on the floor—had to defend himself, had to stop lying helpless on the floor.

It's not me, I'm not getting hurt.

But someone else was and he was doing nothing and Jason—

7

Austin's thumb trembled on the phone's touch screen. Contacts. Esther. The phone rang five times before going to voicemail. "It's Esther D, hey, don't leave a message 'cause I don't listen to them, but when I see your missed call I'll call you back, unless I don't know your number."

Austin hung up and redialed.

"Dude, really, we were going to call you right back."

His hands steadied. "Hey, Livvy. Since when does Esther let you touch her phone?"

Olivia's grin traveled through the line. "Since her hands are all sticky with cookie dough and she saw it was just you. We're making double chocolate chip. You should come over."

The kid knew a pause would follow that, but she always found some reason to say it. Austin leaned back against the couch. He glared at his bookshelf across the room and tried to formulate an answer.

"Dad's not home," Olivia whispered.

Always a good thing, but better tonight. His dad's voice kept merging with the sounds of Marcus Brenner being kicked in the ribs. *"What're you going to do about it, Austin? You going to cry or hit back?"* That man's voice in the background of Olivia's might put Austin's fist through a wall right now. He rose from the couch and paced the geometric design on the rug, phone held between ear and shoulder. Chill out. He rotated his free arm.

"I can't tonight, Livvy, so eat my share of the cookies."

"Oh, for sure."

"What's up with you? Haven't talked in a while." Might as well verbalize the fault now so they could move on, not that Olivia would find fault in the first place.

"It's okay, I know you're busy and stuff. You arrest anybody this week?"

No matter how many times Austin clarified the entry-level nature of his job, Olivia and Esther imagined him breaking down the doors of illegal church meetings, confiscating and burning old Bibles, leading apprehended Christians through the doors of their first re-education session. He couldn't grin at their glamorization tonight.

"Not this week. How's math?"

"I got an eighty-seven on the unit test last week."

"Eighty-seven's good, Liv. Did the mnemonics help?"

"Kind of. When I could remember them."

The chuckle shook his chest.

"What if I text you next time he's working late? Will you come for dinner? You could stay for like an hour or two, and be gone before he got home."

They deserved to see their brother, and he wanted to see them. He dropped back onto the couch and sighed. "Okay, you text me and I'll come."

"And you have to *make* dinner. I want white pizza, and you can do your sauce for Mom and Esther."

"Deal. Let me talk to her."

The phone shifted hands with a blur of sound. "Hey, big bro."

"Just checking in, middle sis."

"We're all clear."

If she ever said, "We're perfectly fine," he would know his father had done something, either to one of the girls or to Mom. But in the three and a half years since he'd left home, the code had never been used.

A fourteen-year-old girl shouldn't have to talk to her brother in code. She should be able to tell him, right in front of Mom, if things blew up. Shoot, Mom should call him herself. Like that would ever happen.

"Austin?"

"Sorry. I'm here."

"Olivia said you'll come for dinner soon."

"I will, Esther. I promise."

"Ooh. I'm going to hold you to that on pain of … I know! If you don't come to dinner within the next two weeks, you have to take me to a concert."

"As in, a not-real-music concert."

"Pop is the most *popular* form of music, Austin. For many reasons."

"Reasons such as the intellectual downfall of Western culture?" The grin split his face. Maybe he should fail to come to dinner.

"You're the world's biggest snob, and you know it, and you like it about yourself. And that's so totally pathetic."

"I'll brave one of your boy bands if you'll let me take you to a folk festival."

"Uhh …" In the background, the cookie sheet was slid from the oven. "I'll think that over, okay? Come to dinner."

By the end of their conversation, Austin could breathe deeply again, but he still reached for his guitar. His fingers picked a Fleetwood Mac melody while he replayed his sisters' voices and envisioned the house he grew up in, ten miles south, white and black with green shutters, a glow through the kitchen window and figures passing in front of it, Esther with that purple streak in her blonde hair and Olivia with her nearly black ponytail, both of them wiping hands on their aprons and eating as much dough as cookies. Around the scene, Austin imagined an invisible cloak of safety.

Maybe Dad would never hit another one of his kids. After all, he didn't have to make a man out of Esther or Livvy. Or maybe gender had nothing to do with it, and the snake inside Dad reared up and struck only in Austin's presence because of Austin.

His fingers blended "Never Going Back Again" into "Landslide" into "The Chain," and his mind blended Dad into Jason and what might happen tomorrow at work.

It proved to be an odd day, except not really, when he thought about it. Putting him on paperwork duty was no doubt Jason's subtle reminder that Austin didn't control his own career or anything else. He set his jaw and got to work, exchanging grins and jokes with the data entry team and concealing the fact that he didn't consider these "agents" really worthy of the title. Look at Agent Stiles, the guy working across the partition. Fifty-something, and before lunch, he'd told Austin about his job as a financial advisor before applying to the Constabulary.

"I didn't want a field post," he said. "Even if I had, I'm too old to start work like that. But I wanted to join this cause, in whatever capacity I'd be useful."

And, okay, the guy *was* useful. Or at least, his photographic memory was.

"What're you doing over here, by the way?"

Austin's face heated. Nothing he came up with sounded true, including the truth. He'd have to paint himself as insubordinate or something. Probably Jason's plan all along, to humiliate him. *Jason's not like that.* Why was his brain still defending the man?

"You're Agent Mayweather's new pet, right?" Agent Fitch tossed over the partition.

Austin gritted his teeth. "No. I am a colleague, though."

Stiles's gaze snapped up to his, as if seeing him for the first time. "Not his partner?"

"Mayweather doesn't do partners."

Stiles nodded. "You do learn fast. Jason put you down here? What'd you do?"

"Nothing." He knew better than to snap. That would only sharpen their curiosity. "And Mayweather had nothing to do with this."

The ribbing went on for another minute, until Austin got up and walked a lap around the building. He closed his eyes and pictured himself slipping into the green coat. Calm. Safe. They were just idiots. He had no reason to bristle. When he returned to his desk eight minutes later, the other guys ignored him. Why the change?

Stiles winked. Hmm, maybe … Austin dipped an inconspicuous nod. *Thanks.* Stiles nodded back.

By lunch break, Austin never wanted to touch a document scanner again. Fifty-something or not, Stiles must get bored, facing forty hours of this every week. Austin grabbed his coat and headed for his car, ready for a long workout with the day only half over.

"Hold up," came a deep voice from over his shoulder.

What could Stiles want? Austin folded his arms, keys still dangling from one hand. "Yeah?"

"Why are you really stuck in paperwork today?"

Austin forced an eye roll that said, *Man, I thought you were cooler than this.* "Wrist slap, that's all. Learning my place."

"Did you question him?"

"Guess I must have."

This wasn't curiosity. Stiles's dark gaze bored into Austin, and he tugged a pen from his jacket pocket and started to walk it through his long fingers. *Hurry up and defuse this.*

"Really, no worries," Austin said. "He's all bark, you know?"

The walking pen froze. The man lowered his hand to his side and took a step forward. "You're obviously not paying attention, kid. Maybe I should walk away and let you learn by experience."

Austin's mouth dried. He pressed his heels into the blacktop. *Don't step back. Don't give ground.* But nothing about Stiles held a threat, other than his voice.

"However, I try not to leave people in their stupidity, so hear me on this. Jason Mayweather is the toothiest pit bull in the MPC. You cross him, he'll tear your throat out."

Maybe it was the reference to a mortal wound, or maybe the pull of Stiles's frown and the urgency in his eyes. Understanding rained over Austin. *Jason, Tisdale isn't the only one who thinks you killed that guy.* But Stiles didn't show any fear. If anything, flickering behind his eyes … that might be hate. The kind that precipitated action. If only this man knew that a mile away, Brenner was …

"You know," Stiles said quietly.

Austin shrugged. "Know what?"

"That it's not just a rumor. What, did he brag to you and then regret it, put you down here as a threat?"

The proximity to the truth sent a chill down Austin's back. He folded his arms. "It's just a rumor, Agent Stiles."

Maybe something could be done. Maybe Brenner could be transferred to official custody, and Jason would … would what? Regardless, a man was being abused to death a mile away. It had to stop. So either Austin stopped it on his own, or—

"What makes you so sure?" Stiles said.

Austin swallowed. This man could be testing him and reporting back to Jason.

Stiles stepped closer until Austin had to lean back, but his feet stayed put. No giving ground. The man's finger poked Austin's chest—not hard, but he had to move his feet to keep his balance. His arm swung up to block and their fists collided somehow and Austin's brain went black as his body surged.

"Whoa!"

The deep voice penetrated the furious haze. Austin blinked. He'd seized Stiles's arms, locked them behind his back, and shoved him face-first against the car.

"Hey, ease up, son, I—"

Austin twisted his arm. "Not your son."

"Sorry. Comes with the graying hair. Listen, I got up in your space, and I apologize. I think we've both had a long week."

True enough. Austin turned Stiles loose.

The man rotated his shoulders and turned slowly. "Agent Delvecchio, if you know anything, I'm asking you to tell me."

"I don't know what you're talking about." The words were like brands on his brain.

Stiles closed his eyes. "I'm talking about Jason Mayweather." His eyes opened. "And the murder of Marcus Brenner."

What are you going to do about it, Austin? Cry or hit back?

He had to tell someone. Someone who, when pinned to a car for no good reason, apologized instead of retaliating.

"Actually, sir … there hasn't been a murder yet."

8

"Go to the kitchen and wash your hands for—"

"Thirty seconds," Violet said from the floor of the car. "And then I'll come find you in the exam rooms. Really, Lee, we've done this a few times now."

Not like this. Sam's *I have a patient for you* texts had never coded the emergency higher than a six. The text she'd deleted half an hour ago still tied her stomach into a knot. No random sentence to make her smile, no *Wassup homegirl*, nothing but the number.

Ten.

She tried to sigh the tension from her body along with her breath. Not effective. Her "six" patient had suffered a dislocated shoulder, tears of pain streaking his face before she even arrived, much less relocated the joint. A ten could mean multiple patients. Burns. Gunshot wound. Anything. She parked behind the clinic and let the headlights shut off before opening her door. Violet sprang up from the backseat and followed her into the windy night. Inside, Violet started to head for the kitchen.

"Wait," Lee said.

Violet glanced past her down the hall, toward whatever case awaited them. "Yeah?"

"You need to prepare yourself before you join me."

"I've seen blood plenty of—"

"I don't expect merely blood this time."

"Maybe there're two patients, and that's why he called it a ten."

Maybe. "If you can't handle whatever it is, you need to let me know immediately and then leave the room."

A month ago, Violet might have rolled her eyes. But she only sighed and nodded, then left to scrub in. Lee hurried to the exam rooms.

Sam sat on the edge of one of the beds, his back to her, shoulders hunched. Twice, she scanned the room. Everything was as she'd left it two days ago.

"Sam?"

He jolted to his feet and faced her, and her heart skipped. He stared at her, eyes too wide, the whites showing between dark irises and dark skin. In one hand, he gripped a pen, as if he'd been walking it through his fingers while waiting for her. Lee stepped nearer. The pen was broken.

"Where is my patient?" she said.

"Sit down."

Understanding whipped away the cold shroud that had dropped onto the room. Sam had brought her here for a discussion, no doubt about her errors in judgment, bringing new patients here herself. "This. Is not acceptable."

"Lee, I need to—"

"You manipulated me into coming here with an emergency code? A ten, no less, and there's not even a patient? I brought Violet and—"

"Good." He stuffed the broken pen into the pocket of his light blue polo, and black ink smeared the edge of the pocket.

"Good?"

"That you brought Violet. Now sit down and let me—"

Lee pivoted on her heel and stalked toward the door. Sam planted himself in front of her, and his eyes seemed even wider now.

"There is a patient. I put him in the guestroom."

What? They'd furnished that room with only a mattress, pillows, and blankets for her, should she ever treat someone who needed round-the-clock, critical care. "The guestroom's not for public use."

"It isn't public. He isn't. I mean—Lee, sit. I have to talk to you. Before you go in there."

"Did the patient die while you waited for me?"

"No, he—he's—alive." Sam scrubbed at his face. "Dang it, Lee, I can't figure out how to tell you."

"Then don't." She headed toward the room. Sam grabbed her arm, but she wrenched free. What was wrong with him? He knew what she saw every day at work. Just today, she'd lost an MVA victim ejected through the windshield.

Violet's voice trailed behind her. "What's going on, you guys?"

"It's Marcus," Sam said.

Lee's feet stopped inches from the closed door. "I'm sorry, I misheard you."

"You didn't." Sam pressed his thumbs into his eyes. "The patient is Marcus. Lee, listen to me, he—"

Her hand flung the door open. Her feet charged into the room. She scrutinized the patient on the mattress, ready to catalogue every feature that proved he wasn't Marcus.

But he was.

His chest rose and fell once, twice, three times, while she stood there and waited for it to stop. It didn't. Lee fell to her knees beside the mattress and pressed two fingers to his left wrist. His heartbeat was steady.

Respiration. Pulse.

Alive.

His eyes were fixed on her, blank. His faint gasp became a cough. His right arm pulled into his chest.

"I laid him down flat," Sam said from behind her. "The pillow was under his head."

Lee blinked. One detail came into focus—Marcus lay propped against the wall with the pillow supporting his back—and then all the rest sharpened too. Gauntness, shallow inhalation, unwashed clothes and hair and beard, eyes too bright. Fever. And the cough … he'd moved because he couldn't breathe.

Lee wrapped her hand around his wrist. Alive.

"Marcus—" She cleared the burning from her throat. "How long have you been ill?"

His gaze didn't waver from her, but he didn't speak.

"Marcus?"

His right arm tightened against his chest.

Sam's voice came nearer. "He hasn't said a word so far."

A fit of coughing seized Marcus, and he jerked his wrist from her hold to wrap both arms around … not his chest. His ribs.

The shirt left human oil on her fingertips as she pushed it up his torso. Behind her, Violet gasped. Black bruising covered most of his body, faded to yellow at his stomach, glaring fresh purple along his right side. A boot print, toe to heel. Not a kick, at least not that time. He'd been supine and stomped on. Lee reached out to raise his arms, but he shrank against the pillow and ducked his head.

"I need to remove your shirt," she whispered.

The brown eyes that locked onto hers held no comprehension, no emotion.

"You can hear me, can't you? If you can, I need you to nod."

A muscle pulled in his jaw. He dipped his head in that single, jerking motion, as familiar as his laugh or his smile.

"You've been—" Brutalized. "Injured. Will you let me help you?"

His hands clenched against the mattress.

"Marcus." She folded her hands on the bed, next to his left one. "Please."

His gaze traveled to their hands, and he watched his own fingers uncurl. Then he met her eyes again and blinked. "Lee."

"Yes?"

"Lee?"

"Yes."

His head bowed. He clasped her hand between both of his and pressed it to his chest. "Lee."

She tried to focus, tried to prioritize the damage, tried to turn and find Violet's gaze. She couldn't move.

A gentle hand squeezed her forearm. Violet's voice choked on tears, but she steadied it. "What should I bring you?"

Thank you. "Stethoscope. Scissors. Ice packs. A water bottle, he's dehydrated. Marcus, when did you last eat?"

He shook his head.

"He needs antibiotics," Lee said, "but not without food. Bring whatever you find."

"Be right back." Violet all but ran from the room.

Lee rose from her knees and sat on the edge of the mattress. Marcus's grip tightened when her hand shifted, but he didn't lift his head. At the edge of her vision, someone moved. She looked up.

Sam stood against the wall. The broken pen had bled a circle of black ink onto the pocket of his shirt.

"They …" The rest of the words remained in her head, screaming. *They had him all these months, and you missed it?*

Sam's voice rasped. "This wasn't sanctioned."

In what way was that supposed to matter?

"The case file still says he escaped in June. But from what I learned tonight, he's been … since …"

One hundred thirty-eight days. He hadn't been dead while she bottled up his laugh, his smile, his nod, his voice saying her name. He'd been breathing all this time. So many breaths in one hundred thirty-eight days.

"It was Mayweather, Lee, all of it. Operating alone, off the books. I knew he was … but I didn't know he was …"

A finger of ice ran down her back. *All of it.* The boot tread on Marcus's side.

"You have to run," Sam said.

"Run?"

"When he finds that room empty … Mayweather's going to come after you, and you're not going to convince him you don't know anything. You need to get out of Michigan. All of you."

"What room? Where was he, what—"

Marcus's grip nearly crushed her hand. She swiveled toward him, but he didn't raise his head.

"Lee," Sam said. He stepped forward but stopped in the middle of the room, well outside her space. "You need to hear me on this, on what has to happen."

She would make Marcus well. That's what would happen.

"You cannot go home, you cannot go to work."

"Obviously."

"What Mayweather did—I don't know what other lines he'll cross. I don't know if he has any lines."

"And where would we go?"

"Personally, I'd suggest Texas."

"Sam." She couldn't imagine it. Well, actually, she could. Safety for Marcus. For all of them. But it was a dream, nothing more.

"Here's everything." Violet plowed into the room and knelt next to the mattress. She held up a Ziploc, its contents blurred by condensation from the inside. "It's a sandwich from last time I was here—PB and J. The bread's a little mushy."

Protein and carbohydrates, good enough for the moment. First things first, though. Lee reached for the scissors, and Marcus released her other hand. His shirt was stiff with old sweat and grime. She cut upward from the hem to the collar, then did the same to the back of it while Violet held his shoulders to keep him upright. The shirt peeled away, taking with it flakes of dead skin. Four months without a shower. The smell registered in Lee's brain for the first time. His muscular build had wasted to skin stretched over bone.

He flinched when she pressed the stethoscope first to his sternum, then to his back. Hope withered at the crackle in his lungs.

She set the stethoscope aside. "Pneumonia."

"What does he need?" Violet said, still propping him up.

A hospital. Oxygen. A saline IV infused with nutrients, analgesics, antibiotics. She pushed away the impossibilities. "Amoxicillin, if it's bacterial."

"You want me to bring you some?"

"In a minute. Marcus, I need to check for rib fractures."

He seemed to understand but didn't respond. She palpated each rib, anterior and posterior. Four of them shifted under pressure, all on his left side. His only reaction was a pause in his breathing, but when she lowered him to the pillow, placing it to the left of his spine, he gave a shallow sigh of relief. Lee settled the ice packs against the darkest contusions, and he held his breath, then sighed again. His eyes closed. The furrow between his eyebrows could have been pain or something else.

"All right." She forced the tremor from her voice. "The ice packs will help with the fever as well as the bruising. For now, the most pressing needs are oxygen, nutrition, and hydration."

Violet offered her the water bottle.

"Marcus," Lee said, and his eyes opened. "You need to drink all of this."

He licked his lips, and one crack began to bleed. Lee unscrewed the cap from the bottle and offered it to him, but he nearly dropped it. She held the back of his head and tipped the bottle to his lips. Violet jumped up and hurried from the room. What was she doing?

Marcus's hand came up to curl around the bottle, brushing hers with too much heat. With a fever this high, he should be sweating, but his skin was only flushed. He gulped the water too fast.

"Slowly," Lee said, but he ignored her. She pulled the bottle back, and his breaths wheezed. "Slowly."

He jerked a nod. By the time he'd finished the water, Violet had returned with a small jar of petroleum jelly.

"Here." She held it out.

Sensible of her. Lee dabbed her finger in the jar, touched it to his bottom lip. He watched her, then closed his eyes, and the wrinkle between them returned. When she'd finished, his lips were coated with a thick shine and her hand was shaking.

She cleared her throat. "Can you eat?"

He opened his eyes.

"Marcus, I … If you can, please answer me."

He nodded.

"Can you answer me?"

Silence swelled until the walls might crack. Marcus pressed his lips together, then whispered. "I can. Eat."

While he chewed each bite of sandwich for a long minute, Lee looked up at Sam. "I can't move him in this condition. He needs three days for the pneumonia to start clearing up, and his ribs—"

"Move him? Where to, Texas?" When no one corrected Violet's sarcasm, her eyes widened. "Really? You're … leaving?"

"If we do, you're welcome to accompany us," Lee said. *She is?*

Yes.

Before Violet could answer her, Marcus pushed aside the second half of sandwich. He shook his head when Lee tried to persuade him to finish it but whispered, "Thanks."

"When did you eat last?" Maybe he'd respond this time beyond a head shake.

"I don't know."

"What sort of food were you given?"

"Bars."

"Protein bars?"

"Granola."

"And what else?"

He shook his head.

Lee laced her fingers to keep them steady. *Make him well.* She no longer knew if she was ordering herself or someone else.

Someone else? Who else was there? The deity that had let a Constabulary rogue abuse him for months?

Lee's hands spasmed, still intertwined, and rose to her face.

"Lee?" Violet said.

Her lungs constricted. Her mind saw the geranium petals she'd ripped apart the last time she couldn't breathe and tried to count them. Fewer than one hundred thirty-eight.

"Lee." Sam's deep voice, closer than he'd been standing a moment ago.

Get away from me, all of you.

"It's … okay." Marcus.

She lowered her shaking hands. His eyes weren't his, not with so much missing from them, but his frown drew down the same way it always had.

"You." His gaze took in Sam and Violet, then returned to Lee. "This. Here. I'm …" He coughed and gripped the edge of the mattress until he could stop. "Going to be. Okay."

Lee pressed her palms into the mattress and catalogued every feature that wasn't Marcus. Empty eyes. Rusted voice. Shrunken body. Broken words.

One hundred thirty-eight days.

9

Most people would have listened to Agent Stiles's parting advice. Austin had listened to half of it, finishing out the workday as if all was normal. Stiles disappeared around three o'clock and didn't return to his desk. Hopefully, Brenner had been hospitalized by now. If he had, Stiles would frown on Austin's failure to heed the second half of his advice.

"Do not under any circumstances go home."

He scanned his surroundings five times as he let himself into the apartment foyer and sprinted up the stairs. Nobody around, yet his arms and neck prickled. He wasn't here to stay, not even to spend the night. He'd grab the sports bag from the hall closet, the one Esther called his "we're perfectly fine" bag, and go to a hotel or something. The duffels he'd packed for the girls—those could stay here for now. They only held clothes, toiletries, and packaged trail mix. Unbeknownst to Esther, hers also held the smallest-capacity iPod model, fully loaded with obnoxious pop music.

The contents of Austin's bag were slightly more practical—clothes and toiletries, of course, but also a wad of cash, a preloaded Visa card, enough beef jerky to sustain him for a week, and his secondary firearm. And yeah, okay, a few books. And the tickets to the last concert he'd taken Violet to, not that he'd admit to keeping them.

He inserted his key into the lock. Before he could turn it, the door swung open on its hinges.

Someone had broken the lock.

Austin drew his gun from the shoulder holster and stepped over the threshold and flipped on the light—

Weight cracked against his wrist. The gun dropped to the floor, safety still on. Austin pivoted toward the source of the blow, stars blinking in front of his eyes. A fist aimed for his throat. Austin ducked to one side, and knuckles clipped his cheek, and something within him exploded. He dived at—yeah, of course, Jason.

Jason staggered back, then righted his balance. Austin threw punches but hit him only half the time, and every landed blow sent searing pain up his arm. A fist crashed into his upper chest, then his shoulder, still trying for his throat. Then Jason danced backward like a boxer and pulled his gun and fired.

Carpet in his face. His voice bursting free now, never a scream but yes a cry. He was on fire. He rolled on the floor and tried to put it out. No, he was shot … everywhere.

"Austin."

He panted through the pain until it melted off him. Tased, then—not shot. He couldn't stand up, so he didn't try. Tennis shoes moved into his vision.

"Where's Brenner?"

In custody. In a hospital. Or … not.

Austin rolled onto his back and cradled his wrist. "I don't know what you're talking about."

Jason holstered the Taser and circled him. *Get up. Hurry.* Austin blinked against the stars. Twin tears trickled down his temples, into his hair.

"You little piece of crap," Jason said. "This is what you do with my trust."

"I didn't do—"

Jason kicked his side, below his ribs. The pain hardly registered. Austin pushed up onto his elbows and rolled to his knees. Jason grabbed the collar of his shirt and yanked him to his feet. This time, the punch didn't miss his throat. Austin crumpled backward, and the couch cushions caught his back and his head. He sprawled, half on the floor. *Black out and you're dead.*

This time, Jason did pull his sidearm.

Dead no matter what. Austin's mouth dried. His heart hammered.

Jason eased the safety to disengage. He leveled the gun at Austin's forehead. "You've forgotten a few things."

Think, think, hurry. Think.

"Such as, I outrank you. I can end your career. I can put you behind bars with one piece of planted evidence. I can do to you whatever I want."

"I can find him." Austin's voice wheezed through the swelling in his throat.

"Certainly hope so."

"Twenty-four hours."

Jason's stare lasted a whole minute. He tilted the gun as if calculating the bullet's path through the air into Austin's skull. He wandered to the bookshelf and browsed titles, then crouched at Austin's feet. With an easy flip of the gun, now holding the barrel, he swung the grip hard against Austin's ankle. Austin bit down on a gasp.

"That's because I think you were planning to run." Jason stood. "You can find him? Go ahead and find him."

"I said—"

"Have you earned twenty-four hours of trust?"

"Yes."

Jason laughed.

Austin stayed on the floor. Let him walk out of the room with the upper hand. But it was pointless. No way Jason would leave him.

"Whoever you have to call, you can do it here and now in front of me. Go on."

"Okay." Austin braced his elbows on the couch cushion behind him and stood. Not as shaky as he thought.

He dug his phone from his pocket. No one to call. He woke his phone anyway and started to dial. The *beep* of the first number made him jump, and Jason made a scoffing sound. Austin kept punching numbers, first a one, then an area code, then seven more and a final eighth digit that he hoped would sound like calling out. He stood with the phone to his ear, eyes on Jason. He'd have to hit the gun first and succeed in knocking it away. Or he'd be dead.

If he didn't try, he'd be dead anyway.

"Well?" Jason said.

"They're not picking up."

"Who're you—?"

Austin dropped the phone and charged, his whole weight crashing into Jason's gun arm. The weapon hit the floor. A few punches hit his midsection and then he was behind Jason, luckily taller. He dropped his arm around the man's neck and squeezed until Jason stopped trying to claw his eyes out and then went limp. Faking, maybe. Austin held on a few more seconds, shook him, trying to get a reaction, but Jason's arms flopped like a ragdoll's. Austin let him fall to the floor and checked his wrist for a pulse. His shaking hand took a minute to find it, and he sighed when it beat against his fingers.

He swept up the phone, raced to the closet, and grabbed his bag. He should tie Jason up, but if the man woke, one of them would end up dead.

10

Austin rotated his throbbing ankle as the headlights approached. The last five cars hadn't been Stiles. This one probably wasn't, either. The guy could be anywhere, could come home anytime.

He slid the seat back until it bumped his sports bag on the floor behind him, then propped his elbow on the arm rest to elevate his wrist. He had to sit here as long as it took. Good thing Stiles lived alone. Doubly good thing he was listed in the white pages.

You don't have to be here. Let Stiles fend for himself.

Not for the first time, his hand reached to turn the key in the ignition.

No. This guy could be in danger, and he'd saved Brenner's life. A good cop. Ironic, considering forty-eight hours ago Austin hadn't wanted to grace him with the title of cop at all. Well, a guy's actions made all the difference.

Twenty minutes later, a black town car pulled into the driveway, and the garage door opened. Austin crossed the street, curtained in darkness. Stiles had parked and was halfway to the door when Austin stepped into the garage.

"Hey," he said.

The man jolted and spun to face him.

"It's Delvecchio." Austin raised his hands to midtorso. "We've got to talk."

In the hours since he'd last seen Agent Stiles, new stress pulled at the man's crow's feet and the lines around his mouth.

"Showing up at my house doesn't qualify as lying low."

"It's important," Austin said. "Things you need to know, about—"

Stiles waved him to silence and hit the garage door opener. The door rumbled shut. "Whatever it is, I already know."

Heat pulsed behind Austin's eyes. He charged closer, pushing at the edge of Stiles's personal space. "Yeah? So you knew he'd threaten to kill me? Could've mentioned it."

"To kill—you went home?"

"Had to get some things if I was going to run for my life."

"You. Went. Home." His voice clipped each word shorter than the last.

"Yeah, well, I'm not dead, so—"

"You absolutely should be."

Yeah, I know. What was Austin doing, anyway, thinking Stiles might be trustworthy? If his mentor could turn out to be a sociopath, so could any other Constabulary agent, even a desk guy like Stiles.

No, not Stiles. Not the guy who'd taken Brenner out of that room and hidden him.

Still, being here was pointless. Austin headed for the side door. He'd get back in his car and …

And what?

"That a limp?" Stiles's voice came over his shoulder, closer.

Austin pivoted to face him, almost stumbling on the stupid ankle. "Reminder not to run."

The man's dark eyes narrowed, scanned up and down Austin. "You favoring that arm?"

"Wrist. I think it's just bruised."

"What else did he do?"

Heat flushed Austin's face. The old shame probably wasn't reasonable when his attacker had a Taser. Still, being beat up did nothing for a guy's self-image. Good thing the jacket collar covered his throat. "Nothing mortal."

"Why'd you come to me?"

"I didn't *come to you*. I came to warn you. Unneeded, obviously."

"Obviously, when I told you not to go home in the first place." He scrubbed a hand over his hair. "But he didn't shoot you."

"He might have. I knocked him out."

"Knocked him out?"

Austin shrugged. "Sleeper hold. And then I got out of there. I don't know where he is now."

"Crap." Stiles scrubbed at his face, and his breath shook on its way out. He couldn't be rattled like this only for Austin.

"You didn't take Brenner to a hospital, did you?"

Austin wasn't certain of it until he spoke the words. If Stiles had denied it, he probably would have believed him. But the man's eyes flickered down to the cement, long enough to be a confirmation.

"Are you …?" Their eyes met. "Stiles, you're part of this somehow, aren't you."

Part of a terrorist underground. Maybe Stiles knew something Austin didn't, something about the entire Constabulary, not only Jason. Maybe they were all less upstanding than Austin's training had taught him.

"I need to know your plan," Stiles said. "Every detail."

I don't have one wasn't allowed to come out of his mouth. Austin pressed his lips together.

Stiles leaned an elbow on the roof of his car, as if his own body were becoming too heavy to hold up. "Well?"

"I—I have an emergency bag with me. Clothes, my other gun. Money. I'll figure it out."

"Highly doubtful."

Never mind that he'd managed to overpower Jason and escape—Stiles thought Austin was a prep school wuss. People often did. It was in Austin's build, lean no matter how much weight he trained with. In his preference for business casual dress. In his vocabulary. He didn't look like a man whose schooling in violence started at the age of six.

Not that Sam Stiles needed to know any of that, but he needed something, so Austin shrugged out of his jacket and rolled up his T-shirt sleeve. The blue bruise spread a few inches up his arm.

"I get it, Stiles. Jason made sure I got it."

"That could be broken," Stiles said.

"Nah."

"Because you'd know if it was, of course."

"I broke it once when I was a kid." *Actually,* I *didn't break it.*

"What—is that ligature marks? On your neck?"

Austin pulled his jacket back on. "He didn't strangle me."

"What, then?"

"It's nothing, really."

Stiles pressed his thumbs against his eyebrows. "Crap."

Yeah, pretty much. Austin headed for the side door.

Behind him, Stiles sighed. "Hold up a minute."

No, thanks. He opened the door and stepped outside.

"I said—" A hand clamped down on his shoulder.

Let go. Austin wrenched the thumb until the hand went slack.

Stiles sprang back with more agility than his hair color should allow. He lifted his unwrenched hand, palm up. Shoot. There'd been nothing threatening in his gesture. Any other day, Austin would have stiffened and shrugged away from the grasp.

"What's wrong with you?" Stiles said.

"Sorry. I'm, uh, jumpy."

"Starting to see a pattern here."

You think? Austin shrugged and turned away. No more delaying.

"You can't just hang out in a hotel, Austin."

He was Austin now? After almost breaking the guy's thumb? "I'm aware of that, believe it or not."

"He's … crap. He's going to find you, and you'll be dead."

The one time Austin had been hoping to have someone talk him down, tell him he was overreacting … Apparently not. Great.

"We can't turn him in," Stiles said. "There's absolutely no evidence linking him to what was done to Marcus."

Marcus. This man was on a first-name basis with the leader of the resistance movement. He didn't seem to notice his slip, unsurprising given the exhaustion in his eyes.

"He'd be investigated, sure, but they'd clear him, and you'd still be dead. And at that point, so would I. And I don't have anywhere to hide you. Obviously, Jason's going to figure out we had a conversation yesterday—people saw us. So he'll look for you here. Even if he doesn't expect to find you, he'll look."

"Sam—"

"I'm not going to let you walk out of my garage and never see you again. Or hear two days from now that they discovered your body. It's not an option, so all I've got is …"

He walked over to the cement steps leading inside and sat. His crossed wrists dangled between his knees, emphasizing his lankiness.

"I can deal with this," Austin said.

Part of him wanted Sam to believe the lie. Part of him shuddered, because Sam might. The words sounded convincing, of course. He'd said them enough in his lifetime to polish them.

"Shut up." Both Sam's hands scrubbed his hair. "You'll have to follow me over there. I don't know what else to do with you."

"Where?"

Sam looked up, and the fluorescent garage lights made the gleam in his dark eyes look feral. "Your MPC career is over. You can never work for, with, or near Jason Mayweather again."

Austin's thoughts hadn't ventured that far into the future.

"If I'm going to do this, you have to understand that, Austin. And you have to realize you could bring a whole nest of Christians to Jason for arrest, and it wouldn't change that you're the reason he lost Marcus Brenner. What's between them is personal."

No arguing that one. Jason had put his hostility on display in that cramped, foul-smelling room. Slowly, the full meaning of Sam's words lit in his brain. Sam was going to hide him … with a bunch of Christians.

"If there were any other way for me to keep you alive … and maybe there would be, if I could spend the next week arranging something, but Jason's going to be setting up a manhunt. Likely already is."

"Sam …"

He stood smoothly and propped his hands on his hips. "Follow me."

Austin shook his head. "If they find out I'm a Constabulary agent, they'll kill me."

Sam barked a laugh. "Right. The violent terrorists. What was I thinking, letting their leader go?"

If Austin went to Jason now, exposed Sam … Surely Jason could get Sam to tell where Brenner was. But Austin had now assaulted a Constabulary officer. Nothing could erase that. And even if it could, then what? Austin would go on with his career, and Jason would go on … abusing people.

Not an option. Ever.

"Well?" Sam said.

No bullying, no manipulation. Austin could say no. But one fact branded his mind, turning all his objections, moral and otherwise, to smoke: Jason probably would catch up with him.

"There's no way resistance members will let me anywhere near them," he said.

"They won't be thrilled with you. But they won't turn you out when I explain."

Austin shut his eyes and tried to process this cage of circumstances, whether any other way out existed. He saw again the barrel of Jason's gun aimed at his head.

He opened his eyes and nodded. "Okay."

"Okay what?"

"I don't have all the facts right now, and you do. So … lead on." For now.

11

Half an hour after Marcus kept down the peanut butter sandwich, Lee administered his first dose of Amoxicillin and Motrin. Half an hour after that, the back door creaked open. Marcus shifted against the pillow, eyes darting to the doorway.

"It's Violet," Lee said. "I'll be back in a minute."

In the kitchen, Violet was stuffing cans of health-brand soup into a cupboard. A stiff-handled brown paper bag squatted at the end of the counter. One of the seams was half torn away from the handle. Clothes peeked out the top.

Violet looked over her shoulder. "I figured I should buy all the soup I could carry, in case we have to hide here for weeks or something. Or we can take them with us, if we actually leave Michigan."

"Sam is adamant."

"What about you?"

Lee shook her head. Over the last hour, the possibility had become less outlandish, but it meant the end of her clinic, her job at the hospital, her ties to … To whom? Sam? Chuck and Belinda? If Marcus needed Texas, Lee would go to Texas. As soon as he was well enough to travel.

"Just so you know." Violet rubbed her thumb against her wrist. "If you blurted that out and then wondered why you said it, or … Anyway, I wouldn't hold you to it. Bringing me, I mean."

"If the situation forces fleeing and you wish to come, then you're welcome to."

It was nothing more than a practical invitation. Where would Violet go if not with Lee? To dissuade a gush of the girl's gratitude, Lee dug through the bag of clothes. A week's worth of boxer briefs and socks, a package of white T-shirts. One pair of black fatigue pants, two pairs of flannel sleep pants, and three pairs of jeans. Four long-sleeved men's shirts, unadorned except for the buttons on the Henley. Several flannel button-downs and a zip hoodie, all of which could be put on without exacerbating broken ribs.

Lee might have believed Belinda stuffed this bag for an unknown patient sized large, if the clothes hadn't all been so … Marcus. Even the colors of the shirts—she'd chosen black, brown, dark greens, blues, one in mustard yellow, one in brick red. No white, no pastels, no patterns.

Violet stood beside the refrigerator, watching her, rubbing her wrist with her thumb.

"You told her," Lee said.

"You knew I was going to."

"You said 'only if it comes up.'"

"Right. It came up."

"When you brought it up." Exhaustion nearly buckled Lee's legs. She leaned her shoulders against the wall. "Is she waiting in the car?"

Violet rolled her eyes. "Good grief, no. I said they can come tomorrow, not before noon."

"Do they understand that he's …?"

"I told them he's hurt, and it's bad, and he's sick with pneumonia. And you're taking care of him and he's going to be okay."

Lee pushed away from the wall.

"Lee, I get that you don't want to deal with Belinda. Really, I do. But for us to let them keep grieving, even for a day, when we know.

I mean, think how it was when they found out he was … I'm sorry, but I had to tell them."

The kindness held a certain logic, and what was done was done. Lee had fifteen hours to prepare for Belinda's barging in the door and dragging Marcus clear off the bed for a hug and crying all over him. Queasiness settled in her stomach. She returned to the bedroom.

"Marcus." Lee waited for him to meet her eyes. "We have clean clothes. You can shower, whenever you're ready."

He absorbed that as if it were a new thought, glanced down at his filthy cargo shorts and bare chest, and nodded.

"You can rest for now, if—"

"No."

Getting him up proved more difficult than she expected. Any way she supported him put pressure on his ribs, and he had almost no muscle strength in his extremities. When he finally made it to his feet, his right leg buckled. Had Lee not already been supporting most of his weight, he'd have collapsed to the floor.

"Your leg is injured?" she said when he tried to continue without comment.

He gritted his teeth and shuffled forward.

"Marcus, I can't treat it if I don't—"

"Knee."

"How did it happen?"

"Not bad now. Stiff."

The shower was only a stall, not a bathtub, so Lee set up the metal folding chair she sat on to debride Ray Donnelly's ulcers. Marcus was silent as she lathered his hair, shoulders, and back with the cheap body soap on hand. Then he took over cleaning himself and rinsing off with the extending shower head. Lee set out underwear, the brown zip hoodie, and a green pair of sleep pants. By the time she'd helped him dress and struggle to his feet, all his muscles shook with fatigue. Lee recruited Violet to support his less injured side and positioned herself where she would least jostle the broken ribs. They reached the bedroom after long minutes, and he slumped down on the mattress. His breathing labored more than when he used to run the park path for miles.

The thought bridged the distance Lee had maintained for the last two hours between her nursing tasks and herself, as if she could be a nurse yet not be Lee. As if Marcus were a stranger brought in by ambulance and charted as John Doe. She'd massaged soap into his scalp and pretended no cowlick twirled at the base of his neck. She'd washed months of dirt and neglect from his malnourished frame and pretended not to remember the muscular power in his arms and shoulders. She'd helped him into secondhand clothes and pretended she didn't know his favorite pair of jeans, threadbare and faded and loosely fitted.

She checked his knee once he was back in bed and found no swelling or heat, but his range of motion was limited. Flexion seemed to cause less pain than extension, but his jaw clamped hard when she asked.

This silence inside him—it wasn't theirs. It didn't hold safety or trust. She needed to understand it, but instead she kept blundering against it and stumbling away, cut by its edges. She had to index the questions he didn't want asked and observe their answers for herself.

So she didn't mention the new scars she'd observed while helping him dress—nearly a dozen of them, dime-sized puckers of skin. On his back, one near the old scar where he'd removed the Constabulary tracker. On his abdomen. On his chest, one below the right clavicle. These compared to no scar she'd seen before.

In minutes, he crashed to a deep sleep.

Violet appeared in the doorway, cradling a steaming bowl of chicken and rice soup. "Oh … I thought I'd see if he wanted to eat some more."

"Let him rest."

"Right. Guess I should've asked."

"No, Violet, it's fine." A thoughtful, sensible thing to do, in fact. One reason Violet was suited to work with patients.

"Lee, are you … well, um …?"

The knock on the back door jolted Lee's heartbeat.

Violet jumped. "Is it Sam?"

Bringing an emergency patient without texting first? He knew Lee was here, but he'd still follow procedure. He was Sam, after all. "I'm not sure. Wait here."

Across the house, the doorknob jiggled, and then a key slid into the lock. Beneath the white blanket, Marcus's legs moved. He opened his eyes, and one knee bent to push himself up.

"It's all right," Lee said. "Only Sam has a key."

"Stay with him," Violet said. "I'll find out what's up."

She slipped from the room before Lee could protest. The back door opened, and Marcus clasped the blanket. Despite the flush of fever on his skin, he was one breath away from struggling to his feet, or trying to. Lee shook her head, and challenge stirred in his eyes. If someone unwanted breached that door, he wouldn't simply lie here. She dipped her head once in comprehension.

We can still speak without words.

Violet's voice punctured the quiet in the house. "He doesn't come in here."

Sam's deep voice spoke quietly for a few seconds, until Violet cut him off.

"No freaking way, Sam."

12

She was standing in front of him. Violet. Just like that. Honey blonde hair longer now, halfway down her back. Green eyes sparking. Curves filled out in the last four months. *She's eighteen now.* And different. His Violet would never have folded her arms and planted her feet in the doorway, facing down Sam Stiles.

"Where's Lee?" Sam said.

"What, you think *she'll* let a con-cop in here? Especially right now. Come on, Sam."

Violet said the man's first name unthinkingly, must have said it hundreds of times. While Austin had chased dead end after dead end in search of her, in search of this ghostly network of people, Sam had known where all of them were. A slow simmer began in the pit of Austin's stomach.

"Violet," he said.

She stared up at him. As her mouth opened to answer, a woman rounded the corner behind her, coming from a hallway. Thirty-ish, taller than Violet, more skeletal than slender, with keen gray eyes and black hair cut just above the crew neckline of her shirt.

Lee Vaughn.

"Sam?" she said.

"We need to talk." Sam propped a hand on the doorframe. "If Violet will let us in."

"Is he a patient?" The woman's eyes raked Austin up and down.

"No." Violet's gaze didn't waver from Austin's. "He's a Constabulary agent."

Even the woman's breath froze.

"In fact, he's Austin Delvecchio."

The woman's lips pulled back minutely, a quick glimpse of teeth, and her shoulders inched back, too, prepared to—what, tackle him? Had Violet told her everything?

Sam sighed. "First, hear me out—"

"Get him out of here," the woman said. "Now."

"He'll be dead, Lee."

"I don't—"

"Because Jason Mayweather will kill him, because he's the one who told me about Marcus."

The very air seemed to absorb his words. Lee drew her hands behind her back and stepped to one side. "Violet."

"But he's—"

"Violet."

Violet backed up, but the blaze in her eyes flickered higher. She faced Sam. "How do we know Mayweather threatened him? Because he told you? He's probably a spy."

Austin pushed past Sam, through the doorway. "Come on, Violet."

"What? It wouldn't be a new concept to you."

"You think I'd turn you over to Jason after what he did to Brenner? You really think that about me?"

She glared at him, and he steeled himself against the sting inside. No, he didn't deserve her acceptance, but this …

"Violet," Sam said. "Austin's in danger. I'm telling you that. Me. Not Austin."

Violet's gaze dropped to the floor, but she slowly shook her head.

Tension danced around these people like lightning bolts in a cloud. Austin's teeth clenched, though no one here looked ready to throw a punch. Maybe he could end the debate. He dropped his bag on the floor and rolled up his sleeve. The bruise had started to throb in the last hour, but it wasn't spreading.

Lee reached his side in moments. "Mayweather did this?"

"And this." He tugged down his jacket collar. Violet peeked upward, then raised her head to stare at the blue and purple mottling his neck. "If Brenner's here, ma'am, you don't have to take my word on anything. Jason brought me to the house yesterday. Brenner will recognize me."

Lee's lips pressed together until they disappeared, further thinning her face.

No one moved from their positions—Sam and Austin just inside the door, Lee several paces further inside, Violet braced with her feet apart, an arm's length from Lee. The air around them still crackled, and they all stood rigid in it, as if a sudden move might bring down the lightning.

"You're a Constabulary agent," Lee said, "no matter what's happened between you and Mayweather."

"No, I'm not. Not practically speaking. Arresting you means paperwork, which Jason would see. So even if I wanted to betray all of you …" Austin shrugged.

"Even if?" Violet said.

"What did I just say? I'm not giving anybody over to that guy, not even legally."

"Not all Constabulary agents are like Mayweather," Lee said.

"And it's clear I can't tell good cop from bad cop. If he hadn't taken me into his confidence, I'd still be an admiring underling."

"You don't consider him an anomaly?"

"Someone trained him. Someone promoted him several times. He's been an agent for almost seven years now, and in that time he's worked with multiple colleagues. In all that time, these people either didn't see what he really is … or they did see it. And did nothing."

Lee angled to face him, and her movement dissolved the friction in the room. "How long ago were you attacked?"

Maybe that question meant a lifting of suspicion. Austin sighed. "A couple hours."

"You need to ice this." Lee took his wrist between her hands and tilted it, then pressed her thumb to each bone. He didn't let himself wince. "I'd need an x-ray to be sure, but I don't believe it's broken."

"It's not," he said, and she arched her eyebrows but didn't comment.

She assessed the bruise on his throat, asked if his breathing was affected, asked if he'd sustained any other injuries. He almost didn't tell her about his ankle, but letting it swell without treatment would be stupid. And pointless. This day had already pulverized his masculinity. One more blow wouldn't make a difference.

"All right," she finally said. "Come inside, both of you."

Sam shook his head. "No time. This is it. You know it is."

"It?"

"You have to run, all of you, tonight. Now."

She shifted to stand like a soldier at ease, shoulders relaxed, hands behind her back. "We've discussed this."

"And we're done discussing. It's time to move. Mayweather knows Austin is either hiding out or on the run. He'll be watching the interstates as soon as he can put a plausible story together and mobilize enough agents. Once that happens, you'll never get out of Michigan."

Something like panic lit her eyes. "He can't travel, Sam."

"Lee, I want you to think about what will happen if he doesn't. If Jason gets to him again."

Austin had never watched someone pale before, not like this, anyway. Lee looked sick. She nodded and breathed deep, seemed to fortify herself from the inside out.

It hit him, what Sam was saying. Why Sam had brought him here. "You want me to go with them."

"No choice," Sam said. "You don't have to live in Texas for the rest of your life. Just lay low there while all this crap explodes. Think of it as a protection detail. You've got a badge and a gun and you're able-bodied."

Protection. Yeah. No way Violet should be driving across the country with a sick, beaten man and a woman who could be made of twigs. He nodded.

Lee's hands, held behind her back, fell to her sides. She nodded back. After a long moment, Violet nodded too.

"You'll take my truck." Sam jingled the keys in his pocket. "I drove it for that very purpose. It's got a cap, and the license plate won't trace to any of you. We'll throw everything we can fit in the bed, including the air mattress for Marcus. Until you get out of Michigan, Austin stays hidden with him. Then you can rotate drivers."

The man had planned their entire trip. For the next hour, a sorting and packing frenzy ensued. They stocked the bed of Sam's truck with everything from cans of soup to medical supplies.

It hadn't taken long to figure out what this house was. Not really a house, not in furnishings, anyway. The spacious living room had been turned into something like a sickbay. Two air mattresses were set up along one wall, white sheets and white woven blankets tucked around them. On the other side of the room sat an actual medical exam table with green vinyl upholstery. Black market medicine. It was the only thing that made sense.

In the kitchen, Austin found Violet stocking a mini-cooler with ice and frozen gel packs.

"For Marcus," she said without looking at Austin. "And your wrist."

"Thanks."

She turned to face him. Her lips pressed into a line of doubt, but her eyes held a depth of care that almost undid his resolution not to sweep her into his arms. The four months of distance evaporated as she stepped closer and tugged down his collar. She studied the bruise on his throat, then lifted her eyes to his.

For once in his life, he understood before he opened his mouth that words would ruin this. The memory of her taste, her touch, pulsed through him, and her eyes were wells of the same memories—except of him.

For about two seconds, he thought she'd let him kiss her.

Violet's hand dropped to her side. She stepped back as if realizing how close they were.

Still nothing to say. He went back to work, adrenaline thrumming in the background of everything else. *I'm leaving. My home. My work. My family.* Not forever, but for now. If only he could call Esther and explain. She'd think he abandoned them.

Both Violet and Lee kept a duffel of clothes here, which probably shouldn't have surprised Austin as much as it did. Something surged in his chest when he shoved Violet's bag into the truck bed alongside his own. Sam had popped the hood and bent over the guts of his truck, inspecting before sending it on a cross-country trek.

Austin stopped beside him. "I won't let anything happen to them."

Sam straightened. "They're good, strong people, Austin. Including Violet."

No one needed to tell him about Violet. "If they stay in Texas, you can fly out for a visit or something."

His lips curved, a smile's ghost. "You haven't thought of it yet either?"

"Thought of what?"

"Someone has to go down for the crimes of the network. The media won't rest without a villain to show behind bars."

Shoot. He was right. "Come with us, then."

"Not enough room in the truck."

"Sam—"

"It'll take a few days to set myself up. If I do it right, they'll have no reason to come after you and no legal justification even if they wanted to."

"Lee's going to—"

"She's thinking about Marcus, and only Marcus, and that's how it needs to be right now. Don't you dare say a word."

"Don't do this, Sam."

"Guard them well. That's all I ask."

13

The truck was loaded, including an air mattress from the exam room. No reason to move Marcus until Lee could assist him from one bed to another. She'd explained everything with as much detail as she could, then asked for permission to sedate him. Raw determination, anger, and maybe fear leaped into his eyes at the suggestion. As a compromise, she gave him an extra dose of Motrin. He didn't argue, but jostling in the back of a truck for two days would put him in more pain than Motrin could dull, and he seemed to know it.

One thing remained before they could leave. Violet had driven down the road to the Vitale house, and in a few minutes, they'd be here, wrapping everyone in hugs and farewells. Lee knelt beside Marcus's bed.

"What's today?"

His voice startled her. Not the faint rasp of it, but the fact he'd initiated conversation.

"Wednesday." Oh … that was an absurd answer. "October twenty-sixth."

The seconds stretched without a reply.

"Marcus?"

"Couple days ago … I thought maybe … Thanksgiving soon."

"Why Thanksgiving?"

"So it … didn't snow then? When it was cold?"

Four nights ago, the record-breaking freeze overnight. How did he know about it from behind a locked door? Threads of her calm began to snap as the possibilities formed in her mind. *Don't ask him.*

"No," she said. "It hasn't snowed yet."

Violet appeared in the doorway. "They're here."

Marcus blinked slowly. "Violet?"

"Yeah. You saw me earlier. I helped you walk, remember? But maybe you were out of it."

"Are you okay?"

"Me? Uh, yeah, of course. Did Lee tell you I live with her now?"

His eyes traveled between them. "What happened to … people, my … my—?"

His family. Fear inched into his eyes, as if realizing he should have asked before now and in not asking might have failed them all.

Violet leaned against the door trim, arms folded. "Chuck and Belinda are good. Mrs. Lewalski got released in August, so she's good now, too. I haven't talked to Clay or Natalia or Khloe since June, but we're assuming they're fine."

Marcus's lips pressed together until they disappeared. He nodded.

"There's no word from anybody else," Violet said, and he nodded again.

The rest of his church was, according to Sam, still in re-education. Lee had never met them, but Marcus had spoken their names. Jim, Karlyn, Janelle, Phil, Felice. All taken.

"Speaking of Chuck and Belinda," Violet said. "They're hoping you're up to saying hi. And good-bye."

His gaze fixed on the doorway.

"Do you wish to see them, Marcus?" Lee said.

He nodded.

Violet left and returned before Lee could brace herself. Belinda glided through the doorway with a tearstained smile.

A smile that froze and shattered.

"Marcus?" Her voice wobbled, the accent drawing his name out more than usual. When he didn't respond, tears filled her eyes. "What's happened to you? Where were you?"

The jagged questions.

Chuck pushed past her, and Violet followed him, and the crowd of them seemed to knock the breath from the room. At least Austin and Sam knew enough to keep away, wherever they were. Both Vitales stared down at Marcus, concern and disbelief and joy battling in their eyes.

"You're here." Belinda charged across the room, and Lee's imagination hadn't exaggerated. The woman was going to lean over him and hug him.

Marcus's left arm snapped up, ready to deflect a blow. Belinda froze midstride, and her mouth opened, finally speechless. His eyes roved the room for … danger?

"Pearl," Chuck said quietly. "Step back now."

Belinda shuffled backward and bumped into her husband's chest. "M-Marcus?"

Marcus's gaze landed on Lee, and the silence now wasn't new but wasn't safe, either. This was the silence that had lengthened while she held her phone to her ear and Marcus drove home too late at night, both of them knowing that if he tried to talk, his voice would shake with the need for whiskey. His eyes pleaded. A piece of the ice surrounding her broke off and drifted away. *You're still there, inside. I'll bring you back.*

"Give us a moment, please," she said.

Violet motioned Chuck and Belinda out first, then followed them without a look back. *Thank you.*

Marcus buried both hands in the blanket. Lee knelt beside the mattress, and one of his hands reached toward hers, then burrowed again. This close, his rapid breathing was audible. He rocked forward, white with pain even before the coughing started. When it was over, he leaned into the wall to stay upright. His breathing didn't level.

He was a patient. She had to do what was best for him. She wrapped her hand around his warm wrist. Physical contact, of a sort, but … "Your pulse is racing."

He reversed her hold on his wrist and wove their fingers together instead.

"Are you afraid?"

"Is—is this you?" He squeezed her hand.

Lee nodded, but he didn't seem to notice. Her hand throbbed in a grip he shouldn't be strong enough for. "Yes, I'm here. Marcus, is this a reaction to Belinda or something else?"

"I d-don't know."

She untangled their fingers and pushed aside the catch in her breath when he tried to hold on. She stood. "I'll see them out."

"No. Wait." He rested his forehead on his good knee. "A minute."

She waited at least that long. His breathing remained shallow but evened out.

"Okay," he said. "They can come back."

"This obviously isn't beneficial for you."

"It … is. Please."

When the Vitales returned, the last vestige of Belinda's makeup had been sobbed away, and Chuck kept rocking back and forth on his feet. Only when Violet brought them each a folding chair from the closet did the stiffness leach from Marcus's shoulders. Lee and Violet sat on the floor against the wall.

Marcus asked if Chuck and Belinda were okay, then asked again. Before the next pause could become awkward, the couple launched into a holiday newsletter of conversation—their children and grandchildren and Belinda's recent birdwatching excursion. Marcus didn't speak, but his gaze never left their faces. Ten minutes passed, and Lee could imagine Sam outside the door, glaring at her for not being halfway to Toledo by now. She stood.

"Time to go?" Belinda said, and disappointment pulled her mouth.

"Yes." Well past it.

Chuck stood up and stretched his back. He stepped close to the mattress in the corner, squatted beside it, and held out his hand. "You'll be all right, son. If it's ever safe to contact us, we hope you will."

Marcus gripped his hand and didn't let go. "Thank you. For ..."

"You're welcome, but I'm just as grateful to you."

When they parted, Belinda approached, more slowly this time. "There wasn't time to fix any food, Marcus. I—I hope you get enough to eat on the way, and get there safe, and stay safe."

Her words choked on tears. Marcus pulled in a deep breath. "Belinda. I'm okay."

"I know, I do know that." She swiped her palms over her cheeks and knelt to place a hand on his shoulder. Marcus lifted his hand and covered hers. "And you're alive. Good-bye doesn't have to be forever."

He nodded. Belinda patted his shoulder but didn't attempt a hug. She pushed herself to her feet with a small grunt and faced Chuck. Even her nod seemed to tremble with tears.

Lee clasped her hands together behind her back. When the others filed from the room, she turned to Marcus.

"I'll be back in a minute."

He nodded.

In the kitchen, they all stood silently as if waiting for Lee to emerge.

"He's really sick," Chuck said quietly. "Feverish, I could tell. And he looks half-starved."

Lee nodded.

"But he's not in any danger, not like that, I mean."

"He's going to live," she said, as if she or anyone else could be certain.

Chuck pinched between his eyes and turned away from her. "Thank God."

"Amen," Violet whispered.

Lee left the room.

One foot in front of the other, step after step, to the other end of the house. Not far enough. She snatched her coat and draped it over her folded arms.

The night enfolded her with a brisk breeze and damp darkness. She doubled over with one hand braced on the side of the house, but she didn't need to throw up. She needed to hold in, couldn't stop now, not while people hovered so near, not while Belinda hovered so near.

They're thanking You? For this?

She crushed the coat against her face and whispered into it. "You have never once watched over him, never once."

She breathed deeply, but the squeezing, shuddering pain in her chest continued to build.

"This is what You do. Nothing. They didn't deserve … They—they didn't—"

They. No, no …

"You're reading my mind, regardless. They deserved Your care. Both of them. And You *don't* deserve anything from me." She stood there, clutching the coat to her chest with both hands, like cradling an infant.

No time for this. She ground her palms over her face, under her eyes. Dry. Calm. It was time to go. She stood.

A few feet away, hunched in his gray jacket, stood Sam.

14

Snap at him, fend him off. Stalk past him into the house without a word.

No.

He was Sam, and she was leaving. Lee stood with her coat bunched in her hands and waited for him to speak. From the garage, the screen door slammed. Austin or Violet, loading final items into the truck.

"I'm sorry." The shadow of the house obscured Sam's face.

"Sorry?"

"I told you he was dead."

"You believed he was."

"I stopped looking for him."

Her next question would not be fair or right. She ventured closer to deliver the blow. "Could you have found him sooner?"

Sam rubbed a hand over his graying hair. "He was within miles of me. Every day."

Lee shuffled to the back porch steps and sank down on the bottom one a moment before her legs gave out. Sam watched her, while the screen door slammed once, then again, in quick succession. Tires ground over the gravel driveway and faded, Chuck's car leaving. For good.

Ask the question.

"Where was he?" Her words might have been snatched by the breeze before he could hear them.

Sam stepped closer and hunkered down, one hand braced on the porch step beside her. "A house behind the admin building, vacant. I don't think Jason was thinking past the next few hours, when he first left him there."

Then the plan had been to kill him. "Vacant?"

"No utilities."

No heat, as she'd guessed. No air conditioning, from June to August. "Was there light, at least?"

Still crouching, Sam shifted away from her. "From under the door."

"Mayweather kept him in a closet?"

"Kitchen pantry."

Lee inhaled the damp air, the faint scent of soil. She assessed her body, the hard step under her backside, the ground under her shoes, her feet in her shoes. Breeze lifted her hair from her neck. If she could concentrate on these things, she could block the image of Marcus, bruised and ill and shivering, eyes on the line of sunlight at the bottom of the door.

Heat surged in her cheeks, and she hid her face against her knees. Breathe in. Breathe out. Forget fleeing, she should track down Jason Mayweather and … The top step creaked as Sam settled his weight, long legs parallel with her hunched back. His knee grazed her shoulder.

"Lee."

She steadied her breathing and lifted her head. "You're not to blame. You saved his life."

"Before you go, I need you to hear some things."

"We're out of time." She tried to stand, but he pushed her knee back down.

"So don't make me repeat myself."

Only the light from the crescent moon illuminated him, the whites of his eyes the most visible part of his face. She'd unscrewed the bulb from the porch light months ago, when she'd first had the electricity turned on. From the outside, the place still had to appear foreclosed.

"Now, you know I'm no mother hen. But for the next month, every time you feed Marcus, I want you to eat something."

"Sam—"

"Hush, girl, and listen."

Girl. He hadn't called her that since … A rock lodged in her throat, and she blinked hard.

"I also want you to picture your uselessness if you try to stay awake for the next six weeks, or however long it takes broken ribs to heal. You'll get sick, and you'll be useless to him. So, sleep. Agreed?"

Lee nodded.

"About Austin, I know part of you thinks it's unwise to include him in this. It probably is, to a point, but he's in danger, and you're going to need him. Still, I wouldn't have suggested it if there was any chance he'd turn on you."

"I don't trust him."

"He's young, and overconfident, and a bit of an egghead, but—"

"I do, however, trust you."

A slow smile curved his mouth, and laugh lines around his eyes created small shadows from the moonlight. "Well, then."

Sam. "We should leave."

This time, he stood with her. "This is going to be hard, Lee. But you've done hard before. You can do this."

"I know."

"Good."

He was right. She'd known the difficulties already, yet she knew them better after helping Marcus into the truck bed. He wasn't strong enough to hoist himself onto the tailgate, much less jump up with one foot springboarding from the bumper, as she'd seen him do countless times. Austin knelt inside the bed, reached down and took hold under Marcus's arms, while Sam lifted him.

Bundling him too snugly could exacerbate the fever, yet he'd be without heat back here, and the temperature was dipping to the low fifties. Lee tucked two white blankets around him.

"Thanks," he said.

"Are you all right? Can you breathe?"

Marcus nodded against the pillow.

"We'll be stopping south of Toledo. No more than two hours."

Another nod.

"Marcus, this will be painful."

One hand shifted under the blankets. "It's okay."

She gauged the feet of distance from his face to the top of the cap. Its sides were opaque, the window at the rear heavily tinted. "Will you be all right in the … closed space?"

He nodded. She had no choice but to believe him.

Austin jumped into the truck bed and burrowed in among the duffel bags and an old sleeping bag Violet had brought to the clinic months ago from Chuck's house.

"If he needs anything," Lee told Austin, "pound as hard as you can. We'll hear you."

Sam shut the rear gate. Lee threw her duffel into the cab, and Violet climbed inside.

Nothing remained but to drive away.

Sam handed over the keys. "They'll freeze everything within the next few hours, maybe already have. Your bank accounts, credit cards, everything."

"I have cash."

"Enough?" Ever the financial adviser.

"Almost forty thousand," she said.

His eyebrows shot almost to his hairline.

"I've been withdrawing a little every week for a while."

"How long is a while?"

"Since last November. No one could do what Marcus was doing forever. It only made sense to plan for a time when we couldn't access bank accounts."

"We?"

"I'm known to plan ahead, Sam."

"But he kept you out of most of it. They wouldn't have gone after you, not then."

The distinction made no sense. Any attack on Marcus was an attack on Lee. She would preserve him at the expense of everything else. Maybe she should explain, but these facts were elemental, not meant for words. She tilted an eyebrow at Sam instead.

He nodded as if she'd spoken. "Right, of course."

"Sam, I ..." That rock again, she couldn't swallow around it. She sandwiched the truck key between her palms. "Thank you."

He nodded. "You'll be fine, all of you. Go on, now."

Lee climbed into the truck. Turned the key. Didn't look back, all the way down the driveway. The truck bounced in a hole or two down the dirt road, and her stomach tensed. She had to drive smoothly.

Violet sat with her chin propped in her hand, facing the passenger window, maybe to allow Lee space, or maybe pondering Austin

Delvecchio's reappearance in her life. If he tried to intimidate her in any way, he'd regret it.

Lee drove south. She merged onto I-75 before she remembered what she had wanted to say. *Sam, you will always be my family.*

15

The truck had been stopped for seconds, still running, when the tailgate lowered and fell the last few inches with a *thunk*. Cool air rushed into the bed of the truck, and Austin drank in the freshness after the stale, metallic taste of the last two hours.

"How is he?" Lee whispered.

"Are we past Toledo?" Austin drew his legs under him to crawl forward, his hair grazing the low cap.

"Austin."

"He might be asleep. He hasn't said anything in a while."

Brenner had spoken five words since they left, four of them "no" when shifts in his breathing prompted Austin to ask if he should get Lee to stop driving. He'd also once said "yeah" when Austin asked if he was sure about the "no."

Lee leaned in, shadowing her face from the glow of the taillights. "Marcus?"

A cough answered her first, then a quiet rasp. "I'm okay."

"We're at a rest stop about forty miles south of Toledo. It's almost four o'clock. We should be safe here for several hours."

"Nothing suspicious so far?" Austin said.

"No." Lee shimmied over the tailgate and into the bed. Austin pulled his knees to his chest to give her room. Her hand ran along the edge of the mattress with a soft sound. "Marcus, I need to take your pulse."

Her breath caught quietly a moment later.

"What?" Austin said.

"His fever is spiking."

She rummaged in the dark, and then an LED light clicked on, bright enough to illuminate every corner of the tight space and make all of them squint. Lee pulled a leather laptop case into her lap and drew out stethoscope and thermometer. Brenner shivered when she unzipped his hoodie. He wasn't wearing anything under it. Austin's breath snagged at the sight of the bruises, at Brenner's ribs visible through the discolored skin.

No belief system could possibly be worth this.

Lee listened to him breathe, took his temperature, and repacked the items into the bag.

"Is he okay?" *Like she'll tell you.*

"One-oh-two-point-six."

When she was a toddler, Olivia once had a fever of 105-point-something, so that couldn't be too bad. Or he had no idea what he was talking about, because Lee's frown might be … fear.

"Join Violet in the cab," she said.

Austin nodded, and his mouth dried.

"When she protests, tell her I apologize."

Lee knew everything. "If you want to sleep back here for a while, I could keep driving."

"No."

She didn't even trust him to take them to their destination.

"Not because it's you offering." He must have scowled more fiercely than he thought. Lee glanced at Brenner and lowered her voice. "He needs a rest from the constant motion."

Of course he did, and if they could freeze time, they could give him a week to heal up. In the real world, even an hour was too long.

They'd barely crossed the state line. But arguing would be fruitless, maybe detrimental. This woman had blinders where Brenner was concerned, and Austin still had a long way to go in earning her trust. He scooted out of the bed and dropped his feet to the blacktop.

Lee had parked under a floodlight. Not the smartest place. Maybe she considered it hiding in plain sight, but this was a rest stop. No one would find it abnormal for travelers to sleep in deliberate shadow. About a hundred yards away, at the north end of the parking lot, a brown brick Visitor's Center squatted alongside an even lower building with an arrow pointing inside: *Public Restrooms.* Austin poked his head into the truck and turned off the ignition.

Violet stared at him from across the cab, and he hoped he only imagined the way she seemed to shrink against the passenger door.

She tugged on the door handle. "Uh, we're not sleeping in here at the same time."

"Lee said his fever's up. She wants to watch him. And she's sorry you have to put up with me in the meantime."

Violet's hand fell into her lap. She rubbed her thumb over her wrist, and something was missing. Her charm bracelet. She'd obsessed over that thing before.

Austin climbed into the cab and shut the door, and there they were, he and Violet, breathing the same air, nothing between them but an arm's length and the gear shift. The cab smelled like strawberries, but manufactured—a plug-in scent hidden under the seat or somewhere.

Violet leaned back into the headrest and shut her eyes. "Fine, I'll sleep in here. But we're not going to talk."

He should respect that, and he did. Would. In a minute. "I have one thing to say, and then—"

"It doesn't matter, whatever it is."

"When I—when I hit you."

Violet's eyes shot open. "Seriously, that's your topic?"

He willed his voice to be steady, in control. "You need to understand."

"It's the cop thing, right? You can't take no for an answer, not even from a girl who wants to keep her clothes on."

He ducked his head, but she could probably see the heat flushing up the back of his neck before reaching his face. *This is how she sees me.*

"The whole thing was so stupid." Violet turned toward the window, and it fogged with her breath. "I was so stupid. 'Come on, Austin, please have sex with me,' and you all, 'Not yet,' and I really don't understand that part, actually. If you'll hit a girl for saying no, why—?"

"I didn't."

"Um, I had a fat lip for a day."

He ground the heel of his hand against the steering wheel. He forced himself to meet her gaze. "I didn't hit you for saying no."

Her eyes widened, and her eyebrows arched, and she might as well have spoken aloud: *Right, sure you didn't.*

"Violet, I …" His hands needed his guitar. Without it, they fidgeted in his lap until he rubbed his gritty eyes.

Violet crossed her arms and leaned on an angle, into the corner of the door and the seat. "Fine, whatever, say it."

"I wasn't hitting you. In my head, I mean. I'd never hit you." Good, his voice was strengthening, and he didn't have to force it now, because this was truth Violet needed to hear. "I would never hit you. You're—you're—"

Kind. Sweet. Beautiful. Strong. And you glow, Violet. With, I don't know, life or something.

He breathed in and let it out. "You don't deserve to be hit, by any guy at any time for any reason."

Violet drew up her knees, heels of her shoes propped on the edge of the seat, and encircled them with her arms.

"That's all," Austin said.

"Okay."

Silence stole in. A long sigh poured out, one he hadn't known he'd been holding. He'd said it, and she'd listened, and she seemed to believe him. He tried to tilt his head back, the headrest supporting his neck, but … ow. That wasn't going to be comfortable in three minutes, much less three hours or however long they were here. If they were going to sit motionless, he might as well sleep.

"Who was it, then?" Violet said.

"What?"

"Whoever you were punching. In your mind, I mean."

A rock fell onto his chest. "I wasn't … it wasn't anyone."

She stretched out her legs under the dashboard and closed her eyes.

"Violet?"

"Like I said, we're not talking."

"I—"

"There's no point, Austin. You can't stop lying."

His right fingers twitched for guitar strings, for the reassuring universality of the chords. He stared out the driver's window. A semitruck pulled into the rest stop and parked on the other side of the lot. The tall gray-bearded driver climbed down and beelined for the restroom. Austin closed his eyes and pulled on the green coat of calm, of safety. Breathe in, out. Now, talk about it.

"My dad," Austin said.

Violet's eyes popped open. She sat forward, legs pulling closer to the seat. "I reminded you of your dad? I'm five-foot-five and, uh, a girl."

"Sometimes my reactions don't make sense. I've done a little Internet research on the topic, and I seem to be pretty typical."

"The topic?"

Maybe this would all be easy, if he'd ever spoken about it before. "Um … abuse. Child abuse."

Violet's lips parted, her eyes widened, and then she sat there like that, open to his stupid revelation, waiting for … what, details? What Dad used to do? How it felt? Like he'd tell her any of that crap. He'd look weak, and she might start to pity him, and … no.

"Austin, your dad didn't … didn't do things to you, did he?"

Things? … Oh. "Nah, nothing like that."

"So he hit you? But I didn't hit you. What did I do that made you think—?"

"Really, it's not important. It was a long time ago, and I'm fine now." His voice didn't wobble, although his heart felt like it was going to pound out of his chest.

"Still, I should know what I did, so I don't do it again."

So you don't have reason to give me a fat lip again, she was thinking. He hid his face in his hands, and it was too hot, flushed. Or maybe his hands were cold.

"Austin."

Violet's voice was soft, and he wanted to brush against that softness, let it hold him for a minute. Let her hold him, and hold her back. But he'd lost the right to do that, and besides, at the moment he couldn't lift his head.

"Austin, listen. I'm not saying I'm scared of you. I just don't want to do something that would … I don't know, hurt you."

"You didn't hurt me," he said into his hands. *I'm not breakable, dang it.*

"Okay. Well, if you don't want me to know, then I get that. It's personal stuff, and I'm not really—we're not really—anything, anymore."

He lowered his hands and rested his forehead on the steering wheel. Another deep breath, then one more, and then he sat up and met her eyes. At least she wasn't crying. And her face wasn't all pinched with sorrow for his tragic childhood, or any of that melodrama. Maybe it would be all right for her to know. Not everything, of course, but a little more.

"You pushed me. I get, um, too defensive sometimes, when people are physically aggressive. But I could still see you and deal with it. Then I lost my footing, do you remember?"

She nodded.

"And I bumped my head on the wall?"

"Yeah, but not very hard."

"No, but it was …" He sighed. "Um … my … my dad …"

Violet inched closer to him on the seat. Her hand didn't take his, but she rested it on the gear shift. Closer. Close enough.

"One of his things was, he'd pick me up and throw me. Not far, not like—you know, a football pass or something—just a few feet. Usually into a wall."

"How old were you?" she whispered.

"When it started? Six. The year my sister was born. I mean, he'd slap me and all before that, but when she came it got …" His throat closed up. Violet waited for him. "Anyway, bumping my head into walls is apparently something to avoid in the future."

The silence wasn't cold anymore, and Austin let his heart rate slow back to normal over the next few minutes. Violet withdrew her hand back into her lap and rubbed her thumb over her wrist, slowly at first the way he'd seen her do it before, then faster.

"Like I said before, I'm fine now." He ventured half a smile.

She didn't return it. "You probably don't want me to say I'm sorry, do you."

"It's not really necessary."

"Then, I guess, thanks for telling me. Even though you didn't want to."

He nodded. They huddled against their respective doors, and Austin imagined his body sinking down on a mattress, swathed in sheets and blankets, with a pillow under his head. He probably wouldn't sleep a minute....

Tap-tap-tap.

He jolted up from his slump against the driver's door and swiveled to face the window. Lee stood there, tense lines drawn between her eyebrows, probably a headache. Across the cab, Violet slept on.

Austin cracked open the door. "Yeah?"

"We have to find a hotel."

"Lee." No words could encapsulate the danger of what she'd just said.

"I understand, but Marcus is—" She stepped backward from the open door and stood with her hands behind her back, a soldier at ease. Her voice evened. "I can't control his fever."

"And you'll be able to in a hotel room?"

"I'll be able to bathe him. And he needs to be indoors, in a regulated temperature."

"We should get farther south first."

"Austin, we can't."

He tipped his shoulders back against the seat and pressed as hard as he could and took a deep breath. No reason to be angry with her. "Give me the keys. I'll find a hotel."

16

Less than an hour later, Austin had found them a room. And not just any room. He'd taken into account all the details Lee had meant to tell him. Ground floor, door to the outside rather than a hallway where they were more likely to be observed by other guests. And he went further, choosing the back side of the building, facing only a parking lot instead of the road. At six in the morning, with the sky washing gray and promising a cloudless sunrise, no one witnessed Austin carrying Marcus inside.

Less than twelve hours with the Constabulary agent, and Lee had to admit Sam was right.

After she unclothed Marcus's shivering body down to his underwear, Austin lifted him into the tepid bath. His eyes lingered on the contusions covering Marcus's torso.

"Let me know if you need anything else, okay?" he said, and Lee nodded, words beyond her reach.

The next two hours nearly wrung her out. Marcus's fever climbed to 103.8 and stayed there, while she sponged water over his neck and arms and chest with one hand and wrapped the other around his wrist. His pulse was fast but strong. She kept him propped up with a pillow against his upper back. She squeezed out the sponge and wiped his face, and his eyelids fluttered but didn't open. She spoke to him, but he didn't seem to know she was there.

Two hours into her ministration, she checked his temperature again—102.9. The coiled wire in her chest loosened, just a little.

Half an hour later, it was 102.5, and the next time she sponged his face, he opened his eyes and whispered, "Lee."

In another fifteen minutes, he coughed and shifted to ease his ribs. "What're you doing?"

"You've been fighting a high fever."

"Where?"

"A hotel room, outside Toledo. How do you feel?"

"Cold."

She checked again. His temperature had fallen another whole degree. Lee lowered her head to rest on the edge of the tub. The throbbing in her temples, behind her eyes, eased at the cool pressure.

"Lee."

"I'm fine," she whispered.

The water sloshed as he lifted a hand, dripped while he held it midair. *Go ahead, Marcus, it's all right.* She couldn't say it. He would lower his hand, and this moment would pass.

But no. His hand came to rest high on her back as she knelt, bowed over. Water seeped into her shirt, just below her neck. Perhaps he touched her because he was feverish and in pain, perhaps because he'd been resurrected, perhaps because he was unchangeably unable to see her struggle without trying to take the struggle onto himself. And perhaps for all those reasons, or for others, she didn't shudder at the weight of his hand.

Long minutes passed. They didn't move. Then he coughed again, and Lee raised her head, and his hand slipped away and left a wet, cold mark on her back.

"I think you'll be better now," she said. "If I help you, can you get out of the tub?"

On the first try, she knew it was no good. She left the bathroom in search of her Constabulary ally, two words she'd never have predicted joining in her mind. She'd never thought of Sam as true Constabulary.

She had walked through the room before without seeing it, trailing behind Austin with Marcus in his arms. It was a standard room—two queen beds, a TV, a small fridge and microwave. Violet had crashed on the bed near the door, not bothering to turn down the covers. Austin slept on the floor in their lone sleeping bag, leaving the other bed empty.

Lee knelt beside his head. "Austin."

He jolted up, eyes darting around the room, then saw her and relaxed. "How's he doing?"

"He's much better, ready to sleep."

By the time she finished speaking, Austin was on his feet, one hand scrubbing at his face, then his fine blond hair. Sleepiness lingered in his eyes, and he didn't look any older than Violet at the moment. He entered the bathroom ahead of her. From inside came a slosh of water.

"Hey," Austin said, "I'm here to help. Sam sent me with you guys to help."

Lee pushed past him into the room. The pillow had fallen from behind Marcus into the tub, and he hunched forward, jaw clenched, breathing labored.

"It's all right, Marcus," she said.

"He's an agent."

"I know. Sam says we can trust him."

"No."

"Marcus—"

"No."

Austin pressed his lips together, then crouched to eye level with Marcus. "You're right, I was there. Two days ago. With Jason."

A shudder seized Marcus. He gripped the edge of the tub, wide helplessness in his eyes. She'd let a stranger see him this way, bruised and exposed. Let a Constabulary agent see him. She should have dragged him to bed herself. She should be strong enough to carry him.

"Bre— Marcus," Austin said. "Hear me, man. Jason's a coward and a psycho. There's a reason Sam came for you after I was there."

Marcus didn't blink, didn't break eye contact.

"Jason threatened me when he found out. Sam sent me along to keep all of us safe, not just you. But I'm going to help you in the meantime."

"No."

"I'm not here to turn you in."

A long silence bridged between them, or maybe widened the gap. Austin crouched there, utterly still, until Marcus shivered and coughed.

Austin extended an open hand. "Lee can't lift you. Will you let me help you up?"

"You told him to shoot me."

He … what?

"I did. Live to save another day."

Marcus studied him a long moment, then nodded.

An hour later, Austin had burrowed back into the sleeping bag, Violet hadn't stirred, and Marcus lay under the sheet and thin comforter in the second bed. He'd thanked Lee as she drew the covers up over him. She sat in a stiff upholstered chair that she'd pulled up to the bedside, feet tucked under her.

"Lee?" Marcus stared at the window, where morning poured stripes of chilled sunlight through the blinds.

"Yes?"

"Sun's coming up."

"It's been a whole night, Marcus."

"I know." He waited almost a minute to speak again. "Could we … see it?"

Of course, the sky. One of the dearest sights in the world to Marcus. She crossed the room and pulled the blinds.

Marcus's hands curled into the blanket. "Thanks."

Even through his coughing spells, his eyes didn't move from the window. The sunrise bled from pink to orange. The ball of fire rose in the sky while his fever dropped to 100.8 and the sick brightness left his eyes. Then he lay still until Lee thought he was asleep, until he half-flexed his injured knee and grimaced. His eyes opened.

"What happened to Indy?"

She should be prepared for this question. She placed the flats of her hands on the arms of her chair. "I don't know."

"She was at home."

"I went as quickly as I could, but they'd already been there. The dog was gone."

"They were … intruders."

"I would imagine so." And as such would have been attacked. Self-defense against Marcus's dog might have involved lethal force. But even if Constabulary agents had bothered to confine her, no animal shelter would offer for adoption a seventy-five-pound German shepherd who had tried to bite multiple people. The why wouldn't matter.

"Thanks. For trying."

"She was yours."

A crinkle formed between his eyes. "She was a good dog."

Indutiae. Truce. Mascot of a friendship's endurance. "Yes, she was."

Around eight-thirty, he fell asleep, and Lee's own eyelids started to droop.

Sam did say she had to sleep.

I'll sleep when he's well. Two more days, and she'd know if the antibiotics were going to help. Until then, especially, she had to watch him.

But if she became fatigued, she could miss something vital. She closed her eyes and drew up her knees. Every muscle remained tense, ready. She reached for his wrist. His pulse thrummed against her fingers, steady, and her body relaxed a bit. He was weak, but he was also strong.

She would sleep. Only for a few hours.

17

"First things first." Violet reached for a case of bottled water, but Austin stepped between her and the grocery shelf. He hefted the twenty-four-pack with one hand and shoved it onto the rack at the bottom of the cart.

"Oh," Violet said.

"What?"

"Nothing, you just make them look … less heavy." She pivoted away from him and marched to the main aisle toward the back of the store, so they could "shop against traffic," she'd said.

Austin pushed the cart behind her. "Why is water first priority?"

"Because in my head, it's last. So if we don't get it now, I'll forget."

"Didn't Lee put it on the list?"

Violet waved the sheet of hotel stationery at him, filled with precise cursive. "Not the point."

Whatever. Shopping in general was the last of Austin's priorities, but Violet refused to drive Sam's truck. Anyway, he wouldn't have let her go alone. Not that danger lurked around every corner in a mostly empty Kroger at 9:00 at night, but still. Violet double-checked Lee's list as she went, and items started to stack up in the cart. Paper plates, plasticware. Peanut butter, a jar of real honey (Violet read the ingredients per Lee's instructions), whole grain bagels, a loaf of whole grain bread. Apples and oranges and bananas and baby carrots. Beef jerky (at least there was that), a whole case of tuna fish, a jar of relish, mixed nuts, string cheese.

"We're going to be eating like squirrels," Austin said.

"She said to get whatever else we want, too, but I can't think of anything she missed. Anything convenient, that is."

True enough. Frozen pizza and burgers on the grill would have to wait until they got to … Texas. *I'm actually doing this, running away. To another state—no, country. With Violet.*

"And why can't we just get drive-through for the next few days?"

"She said this is in case stopping 'becomes impractical or a risk.' Plus she hates fast food, as in, she refuses to eat it."

He'd never expected to meet someone more prepared for the most extreme scenario than he was.

Violet stalled in the snack aisle, wandering past the tortilla chips and biting her lip, then freezing in front of the cheese dips and salsa. "I want nachos."

"Okay."

"Except there's no way to keep all the toppings and stuff. Plus they're messy. Oh, never mind." She huffed and turned away from the chips to the other side of the aisle, grabbed a few boxes of fruit snacks.

"Those are gross," Austin said.

She giggled.

It hadn't changed. The sound of it, a sound he hadn't counted on hearing ever again, caught his breath. She tossed the boxes into the cart and kept moving down the aisle.

"That wasn't a joke. I'm not eating wax and cherry juice."

"They're made with real fruit, I checked."

He shook his head, and Violet shook hers back, a *what-will-I-do-with-you* tolerance in the tilt of her mouth that quickly flattened. He could see this thought too, as if she'd spoken it. *I'm not supposed to enjoy your company anymore.* But … she still did?

They reached the end of the aisle and started to turn before Austin realized what she'd skipped. "Don't forget granola bars."

"Lee said not to get any."

"They're nonperishable and nonprep."

"She wrote it on the list with a line through it *after* verbally telling me not to get any granola of any kind."

"Is one of them allergic? Can you be allergic to granola?"

"I've never heard of it, but maybe." Violet paused in front of the gourmet chocolate and grabbed two bars of intense dark, 85% cacao. "Not on the list, but I've seen this stuff in her pantry. I think before she stopped eating, it used to be her thing. That and Klondike bars, there were two unopened boxes in her freezer."

"Lee stopped eating?"

Violet's thumb traced the wrapper's gold foil lettering. "This isn't normal for her. Tall and thin, yeah, but not … bones poking everywhere."

Before Austin could figure out how to respond, Violet gave a small smile and set the chocolate bars into the cart, more carefully than she'd handled the rest of the food.

At the last minute, she remembered to get a manual can opener. They went through the self-scan and paid cash, and no one looked at them twice. Did Jason have patrols at Michigan's state line, not realizing they'd already escaped it? Could he get jurisdiction to extend the search to Ohio? Austin's scalp prickled with the possibilities.

He and Violet walked to the truck under a few floodlights, shoulder to shoulder. He caught the scent of hotel shampoo when the wind lifted her hair toward his face. While she climbed into the truck, Austin held the bags. Good thing. Otherwise he might have picked her up and lifted her inside, just to hold her. He tossed the bags on the floor at her feet and shut the door.

As planned, they stopped at Subway—soup for Brenner, sandwiches for everyone else—then headed back to the hotel. Their room was easy to spot from down the hall: one of two doors bearing a Do Not Disturb tag. Bags hanging over both arms, Austin let them in with the key card.

Brenner still slept in the bed across the room. Lee sat at the low, wooden table by the window, studying a highway map of the Midwest. She glanced up as Austin slid the bolt on the door.

"Wow, a paper map." Violet set her bags on the floor and bent over the table. "Old school."

"I'd prefer my phone app," Lee said. "But fortunately, the hotel clerk had these. I'm trying to determine if we should go south through Kentucky and Tennessee, or west through Indiana and Illinois."

Austin set down his bags, including dinner—well, breakfast, for them—on the empty bed.

"Shh." Violet glared at the rustle of the plastic bags. "You'll wake Marcus up."

"He's slept fourteen hours. He needs to eat." Lee crossed to the bed. "Marcus. Wake up."

He didn't stir.

Lee leaned close to his head and softened her voice. "Marcus."

His body jerked, rolling from his back to his side, arms snapping up to guard his head, one knee pulling into his chest. Austin's body twitched, recognizing the reflex. A sour taste filled his mouth, but it was in the past. For him, anyway.

"Shh. It's Lee."

Brenner uncurled and lowered his arms. His eyes traveled the room, lingered on Austin, then found Lee.

"Dinner," she said.

After he'd finished the last drop of broth, Lee helped him drink a bottle of water and gave him more antibiotics and Motrin. He fell asleep again almost as soon as she'd lowered his head to the pillow. Perched at the foot of his bed, Lee began eating her oven-roasted chicken sandwich. Violet and Austin split a foot-long roast beef, but she only nibbled her half. Her glances at Lee seemed afraid to break a spell. Oh, right. Bones poking everywhere.

Halfway through her sandwich, Lee planted her heels on the edge of the box spring. "He needs more time."

Austin might think she was overreacting if he hadn't just watched Brenner tremble to hold a cup of soup. But being right didn't make her scenario preferable. Crossing another state line, then another, all the way to their haven—that's what they should be doing.

Violet was already nodding, staring at Brenner's sleeping form. Challenging both her and Lee … Well, the trust around here was tenuous enough already.

Still. "It's not a good idea."

"Leaving is not an option," Lee said.

Austin tried to smooth his scowl. "Tomorrow night, then."

"The night after."

She wanted to stay here two more days? The risk left his instincts faintly buzzing, as if he stood beside an electric fence. "That's—"

"By then, the antibiotics will be working, and the fever should break."

"Lee, by that time we could be in Texas. He could be safe."

She set down her sandwich, only half eaten. "Or he could be dead."

Violet jerked in her chair as if someone had stabbed her. "What're you talking about? You told Chuck he's not in danger."

"I couldn't leave them with futile worry."

"But he—he's eating and sleeping, and the fever's been lower since this morning."

"And they're all reassuring signs. But malnourishment, dehydration, muscle atrophy, fractures—Marcus's body is fighting multiple battles at once, and it's too soon for him to be winning any of them."

If he died … well, what would be the point of all this? Austin sighed. "Two more days."

"Yes."

"You didn't tell me," Violet whispered. "You let me think … for a whole day."

Lee resumed eating.

"I'm not Chuck and Belinda. I'm your—your medical assistant."

At the break in Violet's voice, Lee looked up. Before she could respond, Violet pushed her own sandwich away, shot to her feet, and barreled into the bathroom. The door shut quietly. Lee stared at it.

"It's important information," Austin said. "We should've known before."

Lee gathered the spoon and empty soup cup from the table and threw them into the trash. A muffled sob came from the bathroom, and she froze. If she wasn't going to talk to Violet, then he would, but when Austin moved toward the door, Lee's glare stilled him. She crossed in front of him, tapped on the door, and slipped inside.

18

Violet knelt on the frayed white rug, hands folded in her lap. As Lee shut the door, she turned her face up, tears magnifying the green of her eyes.

"Wasn't I worth telling?"

Lee pressed her shoulders against the door. She'd wounded Violet. Violet, who dusted her furniture and vacuumed while Lee was at work, who studied with flash cards on the couch every night, who made toast after Lee's body finally stopped trying to be rid of itself from the inside out. *Say something. Repair what you've done.* But her mouth was sawdust.

"I know it doesn't matter to you, but Lee, I've been praying the wrong prayer. For a whole day."

This was the reason for the tears? Not Lee herself? Her chest eased slightly.

"I've been thanking God that Marcus didn't die, but maybe he's going to, and maybe if I'd just prayed for him not to ..." She squeezed her eyes shut, and a tear escaped.

Lee crouched beside her. "Violet."

"Go away, I have to pray."

"You believe God works this way? Have you found a passage in the Bible suggesting that He does?"

She swiped at her tears and frowned at Lee. "You don't believe in praying in the first place."

"But you do, correct?"

She gave a teary roll of her eyes. *Duh, Lee.*

"And you believe God cares for you."

"It says we're supposed to pray without ceasing and make our requests known and stuff. And Jesus says the Father gives us gifts."

Far be it from Lee to strengthen anyone's misguided faith, much less Violet's, but applying the girl's beliefs to her situation was only logical. "If you believe that, then you can't believe God would willfully misunderstand you. You can't believe in God's cruelty."

"No way. He gave us Jesus. The opposite of cruel."

Technically no, but all right. Lee rocked back on her heels. "Well, then."

"Lee … He isn't cruel. There's a lot I don't know, but I know that much."

She stood. Now wasn't the time for a war of the worldviews. "I apologize for not communicating with you."

"Why didn't you?"

"I …" *I couldn't say it.* A ball of ice formed in her stomach. "I should have. I'll do better in the future."

Violet's mouth tipped up. "Because I'm your medical assistant."

"Yes."

"I'm okay, you can go. I need to keep praying for a little while, for Marcus, I—I just feel like I need to."

Lee nodded and left her to her futile exercise.

Austin's gaze speared her the moment she'd exited the bathroom. "You're not a Christian."

They'd been heard that easily through the door? "No."

If she wasn't up to a philosophical debate with Violet, she certainly wasn't going to endure a personal conversation. Not with a Constabulary agent, while Violet knelt pleading in the other room, while Marcus lay defenseless a few feet away. She dug through her duffel bag, brushed her fingers against the cash envelope, and found one of the books she'd laid flat at the bottom. The nurse's memoir. Her soul throbbed a moment for the hundreds of books she'd left behind.

She curled into the stuffed chair and opened to page one. Re-center herself.

"But what about the clinic you were running?" Austin said. "And that kidnapping, the Weston baby. You did do it, didn't you?"

Lee turned the page though she hadn't finished reading it. *Stop talking, and stop asking me to talk.*

"I mean, forget everything you did before. Look at what you're doing now. If you're not a Christian, then why would you …?"

When his words trailed away, Lee stretched her legs and settled her feet on the floor. Six pages into her book, Austin started in again.

"There was conjecture about the two of you. Bonnie and Clyde of the resistance movement or something clichéd like that. I didn't give it much credit." He was staring at Marcus.

"We're not Bonnie and Clyde," Lee said.

"Right."

"And we're not …" Together. Not in the way Austin meant. But he wouldn't believe her if she said it, given what he'd observed in the last day.

After all, her behavior was extreme, the kind that typically resulted from love. She couldn't fault the rationale behind Austin's conclusion. And if she tried to clarify, he would return to his original question.

What was she doing here … if she didn't love Marcus?

Lee glanced up to find Austin studying her, and she attempted a glare, but logic was worming in to distract her. Her actions didn't make sense without …

You don't love him.

No. She didn't.

He's a friend.

The friend of her heart. The friend who would die for her, who hadn't walked away in ten years. The man whose body she'd now seen and touched, washed and tended.

Lee rubbed her thumb along the book's spine and turned another page. Her eyes refused to focus on the words. Perhaps for no reason or perhaps because Austin had just mentioned Elliott Weston, her memory echoed with Aubrey's voice.

"You should think about it … him and you."

She had. Regardless of what Aubrey or Austin or anyone else thought they observed, she wasn't able to love Marcus. Love was giving—not merely giving up an established life, but giving one's soul. And Lee's soul could hardly be called a gift.

19

Time. Wore. On.

Hours. A night, a day, and a night. The third day's sun rose behind clouds like wool. If Marcus's fever didn't break in the next twelve hours, then the antibiotics weren't working, and Lee tried not to think about the prognosis in that case.

The fever stayed below 103 degrees, but his sleep never seemed restful, more his body's shallow attempt to hide from the pain. Lee monitored his temperature, pulse, and breathing, and woke him long enough to feed him and help him to the bathroom. He didn't worsen but didn't improve.

Austin and Violet passed the time with restaurant runs, reading (good thing Lee had more than one book), philosophical debate—which Violet usually lost—and squabbles for the TV remote, which Violet usually won. All three of them watched the national news every few hours. Otherwise, Violet alternated between ocean ecosystem documentaries when she could find them, and soap operas when she couldn't. Austin did force her into a U2 concert special that he spotted while surfing, and over the next few hours he absently, quietly kept breaking into "Beautiful Day." His tenor had perfect pitch.

By the overcast third day, Lee needed a good workout at the gym and at least twenty-four hours of solitude.

"News," Austin announced around noon, and Violet changed the channel.

Their faces hadn't shown up so far. At some point, though, Jason would realize Lee was gone as well as Austin and Marcus. Hopefully, Violet had been invisible long enough that the Constabulary wouldn't think to include her in the search. At least one of their group needed the ability to walk into a gas station and pay cash in view of security cameras.

Local news rolled first. Yesterday, Violet and Austin would have talked over it, but quiet reigned today. Maybe Lee wasn't the only one wearing down. The first national story caused subtle shifts in all of them, straightened posture and eyes trained on the screen.

"There are still more questions than answers in the matter of the state of Texas, which ratified a motion to secede late in June this year."

As if anyone didn't know that. Lee rolled the tension from her shoulders and sank onto the edge of Marcus's bed. His hand twitched, then his eyes opened. They closed again after a quick gauge of his surroundings, but based on his breathing, he remained awake.

"Latest on the list of unknowns is what kind of measures would be taken to secure fugitives who have committed crimes in other states. The border of Texas is being reinforced daily—they claim in order to preserve their sovereignty as a nation. But many people see this as a way to defy the American legal system, particularly the Constabulary."

Marcus opened his eyes.

"The federal government has petitioned on behalf of state Constabularies for authority to enter Texas and bring back philosophical criminals. So far, Texas is denying this request." The news anchor took his story "to the streets" for a poll, in which people seemed to be split fifty-fifty. Half said the federal government had the right and duty to pursue criminals into Texas, especially Christians.

Half said that if Texas wanted to welcome terrorists over its borders, why not let them? Taxpayers could save money on re-education.

"This already got resolved," Violet said. "The President said so. Texas is sovereign. This guy's talking like that never happened."

Austin shrugged. "There's still a ton of controversy on it, and one speech didn't change that. So now they'll show the public a neutral poll and watch their reaction."

Violet shook her head. "You seriously think they might decide to—oh! Hey, Marcus. You're awake."

Marcus's eyes darted to hers, clear and focused, an acknowledgment despite his silence.

"We're checking the news for your face." Violet ventured a smile. "So far, so good."

He nodded against the pillow and turned his attention to the television. A few stories later, Violet cartwheeled the remote between her hands, ready to change the channel back to her special on the Great Barrier Reef. The camera cut back to the anchorman.

"Michigan Philosophical Constabulary officials had the task of arresting one of their own this morning. He's been identified as Agent Samuel Stiles of …"

No. No, no, no. His face appeared, filling half the screen. A mug shot.

"Lee," Violet said.

"Quiet." She had to listen.

"The ongoing investigation is being aided by the cooperation of Stiles, who has confessed to a variety of crimes previously suspected as being the work of more than one Constabulary dissenter. Further details aren't being released at this time. The …"

Lee tried to hear it, process it. "He set himself up."

"You … you really think so?" Violet said, as Austin nodded.

The certainty on his face sent a surge of heat through Lee. Austin didn't know Sam, not really. Which could only mean …

"You planned this together?"

"No," he said. "I didn't want him to do it."

Of course, Sam hadn't revealed his plan to her. She might have refused to go. Lee's eyes burned. No, she wouldn't have refused, not with Marcus's life in the balance, and Sam knew it. He spared her the choice.

His picture was replaced by a weather map, and she pressed her hands to her face. If Jason somehow got hold of Sam …

"She's starting to hyperventilate." Violet's voice drifted from the other end of a tunnel.

"Talk," Marcus said. "Talk to her." The mattress shifted. He was trying to move.

Lee's lungs opened enough for an answer. "I'm fine."

He studied her, concern etching into his face, deepening the grooves of pain.

"Marcus, I'm fine."

He pushed himself up as Austin switched off the TV. "Where are we?"

"Ohio," Violet said. "Toledo-ish."

Marcus's eyes roamed the room, then rested on Lee. "How long?"

"Almost three days."

"In the same place? Why?"

"You've been very ill. You still are."

An old, stubborn fire flickered, so far behind his eyes Lee had to be imagining it, seeing what she wished was still there. Or maybe it truly was. Marcus shook his head. "No."

"The fever—"

"We're leaving. Now."

Austin began to pack away what few possessions were scattered around the room. He tossed Lee her book, and she caught it against her chest.

"He's awake and coherent for once, and he's right," Austin said. "We need to keep moving."

Because of Sam? Or because Austin finally had an ally in his push to get them as far from Jason Mayweather as possible? Lee glanced to Violet, and the steady gaze that met hers promised to back her, whatever that meant.

Marcus leveraged himself upright. "No one's safe here."

Including him. Lee shut her eyes. Think.

They didn't have to drive straight through. If the fever rose again, or if he simply needed rest tomorrow, they could get another room for at least a few hours. And every mile that widened the distance also opened more route possibilities for Mayweather to track.

"All right," she said. "We'll go."

She opened her eyes, but Sam's mug shot was burned on her vision. *Sam, you gave too much.*

20

Indiana blended into Illinois without much change as far as Austin could tell—flat farmland, green and brown patchwork fields, and the road in front of him. The highway widened and narrowed as the miles rolled by. Sometimes there was only one worn blacktop lane for each direction, winding through low hills of harvested crops and dry grass that soon flattened again. Right now, two lanes headed west, two east, separated by a wide stretch of grass and, as Violet had pointed out, some yellow wildflowers.

The sun's last rays reached up from the horizon in front of him, but their pink glow was waning. Austin had squinted into the sunset for the last two hours, while it stretched and shifted color and turned the highway signs into silhouettes. Driving behind a semitruck for a few dozen miles had helped. Now dusk began to settle, and headlight glare left him less blinded but no less tired. All he wanted to do was park somewhere and shut his eyes, and he'd been driving for only six hours.

"How's your head?" Violet said.

He massaged his right eyebrow, which felt bruised to the touch, but it helped the deeper ache. "What's in that bag by your feet? Any beef jerky?"

"What if there's only"—she gave a theatrical gasp—"fruit snacks?"

"Violet, seriously."

"Sorry." The bag rustled. "The jerky must be in the back. There's peanuts in here, though."

His stomach rumbled. "That'll work."

The top of the canister popped off, and then she tapped his right elbow. "Here."

He must be starving, because the salty pittance she poured into his hand was kind of delicious. He turned up his palm for more, and Violet giggled.

Motion in the rearview mirror captured his peripheral vision. He glanced over. His blood froze. Cop lights.

Red and blue, not green. A regular cop. But … Austin pulled the truck over to the concrete shoulder. What had he done wrong?

"Oh, no," Violet whispered.

In the mirror, the police car's door opened. The officer stepped out.

"Please, please, Jesus—"

"Violet!" Austin gripped the wheel to keep from grabbing her arm. The officer would see any sudden motion. "Let me talk, but if he asks you a question, answer him. We're driving to see my relatives in … uh, Missouri. In St. Louis."

A suburb would be more believable, but he'd have to know the name of it, and he'd never been further from his birthplace than Ohio, until today. St. Louis proper it would have to be.

"What'd you do?" she said.

"We'll find out in a …" Wait. "You think I planned this?"

She ducked her head.

He had to process that later. The cop looked to be about fifty, dark-haired and stocky. He wore a tan uniform shirt, dark green pants—*not gray, not a con-cop, you're fine, keep calm*—and a badge on his chest, a nightstick and a radio and a gun on his belt.

Austin reached toward the glove box, where Sam had mentioned he kept the registration.

Shoot. The registration.

This wasn't Austin's vehicle. Not a criminal offense in and of itself, of course. But the vehicle's owner *was* now a criminal, whose property would be investigated. *Could've held off getting arrested for one more day, Stiles.* No, this was Austin's fault for agreeing to kill two and a half days in a hotel. And for not figuring out sooner that they needed to ditch this truck.

Violet's trembling hand curled around the can of nuts as the cop reached Austin's window. Austin hit the button to lower it. *Come on, Violet, keep calm.*

"Good evening," the cop said. "License and registration, please."

Austin took a slow, natural breath, and his chest expanded as if filled with light. He could do this. He flipped open his wallet slowly and angled it toward the officer. The gold badge gleamed, even in the dusk.

"Michigan Philosophical Constabulary, sir. Agent Delvecchio." *I outrank you.* Even if he'd left his jurisdiction long behind.

"Let me see that." The cop held out his hand.

Austin's hand spasmed around the wallet, but he handed it over.

After a few seconds, the cop handed it back. "What do they do in Michigan, recruit you from undergrad?"

"They did with me."

"How about that." He propped a hand on his gun belt and smirked.

No words could wield a barb any sharper than the next quiet second, as Austin was sized up and deemed laughable. Heat rushed into his face, and the man's mouth curved outright.

"I pulled you over for doing sixty-seven in a fifty-five."

"Fifty-five?" On an interstate?

"Speed limit doesn't go up until you're past Effingham."

He forced out the necessary words. "I apologize, sir. The sun's been in my eyes for a while."

"All the more reason to slow down, wouldn't you say?"

"I will."

"Now get out of here."

"Thank you."

The cop walked back to his car. Austin rolled up the window. Violet turned to face him, and he waved her to silence, his hand skimming above the center console, out of the cop's sight.

Back on the road, he tossed Violet his wallet. "Could you pull the badge out for me?"

She tugged at it until the clip came free. "Here."

Austin reached up to his sun visor and fastened it so that the gold glinted in plain sight. His hand shook, caught between nearly being manacled and hauled back home, and still wanting to punch that cop's condescending lights out. He tried to calm his breathing. He'd been able to, only seconds ago. But now a blaze coursed through his body, and deep breaths only fueled the rush. In his mind, he tried to put on the green coat from second grade, but he couldn't feel the warmth or the softness.

"You saved us," Violet said. "If anybody else had been driving, that cop would've run the registration."

Good for her, putting together the consequences. Maybe he underestimated her street smarts. Then again, she'd blurted a prayer to Jesus five minutes ago.

"Austin?"

She could see it. He had to calm down. The rage hadn't grabbed him this hard in over a year. Why now? Because some state cop thought him young and ridiculous?

Violet's eyes bored into him until he had to glance away from the road.

"What?"

"You don't look right, that's all."

The laugh was a bark. "Okay."

"Is it your headache?"

Thanks for reminding me. He sighed.

"There's a rest stop in two miles, that sign said."

"We need to keep driving. No, we need to find a used car lot and then abandon this one in a field somewhere."

Except there was no way they had enough cash for that. What was the most they could pool together? A few grand? His stash was down to eight hundred. Lee had tried to pay for everything, insisting she had the most to spend, but a guy didn't let other people pay his way. Not even on a protection detail.

"I know there's something else wrong," Violet whispered. "Will you talk to me?"

"Considering you thought I orchestrated that whole thing, I'd rather not." The bite in his voice stung even him.

Violet bowed her head and rubbed her thumb over her wrist. "Okay."

He drove another mile and knew he had to stop. He barely made it to the rest stop without bashing his fist on the dashboard. He parked the truck but left it running, said something to Violet, and left all of them behind.

The place was a sort of park. He stepped over a low guardrail onto a pine-needle path that ran parallel with the parking lot. He inhaled the smells of wood and sap, stared up at the towering evergreens. What he needed was about half an hour with his home gym, bench pressing until the weight on his chest morphed into the weight in his hands. He glanced back at the truck. Nobody could see him right now. He dropped to the chilled ground and started push-ups. Dirt and pine needles crushed against his palms. One, two, ten, twenty, fifty, a hundred, not enough yet. Not until his body weighed more than that cop's disdain. More than Jason's gun cracking against his ankle and wrist, both still sore. More than Jason's form standing over him while he couldn't fight back.

"What're you going to do about it, Austin?"

Shut up, Dad.

Sweat broke out between his shoulders. He stopped counting.

He lifted his body up from the ground one last time and held the pose, and his arms didn't shake. For a long minute, he let his breathing slow, then drew himself to his feet.

Violet stood on the fringe of the path, watching him.

Not fair. This was his. She had no claim on this ritual, no right to watch it. He stalked past her toward the truck.

"I'm sorry," she said.

He halted, letting his profile face the headlights. Head on hurt his eyes. "What?"

"I know this is because of what I said."

He rubbed his eyes and started walking back. "Did you check on them?"

Violet fell into step at his side. "Lee said Marcus's fever broke an hour ago. I think she's not as worried. But I think his ribs are … bad."

Yeah, nothing hurt like a rib. Austin blinked against the image of a blurred arm swinging, the hand holding a skillet about to be set on the burner for Saturday breakfast. He winced at the phantom impact against his left side. And that had been only one rib, one hairline fracture, one bruise curving over his otherwise unmarred skin.

"Oh, I told her what you said about the truck. She said we'll ditch it in the morning."

Violet's voice pushed away the rest of the memory as they got back into the truck. Austin put it in gear and headed back toward the expressway.

"Is she planning on raiding a junkyard or something?" he said.

"No, she'll buy something."

"We don't have that kind of …" But Violet didn't seem surprised by this plan. "How much cash does she have with her?"

"I'm pretty sure she's rich, so …" Violet shrugged.

"Pretty sure? Based on what?"

"Uh, living with her."

Right. He'd put that together days ago. All the time Lee Vaughn had, to him, been a name and picture paper-clipped to a case file, a kidnapping suspect, a close associate of Brenner's … to Violet, she'd been a roommate and a friend.

When the silence weighed too much, he turned on the radio and found a station that claimed to play "everything but the Top Forty." Perfect. He was humming along to James Taylor when Violet's soft voice broke in.

"I don't know why I said that, earlier. About the cop."

"It's fine."

"No, it's not. I don't even believe it. I mean, obviously, God set this up, you coming with us. I don't think He's going to do that so you can change your mind halfway there and turn us in."

Oh, so she didn't trust Austin, but she trusted God not to let Austin screw them over? *Thanks a lot, Violet.* He focused on the white line, on the highway exit signs. Effingham. That about summed it up.

"Can I ask you something?" she said.

"Sure, why not."

"Are you still mad at me?"

"I'm …" Why did she have to keep digging at the scar, even when she didn't know it? "It wasn't you in the first place. Though I clearly have more to prove than I thought."

"Oh." The silence stretched out. "That, um, that wasn't the question. I have a … a thousand-dollar one."

A sad smile tinged the words, because she had to know they'd both outgrown what they'd had before. Muggy June nights in her room or in the park, posing hundred-dollar and thousand-dollar questions, getting to know each other's thoughts and … A ghost of the soft skin at her collarbone brushed against his thumb, and he grasped the steering wheel with both hands.

"It's okay, go ahead," he said.

"Well, you spent a lot of time at Elysium. Our small group, and I know you were a leader for the middle school boys every Saturday. And I know the church didn't pay you to do any of that, because you told me."

At least she wasn't questioning everything he'd ever said to her. He nodded when the pause stretched on, though her destination in this discussion wasn't hard to guess.

"So, did you report to your head agent, or whoever? About Elysium?"

"No."

She sighed. "Okay. Um, good, I guess. But … do you believe the stuff you were teaching?"

Stuff like God wanting the human race to realize its own God potential. That belief would appall her, now that she'd embraced archaic Christianity. He fought a grimace and lost.

"For me, Elysium is—was—a sociological field trip."

She shifted to face him. "You're over my head, scholar."

The nickname was a knife, coated in four months of rust. Only Violet had ever called him that. "I told you this before. I enjoy listening to people talk about their belief systems. It's fascinating to me, what they lean on to cope, what philosophical constructs they choose to regulate their behavior."

"But what do you believe, then? Seriously, Austin, this one's worth more than any dollars."

Of course it was, to her. "I don't think about it much. Not beyond the theoretical, anyway. I'm not sure there's a single truth out there, and … if there is, it's never bothered me that I don't know."

"Oh." The music filled the cab again. Ten miles later, Violet said, "For the record … I'm not a terrorist."

21

Lee took two steps out of the rest-stop women's room and almost collided with Violet, who motioned her to the corner beside the drinking fountain.

"This isn't a bathroom break." Violet glanced over her shoulder at the men's room. "I mean, it is. I didn't lie to him. I did have to go. But this is actually an intervention."

"Excuse me?"

"You need to beat Austin to the driver's seat. Quick."

"Violet, I already planned on relieving him. He's been driving nearly ten hours."

"I know, but he won't let you. After that cop pulled us over, he got it in his head that he has to drive us all the way to Texas. Even once we get rid of the truck."

Lee rubbed her arms against the brisk night. She'd half expected a year-long, night-and-day sauna this far south, but apparently, October nights could be as cold in Missouri as in Michigan.

Well, maybe not quite.

"All right, I'll talk to him."

"Talking isn't going to work. He—I said something, and now he's all stubborn."

Lovely. Lee let out a sigh and headed back to the truck. Leaving Marcus alone, only for five minutes, only a few hundred feet away, left a small knot in her stomach. He'd been silent for hours, clutching fistfuls of blanket, sweating from the pain.

Lee opened the driver's door, and Austin's voice came from behind her. "I'll drive."

She turned to face him. The light of the parking lot threw a stark shadow over one side of his face, but his knit brows gave away the headache. "You need a rest."

"We could get pulled over again."

"For crossing the median when you fall asleep at the wheel? Yes."

"I'm not that tired."

His eyes were bloodshot, fighting to focus on her. Lee opened the driver's door and climbed inside. Violet had already taken her place on the passenger side.

Austin sighed and rubbed his eyes. "You'll have to get gas soon."

"I believe we can handle that."

He nodded and disappeared around the back of the truck. In a minute, two taps came from the front of the truck bed. All clear.

An hour later, after they'd passed the sign welcoming them to Oklahoma, the gas needle dipped to an eighth. Violet scouted for a sign indicating where they could fill up, and less than ten minutes later they were pulling in, squinting in the lights over the pumps.

Per routine, Violet got out and pumped the gas, enough cash already shoved into her pocket to cover the cost. She headed inside, and Lee kept an eye on her as she stepped up to the counter. Behind her slouched a young man in a yellow hoodie, and behind him stood an artificially redheaded woman. As Violet passed them after paying, the man said something to her, and she smiled.

Violet was halfway to the truck when the man finished paying and exited. She was mere steps away when he lengthened his stride toward the rusted, maroon sedan one pump over. She reached for the door handle as he called, "Hey, hold up a minute."

Violet's hand dropped to her side, and she turned to face him. He crossed the space between the gas pumps, and Lee's instincts screamed.

"Don't," she said, as if Violet could hear her.

He hooked his arm around Violet's neck. Lee threw her door open. He reached his other hand behind him and—

He had a gun he had a gun he had a gun.

He pressed the barrel under Violet's chin, looked up into the truck cab, and his eyes met Lee's. Gray like her own, pupils like pinholes.

He raised his voice, the first Oklahoma accent she'd heard. "I know y'all got money. She paid with a hundred-dollar bill. Come on down and give me what you got before I do something bad."

Austin was armed.

Austin was asleep.

If Lee screamed, he would wake up and shoot this animal in the head.

If Lee screamed, this animal would shoot Violet.

She gripped the handle of her duffel and slid to the ground.

Inside, the redhead was chatting and gesturing with the girl behind the counter. Lee walked around the back bumper of the truck. She could punch the tailgate once, and Austin would be awake.

The man pressed the gun barrel into Violet's throat. She choked, and he gave her a shake. "Faster," he said to Lee.

If she did anything to startle him, threaten him, he could pull the trigger. She stood in front of him, her back to the lit store windows and the potential witnesses. She unzipped the bag, withdrew a bulging bank envelope marked with thick black Sharpie scrawl, *$20,000.* Her deductions in black pen crossed out the original amount and subtracted gas money, meals, groceries, hotel fare.

"Hoo-ee, who'd rob the gas station when the customers got twenty grand in cash? Now don't throw it at me or nothing. Go put it on the roof of my car there."

"Please don't—" Violet choked as he turned the gun barrel and pressed harder.

Lee set the envelope on his car and stood beside it. *Now what?*

"I bet you didn't put it all in one envelope. I know I wouldn't."

"That's all there is." Her voice and her hands didn't tremble, despite the cold shudder in her spine.

"Ain't this girl worth more than whatever you've got left?"

"We have nothing left."

"Turn that bag upside down, then."

Violet's eyes locked with hers, whites showing, unblinking, her face pale and frozen as if she were already halfway to death. Lee reached into the bag and drew out the second envelope, unmarked except for the amount. Twenty thousand dollars, unspent. She held it up.

He nodded toward his car. "Go ahead."

Lee set it beside the other envelope, crossed back to the truck.

The man shoved Violet to the ground, sprinted the five steps to his car, swiped the envelopes off the roof, jumped inside, and nearly hit a car pulling out. Brakes screeched.

Violet huddled on the concrete, staring at the abrasions on her hands. Behind Lee, voices poured into the night.

"We saw everything, we called the police, they should be here any—"

"Are y'all okay?"

Called the police.

Lee hauled Violet to her feet and pushed her into the truck. The women's voices didn't pause, but the words didn't register. She grabbed her bag, though nothing remained in it but clothes and books. She dashed to get behind the wheel and pulled into traffic. Horns beeped behind her.

She drove. She trembled. She bit her lip until she tasted blood.

Violet drew her knees to her chest, shoes planted on the truck seat. She held her bleeding palms away from her, open to the air.

Lee's lungs tightened, and a gray frame boxed in her vision. Her hands tingled. She saw everything that could have happened. The bullet piercing Violet's throat, tearing through her carotid. The pulsing blood.

The truck swerved. Lee gripped the wheel. Breathe. Stop the spiral now. In another thirty seconds, she—she—

Violet. Grabbed from behind. Held against the man's body. Treasured Violet, forced and powerless.

"Lee?" Violet turned and lowered her feet to the floor. "Lee, say something."

Lee's gasps rent the air. Her hands quaked on the wheel. The truck weaved again.

"Lee! You have to pull over."

Violet, smothering in a black hood while he pulled her jeans down her hips. *That wasn't Violet, that was—*

"Jesus, help her. Please don't let us crash. Lee."

Through the gray tunnel, Lee found the shoulder of the road. There, a driveway. She should brake.

"Oh, God, thank You, Jesus."

The truck jarred her. Someone had put it in park. Lee's numb hands fell from the wheel.

"Lee, look at me. Come on."

Yes. Look at her. The tunnel allowed Lee to see only one piece of Violet's face at a time. Focus on the eyes. Green.

"Good. Awesome. Okay, so you can hear me. Should I talk about something? Would that help you?"

Nod.

"Okay. Um, I, um. At my mom and dad's house, I had fish. An aquarium. When I got stressed out, I liked to watch them. Well, actually, I liked to watch them whenever, but especially then, because fish are so peaceful and oblivious, you know? Like, they just … float. And explore the rocks and the coral like they've never seen it before, even though they've been living there for a year."

Breathing. Fingertips prickling. The tunnel widened until Violet's whole face showed through.

"And they eat whatever you toss on the water and have no idea where it came from. And I had an air stone, so my room always had this nice bubbling sound. Calming."

Lee nodded. Glanced at the clock. Habit had caused her to register it, subconsciously, when the attack hit. She'd come out of this one in four minutes.

"Are you better?" Violet said.

"Nearly. Thank you." A slow heat blossomed on her face. The incident had become all about her, when Violet was the one—she quelled the images that squeezed her lungs again. She had to be all right.

From behind them, Austin pounded once, twice, three times. A pause, then again and again.

"He's been doing that," Violet said.

"We're too close to the scene. We'll have to explain to him later." Lee put the truck in gear.

"You're sure you can drive?"

"Yes. Are you all right?"

"I'm—" Violet shuddered. "I didn't die. I didn't even get hurt. So yeah, I'm good."

They'd never before been in a situation that caused Lee to ask the question. She had to trust that Violet, unlike Marcus, wouldn't claim to be all right unless she was.

For ten minutes, Lee drove. She took them off the highway, down roads that seemed more or less to run parallel with it. Temptation nudged to reassemble her phone and find a non-highway route, but that would be stupid. When Austin began pounding again, she parked under the brightest light she could find, in the parking lot of a church. *Avalon Fellowship of Believers,* read the lit sign. The moment she turned off the truck, the tailgate crashed open.

22

They'd been car-jacked. Had to be. They must have stopped to get gas. Someone must have jumped into the truck and forced Lee at gunpoint. Probably left Violet behind. The second time they swerved, hard enough to send him almost on top of Brenner, Austin thought they were about to crash. But they didn't. And now they were stopped again. He wasn't waiting any longer.

"Stay here," he said to Brenner, because the idiot was trying to get up.

Surprise wasn't an element Austin could hope for after pounding on the side of the truck, so he opened the tailgate, let it crash down, and leaped outside, gun trained forward, safety off.

Nobody shot him or grabbed him. Nobody stood there at all. They were parked at a … church? He pressed his back to the side of the truck and side-stepped forward. He half spun to level his gun on the window, in case Lee wasn't driving.

She was. Beyond her, Violet sat staring at him.

His lungs released. He reengaged the safety, pointed his gun skyward but didn't holster it yet. Adrenaline bled from his system, and his knees trembled. He locked them.

Lee opened the door. "We're all right."

"Great," he said. "What the—?"

"There was an incident."

No kidding. Lee opened her door and nodded to Violet, who crawled over the gear shift to exit on Lee's side. Under the floodlight, they were both pale as wax.

"Tell me what happened." He shouldn't have to ask.

"We have to leave the truck," Lee said.

"We established that."

"No, we have to leave it here. The police will be … The license plate was facing the witnesses, and …"

Austin raked a hand through his hair. His pulse still hadn't fully lowered. "Okay, did you stop for gas?"

Both of them nodded.

"So Violet was pumping it, and she finished? And then …?"

"I paid. And c-came back out. And then—there was this guy—and he wanted our m-money—"

His body felt freezer-burned, fingers and toes and limbs ready to snap off. "Did he threaten you?"

Violet's mouth opened. Her eyes widened.

"Violet." The cold disappeared. "Did he?"

"He had a—" Her hands wrapped around her neck. Demonstrating? The guy had strangled her? No. Shielding. And she didn't know she was doing it.

"He held Violet at gunpoint while I gave him the money," Lee said.

"Right here." Violet pressed her fingers to one side of her throat. Her palms were scraped red. "He was going to shoot me right here."

Coherent thought boiled away. Austin was going to find him and shoot him. In the throat. But in the kneecaps first. And a few other places.

"But Jesus protected us. I'm not dead or anything. Or shot, even."

Austin pulled her against his chest. He'd stepped closer without thinking. She melted against him. His hand cradled the back of her head, and she buried her face in his shirt.

"Shh," he said. "It's over, Violet, you're safe."

Violet curled her fingers into his back. "I was so scared. I thought, maybe I'm going to die tonight."

"You didn't. You're right here with me."

"I know, but don't let go."

He rocked her and set his chin on the top of her head. A few tears soaked through his shirt to his chest, and her arms tightened around him. Over her head, he met Lee's gaze and held it.

Lee had adopted the soldier pose again, hands behind her back. She nodded to him. Gratitude? He nodded back. She stepped past them, head down, toward the tailgate.

Austin hid his face in Violet's soft golden hair. She could be dead now. One slip with the gun. One moment's delay from Lee. One decision from that animal—wanting to know what killing felt like, wanting to see some blood. Violet's blood. Spilled out of her until she was gone.

It hadn't happened. Wouldn't. He wouldn't allow it. He'd hold her for the rest of their lives, until their skin wrinkled and their hair turned gray.

23

The truck bed smelled like metal and sweat. Before Lee's eyes could adjust to the dimness, a hand curled around her arm. She jerked backward and nearly fell off the tailgate.

"Lee."

She skimmed her hands over the air and found his shoulder, then his arm. He'd been crawling forward on hands and knees, or one knee, more likely. His breaths labored.

"Lie down," she said.

"What happened?"

"Marcus, you need to—"

"Tell me."

She did, omitting the panic attack. Even without that detail, he asked three times if she and Violet were okay. He didn't crawl back to the mattress until she'd finished the story. As he settled, a coughing spell racked him. They came more frequently now. A good sign where his prognosis was concerned, but the effort and pain drained him. Lee propped him forward with one arm, an easier position from which to expel the phlegm from his lungs. When he could draw a full breath, she eased him back to the pillows.

For a minute, he could manage only a rasping "Thanks." Then he met her eyes. "You're right about the truck. We can't drive it again. They'll run the plates and put everything together."

"And you can't walk." As if any of them could walk to Texas.

"I can make it for a while."

"Don't. Please. I need—" Her voice splintered.

"Lee?"

"You can't help me form a strategy if you won't factor your condition into the scenario."

This silence was the new, jagged one. It sawed through the reserves she had left. She turned her head and pushed away from him. She clasped her hands together. Holding in.

"I'll discuss this with Austin and Violet and inform you of the plan."

Her feet hit the cement as he said, "Wait."

She turned back. "Yes?"

The word wasn't supposed to bite. But shock and the flashback had worn off, and now all the things she should have done pounded in her brain. Pull half the money out of the envelope and leave her bag in the truck. Drive after the man. Something. She could only move forward, though, not back, and if Marcus couldn't be honest enough with himself to help her, then she had to do this without him.

"Don't ..." he said.

Don't what? She waited, but he was quiet. *What did Jason Mayweather do to your words?* He'd never had many to begin with, but this ... She pushed away everything but the present juggernaut and scooted back into the truck.

"I don't know what to do, Marcus. We have nothing."

"I know." Another, different silence followed, not a wall but a cracked door. "How much is left?"

Realistic focus on the physical plight. Exactly what she needed. "I believe Austin has around five hundred dollars."

He closed his eyes a moment.

"Yes," she said.

"The faster you can move, the better chance you have."

"You mean … go on without you?"

"You won't make it with me."

"That is the most absurd—"

"When you had … resources …" He coughed. "I lowered them. Now you've got nothing. So I'll put you in the red."

"Marcus, we all consume resources."

"But you each give things back."

A slow pressure built in her chest. She was going to scream at him. Instead, her words emerged on a whisper. "You idiot."

Confusion gathered between his eyes. "It's the truth."

"What do you think I'm doing right now? Giving you an opportunity to contribute. Asking for strategy assistance from the man who coordinated the efforts of an entire resistance organization. Asking for … for …"

For you to anchor me. As you always do.

She drew her knees up. "Would you leave me?"

He growled.

"All right, that's settled."

"Lee, I—" He coughed once, twice, couldn't stop. His right arm pressed against his ribs. Lee held him forward again, and by the time this spell ended, he was limp in her arms. He moaned as she lowered him.

"Shh," she said. "Easy."

He squeezed his eyes shut and turned his head away.

"Marcus?"

No response. Not even a quiet *thanks*, his mantra for the last few days, which she noticed only in its absence. She leaned nearer, circled his wrist with her fingers, and Marcus jerked his arm.

"What is it?" she whispered.

"I can't."

"Can't what?"

The silence shouted the answer. Marcus couldn't do anything. It was an absurd overstatement, yet she knew his thoughts as if he spoke them. In fact, she should have seen long before now. He couldn't walk. He couldn't sit upright. Until today, he couldn't feed himself. Yet his own list wouldn't stop there. She could imagine it written out in his block handwriting.

Can't drive. Can't help. Can't protect.

And the rest of the list, unrolling like a scroll, because Marcus would be aware of every small thing his body was incapable of. He would hate every disability. No, more than that, he would be …

"Marcus, look at me," she said.

He turned his head to face her, and even in the dimness, with the floodlight sneaking in the open tailgate, the flush in his cheeks was obvious. Yes, she should have known. She'd seen the same reaction so many times, but on a smaller scale. Attempting to treat lacerations on his own, until she made him promise to call her anytime he bled for longer than ten minutes. Fully using his hands while they healed from his latest work injury and ignoring pain any logical person would consider the body's warning sign. Slicing the Constabulary tracker from his own back and intending to dress it himself (how, Lee still didn't know) until Aubrey Weston intervened by calling her.

But he couldn't push through it now, this degree of physical incapacitation. Again she saw Austin standing over him, Marcus's hunched posture in the tub. Humiliated. Ashamed.

"You're mending," Lee said. "In time, you'll be whole again."

His mouth quivered. "I don't know."

"You will. But that's irrelevant."

His stare was as loud as any words. *It's not irrelevant. It's the whole point.*

"Listen to me. If you were in a coma right now, or you had lost your four limbs, or you were deaf and blind and wheelchair-bound—you would not cease to be yourself."

He stiffened against the pillows. *Yeah, I would, Lee.*

"No," she said. "You would be Marcus. And I would not leave you."

His hands curled. Lee grasped his wrist and sat for a while, letting his pulse beat against her fingers. Then she took a deep breath—*I can do this*—felt again his wet handprint on her back. She slid her fingers along his hand until he opened it. She nestled her hand inside his, and he gripped it like a man in the dark who'd been offered a guide into the light.

24

You wouldn't expect a town like Vinita, Oklahoma, to be crawling with law enforcement. But on his first pass down Main Street, or whatever it was called, Austin passed three Constabulary squad cars in less than two miles. One was headed the other direction. One made a left in front of him at a traffic light that didn't give the agent the right of way. One sat in the parking lot of Edie's BBQ Catfish. (Hopefully, those two weren't served together.) Technically, the agents in those cars were still his colleagues, yet all three sightings quickened his pulse. As if he were a fugitive now. Well. Yeah.

What had happened to his life in the last five days?

At the sight of the first gray car with its green light bar, Violet's face blanched and stayed that way. A low flame ignited inside Austin. She shouldn't have to be afraid. Ever.

He left his three charges at the first motel he spotted—a Super 8 that looked like it had been there at least several decades. His insides continued to simmer as he abandoned the truck in some woods near the locked gate of North Park. As he tossed the license plate into a drainage ditch. As he walked back to the Super 8.

He walked east for a while, hit North Wilson, and made a left toward the motel. Most of the detached buildings were one story. Some of the weather-stained brick storefronts, with parallel parking the only visible option, had been built a little taller. On the whole, the town wasn't rundown so much as frozen in time. Austin stripped off his jacket and carried it over his arm. How did it get so warm?

They'd only driven two hours south, and it had to be sixty degrees here. At midnight.

That, or the fury was an actual fire, pushing up his body temperature. A large part of him still harbored a white-hot desire to kill the guy that had held a gun to Violet's neck.

He ought to get hold of himself before he faced her again. He slowed his pace and reached in his mind for the green coat. It hung right there, on the wall peg in the mud room, in the house on Chestnut Lane, the house they'd brought Esther home to when she was born. Austin imagined shoving his arms into the sleeves. Weird thing about that memory—he could adapt it, somewhat. The coat was the same, but his arms weren't stubby second-grader arms. He stayed in his adult body when he put on the coat, and it fit him just as well, like a garment from a fairy tale.

His heartbeat slowed as he made another left, down the sidewalk along the storefronts. Two miles from the motel. A million from Texas, from the ability to reassemble his cell phone and let Esther and Olivia know he was okay and would be home … When?

Once they made it over the border—because they had to, no *if* allowed—Violet might want to stay with Lee and Marcus. Letting Austin hold her once, under extreme stress, didn't mean she was ready to let him back into her life. Much less follow him wherever he was going next, wherever that was.

He sighed and picked up his stride. Better get back. He passed a Sunoco, a few family-style restaurants, and a one-story, brown brick church—First Paradiso Fellowship of Believers. Interesting. There didn't seem to be a Second Paradiso. No wonder the names were getting rehashed, though. You could only invent so many synonyms for Happy Place.

A car pulled closer, on his right, doing about fifteen miles an hour. It didn't pass him. Odd. Behind him, a window rolled down with a mechanical *whir.*

"You lost?"

Austin swiveled to face the male voice, carefree with a hint of twang, and his stomach knotted. Constabulary.

"Just walking."

"Kind of late for that." The agent leaned out the window, and a flickering streetlight reflected on his bald head. "Not from around here, huh?"

Well, that didn't take long. "Michigan. Here visiting family."

"In Vinita?"

Austin's scalp prickled. None of this was a con-cop's jurisdiction. The guy shouldn't be asking. He shook his head and shifted his weight from one foot to the other, allowing curiosity to show but not alarm.

"Shawnee. I've still got a few hours to drive, but I was getting tired."

"Scared of flying?"

Okay, really, this guy had crossed the line. Austin shook his head and clamped his jaw. He had a whole story—sick relative, going to be spending a month or more—but he shouldn't have to tell it. He'd threatened no one.

"I'm not a terrorist." Violet's voice flashed through his head. She must feel this way all the time. As if her society was backing her into a jail cell for no tangible reason.

The agent leaned a muscular arm in the window. "If you're that wiped out, I'd expect you in bed by now."

He wasn't a kid with a curfew, dang it. But he didn't blink, didn't pause. He quirked a self-deprecating smile. "Insomnia. Have to walk to help me unwind, if I've been driving too long."

"Two miles in one direction?"

"Nah … wait, did I walk that far?"

"If you're at the Super 8, you sure did."

He gave a short laugh. "I must be more wired than I thought."

"Must be."

Distant traffic broke up the silence, along with a chattering group of teen girls emerging from the little movie theater across the street.

"Are you a Christian?" the agent said.

Austin froze. Technically, the question was perfectly legal. But Constabulary didn't simply walk up to random pedestrians and ask without evidence. It would be like searching without a warrant. *We can do that too.* But they didn't. That was the point.

The man's gaze drilled into him.

"No, I'm not."

"You seem nervous."

No flashing the badge. Invisibility was more important now than ever, and a twenty-two-year-old Constabulary agent might be as exceptional in Oklahoma as in Illinois. Plus, the longer he delayed, the more suspicious it would be if he did have to reveal his occupation.

"I wouldn't say nervous." Somehow he sounded calm, even bored. "Wired, sure, like I said. Although I don't think Constabulary agents in Michigan poll random people like this."

"Poll?" The agent laughed, thumped his palm on the window frame. "Michigan must be a wishy-washy state, just like I've heard. You get on back to your room and get some sleep now."

Austin nodded and resumed walking, his heartbeat like a double bass drum. The agent's car coasted along behind him for a whole block before turning down another street. Austin broke into a jog. He had to warn all of them, as if it would change anything. He knew only one sure thing about Marcus Brenner. The man would have said *yes* to that last question.

So would Violet.

25

"We can't steal a car."

If Violet's volume increased any further, Lee would have to remind her that hotel walls were essentially paper.

Austin leaned against one of said walls and rolled a can of peanuts between his hands. "Sure we can, I just told you. I haven't hot-wired anything since high school, but once you know how, you know how. I'm not going to blow up or—"

"That's not why we can't." Violet pulled her feet up to sit cross-legged at the foot of Marcus's bed, the only bed. She swiveled to face him. "Come on, Marcus. You do the right thing, I know you do. From experience."

Marcus didn't cringe away from Violet's invasion of his space, simply studied her. "This isn't the same."

The same as setting Violet free last summer, despite her status at the time as a Constabulary spy, because the alternative was kidnapping. Marcus was right. Their current situation robbed someone of an object, not a choice.

"Close enough," Violet said. "It's doing something wrong to get what you want."

"We don't want a car." Austin juggled the peanut can back and forth, low in front of his body. "We need one."

"Good grief, Austin, you're a cop."

"Theft isn't my jurisdiction."

Violet marched into his space and took the can. "Are you serious?"

"If we're talking about what I should be doing according to the oath I took—you really don't want to go there."

They stood too close, matching glares and wills, the silence a wick that sparked toward detonation. Lee uncurled from her position in the stuffed chair and set her feet on the floor. Business at hand. No more, no less.

"All right," she said. "We need a vehicle, and we don't have the means to purchase one."

Austin shrugged. "I don't understand why we're still debating it."

Neither did she. If their method was democracy, Violet had already lost. Lee nodded to Austin. "Do it."

Violet stared at Marcus, who met her eyes but said nothing. After a moment, she turned her back to all of them, ducked her head, then squared her shoulders, and headed for the door.

Austin pushed away from the wall. "Where're you going?"

Violet spoke without facing them. "The hallway. The vending machine, I don't know. Look, I'm not going to pull a Khloe. Obviously, I'm coming with you, whether it's in a stolen car or not. But I need to … think about this and talk to Jesus for a little bit."

Austin swiped a key card from the table and pressed it into her hand. The door shut after her with a quiet click.

He tossed the peanut can in his hand and caught it. "She needs to stop talking about Jesus."

Marcus didn't move from against his pillows, but his glare emanated heat across the room.

"Jesus is legal," Lee said.

"Her version obviously isn't if you listen to her talk about Him for more than thirty seconds."

"You have?"

"A road trip means a lot of conversation, and she trusts me. But I think she'd say the same things to someone she didn't trust. One more reason to get out of here, especially with Agent Baldy patrolling the streets."

Yes. Time to act. Lee pressed her palms to the arms of the chair. "Find the most dilapidated car you can and hotwire it."

"No." Marcus flexed and stretched his good leg. "It might be uninsured and the only car they have. Find something newer."

"Am I doing this now?" Austin was already halfway to the door.

"Better than broad daylight."

"Right." He opened the door.

He was halfway into the hall when Marcus's voice fell like a gavel. "Wait."

Austin slipped back inside and let the door close. "Yeah?"

Marcus sighed, shook his head. "We can't."

Austin crossed his arms and waited. For Lee to argue instead of him? She'd oblige.

"Why not?" She let the words snap.

"Because."

Of course his sense of morality had anchored itself to biblical principles once he embraced Christianity, but he was driven by other things as well, sometimes equally, sometimes more so. Things like the protection of those he cared about. Stealing a car was necessary for their safety. He couldn't protest it.

"We won't be endangering anyone, merely inconveniencing them."

"That's not the point," he said.

"You believe God will hold it against you as a sin."

"Lee—"

"Enduring torture for Him earns you no leniency."

"God doesn't ..."

He said more, but a roaring grew louder in her head. She knew well what God didn't do. He didn't esteem Marcus's sacrifice. Didn't allow him freedom, only one state's border away. She pushed up from the chair and stalked to the window. Her fingers tried to wring themselves out until one of her nails caught the other hand and broke skin.

"Lee."

The gentling of his voice wasn't necessary. She was fine. Marcus, on the other hand—"You continue to cling to Him, of course."

The corner of Lee's eye, the corner of her mind, acknowledged that Austin was standing against the door, the peanut can motionless in his hands. But his presence couldn't matter in this moment. Marcus didn't give him a glance, either. He drew up his good knee as though he'd try to get out of bed. His eyes burned into Lee. This was not the new Marcus of sharp silences, nor the old Marcus whose convictions and heart blazed behind his eyes. This Marcus was himself a fire, and Lee was seared.

"I prayed," he said.

Of course you did.

"For all of you, for protection. I couldn't do it, so I said—God, all of them. Hold them—" He extended his left hand, cupped and shaking. "Safe. Like this. I—I held my hand out. I said, please. And if nobody else, then Lee. Please, God."

Lee's entwined fingers spasmed against each other.

Marcus swept the heel of his hand over both cheeks though his eyes were dry. "He held you all."

No. *You do not hold me. I won't allow You to.* Her safety was her own doing.

"So if ..." Marcus strained for another breath. "If He could keep you safe then, He can now, too. Some other way ... that honors Him."

She could ignore his wishes. Austin would back her, and Violet wouldn't challenge her. If Austin carried Marcus to a stolen car and deposited him inside, Marcus couldn't fight back. The image was an IV of ice water. Lee couldn't make him helpless. She could steal a car without a prick of conscience, but she couldn't steal his choice.

"All right," she said. "Some other way."

But there wasn't one, and judging from the slam of the peanut can onto the desk in the corner, Austin knew it too.

26

If Austin heard his own voice say "There's not another way" one more time, he'd put a fist through the TV. He sealed his lips and sat with his knees up in one corner, back to the wall. Probably looked like he was sulking, but there were no other chairs or beds, and besides, who cared what Lee and Brenner thought of him?

If only leaving them behind wouldn't defeat his purpose in coming here.

Well, would it?

Yes. Because no way would Violet leave them too.

She'd been gone at least fifteen minutes. How long did she think she needed to pray? Austin pushed to his feet. "I'm going to find—"

The lock clicked, and the door swung open. Violet slipped inside and let it close.

"Are you …?" Austin didn't have to finish the question. Her eyes shone.

"You won't believe it." She clasped her hands in front of her. "I found it, guys, the answer to everything."

From the stuffed chair, ankles and arms crossed, Lee cocked an eyebrow at her. "Please elaborate."

"Okay, this is going to sound crazy, but …" She turned to Austin. "When we checked in, remember the hostess asking us about the room? Where we wanted to stay? Do you remember the words she used?"

"Not really." The question had been oddly phrased, but not oddly enough to stick in his memory.

"You told her that this room was fine, and she asked, 'Is that where your heart is?'"

Oh, right. "And …?"

Violet stepped further into the room and included all of them in her gaze. She set the key card on the table. "The question was half of a password, but we didn't know, so we didn't say the other half."

"And you know this how?"

"I went for a walk and got all the way to the check-in desk. I was going to turn around, but somebody came in, and when she asked that question, the guy said, 'My heart is where my treasure is.'"

Brenner shifted under the blanket, and Violet nodded.

"It's a Bible verse," she said to Austin and Lee.

"Violet," Brenner said. "Did you—"

"I knew it wasn't an accident that I figured it out. Or that the person said it before I could come back here. So I talked to her."

"No." Brenner pushed to the edge of the bed.

"It's okay, Marcus." Violet's thumb rubbed at her wrist. "She helps Christians."

She opened the door halfway and beckoned. Lee sprang to her feet. In walked the hostess, short and curvy with shoulder-length, red curls, clad in a white button-down shirt and black pants. A dimple appeared with her smile, warmer than the automatic one she'd bestowed on Austin and Violet at the check-in desk.

"Guys," Violet said, "this is Tatum."

Tatum's eyes darted around the room to encompass everything—their duffels piled in a corner, the four of them crammed into this single-bed space. She swiped her bangs out of her eyes and continued to stare for another moment. Her eyes lingered on Brenner, who had lowered his feet to the floor but stopped there, hunched at the edge of the mattress.

"Well," Tatum said. "Let's get y'all moved to a better room."

Lee blocked her without entering her space, soldier-stiff and steel-eyed. "This is sufficient."

"I don't charge Christians, ma'am, so put that out of your mind, what you can afford and what you can't." When none of them relaxed or responded, she sighed. "It's pretty clear y'all are in dire straits. If you let me help, maybe you can make it to Texas. If you don't, the Stab will get you for sure. Vinita's no safer than the city."

More silence.

Screw this. Didn't Lee and Brenner want another option? They weren't allowed to reject one delivered to their door. Austin sidestepped around Violet, and now they all faced the woman. She tugged the hem of her shirt, more an absent gesture than a nervous one, and appraised Austin. Probably assumed he was as young as Violet.

"The Stab," Austin said. "Is that what you call the Constabulary down here?"

"Down here? Thought that's what everyone called them."

"We call them con-cops in Michigan," Violet said.

Tatum snorted. "You make them sound like superheroes or something."

"They are to most people."

"Not in Oklahoma." Tatum tugged her shirt again, this time with something like pride. "The Stab's not wanted, and they know it, and we pay for it. But so do they."

There was no decision to make here. Austin crossed to the corner and grabbed his bag and Lee's, which both now bulged with additional items—Brenner's clothes and medicine. Violet scurried to his side and picked up her own, and the brown paper grocery bag containing Lee's medical kit and the rest of their food.

Lee nodded to Tatum. "Where would you take us?"

"To a safe room."

"Hidden?"

"No, but it has a safe in the floor. For your contraband, if you have any." She produced two room keys from her pocket. "Two-seventeen, suite with a connecting bathroom. All of you crowded in here—I don't know how you snuck in, but this many people with one bed? The Stab would be suspicious right off."

Good point. They couldn't consider only the cost of things, no matter how little money they had.

The safe rooms were all located on the second floor, and the hotel didn't have an elevator. The five of them rushed as much as possible. Violet mouthed prayers for concealment the whole way down the hall to the stairs. Halfway up, Brenner collapsed against Lee, and her balance wobbled on the narrow step. Austin hurried to support his other side, and Tatum picked up their bags.

Austin's mouth dried. What if she asked to search them? If she found his badge, she'd throw everyone out, with good reason. Well, maybe then they'd admit to the necessity of grand theft auto.

Who are you becoming?

When all this was over, he was going to … Australia or somewhere … to straighten out his head.

At their second-floor room, Tatum let them in and handed the room keys to Violet. "The rooms on either side aren't occupied right now, but if they are later, it'll be with folks like you."

She also told them about a true safe room on this floor, concealed in the ceiling at the other end of the hallway, above the vending machine. If Constabulary showed up at her desk, Tatum would ring their room phone twice, a signal to hide. She didn't mention what everyone had to be thinking: Brenner would never be able to climb into an attic.

The room was double the size of the one they'd shared before, with two beds, a night stand, a table in one corner, and a low couch. The dark green curtains were drawn against the night, and green-and-navy-plaid comforters covered the beds. The connecting door stood open, and past the suite's bathroom lay another room identical to this one. Four beds. Austin's shoulders caved with the anticipation of sinking into a mattress.

He eased Brenner down to the nearest one. The man tried to stay upright, but for him, the move down a hall and up a staircase might as well have been a hike up a mountain. He coughed, fought to catch his breath. Austin propped the pillows against the headboard and lowered him. The guy didn't weigh anything.

"Thanks," he whispered, and Austin turned at the prickling sense of eyes on his back.

Tatum propped her hands on her hips. "Any idea what's wrong with him?"

Lee deposited their bags together in the far corner. "Pneumonia."

"Dear Lord," Tatum said with the reverence of a prayer. "But it's more than that. If I could get a doctor here—"

"No." The snap of Lee's voice stiffened Tatum's shoulders. "I'm a nurse. We don't need anyone else."

Get it, lady? Go back to your desk. So he could remind Violet not to trust. Anyone. Then again, Tatum might find a way to get them over the border. Austin sighed. He, of all people, couldn't upbraid someone for trusting the wrong person.

The frost encasing the room must be getting through to Tatum. She glanced at each of them in turn, measuring them, deciding they were all right alone, or simply hoping for an acknowledgment from someone.

Violet's smile rescued the rest of them. "Thank you so much. You're amazing."

"Doing what I can, that's all." Tatum smiled back. "Sleep well. Continental breakfast is at seven."

The door whispered shut behind her. The lock mechanism clicked. Silence descended.

Brenner propped himself up on his elbows. "Violet."

She turned. He gave her a glare to melt iron.

"We—we needed help," Violet said.

"Not from people."

She rubbed her wrist. "God sends people sometimes. I think He brought us here. To her."

Both of them missed the point. Austin sat on the edge of the far bed, and his body became a weight. Lie down, relax, sleep. In a minute. "You shouldn't have talked to her. Not without talking to us."

"Why? You'd already decided what to do. Anyway, this is how it works. Right? Christians trusting each other."

By the end, her words were directed to Brenner. He didn't skirt her gaze, but the silence lasted too long.

"I don't know," he said.

At one time in his life, he probably had. Some people were who they claimed to be—safe, helpful, innocent. Qualities Austin never expected to ascribe to a Christian, but nothing about Tatum (or Brenner, but he wasn't himself right now) suggested danger.

"Well, I'm not going to apologize," Violet said.

She trudged toward their other room, head ducked, but for all Austin knew, she'd done the one thing that would save them all.

27

A pushpin of light jabbed her eyes. Lee turned her face into the pillow. She must have fallen asleep, after all. But what was this piercing shaft? Not morning. She'd pulled the thick drapes before they went to bed, leaving a strip of the streetlight outside so she wouldn't awake in the dark. Lee rolled onto her back and cracked her eyelids. The lamp had been turned on its lowest setting.

"Violet?" She swallowed the wasteland from her voice. "What's—?"

Marcus.

Lee sat up, but Violet wasn't standing over her. Nor was anyone else. "Violet."

"Sorry." The word quivered up from the floor.

Lee looked over the side of her bed. Violet sat cross-legged beside the floor safe. The empty floor safe. Marcus's Bible lay open across her knees.

"What are you doing?"

Violet glanced up, then ducked her head, but not in time. She'd been crying for a while, eyes bloodshot and tears blotting her sleeve where she'd wiped her face on her shoulder.

"Violet." Lee pushed aside the covers.

"I'll turn the light off."

"Why are you—?"

"Don't." The word ruptured on a sob.

Had the Bible caused this devastation? No, she must have gone there for comfort. And of course, she didn't want to discuss it—the cold barrel pressing under her chin, the warm body pressing her too close. Lee shuddered.

"I thought if I let myself sleep, I'd get stuck in a dream. You know how that happens sometimes? You know you're dreaming but you can't wake up?"

No. Lee's nightmares were reality as long as they held her. She drew her knees up and planted her heels on the mattress.

"I started reading in Matthew, but I was getting sleepy, and I thought maybe it would keep me awake to read Romans, because I can't understand all of Romans, and … and …" Violet hid her face in her arms.

Should Lee talk to her? How? Words couldn't erase this.

The tears broke off, stifled by a long breath. Violet's hands, palms scabbing now, wiped her face. She closed the Bible and placed it back into the safe and locked it.

"My eyes are adjusted to the light," Lee said. "I'll be able to sleep if you—"

"No." Violet pushed to her feet and crawled into bed. "I can't read anymore."

She shut off the light, and Lee kept her eyes on the crack between the drapes. "If I can help in any way, please say so."

Only quiet answered her. A few minutes later, someone stomped past their room, and clanking began from the ice machine. Hazard of sleeping toward the end of the hall. When the noise stopped and the person had tramped back the way he'd come, Violet rolled over with a rustle of sheets.

"What would it take?" New tears trembled in the whisper.

What would it take … to sleep without nightmares? Surely that was the cause of her distress. *If I knew that, I'd mend myself as well.*

No, she wouldn't. Her own flashbacks had been earned with her choice.

"I don't know, Violet. Perhaps you only need time to process what happened."

"No, Lee. What would it take … for you to believe?"

Frost slithered around her. She stiffened to prevent a shudder. *What would it take?* A meaningless question.

"I don't wish to discuss Christianity with you."

"Why not?"

"It would be pointless." And she must not wound Violet.

"Why?"

"Because you won't be dissuaded from your trust, and I won't be convinced to join you in it."

"I know you believe God exists. And I think you believe Jesus does too."

The stripe of parking lot light fell onto Lee's bed, across her ankles, and sliced up the far wall, over the only piece of art in the room. The glass wasn't anti-glare and reflected even the dim light, so that Lee couldn't make out details of the still life she'd noticed earlier—a wooden table set with a vase holding a single rose, a plate of fresh bread, and a small glass pitcher of water with ice cubes.

"You do," Violet said, "don't you?"

"Yes." Maybe one-word answers would deter her, if silence wouldn't.

"Do you think Jesus is alive? That He's God?"

"Probably." Based on her historical research after Marcus's conversion, it was the simplest, if most incredible, explanation for certain facts.

A sigh poured from the bed beside her. "Oh, wow. Okay."

Could they sleep now? Lee closed her eyes.

"You said trust, so why don't you? Trust God, I mean?"

Not a yes/no question. Lee draped an arm over her face. This could only be coming from Violet's brush with mortality, for some reason a reminder that Lee was headed for eternal damnation.

"Lee. Are you asleep?"

An escape. She pressed her lips together and lay still, but the silence ached in her stomach. "Do you believe God has the power to disallow evil?"

"Of course. He wouldn't be God, otherwise."

"Yet evil exists."

"Well … yeah."

"There you are." Lee turned over to face the wall and the obscured painting.

"So you would trust Him if we couldn't do evil things?"

If no one could hold a gun to the throat of a child. If no one could beat a man until his ribs broke, starve a man until his muscles began to consume themselves. If no one could pin a woman to cold cement and pull off her clothes and force—

If no one could boost herself onto an exam table and open her legs and nod to the doctor, *Take my baby and throw her away.*

"Yes," Lee said. "I would."

"But … well, yeah, I guess you would, because everyone would."

Perhaps, though that wasn't relevant.

"So you want God to … force us? To do what's right?"

If she wanted to phrase it that way.

"But you're Lee."

"Meaning?"

"Choosing matters to you. I—I mentioned it to Sam one time, and he said yes, I was right. So I'd expect you to want the choice. Between good and evil."

At least Violet was no longer crying. Lee could tolerate this dead end of conversation a bit longer for that. "Perhaps God could permit the choice, as long as evil wasn't chosen."

"So He only creates people who choose to do right?"

"Precisely."

"Then the other people never even get to exist? How's that more of a choice?"

"Violet." Lee let her hear the sigh.

"Anyway, what if you did love God, and then at the end of your life you got to see for a second that the reason you loved Him was because He forced you to all this time and didn't even let you know He was doing it. Wouldn't you all of a sudden hate Him?"

A meaningless hypothetical, since clearly God had not forced Lee to love Him.

But if He had.

What would she be, then? A cheery machine programmed for adoration. Not herself, surely. A despicable, subservient version of herself. The image was sour on her tongue.

"Wouldn't you?" Violet said.

"All right, I suppose I would." *But it's immaterial.*

"So you'd hate God for forcing you to be sinless. But you also hate Him for *not* forcing you to be sinless."

No … yes?

Silence stretched over minutes. The ice machine clanked again. The air conditioning kicked on—in October, proof they'd left Michigan far behind.

Hate was an inaccurate word, an emotional word. Lee's reasoning was solid, and solid reasoning couldn't be shaken by … by Violet of all people.

"So what would it take?" Violet whispered.

Logic demanded an answer. If one rejected God based on His nature, then a change in His nature should produce something other than rejection.

What would it take?

Violet was silent, likely praying for Lee. That God would change Lee's mind, as if they hadn't just discussed the repulsiveness of that prospect. Lee closed her eyes.

Sterile, white room. Feet in stirrups. Gentle swell of her belly under the thin gown. Good-bye, *and* I'm sorry, *and* I have to do this, Dad says so.

Instruments inside. Discomfort spearing into pain.

Flutter inside, felt before, then something new. Writhing, jerking. Hand to her belly. That's you, isn't it. You, dying. *Tears on her face. Sweat on her neck. Time.*

Pain squeezing around stillness.

Blood on the table.

Someone small wrapped in something disposable. Disposed of. You were a girl. A daughter. *No one told her. No one had to.*

Lee convulsed awake. Sweat plastered her hair to her neck. Tear stains stiffened her cheeks. She panted into the pillow. Her hands pressed her abdomen, and her knees drew up, but nothing eased the twisting pain. Somehow her body could reenact her crime again and again, even without a womb.

She waited for Violet's voice. The girl must be exhausted not to wake up. This nightmare wasn't as loud as the other one, but it wasn't quiet.

Lee's body uncurled as the cramping abated. Her breathing leveled. One hand settled at her side, and one remained tight against her belly. Her right hand. The one that had signed the consent form. Eighteen years old. An adult. Culpable.

God hadn't stopped her.

28

The room was too dark to see the ceiling, but Austin stared toward it anyway. He'd crossed the line between exhaustion and too-far-gone-to-sleep. His eyes were dry, too wide, blinking maybe once a minute, yet they refused to stay closed. The edginess wasn't about Tatum, was it? Maybe it was Agent Baldy. Or the piece of dung that had threatened Violet. He held in a growl. He needed to relax, or he'd be dead on his feet in the morning. Not the greatest condition to guard vulnerable people, and if they'd ever needed protection on this trip, they needed it now.

Sand gritted against his eyelids, and his eyes sprang open again. He held back a growl.

Bump.

Austin sprang up in bed and tossed off the covers, heart hammering before his brain could dial back his reflexes. Probably someone in the neighboring suite had—

A shuffle and another bump. No, that was in this room.

"Brenner?"

A cough.

Austin turned the old switch between their beds, and both reading lamps flooded the room with light. Ow.

Brenner was on his feet, bracing one arm against the wall, halfway to the bathroom.

Austin jumped out of bed. "You should've asked for help, man."

"I'm okay."

The man took another step and had to catch himself. Nothing but the wall was near enough to grasp. He swiveled to brace both arms and bit down on a whimper.

Austin reached him in five steps. "Don't be stupid."

"I don't need—" A cough broke off his words.

Austin lifted Brenner's arm over his shoulder and circled his waist below the ribs. Together, they hobbled to the toilet, and Austin kept a supporting hand under Brenner's elbow while he used it. By the time they got him back into bed, sweat had broken out on Brenner's forehead. He glared when Austin tucked the covers around him.

Whatever. Austin dived back into his own bed and switched off the lamp.

A minute later, Brenner said, "Thanks."

If he thought about it, Austin would cringe at the idea of being in Brenner's place. Maybe he should say so. Probably not.

"Why'd you come?"

Austin folded his arms under his head. The truth might not be the best thing to tell this guy, but he didn't feel like lying. "For Violet, I guess."

"You think we'd hurt her?" The tension in the words constricted into a cough.

"Not intentionally. But you also couldn't protect her from a hornet right now."

Brenner coughed a few more times, then filled the room with shallow breathing he tried to mute.

"See, you're not even going to argue the point." Austin shifted the pillow under his head.

"No," Brenner said.

"Nothing personal, man. Just a fact."

"Yeah."

For some reason, Brenner didn't point out Austin's hypocrisy in bringing up the whole protection thing. And at least Brenner had an excuse. Being bedridden was about as excused as you could get. Austin had been *asleep* when Violet and Lee got robbed. He shut his eyes and ground his palms into them. How could he spend minutes or an hour not thinking about it and have to be jolted back to the reality? It should be in his head like a song on repeat, a grunge song with gory lyrics.

Brenner cleared his throat and shifted in the bed. "Thanks."

Any response he gave—*sure, no problem, you're welcome, anytime*—would be accepting the gratitude. He searched for some change of subject, but maybe he didn't need one. Brenner would probably fall asleep in a few minutes.

And then Austin would lie here until daybreak. The quiet settled onto him, heavier by the minute. He squirmed under it but couldn't set words loose in the room, not even to push away the weight.

This was the Christian resistance leader. Austin should be volleying questions into the dark. Sociological data to explore. A criminal—the prime criminal—to interrogate.

"You would've died."

Not the words he meant to say. Not that it mattered, because Brenner didn't even cough in response. Austin rolled onto his side and propped his head up on his hand. Facing Brenner, he could barely make out the guy's profile—the hand at his side, the low mounds of his legs under the bedspread—yet even in the near-dark, the emaciation was obvious. *You have no right to ask him this. Last week, you were strangers and enemies.* But he wanted to understand. Probably had since the first time their eyes met in that reeking pantry.

"You went out of your way to clarify that you wouldn't recant. What was the point, antagonizing him like that, when you were already …?"

Dying.

"You knew what he'd do," Austin said quietly.

Brenner stared forward.

"Nothing you did—nothing—upped your survival odds."

His gaze snapped to Austin's, then back to the wall.

Austin flopped onto his back and shut his eyes. He didn't regulate his tone, let surface in it the frustration and whatever else nibbled at him. "Yeah, I don't know why I expected an answer to that. Forget it."

"Why does it matter?" Brenner said.

"Call it a hobby. Understanding people, motivations, etcetera."

"It would have been wrong. To deny Him. So I didn't."

Black and white the guy might be, but he couldn't think it was that simple. "And if you did, what do you believe would happen? You'd go to hell?"

The pause lengthened. Surely Brenner wouldn't say yes.

"Just because God would forgive me … doesn't mean it would be okay."

Fair enough. "You may be in the minority on that opinion, but …" Austin could respect it, although it still left the question of survival instincts and where Brenner had misplaced his.

"I'm not in the minority. Or you wouldn't have so many people locked up."

"True, but we've released a lot too, clean bill of mental health."

A quiet scoffing sound punched the darkness.

"Come on, you don't know anyone who was released? Hard to believe."

The silence again, but Austin was learning its ebb and flow. Brenner was collecting thoughts or words or something. He'd answer in a minute.

"I knew someone," he said quietly. "But she had more to lose than I did."

"More than her life?"

"She was pregnant."

And what, she didn't want to raise her baby in re-education? "Not following, man."

"The agent told her she could recant or she could have an abortion."

"No way." The words burst from Austin as his face flushed. No Constabulary agent would threaten a woman like that. They weren't Nazis.

Right, because you know this organization so well. And here he was, proving his … bias? He'd been trained by them, after all.

"Her name was Aubrey Weston," Brenner said, and … yeah. She *had* been in re-education last year, before Austin was recruited. He knew her case file, not well but well enough. She had been pregnant.

"Did you … 'save' her, after she got out? Get her to Ohio and beyond, or whatever it is you do?"

"No. She's dead."

The heat in his face drained away, and cold crept up his fingertips. "How?"

"An accident." Brenner's voice had flattened to hammered steel. No more questions on that topic. At all.

Austin waited for him to change it, but of course, silence took over. Maybe he could sleep now. As his muscles loosened, so did his lips.

"So according to your belief system, did Aubrey Weston get forgiveness?"

"Yeah." No hesitation there.

"The rooster story, right? That Peter guy." In his own ears, his words began to slur.

"Um … yeah."

"I figured you guys use that one a lot. Positive outcome and all that."

"You've read the Bible?"

"Some. It's recommended, under supervision of course."

"So you can play the part. If you need to."

"Well, I think it's more the idea of understanding your enemy, but sure, some guys have used it for undercover work. It's surprisingly effective."

Another pause, and as Austin's thoughts disintegrated into slumber, Brenner said, "Yeah."

29

"I don't sound Canadian," Violet whispered, leaning close enough to brush her arm against Austin's. She didn't flinch. Comfortable with his touch, or immune to it? *Analyze later.*

"Okay." He slathered cream cheese on his bagel.

"I'm serious. Haven't you ever talked to a Canadian?"

"Sure, but maybe these people haven't. Anyway, our vowels are similar."

"No, they're not. Good grief, we don't have accents in the first place."

"Pretty sure we do."

Already three people had asked where they were from, and Violet and Austin hadn't even joined Lee at the table yet. One older guy insisted they were North Dakotan and talked "just like what's-her-name in that one movie."

"What kind of cream cheese is that? I can smell it." Violet wrinkled her nose.

"Chive and onion."

"Oh my gosh. In the morning?"

"Says the eater of fruit wax."

He headed with his tray toward Lee's table—in the corner, of course. He took his time, stepping around strangers who didn't meet his eyes and exchanging small talk with those who did, though when destinations came up, he didn't cop to Texas (and had warned Violet not to, either). It was refreshing, the reminder that people existed other than him and Violet and Brenner and Lee, that some people traveled and mingled and laughed, free of desperation. A smile pulled Austin's lips as he sat down.

Across from him, Lee nibbled her strawberries and melon, ignoring her oatmeal. "Good morning."

"Hey," he said. "How's the gym? I want to go run, at least."

Lee lifted an eyebrow at him.

"Violet said you already worked out this morning," and now her eyebrow arched at Violet.

"What?" Violet said. "You did, didn't you?"

"I did."

"Well, then." Violet dug into her cold cereal—something with marshmallows—as if it were edible.

"Please let me know if you spot Tatum before I do," Lee said. "As for the gym, there's a treadmill along with a few weight machines."

Perfect. Austin started on his eggs. A little runny, but after the last few meals of beef jerky, he could hardly complain. Halfway through breakfast, a young dark-haired couple approached with laden trays. The girl beamed at them through red-framed glasses. The guy, about her height and hefty, hung back.

"May we?" the girl said.

"Sure." Violet moved her chair closer to Austin's as the strangers settled in.

The five of them didn't exchange names. The small talk steered toward impersonal topics. Finally the couple enthused over the latest movie to shatter the box office—a character-driven epic about a matriarchal alien society. The more they described it, the surer Austin became that he'd never be able to sit through it.

He couldn't place their accents. Probably wouldn't have tried if his own hadn't been pointed out to him three times in as many minutes. East Coast, somewhere. They might be hiding contraband in a floor safe, envisioning the border between them and freedom while they sat here eating bagels and oatmeal and discussing movie trends.

Austin cleaned his plate before Tatum flitted into the dining room, wearing her standard black pants and white button-down.

"Hey," he said in lieu of Lee's name, and nodded over her shoulder to where Tatum refilled the two coffee machines. Lee glanced back as Tatum took in the room. She must have signaled with her expression somehow, because Tatum beelined for them as soon as she finished setting up the coffee.

"Hope you all slept well." The smile was for their whole table, but the lingering look was for Lee.

"You have a sign prohibiting the transporting of food to the rooms," Lee said.

"Yeah, if we didn't, people would—oh. That's a problem for you, I guess."

"I don't see anything here but paper plates. I was hoping you'd provide something sturdier."

"Can do. *Uno momento.*" She held up a finger and then disappeared the way she'd come.

Their dining companions eyed Lee with unmasked curiosity. She ate her oatmeal without bothering to meet their eyes.

When no one offered an explanation, the couple glanced at each other. Their confusion hadn't dissipated a few minutes later, when Lee left the table. Austin followed her.

"I'm going back to the rooms," Lee said. "Would you bring up whatever Tatum gives you?"

"Sure." He returned to their table and Violet.

The hostess kept them waiting only minutes. She offered Austin a glass dish with a center divider, one side half-filled with scrambled eggs, the other with oatmeal, its dollop of butter and brown sugar melting. To Violet, she handed a small bowl of the fruit mix—berries, melon, grapes.

"Will this be enough?" she said.

Enough times ten, given Brenner's eating habits. Violet's smile didn't reveal that, though. "Perfect. Thanks so much."

"I'll be up in a bit," Tatum said. "There's things to talk over."

Austin nodded. So far, Tatum didn't know they were without a vehicle.

They found Brenner awake and claiming hunger. He fed himself with a slow but steady hand and didn't leave a single bite. As Lee took the empty dishes from him and set those on the table, a smile eased the lines of weariness from her face.

Brenner repositioned the pillow at his back and leaned forward. "Have you seen any Constabulary in the hotel?"

"Not so far," Violet said, and Lee echoed, "No." Austin shook his head.

"How far are we from the border?"

Lee sat beside him on the bed. "We're just into Oklahoma. I'd estimate another four hours, no more than five."

Brenner nodded, and quiet settled over them as he absorbed, calculated … sighed. "I don't know how we'll get there."

"Tatum will help," Violet said.

Brenner studied her a long moment, and Violet didn't avoid his eyes. Her smile all but held words. *We'll be okay, Marcus.* How had she grown so comfortable with him? She couldn't know him well, not given the timing of her disappearance and his arrest. Brenner's gaze traveled to Lee and flickered.

"It's true, we don't know her," Lee said as if answering something he'd said. "We're also without options, and Violet did observe her assisting other fugitives."

Brenner nodded. "Okay. What's going on at the border?"

"What do you mean?" Austin said.

"Well. In June …" His mouth crimped, and the quiet teetered on the edge of something. He cleared his throat. "Texas had been talking about leaving, but nothing had happened."

Right. The man had missed four months of news coverage. Austin had to stop forgetting that.

"They seceded before July, I don't remember what day it was." Violet sat on Austin's bed and leaned back on her hands. Her hair brushed the bedspread behind her. "Last week, the government was all about respecting their borders and stuff. This week, it's like no one ever said that, and they're still deciding whether they can go into Texas and capture fugitives. There's a federal border patrol now to keep us here."

His brow furrowed. "They don't want us. Why keep us?"

"You're terrorists." Lee bit the words, though not at him. "A clear and present danger to peaceful citizens if you're allowed to amass on our doorstep. Who's to say you won't acquire weaponry and try to claim America for God?"

Brenner stared at her and hadn't blinked yet when someone rapped on the door.

"It's Tatum," came her soft drawl.

Violet hopped off the bed and hurried to the door. No one spoke until Tatum had slipped inside and the door was shut again.

"How's everyone? Get enough to eat?" Tatum's eyes darted to Brenner.

He nodded. "Thanks."

"It's what I do, sir." Her smile appeared and faded in a moment, and her hands swept her curls into a ponytail and held for a moment. "Now, here's what's up. You need to be out of here within the next three hours."

The stutter of Austin's heartbeat must have reflected on his face as well as everyone else's. Tatum held up her hands, palms open.

"We've got a system here, an oiled machine, so don't worry. When the border patrol got called up, a young man of ours—decorated cop, shot in the line of duty and God spared him—he volunteered to serve. Was accepted without question, if nothing else to fill a quota, given his injuries keep him from active duty on the force. This man is our weak link in their chain."

Brenner shook his head. "What happens in three hours?"

"Eight, actually. He gets off work. They do ten-hour shifts. He won't work another one for two days."

Eight hours. Four or five to drive there, so yeah, they had to be on the road in three at the most. A clock started ticking in Austin's skull. They should leave now.

If they could.

Tatum gathered up the breakfast dishes with a smile that said *why are you all frowning at me?* "I'm sure it won't take you more than three hours to pack up."

"We don't have a car," Violet said.

"You … what?"

Violet shook her head.

Tatum's eyes darted to each of them, seeking contradiction.

Austin ground his knuckles against his thigh. *Don't be angry.* But she'd just waved their greatest vulnerability like a bullfighter's cape, without a discussion first, without … *Chill.* It wasn't as if they could avoid telling Tatum.

"We didn't have a choice." He flexed his hand. "It's complicated. What matters is, we had to ditch our vehicle."

"Where?" Tatum set the dishes back down.

Violet's face had flushed the moment after she spoke. Her right thumb rubbed a frantic rhythm along a bone of her left wrist.

"Not important," Brenner said. Oh, so he was taking the lead? Fine.

Tatum's eyes narrowed, and she stared down at the dishes, tapping her finger on the edge of the fruit bowl. "Hm. I think I can get you … yeah, I can get someone to drive you within an hour or so, but … shoot. He has a pickup truck. Not room for five people including himself."

If another vehicle could be recruited, Tatum would know. They had to take this truck. In the pause, everyone circled around to the same conclusion. Austin watched it happening on their faces, one by one, Violet's last as she lifted her head to stare bug-eyed.

"Someone could hide in the bed," she said. "Like we did before."

Tatum's eyebrows arched. "Not a chance. Even if this truck had a cap—which it doesn't—Danny would have to search it, or he'd look suspicious."

"So we have to split up?" Violet's voice trembled.

"I don't see another way."

Brenner and Lee were already nodding. Brenner's gaze targeted Austin, grimness tugging his mouth. "You and Violet. We'll follow in two days."

"But—but, Marcus." Violet hugged herself and hunched forward. "You're sick. You should go first."

"Agreed." Lee's voice held an edge.

"No," Brenner said.

If the man wanted to stay behind, Austin wasn't going to argue with him. He folded his arms and leaned against the wall. "I'll take Violet now."

"Good."

"You are the primary target." Lee pinned her glare on Brenner. "And if hiding becomes necessary, you won't be able to move quickly."

"And there's con-cops everywhere," Violet said. She shot a glance at Austin, frowned when he said nothing. "Come on. You guys know we're right. It should be Marcus."

"No," he said. He shifted his attention to Tatum, who answered before he could voice the question.

"One cryptic phone call, and he'll be here in forty-five minutes."

Brenner nodded. "Thanks."

Packing would eat about one tenth of that time. Then they'd wait. And then they'd set out, Austin and Violet, and he'd get her over the border, and then … *Who knows?* His entire life had become one endless, shadowed maze to be navigated without a map, without a flashlight, without even the assurance that Violet would be feeling her way forward alongside him.

Brenner looked at him again, part challenge, part trust. Austin nodded, and Brenner nodded back. First things first.

30

Violet's embrace tightened around Lee and refused to let go. When Lee tried to step back, Violet stepped with her. Austin stood in the doorway, mussing his hair with one hand, his duffel in the other.

Perhaps Lee should tell her everyone would be fine, that they'd see each other again in three days. But they might not. Lee set one hand on Violet's back, and the girl squeezed harder. About the time Austin began to shuffle in place, she dropped her arms to her sides. Lee took a deep breath.

"I have to say something to you," Violet said.

Lee tried not to react, but her lips tightened. If only Violet would walk away, but no, she had to try to evangelize first. Strange that for all her pushing, Lee still dreaded her absence. If circumstances did make this their last interaction, Lee's life would be emptier. Evangelism notwithstanding.

Violet gave a tiny smile. "I love you, Lee."

You … what?

Another quick smile, a squeeze of Lee's hand, and Violet turned away as if Lee's response to that outlandish statement didn't matter. Lee should say something, but what?

Violet stepped over to Marcus and whispered, "Hey."

He sat on the side of the bed, his good leg hanging over, foot propped on the bed frame. His damaged leg stretched to the side, along the edge of the mattress. An awkward position, but a good sign that he'd gained the strength to sit up without the aid of pillows and headboard. As Violet took his hand between hers, creases of a smile formed around his eyes. He placed his other hand on Violet's.

"I have to tell you something, too," she said. "Thank you. For letting me go."

Marcus nodded.

"Thank you for showing me Jesus."

His grip tightened on her hands.

"I'm glad and—and honored—to call you my big brother."

"Violet."

"Yeah?"

"I'll see you again."

His words dug into Lee's chest. Hope, assurance, trust—parasites all.

Violet stared down at their hands for a long moment, then looked up and smiled. "See you soon."

"Or later."

She nodded, let go, and hurried from the room. Austin turned to follow.

"Wait," Marcus said quietly.

He slung the bag over his shoulder and faced them. "I'll protect her. However I have to."

"I know."

"We'll meet up in a few days."

Marcus nodded. "Hope so."

He shifted from one foot to the other, eyeing Marcus.

"I … I've got to know something." Marcus coughed.

"Okay."

"There was an undercover agent. Clay Hansen. Did you know him?"

Lee's body chilled from the center outward, ice creeping toward her hands, her feet. Undercover. A member of Marcus's church.

"Hansen?" Austin's brow furrowed, and he ran a hand through his hair again. "He's a civilian. Wait a minute, how do you know about—what do you know about Hansen?"

Marcus's hand clenched around the mattress.

Austin's eyes widened. His next words were hushed. "Jason made sure you knew, didn't he. Who it was."

Who it was that … *turned him in.* Lee's fingernails gouged her palms.

"He wasn't an agent," Austin said when the silence threatened to asphyxiate. "Just a guy who'd do anything—literally anything—to protect his family."

Lee snapped her gaze to Marcus's face and nearly missed the flinch. He blinked, and the lines in his face smoothed away. Hiding. But Marcus didn't hide. Ever.

Except.

The day eight years ago when she'd told him she wouldn't date him if he was "the last person on earth."

The day four years ago when he'd put his dog Tessa to sleep because the arthritis in her joints had progressed too far for her to walk down his porch steps.

The day last year when he'd driven to her house in a blizzard to tell her he'd found out about her abortion and wanted to help her, and she'd slapped his face.

This flinch was the same, this blankness was the same, and Austin couldn't see it, of course. Didn't know Marcus, didn't understand what his words had done.

"Anyway," Austin said. "We should go."

"Yes." Lee stood.

"See you in a few days." He disappeared after Violet.

Marcus swung his good leg up onto the mattress and eased back against the pillows. His face was a wax figure's, expressionless, and Lee was probably the only person alive who could interpret that lack.

"Marcus."

He shook his head.

"Clay Hansen—"

The crumpling of his face broke off her words. She had to leave this alone.

"All right," she said quietly. "We won't discuss it."

He nodded. In a few hours, he would be with her again. The wax, the shell—he never remained inside, only crouched behind it when some unexpected wound tried to bleed him out. She would never understand the care he felt for his church, care that gave them power to hurt him. The responsibility he took for them, the …

Love.

They probably didn't know. He'd never verbalize it. He wouldn't know how.

"You'll be all right?" Lee said, and he nodded again. "Then I'll give you some time to yourself."

Another nod.

Marcus, if I could make him pay, I would.

She left her purse in the room, slid a key card into her pocket and left. Halfway down the stairs to the hotel's main floor, she met Tatum. The woman peered up the stairwell, then down, listened a moment, and motioned Lee to the corner of the landing.

"You said you're a nurse."

"Yes."

"There's a woman who came in last night, your neighbor on the right. She's got something wrong with her, but she won't tell me what it is."

Neighbor on the right. A fellow fugitive, then. Lee quirked an eyebrow at her. "Her health is her own business."

"Well, she told me she'd talk to you. If you're really a nurse." Tatum tugged at her shirt hem.

Being memorable to a stranger was inadvisable, fugitive or not. But if this woman was truly ill and couldn't see a doctor … Lee trailed Tatum back upstairs, down the hall of beige walls and beige carpet.

The hostess stopped at the door past Marcus and Lee's and knocked. "It's Tatum."

In a minute, the door opened. Lee slipped in after her and shut it.

The room was a carbon copy of next door with one exception. The painting on the wall wasn't a still life but rather a close angle of a dusty road. In the foreground stood an open gate, through which several sheep—some black, some white, some gray with black faces—rushed, hooves blurring with motion, into a lush pasture. Interesting art choices.

"Who's she?"

The woman had already retreated to sit in the stuffed chair, arms folded. She wore a modestly cut, pink camisole and a plaid pair of lounge pants. In her forties with an average build and a brunette pixie cut, she stared up at Lee without any sign of trust.

"The nurse," Lee said.

The woman slapped her palm on the arm of the chair. "I said I was fine."

Lee faced Tatum. "And I said it was up to her."

"Listen to me now, Debra, this woman is a fugitive herself, and she's caring for—"

"Stop." The word snapped from Lee, too loud. "Debra, I apologize. It wasn't my intention to force my help on someone who doesn't want it."

She'd nearly reached the door before Debra sighed and stood up. "I know what's wrong with me, and you can't help, ma'am. Not unless you could write me a prescription. I have a bladder infection. It's not the first one."

Debra listed her symptoms, and the localization of the pain as well as her other complaints suggested her diagnosis was correct. She wouldn't get well without antibiotics.

The medical bag on the other side of the wall became a magnet, tugging at Lee's brain. *I can heal this person.* For a cost.

Debra didn't seem to have a fever, but if the infection spread to involve her kidneys …

Her life could be threatened.

Lee excused herself. Tatum nodded too hard and tugged her shirt hem. Debra didn't nod at all, as if convinced Lee wouldn't bother to come back.

She slipped inside and eased the door shut, but Marcus wasn't asleep. He sat up in bed with the book she'd left on the nightstand. Not reading it, of course, but rather using it like a dumbbell, curling his forearm toward his shoulder. Lee picked up her medical bag and opened it on the other bed.

He set the book aside. "What's going on?"

Lee opened the bag and counted the pills. They didn't multiply because she couldn't multiply them, and because God didn't.

"Lee, I heard your voice in the other room."

"There's an ill hotel guest, a woman. A fugitive."

"Can you help her?"

Lee's teeth fused. No. She could not help. Not both of them.

As if she'd told him everything—but maybe no real leaps were required when she stood cradling the Amoxicillin bottle in her palm—Marcus sighed. "Do it."

"You need to stay on this for three more days. You could relapse." Her fingertips were numbing around the bottle. She pressed the cap end to her forehead and closed her eyes. *Isn't there an end to the games You play on us?*

"It's serious, what she's got," Marcus said.

"Yes."

"And a few days without a doctor could make a difference."

"It's possible."

"Could she die?"

Lee tried to respond and could only swallow around a sour lump in her throat.

"Give her the medicine."

"You're not strong enough, Marcus."

"I can breathe. I can eat. Give it to her."

Lee hurled the bottle past him into the wall.

He didn't blink at the impact, but his mouth tightened. "I'm mending. Like you said."

"Look at you. Look."

His lips pressed tight to hide the wince, but his eyes failed to. He drew in a breath that shook his body, or maybe her words did that. He bowed his head and looked at his ravaged frame.

And she'd wanted to throw Austin out of the room for saying something to wound him. *Hypocrite.* Still she couldn't stop the words. "For once in your life, you should have done the sensible, selfish thing and gone first. I should have dragged you out of here if it came to that."

He met her eyes, earnest. "Then Austin and Violet would be waiting instead. Without medicine for that woman."

More convolutions. More circumstances for Marcus to credit to God. Lee crossed the carpet and picked up the bottle, and the pills rattled inside. Too few. Enough to keep Debra from developing a kidney infection? Probably. If she took them all.

"Lee," Marcus said. "It's the right thing."

"There is no right thing."

She strolled next door. Set the pills on Debra's nightstand, endured the woman's grateful tears, and promised to follow up tonight. Fled to the gym minutes later and worked until sweat poured down her back, until her lungs guzzled the air, until her muscles quivered. Until for one betraying second, she forgot everything but the power and proficiency of her own body. Then she left the machines behind and returned upstairs.

31

The driver of the truck was short, probably in his mid-forties, and called himself Graham, which might or might not have been his real name. Austin wouldn't give his name in the guy's position, but who knew. Graham wasn't a talker and didn't protest when Austin turned on the radio. In the middle seat, Violet sat like a fireplace poker, more rigid with every passing mile.

Austin tapped her arm. She gave him a questioning look.

No way to say this out of Graham's hearing. "You okay?"

"Sure," she said.

"I didn't think about it before, but we can, um, switch places if that would be better."

"Why would that … oh." She shuddered. "That. No, I'm good. Thanks, though."

Graham didn't even glance in their direction.

If she rebuffed once more, Austin would let it go. "You're tense, that's all."

"Well, yeah." She rolled her eyes. "Either I'm going to be free today, or I'm going to be arrested today."

Right, of course. He'd better guard his comments, or Graham might suspect something was off. Austin should feel tenser, anyway. Not as if he had nothing at stake here. But an odd serenity cloaked him, as if he'd gone back to second grade and put on the green Safe Coat.

The sun crept past noon and inched toward the west. Songs on the oldies station began and ended. Austin rotated his mostly healed ankle. Maybe he should try to start some small talk, but then Graham might ask about him, what he'd done before, and how could Austin lie with Violet sitting here, her eyes open windows that might stray to his bag? How would Graham react to his badge, his gun?

How would Texans react? The gun wouldn't faze them, from what he knew. They were one of the only states that hadn't established a federal program to recycle firearms. But the badge …

As the sun was dipping low enough to cause a glare on the car's bumper ahead of them, a sign came into view. *Texas Border 10 Miles.*

Violet pulled her knees into her chest. "Almost there."

"I never lost anyone at the border yet," Graham said. "Danny knows his work. He'll get us in and out."

"I guess I shouldn't sit like I'm watching a movie and the intense, awful part just started." She lowered her feet to the floor and sighed.

The lanes to customs, or whatever they were calling it, were all at a dead stop. Austin shot a look at Graham, who shrugged.

"Pretty normal."

"For this time of day?"

"For any time."

When the row of booths appeared ahead, a mile and an hour later, Graham shut off the radio and peered forward. "Yup, that's him, sixth line from the left, just like he said."

The border guard checked out the entire truck, asking each of them several questions about their trip, work in their home state (Austin said he was a student), and their upcoming stay in Texas. Finally he snapped on a pair of latex gloves, stood between his booth and their bags (blocking them from a camera?), and asked them to show him the contents. Well, this was it. Austin unzipped his sports bag and let the guard tug the opening wider and sift through it. He didn't lift any of the items out and didn't blink at Austin's sidearm. He didn't open the wallet, and Austin sighed.

Violet's hands trembled as she handed over her bag.

And no wonder.

The guard didn't react to the leather book buried under her clothes. Austin tried not to, either. *But really, Violet? Really?*

No one spoke until the guard handed Violet's bag back and waved them through. The lanes funneled and merged back onto the interstate, and in a mile, green signs welcomed them to Texas.

"Did we make it?" Violet whispered.

"Sure thing." Graham sighed, then grinned. "Welcome to Texas, folks."

"Omigosh." She rubbed her thumb over her wrist and stared out the windshield as another sign passed: *Drive Friendly, the Texas Way.* "Oh. My gosh."

"I'll take you into Burkburnett. It's a few minutes off the expressway."

"That's fine," Austin said.

He let out a sigh. Texas. Here he was. Jason couldn't touch him. He reached into his sports bag and pulled out the Ziploc holding his phone and a screwdriver to reassemble it.

"Oh!" Violet fished out her phone. "Here, after yours is back together."

"This should only take a minute." But each bump in the road jarred the tiny pieces until Austin sighed and set the screwdriver on his thigh. "Okay, maybe this should wait."

"We're almost there," Graham said. "That's our exit up ahead."

"Do you bring everyone to Burkburnett?" Violet shoved her phone back into her bag.

"We have a few towns in rotation."

Alarm widened Violet's eyes. "You can't rotate us, or we won't be with Lee and Marcus."

"I know, Tatum told me. I'll bring them here, too." Graham took the exit.

They'd passed the welcome signs less than ten minutes ago. Austin rolled the screwdriver under his finger. "What's the next closest destination?"

"Kearby, about a hundred miles south."

"Would you be willing to take us all there?"

Graham thought about it a moment, then shrugged. "Shouldn't be a problem."

"Thanks."

Violet crinkled her face at him, but he shouldn't explain in front of Graham, even if the man did seem to be safe and helpful. Instinct was loud, though—settling five minutes from the border wasn't the safest option for a resistance leader.

Violet dug into her bag and withdrew the Bible. She held it on her knees and laid her hands side by side on the cover.

A sour taste filled Austin's mouth. Why did her having a Bible make him so …? *Upset* wasn't the word for it. He wanted to throw the thing out the window. When Violet set it in the center of the dashboard, he grabbed it and put it back on her lap.

"Don't, Austin."

"Why do you want it up there?" His voice was more a growl. Graham shot him a brow-furrowed look.

"B-because. Anybody can drive by and see it and not arrest me or take it away from me."

"It don't bother me." Graham shrugged and took the entrance ramp back to the interstate.

"Never mind," she said quietly. "It's okay."

They drove drenched in a silence like kerosene. Violet kept the Bible on her lap. Austin stared out the passenger window. He needed to calm down. She hadn't done anything. She was a free Christian, of course she wanted to express that, and she was Violet, not some violent head case. Why was his chest so tight?

He waited for his body to get over it, ease up. He waited over an hour. Maybe he was reacting to more stressors than that stupid book. Graham took the exit to Kearby and turned onto East Third Street, and still, Austin couldn't relax.

"I usually drop folks at Grace Bible Church," Graham said. "They're running a shelter, and I know you've had some losses along your way. They'll be able to help you."

"That would be awesome," Violet said.

"No."

Both she and Graham looked at him, Graham with half-raised eyebrows.

Violet folded her arms. "You know we can't afford a hotel."

Austin ground his teeth against the tingling heat in his hands, the only warning his body ever gave him before—no, he had to get control, now. "Violet, I'd like to get out here. Walk around town. Okay?"

Her arms dropped to her sides. Her eyes widened, and he concentrated on them, green and guiltless, but the lava still pulsed in his veins. Did she see?

She turned to Graham, and the smile lifted her voice. "Could you tell us where the church is, so we can head there later?"

"Well, sure, if you want." Graham turned down a residential street and stopped in the middle of it. "If you walk about three miles south, you'll hit Hayes. Make a right, you can't miss it. Tan-colored brick building, big sign out front, on the corner of Hayes and Third."

"Thank you so much."

Austin threw the truck door open and pulled back before it bounced on its hinges. He hopped down and stood in the street. *Run.* No, he had to wait for Violet. *She shouldn't be around you right now.* She would be alone without him, in a strange … well, country. All these thoughts could form in his mind, cogent and reasonable, but none of them cooled the need to throw something breakable.

Violet's voice filtered to him as she climbed down from the truck with both their bags in her hands. "We'll be totally fine. I'd like to walk around too. Thanks, Graham, you're amazing."

Graham said something. The sound of tires on blacktop faded. Austin clenched and unclenched his fists.

"What's wrong with you?" Violet said quietly.

I wish I knew. He huffed. "I'm going to jog for a minute. Stay here."

"Seriously? You're going to leave me standing in the middle of the street? I can jog too, you know."

"No, I—" Red blinded him. He stalked down the street. *Have to move.*

"Oh," she said behind him, and then her tennis shoes slapped the pavement, one pace behind him.

A vacant storefront sprawled half a mile down, backed by a parking lot. He jogged across it, not intending to stop, but … there. A whole pile of broken concrete, some slabs, some fist-sized chunks or smaller. He stooped down and picked up a piece and hurled it back at the pile. It broke in half. *Take that.* He scooped up one half and hurled it again. *And that.* Again. Again. Again. Until the remainders were pebbles too small to shatter. He found another chunk and threw it, too, counting this time to slow his heartbeat and flush the heat from his body. One, two, three … five, six, seven … twelve, thirteen fourteen … This piece didn't break like the other one. *Stop now. You need to stop.* Eighteen, nineteen, twenty, twenty-one, twenty-two, one for every year he'd lived. He dropped to his knees in front of the cement mound, able to think again, able to act on thoughts instead of … *What's wrong with me? Why do I get like this?*

Violet knelt beside him. "Can I … help?"

He scrubbed at his face. Ow. Crumbs of cement stuck to his hands.

"You don't want to be here, do you? You hate this. I mean, of course you would. You're a con-cop."

"Not anymore, clearly." Shoot, he hadn't meant to bite her head off.

She stretched her legs to the front and sat on her bag. Oh … she'd carried his, too. *Nice going, loser.* Had he really been that out of it?

Her right foot nudged the rock heap. "You'd be in Michigan still, with your job and your family and everything. If you hadn't rescued him."

"I'd also be working for a psychopath, and Brenner would be dead by now."

Violet wrapped her arms around herself. "I wish you'd stop that."

"What?"

"You never call him Marcus. He's always Brenner, like he's some case to you. Instead of a person. It's like … I don't know, like you think all of this is his fault."

Whoa. Okay. He had to process this before he responded.

The overcast day had given no heat to the blacktop. Austin shivered as the chill sank into his knees and up his legs. He pushed to his feet, picked up his bag, and held out his hand. Violet took it but didn't smile. They headed back to Third Street. South, Graham had said, about three miles.

"Austin?"

He waited for the anger to hit over her ridiculous conclusion, but he'd spent it all on some other stupid trigger he couldn't even name. "I don't consider any of this his fault."

"Okay. Um, good." Her voice fell, and she quickened her step to walk beside him as they reached the cement shoulder of Third. "I guess it's stupid for me to think you guys could become …"

Friends? Yeah, that was stupid. He couldn't answer it, so he reached for something he could answer. "He's been Brenner to me for months. I wasn't attaching any significance to it."

"He was Brenner because he was a case. So in your head, he's still a case."

"I—okay, maybe so, but it isn't because I hold him responsible for this whole …" He couldn't think of a non-vulgar way to finish that sentence. "If I were going to blame someone besides Jason, it'd be Hansen, not Bre—not Marcus."

Violet froze.

Austin kept walking a few strides, then turned back. "Violet?"

"H-Hansen?"

Crap. She was never supposed to know this. Clay Hansen had been like a father to her, and Austin had just blasted a shotgun-sized hole in her perception of the man.

"Austin, tell me. What about Clay, what did he do?"

He stepped closer as if he could absorb the tremors in her frame, in her voice. "The Constabulary told Clay that we had Khloe in custody. We thought we could get him to panic, betray himself somehow so we could make the arrest. He'd been one-hundred-percent reactionary thus far, so it seemed like a decent play. We didn't have any idea where Khloe was. Where you were."

"Of course not, because Marcus hid us. We were totally safe from you."

Right. And with every *we* and every *you*, a canyon opened between him and Violet while they stood there, feet apart. A canyon that began to crack inside him, too, but Violet didn't feel it. Not yet.

"So," she whispered. "What did he do?"

"Clay shocked everybody, Violet. Jason Mayweather included. He came forward with a bargain."

The blood drained from her face. "He wouldn't do that."

"He did, babe."

"Don't."

He gritted his teeth. The old endearment had slipped out, but she might think he'd done it to manipulate. "Violet—"

"He gave you Marcus? Uncle Clay gave you Marcus?"

"He wanted his daughter back."

She swayed. Her bag dropped to the pavement. Austin reached for her, but she stepped back and bent over, head in her arms. "Oh, God."

Two words he hadn't heard her use in the last week. She held that name as sacred now. But this wasn't casual use. Violet was crying out to Someone she thought could hear her.

"Oh, dear God. Jesus. I'm sorry. I'm so, so sorry."

Sorry?

Oh no.

"Violet, you had nothing to do with—"

"Shut up, I had everything to do with it. It was me, all of it was me. Marcus—oh, God, I am so sorry."

Austin put his arms around her. For a long moment, she melted against him, clinging to the back of his shirt, her tears dampening his chest, and then she pushed him back.

"No. You—you're still a con-cop."

There it was, the crack inside her. The title he'd worn with pride, the slang his sisters had bestowed on him with awe, skewered him. He didn't breathe.

"I'm sorry. I'm not mad at you. But I have to be by myself. I have to talk to Jesus about this." She pushed past him and grabbed her bag.

"Violet. Wait."

"Don't follow me. I mean it. I'll go to the church later, I promise, but I have to …" She sprinted away, and her golden hair streamed out behind her.

32

One dose of antibiotics wasn't enough to fend off a kidney infection, but the lack of fever ten hours later remained an encouraging sign. Lee latched the leather medical bag and stood up.

"Thanks for coming by again." Debra stood to see her out, though the door was only five paces away.

"I'll check your temperature again in the morning."

"Has Tatum given you a departure date yet?"

Lee stilled with her hand half-outstretched for the door handle. "I don't believe we should discuss that."

"I know someone left this morning, and someone else is leaving in a few days. I have to wait until Monday, she said. I was just wondering if you'd be the one leaving before me."

"As I said—"

"It's not idle curiosity, ma'am. What you're doing for me—I know I could wind up in a hospital without your help, and from there … Anyway, I'd be willing to trade dates with you, if it'll get you out sooner. You know, before the Stab search the place. I owe you."

"You don't."

Debra looked down at her feet, then back at Lee. "If you change your mind, let me know."

Lee gripped her bag and stepped into the hallway. "I'll talk to you later."

She let herself back into her own room and dropped the bag at the door. "Marcus, we …"

He wasn't in bed.

He stood on the other side of the room, one hand curled around the old wooden molding halfway up the wall. He took a step forward, then another. Sweat dampened his hair into curling at his neck and temples. The corners of his mouth pinched downward.

Lee stepped toward him. "*What* are you doing?"

He labored for breath.

"Marcus, do you need something?" He wasn't moving toward the bathroom.

He shook his head. He took another step, slow, firm, certain. The next one wobbled on his damaged knee. His free hand fisted and pulled into his side as he steadied himself.

"What are you doing?"

Another head shake.

Lee moved beside him to take his weight. Stiffening, he withdrew, and the knee gave out. As he pitched toward the floor, he reached for the wall and found nothing to grip. Lee stepped into his fall and planted her feet. A cry burst from him as they collided. She held him up. His back was warm, almost feverish, under her hands.

"It's all right," she said. "I've got you."

He turned his face away and tried to pull back, but he lacked the strength to resist her. The sound that seeped between his lips was half growl, half moan, wholly helpless.

Lee dragged his spent body to the bed, but he pushed away from it. She took him to the stuffed chair and lowered him as gently as possible. One arm circled his ribs as he rocked forward.

She should talk to him. She shouldn't want to break out the windows, pound a hammer into the walls, shatter the mirror and the television. She retrieved a water bottle and the Motrin from their place on the nightstand and brought them to him. He'd be ready for another dose in an hour anyway. He took the pill without argument. Lee went to the small refrigerator and pulled out a gel pack. The unit didn't have a freezer, so the gel was soft.

She crouched in front of him. "Can you sit up?"

He shut his eyes and uncurled slightly. Lee held the cold pack to his side.

"What were you doing?" she said.

"Getting … stronger."

"Obviously not."

In one blink, the depleted haze left his eyes. "No. You don't get to do this."

"I'm only pointing out—"

"You can't be angry I'm not strong enough. And then be angry I'm trying to fix it."

Was that how he saw this? "I'm not angry, Marcus."

"That's crap."

Fine. He didn't look inclined to give up her chair, so she settled on the bed where Austin had slept and opened her book.

"Lee. I get it."

Not likely. Lee tossed the book onto the bed. "I want your permission to sedate you, should the Constabulary search the hotel."

His eyes blazed.

"You'd prefer to be delivered to Mayweather in handcuffs?"

The blow struck center mass, as she'd intended. He punched down on the arm of the chair.

I'm sorry. Yet not, if it convinced him. "Please. Let me do this."

"No."

The look held. Knowledge and trust see-sawed between them.

"It's a simple way out, Marcus. A sensible way out. You won't be denying anything."

"I'm telling you," he said. "No."

They passed a silent hour. Marcus tipped his head back against the chair and shut his eyes, but strained respiration gave away his wakefulness. Lee stared at her book and allowed the words to blur. While Marcus had struggled around the room, his ribs hadn't been the main source of pain until she'd caught him around his torso. She evaluated his every sign in her mind's eye. She waited until he stirred … and leaned forward to grip the inside of his knee. Nothing like a patient's actions answering her question before she could ask it.

"Is the pain constant?" she said.

He looked up, then down at his knee. "I don't know."

"There was no swelling when I first examined it. I assumed the injury was minor."

An error on her part. The injury was old, past the point of swelling, but it could still affect function if the original damage had been severe. She was a trauma nurse, not a physical therapist, and the dangers of the pneumonia and rib damage had superseded anything else at the time. No excuses, though.

Marcus shrugged.

"Can you tell me now how it happened?" she said.

His eyes dimmed. He shook his head.

Lee pushed off the bed and crouched beside him. "Can you point out the specific location of the pain?"

"My knee."

Tread lightly. Even that obvious confession drew a blush of embarrassment up his neck, into his cheeks. He'd bury this subject any moment. All right, then, she wouldn't require words. She pushed the lounge pants up to his mid-thigh. Her pulse throbbed in her thumbs, in her chest, as she placed her hands on either side of his knee.

"Tell me if this causes you any further pain. Will you do that?"

He nodded.

For ten minutes, she massaged. Marcus's head fell back against the chair cushion, and for a moment she hesitated, but the crinkles that formed around his mouth, his eyes … no, not pain. Relief.

"Marcus?"

"It's helping. I think."

Lee kneaded lower, into his shrunken calf muscle, knotted with disuse. He breathed harder when she dug her fingers in, but she massaged his entire leg, down to the ankle and back up, then moved to the other one. The atrophy in those muscles was no less severe. He'd lain immobile for weeks, probably months. Finally she worked the injured knee through a few gentle exercises, and Marcus gritted his teeth and let her. Therapists had tests she didn't know, but a valgus and varus stress test was an obvious choice. And telling, when she applied stress to the inside of the knee. He had probably injured the MCL. Somehow, he'd bent his knee inward.

She could rig up a moist heat pack from hand towels and water that ran from the tap until it steamed. But first, after the exercise, she should massage a few more minutes. The bones of his knee ground against her palms, a knee that had carried him all his life, allowed him without a second thought to run the park paths, jog with Indy, hop up into his pickup truck, pace her living room rug …

She was touching Marcus.

"Lee?"

Her hands had retreated to her lap. Her gaze was fixed on his knee, but she was seeing … his body. Unclothed, lathered, rinsed, bruised, shivering … his. His hair between her fingers, stiff and oily, then softened and wavy after the shampoo.

"It's okay."

Lee blinked and looked up. His eyes held hers, steady, seeing. "I …"

It's not that I don't want to.

"I know," he said.

33

Violet had made it to Grace Bible Church. Austin trailed her there, out of sight, not leaving until she'd been inside for an hour. He tried to make himself go inside, but the doorway seemed too narrow, and he imagined the questions they would ask him. He shouldered his bag and wandered without anything like a destination.

The town was the sort that made you want to smile even if your life had recently gone up in flames. Black lampposts held guard duty along the commercial streets, while oak trees older than his favorite music groups shielded the neighborhoods. Every pedestrian he passed waved or smiled or said hello-and-how-about-this-weather. And the space. The sparseness of the population revealed itself in more obvious things like the non-existent traffic, but there was also this strange sense that everyone here had plenty of room. Real front yards, buildings constructed outward, not upward. Nowhere Austin walked did he ever feel crowded. In Michigan—the southeast suburbs, anyway—these people would suffocate. He passed too many churches, a children's learning center, a library, a volunteer fire station, an actual "general store," and more churches.

Austin kept walking.

By the time dusk settled, his stomach was growling. Two hundred thirty-five dollars nestled in a white security envelope in the zip pocket of his bag, alongside his wallet and gun. Technically his money, since his was all they had left, but …

Forget it. He was hungry.

He fast-walked back to Third Street and watched for a fast-food place, but there didn't seem to be a single one. At last he found Rosita's Burritos. He'd rather have a steak burger, but this would do. He shouldn't text Violet. She'd been clear, and she wouldn't go hungry at a church acting as a shelter.

The restaurant was brick, like most everything around here, set across from a quilt shop and alongside, wow, another quilt shop. He'd have called that a small-town stereotype if he hadn't seen it for himself. On its other side was a furnace/AC business.

While he ate Rosita's chimichanga with ground beef, sitting in a white metal chair at a cement table outside the café-sized restaurant, he reassembled his phone. It involved frequent napkin use, but whatever. He wanted his phone back.

He used the last bite of tortilla to wipe every hint of signature sauce and sour cream from the plate. He wiped his hands on the paper napkin and pressed the home/power button.

By the time he disposed of his trash, the phone was vibrating and pinging and generally overloading. Eleven voicemails, twenty-nine texts, a few emails. At least his social media apps were set to the least aggressive settings. He had to check those to know if anyone had messaged him.

Of the voicemails, a few were buddies wondering what was up, one was Tamara, that girl from Elysium, and six were, of course, Esther. Of the texts, she had about the same ratio. She had even emailed him once:

big bro,

please let me know if you're dead. j/k ...... right?

middle sis

He listened to every voicemail, waiting for the words. *"We're perfectly fine."* She'd say them for the first time now, while he was thousands of miles away. He couldn't move while the phone played each minute-long tirade, all starting the same way: "It's me, big bro, and we're all clear."

Her last message wasn't boisterous or demanding or sarcastic. She had left it two hours ago.

"It's me, big bro … um, we're all clear … I—I'm getting scared, Austin. You don't do this to us. Olivia has it all figured out, that you went undercover on some big Constabulary mission and you couldn't tell us about it. But you would never do that. Even if your boss said, 'don't tell a single living person,' you'd tell me. I know you would. So … if you could … call me? Please?"

She hung up without a good-bye.

He almost hurled the phone against the table. Esther was right. He would somehow find a way to tell her about a deep cover mission, if the Constabulary ordered such things. So why hadn't he found a way to tell her about this?

Because you were running for your life and any contact would have probably gotten you killed?

It didn't seem like much of an excuse. He drew in a shaky breath and pulled up his phone contacts. A breeze wrapped around him, cooling as the sun dipped away, but the chill up his back had another source. Jason would be watching for this number to ping somewhere. Monitoring their phones, Mom and Esther and Olivia, even his Elysium friends and acquaintances, figuring at some point he'd commit the ultimate living-off-the-grid sin and call someone for moral support.

Well, it didn't matter. Jason had no jurisdiction here.

He thumbed the number and listened to the ringback, something obnoxious and synthetic. It was new. Probably only been in the Top 40 for a few days. Esther wouldn't delay. He smiled as it looped. He'd have rolled his eyes at it last week.

"Uh … Austin?"

"It's me, middle sis."

"What the—" A stream of words he'd never heard from her followed for several seconds. "What is wrong with you, what did you do, drop your phone in the toilet? And your computer? And then take off to Europe with some porn star?"

"Esther, listen—"

"Because your apartment has been locked up with your car in the lot for at least the last four days, and I totally thought you were totally dead!"

"I'm not dead. Totally or otherwise."

"Shut up." A sob burst over the line.

"Okay."

She cried into the phone, hiding nothing. Austin blinked hard and looked up at the indigo void above him, shot through with waning pink sunbeams. In a minute, Esther sniffled and said, "Tell me why I should forgive you."

"Olivia was … about twenty percent right."

"You're undercover?"

"No, not that part."

"Your boss told you to swear off your family and give your all to the cause and focus on your cases?"

"Um … Olivia came up with all that?"

"No, numbskull, this is me mouthing off at you. Can't you tell the difference anymore?"

Austin propped his arms on the table and let the cement grind into his elbows. An elderly couple, both with walkers, shuffled into Rosita's and angled curious glances at him as they passed.

"You're not going to tell me anything about it, are you?" Esther said.

"This is what I can tell you. I'm not in Michigan right now"—he didn't let her gasp turn into more cussing—"and my job is the reason I had to leave. And I don't know when I'm coming back, but I won't have to go dark again. You can call me anytime, and I'll answer."

"Is it the same time zone?"

She might figure it out, but anyone who could use it against him already knew. *And can't get to you here, anyway, remember?* "I'm an hour earlier than you."

"So … west, but not as far as, say, Colorado." But that topic must not hold much interest at the moment, because she continued before he could determine the wisdom of blurting out his location. "And you left because of your job, but not because of undercover. Was there danger?"

Austin sighed and stood up. He shivered. Maybe he ought to try to find some shelter for the night. A few bucks on a fast-food-priced chimichanga was one thing. A hotel room … no. Maybe Grace Bible Church wasn't the only place offering aid, though it soured his insides to consider begging.

"Well, was there?"

"You need to let it go, Esther."

The laugh she barked in his ear was one that wanted to be angry instead of hurt, the one she'd been using since the day Austin moved out. "Sure, that's fair. You up and disappear and I let it go."

So easy to forget she was still a kid. She'd grown up as fast as he had … well, maybe not quite.

"I'm totally entitled to …" A quiet gasp, and her voice dropped. "This is about that guy, isn't it, the dirty con-cop. Samuel Stiles."

The man's name hit him in the chest, the last thing he'd said to Austin. *"Guard them well, that's all I ask."*

And here he sat in solitude, guarding no one. *Sorry, Stiles. I've mangled the whole thing.*

"Well," Esther said, "you can come home then. He's in jail."

"I know he is. But he's not the reason I have to stay … away, for a while."

"Austin—"

"Hey. It's your turn to shut up."

She was silent.

"This is not because you're fourteen, honey. It's because I am not able to talk about it. To anyone. It's for your protection, my protection, and the protection of some people …"

"Some people you care about."

What? No. That is, not other than Violet. "I guess I do." All right, maybe a little.

"So … I should get someone else to take me to the concert this weekend."

"Unfortunately."

She sighed.

Austin paused in his trek down Third Street to eye the lit sign to his right. *St. Jude Assistance Mission.* He walked toward the door, and his feet froze to the concrete. Esther's voice in his ear, her image in his head, tucking the purple stripe of hair behind her ear and rolling her eyes rather than succumbing to disappointment—he couldn't check himself into a homeless shelter while her repaired faith soaked through the phone line. Prying and pouting and all, Esther still believed in him.

"Esther, I have to go."

"Oh."

"I'll call you tomorrow, okay? That's a big bro promise. We need to catch up."

"Okay." Her voice perked a bit. "And I can tell Livvy and Mom that you're okay?"

"Sure."

"Bye, then."

"Bye."

He shoved the phone into his pocket. He gulped down whatever pride he had left. As he opened the door, a bell rang above it. From nearby, a faucet ran, dishes clanked, and quiet chatter tried to embrace him. *No, thanks.*

A woman approached from around a partition wall. Older than him by multiple decades, she wore a ruffled yellow apron over her jeans and sweater and dried her hands on a dishtowel.

"How can I help you?" She smiled.

Austin glanced around, up, down, anywhere but her eyes. "I was hoping you could … I mean, I thought if you had something … Actually, I only need a …"

If he finished any of those sentences, he could never call himself a man again.

He returned the woman's smile and tried to smooth his voice. "I'm sorry, I've made a mistake. Thank you, though."

Her voice followed him out, but the roaring in his ears muted the words. He broke into a run, slung the handle of his bag over his shoulder and gripped it while he retraced the steps of the day. Headlights passed on his right, and at least one person tried to offer him a ride. He ran faster.

Until he reached that vacant parking lot and dropped to his knees beside the rock pile. He tossed his bag down and pulled out the shirts, the jeans, and layered them over his body. He left the gun unloaded but settled it near his right hand, in case a bluff was necessary. Then he lay back with his head on the mostly empty bag that barely pillowed him from the blacktop. He shut his eyes and, for the sake of exploring every angle, tried to find reasons to stay in this country that didn't want him.

34

Lee sat at the side of the covered pool, legs crossed at the edge, next to a *7'* warning painted on the concrete. She wished this was an indoor pool, or that it wasn't October. Marcus might be able to manage water exercise, and it would certainly benefit him. She'd just have to make sure he didn't become chilled, that was all.

Futile thoughts for now.

Voices drifted around the brick corner of the hotel, raised to carry. Lee stood. She'd come out here for space to breathe outside their room and the narrow hall, away from the scents of carpet cleaner and cranberry room freshener. Ever since breakfast, when Marcus devoured another meal of scrambled eggs and oatmeal, something had chafed inside Lee, like sandpaper between her organs and her bones. Conversation wasn't something she could endure at the moment.

She rounded the pool. Who else would be out here? The nearest entrance to the building was at least thirty yards away. She'd be seen, and Southern people didn't ignore strangers. They smiled and greeted at the very least.

Ducking behind the shrubbery qualified as absurd behavior.

No one would ever know.

But herself. She wasn't a social invalid.

The voices floated nearer. "Right, but you know Tatum Murphy. She's got one eye on the parking lot at all times. Bet she already spotted the cars."

"Bet she's barricading the door as we speak. 'Keep out the filthy Stab.'"

"You bring your battering ram, Jones?"

Laughter.

Lee slipped between a gap in the shrubs and crouched. Their words were even plainer as they strode into sight. She held her breath, though they couldn't hear it from across the pool. Four Constabulary agents, three male and one female. Gray uniforms. Guns and badges.

"I'm thinking we enter back here," the woman said. "Throw Ms. Murphy off her game. If she wants to make her remarks, she can come find us this time."

"Good call." The tallest of the men, well over six feet and shaved bald, propped a hand on his sidearm.

The back of Lee's neck tingled. Did he sense her?

He scanned the pool area and shrugged. The hand on his gun must be habitual. "Jones"—the woman nodded—"you take our rookie through the upper level."

Jones nodded again and motioned to the stockiest of the men. He appeared Mexican, and his haircut wasn't the standard cop buzz of his two male colleagues but rather curled past his collar, almost long enough for a stub of ponytail. He and Jones entered the hotel first, and Baldy and his partner followed after another quick glance back. The weighted door shut behind them.

Lee jumped to her feet and dashed across the cement aisle between the shrubs and the pool. She had to draw up the sedative and inject Marcus before they got to him. Would it have time to work?

He would never forgive her.

He would be safe.

When Lee burst in the front door, the hostess station was empty. Maybe someone else had warned her. Lee ran to the stairwell and took the stairs two at a time. She emerged into the hall and padded forward at a normal pace. At the other end, doors stood open.

They had a master key.

Room two-seventy-three drew her eyes. Open. They were already inside. Bile rose in her throat. *Marcus, please.*

She folded her arms. She swallowed, and her throat burned, and she stepped into the room. Marcus slept in the bed.

"Can I help you?" Lee said.

Agent Jones had unzipped their duffels and was pawing through Marcus's clothes. "Just a routine check, ma'am. My name is Agent Nina Jones and this is Agent Daniel Gutierrez."

Her partner stood beside Marcus's bed. "Are you Christians?"

Lee's heart skipped. "No."

"Are you sure?"

"Quite." She stepped farther into the room and perched on the other bed, crossing her ankles.

"Does any of the property in the hotel safe downstairs belong to you?"

She kept her eyes away from the rug that covered the subtle seam in the carpet. "No."

"We'll be searching it as well. We'll get a list of items and owners from the hotel manager."

"Of course."

Jones stood up and carried Lee's bag to Marcus's bed. She poured the contents out over his feet and rifled through the pile. The bag bumped his legs. Lee's lungs shut down. Any moment now, he'd jerk onto his side, shielding his head.

Jones opened Lee's wallet and eyed her ID, glanced at the credit card and the three hundred dollars in twenties, and set the wallet aside. She shook out a denim button-down shirt and looked down at Marcus, still holding the shirt up by its shoulders.

"He's a deep sleeper."

Except … he hadn't been for the last week. Lee had roused him with a word close to his ear.

Jones shook his leg—the injured one. Marcus didn't stir. "Is something wrong with him?"

Lee had to be still. She had to respond. But something must be wrong. The clearing sound of his lungs through the stethoscope, the smoothness of his forehead that spoke of less pain, the strength returning to his voice—had all these signs this morning been false somehow?

"Ma'am, if we can't wake him, there could be a medical danger here."

"No." The word snapped from her. "He's fine. He takes sleeping pills."

"At eleven in the morning?"

I have to do this. I can do this. "He suffers from post-traumatic stress disorder. He sleeps better during the day."

Betrayal poked her. Marcus might very well have some form of PTSD. But she'd mix truth and lies if she had to.

"Are you friends or lovers?" the man said.

"Excuse me?"

"Well, you're pretty defensive for a friend, but there's two beds here, so …"

"We don't sleep together."

Neither of the agents was buying that. They exchanged a glance and shrugged—*let her lie to us as long as she knows we know it*—and

Jones finished her ransacking and tossed the bag onto the floor. As she prowled the perimeter of the room, her partner placed himself between Marcus and Lee. Closer to Lee. She tried not to shudder.

"I mean that we don't *sleep* together. He needs his own bed. Night terrors."

"Ah." The man grinned.

"Let it go, Gutierrez," Jones said.

He shrugged again. Maybe the motion was supposed to convince Lee that his questions were nonchalant. "So why are you hanging out in a hotel in the middle of the day? Your accent's northern—"

"Michigan," Jones said.

"Right, okay, so I assume you're traveling, and most travelers try not to drive at night."

Lee uncrossed her ankles. "I believe I just explained that. He sleeps in daylight whenever possible. So yes, we do drive at night."

Jones joined Gutierrez in facing Lee down, both of them standing too close to her, a wall blocking Marcus.

"Once more," Jones said. "Are you a Christian?"

"No."

"Is your companion a Christian?"

"No."

Jones nodded. "Thank you for your cooperation, Ms. Vaughn. This is only a routine check, but if you have any questions or concerns, you are free to call the national Constabulary contact number."

Gutierrez's mouth twitched at the futility of the suggestion.

"Good afternoon."

They marched from the room and left the door open. As Lee shut it, one door down, the master key card clicked. Hopefully, Debra had made it to the safe room.

Lee barreled to the bed. The pulse at Marcus's wrist was steady. Strong. She knelt to pull the rug aside and pried at the carpet until it peeled up the requisite three inches. The knob of the safe was sunk down into the floor, difficult to grasp. When she raised the door, the cut seams allowed the carpet to come up as well. Lee retrieved her stethoscope, leaving the medical bag in the safe.

Even the cold disc against his chest didn't wake him. His breathing still held a faint crackle, exactly as it had three hours ago.

"Marcus?" she said.

Something thumped on the other side of the wall. Lee crossed the room to press her ear against it.

"Maybe it's not occupied," Gutierrez said.

"Then why's the Do Not Disturb tag on the door?"

"An oversight, Jones. Come on."

"Maybe. We'll find out when we take a look at the registry."

A few muffled slamming sounds—shutting of drawers?—were followed by silence. Lee went to the door but didn't open it. Gawking into the hallway would only get her noticed. She padded back to the chair and pulled it close to Marcus's bed. She checked his pulse as if it might have stopped in the last few minutes.

"Marcus, I need you to wake up."

A few minutes later, the phone rang twice, Tatum's all-clear. Lee released his wrist and curled into the chair. A tremor gripped her body. Those agents had been in the room with him for … two minutes? More? Had they done something to him? Yet why act baffled by his sleeping?

"Marc—" Her voice broke. She cleared her throat, but her voice wouldn't squeeze out any louder. "Marcus."

He opened his eyes. No gasp, no defensive posture. He turned his head toward her and frowned.

"Are you all right?" she said.

He turned onto his side, trying to sit up. "Yeah."

She stood and helped him upright. "You're certain?"

"Yeah. What's going on?"

Her legs liquefied. The edge of the chair cushion caught her, and she gripped its arms.

"Lee."

"They were here."

"Who?"

"There was a Constabulary search of the hotel. They stood in this room and—" She jerked a gesture at her clothes, strewn over the bed.

"Why didn't I wake up?"

"I don't know. I told them you took a sleeping pill."

His eyes widened, then narrowed as he shook his head. He clutched handfuls of the bedspread. "I told you not to do it."

"I didn't sedate you, Marcus."

"Then why?"

"I don't know."

The frown didn't ease, but he sat up straighter and looked around the room, taking in the disarray. "Is everybody safe?"

"The agents left only minutes ago. Debra wasn't in her room next door, so I assume she was in the safe room."

"Go make sure they're okay. All of them."

He wouldn't relax until he knew. Lee nodded and went in search of Tatum.

In front of the check-in desk, someone had piled generic black luggage and two child-sized backpacks, one pink and one green. Two girls stood near the potted tree in the corner, engrossed in their cell phones. Lee glanced out the glass door to the parking lot. Two women gestured to each other, either furiously or rapturously, beside a beige minivan.

Tatum stood behind the check-in desk with a small computer to her right and a legal notepad to her left. Between them, she typed numbers into an old adding machine that spit out a ribbon of receipt paper, squeaking a prophecy of imminent demise for the rollers inside. She didn't look up as Lee approached.

One finger held up, she kept typing with the other hand. "If I mess up this total …"

She hit a final key, and the ribbon fed forward with a final squeak. As she met Lee's eyes, her mouth curved and pursed at the same time, cordiality and concern.

"How are you folks?" Her eyes blanked to cancel the smile. "The Stab don't usually show up in the middle of the day like that. I hope there wasn't too much inconvenience."

Those women could enter any moment, and the girls appeared to be of middle school age. Perhaps Lee should sing Constabulary praises, but even if she were capable at the moment—*Agent Jones shaking Marcus's leg, standing over him*—Tatum had invited her not to.

Lee folded her arms. "They showed no respect whatsoever for my property."

"Don't blame you for being upset, ma'am, but they do have authority to toss things around."

"Surely you're not suggesting I'm the only one with a complaint against them."

"I've got a few others that feel about the same as you."

Yes. But that didn't answer the question of their safety. Lee arched an eyebrow. *Tatum, this code talking won't work if you over-complicate.*

The door opened, and the women neared Lee to claim their belongings. Both of them cast her a quick glance, not followed with a smile.

"Why don't you go on back to your room for now, ma'am?" Tatum beamed at her.

"All right." Lee unfolded her arms. "You can accompany me and see the damage they caused."

Tatum huffed and tugged at her shirt hem. She leaned over the desk to hand key cards to the shorter of the women. "You all need anything else now?"

"No, thank you," the woman said.

"Okay, you're room one-sixty-eight."

No safe room for them. Tatum emerged from behind the desk and tugged her shirt again and motioned for Lee to go first.

When they entered the stairwell, Tatum grinned and threw her arms around Lee. And didn't let go. "Dear Lord."

Lee set a hand on the woman's back. One. Two. Three. Long enough. She stepped back.

Tatum released her, still grinning. "I knew He wouldn't bring you so far without taking you all the way. But when I saw them, and I called your room phone to warn you—I knew you couldn't make it to the safe room, not the way they snuck in the back this time. Not with that man as weak as he is. What did you do, pick him up and run?"

"No."

"I felt sick, I was so worried for y'all, until they marched out of here empty-handed. What happened?"

"They searched the room."

"Well, I figured, but …" She looked up the stairs, wrung her hands, then refocused on Lee. "With you in it?"

Lee nodded. "You said empty-handed. There were no arrests whatsoever?"

Tatum shook her head. "But didn't they … ask you the question?"

No arrests. Lee's body felt lighter. She started up the stairs.

"Didn't they ask you?"

She'd left Tatum on the landing, staring up at her. Lee planted her feet on the stair. "They did. I lied." Partially.

Like a butterfly losing its color, Tatum's entire body wilted. "Oh. And Marcus?"

"He was asleep."

"Oh, right, he would be."

Lee didn't owe this woman an explanation she didn't have herself. Or a defense for some alleged sin. She turned back toward Marcus.

"Lee."

Please stop talking. But Lee couldn't ignore her. Couldn't sigh down at her, not while sincerity poured from Tatum's shimmering eyes. "Yes?"

"Do you think … we'll go to hell?"

We.

"It's that verse that says if we deny Jesus, He'll deny us before the Father. It keeps me awake nights. I know—I know Jesus forgave Peter and all, but he was *Peter*, and I'm—not."

Lee laced her fingers behind her back. *Well, Jesus Christ? I hope You didn't set this up for me to reassure her.*

"But if I—if I told the truth." Tatum's tears overflowed, but her face turned up to Lee, open, broken … alight. "It wouldn't only be me. That first time, they'd have shut down the hotel. They'd have searched high and low until they found the room, until they found the family hiding in there. And since then I've helped protect so many. Like Corrie ten Boom, or Rahab. They lied, too, to protect God's people."

Lee couldn't muster curiosity for people she'd never heard of. She stood, waiting, because nothing she could say right now would benefit.

Tatum apparently didn't need an answer as much as she needed to confess to someone besides her God. "I know it isn't the same. I've confessed it every single night for the last year."

Lee nodded.

"You've only denied Him once?" She continued without waiting for Lee's nod or head shake. "Still, it'll eat at you, believe me. You'll hardly be able to face Him."

I prefer not to.

"Sometimes the sin is all I can feel in my heart, but sometimes … I can feel peace, too. And that's when I think maybe I'm forgiven."

It was a paltry crime, a crime of words. Tatum had harmed no one. Killed no one.

"We don't have to talk about it," Tatum said, wiping her cheeks.

"Thank you."

"I'm sorry."

"It's fine."

"I—I wanted to tell you, too. About our border guard. He got an extra shift, so we can move you both tomorrow, instead of the day after. If you're ready by seven tomorrow morning, my driver can be here then."

"Yes." Lee inched backward, up one step. "We will be ready."

35

"You lost, boy?"

The voice came from the yard to Austin's right, not the porch but several feet away from it, where a man sat in a sagging canvas patio chair on the walkway leading to his front door.

Austin tried not to bristle. Boy? The guy could be his dad but not his grandpa. "Just walking."

The man crossed his ankle over his knee, and the chair seemed to strain. He nodded as if giving Austin permission to walk past his house.

Austin ambled down the sidewalk and stuffed the wrapper from the second of Rosita's breakfast burritos into a side pocket of his sports bag. He probably looked like a vagrant, carrying it over one shoulder, wearing day-old clothes. Felt like one for sure. Around three o'clock this morning, jolting awake next to his rock pile with a stiff neck and a bruised tailbone, he'd cursed himself for running away from a bed and a shower. By six, he admitted he could've at least found some grass to sleep on. Maybe this was unconscious penance, though he couldn't think of what he'd done wrong. Maybe he wanted to know how Brenner—fine, Marcus—had felt lying on a floor for months.

Violet had texted his phone several times last night, urging him to come to the church for the night. He'd told her he was fine and would see her in the morning.

But he hadn't been to the church yet. He explored for hours, getting to know the town, the layout of the commercial district and the side streets of a residential neighborhood nearby. Geographical awareness could be helpful at some point, and he had nothing else to do. He'd call Esther tonight, after she got off work at the deli.

Meanwhile, he walked. Mapped this portion of the town in his mind. He should go spy out Grace Bible Church a little better, but it was sure to be a safe place for Violet, though its presence still felt to him like a repelling magnetic field.

A scowl tightened his face. Bible Church, a safe place to leave his girl.

His? Violet wouldn't agree. Maybe he should try to stop thinking of her that way.

Good luck with that, numbskull. Great, now Esther's voice was coming from his own head.

By the time he was hungry again—maybe he'd try a couple tacos this time—his phone said it was two o'clock and he'd explored several square miles, probably walked ten. He no longer had to think about the route to Rosita's. He let his feet head back there.

His phone vibrated in his bag. He pulled it out—not a call, a text.

I'm sorry.

Violet.

He texted back. *For what?*

Her response came seconds later. *For running off and telling you to leave me alone.*

I'm sorry too, he typed, and then stood staring down at the words. If he sent that, she'd ask why. This last week of her life? She was grateful for it. She was free. The months that he'd failed to find her? She hadn't wanted to be found, after all. His thumb hovered over the keypad, then typed again. *For letting you spy for us.* There it was, the *us* again, but he couldn't phrase this any other way. Facts were facts.

He hit Send.

And waited.

Where are you?

His breath poured out. His thumbs flashed. *I'll come to you.*

I'm not at church. I tried to find you.

She'd get herself lost. And talk about a target, hefting all her possessions on her shoulder in a town that knew about its fugitives. Austin rocked on his feet and couldn't type fast enough. *Where?*

Chill. I didn't go far. At the park, about a block to the left of the church. By the playground.

To the left of the church. Austin shook his head. She would never learn how to give directions. Good thing he'd walked past the playground a few hours ago. *Don't leave*, he texted.

Duh.

He jogged most of the way but slowed his pace in time to level his breathing before she saw him. He passed the monkey bars first and caught a scent of heating rubber from the tractor tires sunk vertical into the sand. The playground felt warmer than the rest of the park, the difference between sand and grass. It was deserted other than one stoop-shouldered, silver-haired woman sitting on the lip of the sandbox while a toddler tossed damp sand into the air and let it fall into his hair. She laughed and waved to Austin, and the little boy waved, too.

On the other side of the playground, Violet sat in one of three vinyl-seated swings. She turned the chains above her head, watching them crimp tighter and tighter. Before she could spot his approach, she raised her feet and leaned back. The swing spun. She tilted backward, and her hair brushed the sand.

An empty merry-go-round sat a small distance from the monkey bars, freshly painted red. Austin perched on the edge. Even motion-blurred, Violet was beautiful. At last, she came to a stop, and her dizzy eyes found him. She smiled for only a moment.

He stood and approached when she didn't. "Hi."

"Hey." Violet kicked her toes against the sand beneath the swing.

Austin sank into the swing beside her and pumped his legs twice. Olivia still loved these old things, loved pumping as high as she could and then jumping off.

"I'm sorry," Violet said.

"It's okay, really."

"I've been horrible to you for the last week."

"What are you talking about?"

She lurched to her feet and spoke to the merry-go-round, her back facing Austin. "Telling Sam you couldn't come in after your boss threatened to kill you. Not wanting you to come with us. Accusing you of setting us up with that cop. Staying mad about … I don't know what."

She hadn't wanted him to come … at all?

"Where did you sleep last night? You obviously didn't get a hotel room."

His mouth curved. "So observant."

"You smell a little."

"Good to know."

She turned to him, eyes shimmering. "I've been awful."

Austin stood and narrowed the distance, his hands pinned to his sides. She smelled too—like apples and flowers. "You haven't been awful. Okay? But we need to talk, I think."

Violet inched closer, one step, two, three. Austin's chest tingled.

"Violet, we—"

She curled one hand around his bicep, lifted her face, rose on tiptoe, and kissed him. A soft kiss of apology, all she meant it to be, because she started to ease back before she … didn't. His hands found her hair, heavy and thick, the slightest bit coarse. He threaded his fingers through it, and they melded together like they used to, her head fitting into his hand, her arm curving at his back so her hand nestled against his left shoulder blade. He leaned down and deepened the kiss, and she pressed their bodies closer, and—

Violet broke the kiss with a strangled sound and turned away from him, hands over her face. She groaned.

He kept himself from echoing that. "What?"

"I promised."

Promised … The heat in his body froze solid. Promised who?

"I told Jesus I'd honor Him."

The momentary ice thawed into a low simmer of … well, he couldn't resent a God he didn't believe in, could he? "We didn't do anything."

"You don't understand."

"Definitely not."

"Austin." She faced him. Her thumb found her wrist bone. "It's not just sex. It's … walking this line. The almost-sex. I can't do that anymore."

"Violet, it was one kiss."

"No, it wasn't. Isn't. Don't you know that? I still want it. All of it."

She actually blushed. Over something they'd done, something they'd shared, dozens of times. She'd always been the one sighing with disappointment when he told her to put her shirt back on because if she didn't he was going to quit caring she wasn't eighteen yet.

"I should've known I couldn't kiss you. You're too—too—" Again, the blush.

Austin wasn't one for wordlessness, but she'd knocked every syllable out of his brain.

She twirled a strand of hair around her finger.

The silence stayed. He stared at the merry-go-round and hated the flash of memory, another park, another merry-go-round, this one painted blue. A night he hadn't known would rip what he and Violet had into shreds he couldn't stitch back together.

36

At 6:58 in the morning, a red pickup truck pulled around the back of the hotel, and Marcus and Lee met their driver, Graham Henderson. He was of medium everything—height, build, temperament, even the brown of his hair and eyes—and he didn't grill them or crowd the cab with small talk. It was crowded enough, especially for the person in the middle. Lee breathed through her mouth and tried not to smell Graham's cologne—the only noticeable thing about him. Marcus leaned against the door and tried to hide his wince at each pothole, hands curled in his lap, his body coiled with watchfulness, his gaze fixed out the window at the flat fields, the cloudless sky.

At 11:42, their vehicle slowed to a crawl in the lineup to cross the border. Texas wasn't requiring passports, but of course, Oklahoma was requiring an interview to prevent terrorists from escaping. Lee still couldn't wring any logic from that.

The border guard, Danny, gave Graham a companionable glance that wouldn't translate to a camera. He asked them a series of innocuous questions—would they be in Texas long, did they have any weapons with them. Graham shook his head with conviction. Danny looked at their IDs, peered into the truck bed and under the chassis, and waved them on their way.

At 11:53, a green sign came into view to the right of the highway, maybe three hundred feet past the guard stations, adorned with a red, white, and blue flag bearing a lone star. *Welcome to the New Republic of Texas.* Below the bold, white script, in block letters: *Bienvenido a la Nueva Republica de Texas.*

Here they were. She and Marcus. Lee should feel something about this, something other than an inching dread that she was about to awaken from a dream.

The highway unrolled for another mile before Graham cocked his head at both of them. "Most folks are happy to see that sign."

"We are, of course," Lee said.

He grunted. "I'll drop you off in Kearby. Shouldn't take us much more than an hour, and it's where I dropped off those two blond kids. Austin and Rose?"

They were the most words he'd spoken since meeting them. Lee stretched her legs to the vent under the dashboard. "Violet. Yes."

"Austin suggested I not take you to Burkburnett. He wanted to be away from the border."

That was sensible. Lee's shoulders lifted. She hadn't feared for them, not even worried. Violet would be guarded well. The tough confidence Austin wore was the sort to rely on, genuine and earned. He didn't waste energy on bravado because he didn't need to. So yes, they were fine, yet Lee now peered through the windshield with new anticipation. Seeing Violet would be … refreshing.

Graham knew his routes. In just over an hour, they left the expressway for East Third Street and were ensconced in a town barely larger than Vinita. Sparse traffic, parallel parking. A few minutes later, Marcus jolted forward. His head turned to follow as they passed … oh, the church.

"Marcus?" Lee said.

"There was a cross." His voice was low and too even. "Above the door. And the sign said 'church.' Not 'fellowship of believers.' It said 'church.'"

Graham nodded. "You'll see quite a few of them in Kearby."

He signaled and turned right at an intersection occupied by two quilt shops, a Mexican restaurant, and a long green building, Clive's General Store. They drove down a block of one-story brick houses and oak trees that hadn't begun to turn color yet. Two stop signs later, Graham pulled a U-turn in the middle of the quiet street and backed into a parking space alongside a flat-roofed brick building the color of sandstone. This sign bore not one but three crosses. Grace Bible Church of Kearby.

"Is there …?" Lee swallowed the taste of gravel from her next words. She had to say them. "A shelter of some sort? We're not able to book a hotel right now."

"This is the shelter. The church has been aiding people for a few months. They're pretty good at it by now—efficient and all."

But … a church. *I can't walk in there.* Especially not to beg assistance.

Marcus cleared his throat. His hand curled around the door handle as he held Lee's eyes.

Perhaps for him, she could do this.

The truck, like his old one, was high enough for running boards, but helping Marcus down was marginally easier than helping him up. Lee supported him from inside the truck and Graham managed, despite his lack of height or bulk, to bear Marcus's weight and lower him. In full health, Marcus would outweigh him by fifty pounds or more. Lee forced down another lump of gravel.

A sturdy concrete awning over a set of glass doors jutted out from this side of the building, a miniature foyer.

Lee unzipped her bag and drew out three twenty-dollar bills, a quarter of what they had. "Thank you for your assistance, sir."

"Oh, put that away." Graham waved her off. "Don't insult me."

"But you—"

"I helped out family. That's what we do, right? Maybe your Michigan church dropped the ball on that, but it's different down here."

Lee opened her mouth to argue, but her words had dissipated. She shoved the money back into her bag.

Graham took a step toward the doors, Marcus's arm over his shoulder, but Marcus stiffened and shook his head.

Graham sighed. "What now?"

Lee set the bags at the curb and offered her shoulder. Marcus withdrew his arm from Graham's support and took Lee's instead. Yes. He was right. They needed a minute to process, to discuss their options.

"We'll be fine now," she said. "Thank you."

Graham's eyes roved a full circle, though there was no one to see, not even another vehicle within a hundred feet, and those farther off were parked and empty. He sighed and smiled for the first time. "Okay, then. Godspeed."

"You, too," Marcus said quietly. "Thanks."

Graham nodded and got back into his truck. It disappeared down the block, past the small homes and tall trees.

As if they'd spoken it aloud, she and Marcus shuffled toward another entrance, this one up three brick steps with a wrought-iron railing. Lee settled him onto the first one and sank beside him and shivered at the cold cement against her thighs.

"All right. We have two-hundred thirty-five dollars, and Austin has the other …"

He wasn't looking at her, maybe at anything. No, he was gazing past the parked cars across the narrow street, past the wide parking lot, at … the trees?

"Marcus."

He coughed and breathed through it, pushed it down. His arm guarded his ribs.

"Are you all right?"

Still, he didn't look at her. He tilted his head up, squinted into the sun, closed his eyes. Lee linked her fingers between her knees and waited for him. A faint tremor washed over him, and then he was shaking. He bowed his head.

"Marcus," she whispered.

His hands splayed over his face. He tried to clear his throat, but the sound choked into a sob. His shoulders, shrunken but still broad-boned, heaved with the effort of control.

"I'm here," she said. As if it mattered in this moment.

It could matter. All she had to do was tuck an arm around his shoulders, rub his back. Place her thumb below the cowlick at his neck and massage a slow circle of comfort. Her hand ached to do it. She lifted it toward him. Lowered it again. If she'd pictured only her arm around him, perhaps she could have managed, but the intimacy of her fingers on his neck, in his hair, was seared into her body now, into her mind, and it spiraled into other images, nearer, more intimate, and … she couldn't even touch him.

Long minutes later, he coughed again and lifted his head. His eyes were dry, but he pawed at his cheeks anyway. He drew in a slow breath before he met her eyes.

"Are you all right?" she said.

"Thanks."

"For?"

"Being here."

"Of course."

He rubbed his neck, and the old habit hit Lee in the chest. Perhaps pieces of Marcus would continue sifting into place. Perhaps one day, none of him would be missing. She shifted on the step. Words, she could manage. Most of the time. But now she couldn't even say what she'd said before, when he was probably too fever-spent to remember. *I will not leave you, ever.*

She helped him around the side of the church to the front entrance, the one without stairs. Did one knock at the door of a church? She pressed her face to the glass. No one stood in view.

"Lee, you just go in."

"But we have no invitation or … or …" Right to these people's help. *I have no right.*

"Church doesn't need an invitation."

"Not on Sunday, I understand that, but this is the middle of the week and the middle of the afternoon, and—"

"Heck, Lee." Marcus tugged at the door, budged it a few inches and leaned into her with a growl.

"Stop." She shuffled his weight to one side and opened it herself. *They'll assume you're one of them.* And that was the problem. But to remain with Marcus, she would lie to them.

She juggled Marcus's weight and the door's, neither of which seemed much heavier than the other, and then they were inside a navy-carpeted entryway. White walls, a scent of nutmeg and coffee, a long hallway to the left and a yawning auditorium directly ahead. Over the six doors, all of which were propped open with small rubber doorstops, the three crosses loomed.

Yes, Jesus Christ, it's me. I didn't intend to trespass in a place like this, but it can't be avoided.

She could see no camera above the auditorium, and no bell had jingled when they opened the main doors. Well, of course not. A bell would not be reverent.

Somehow, though, their entrance was noticed. From down the winding hall came a man in khaki pants and a muted orange shirt. He seemed to grow in height as he neared, until he towered over both of them, six-foot-five at least. By then, Marcus stood straight, weight on both legs, and had lowered his arm to cling to the back of Lee's T-shirt.

"Welcome, travelers." The man's voice should echo or boom, but instead it came gently, with the twang Lee was learning to expect.

"Thank you," Lee said. "We were told to come here for … We were told that you …"

"Yes, we offer sanctuary." The man grinned and took their bags. "I'm Heath, and you can follow me."

After a few steps, Marcus hooked his arm around her shoulders again. Heath's long strides set a quick pace, and he hadn't glanced back to notice they fell behind after only a few seconds. They reached a section of the hall well lit by a row of windows on the right. Outside, a garden with a waterfall was circled by padded benches and a stone path. Marcus stumbled, and Lee focused on the path in front of them. It forked at a small gymnasium, one door propped open, spilling the sounds of a dribbled basketball, squeaking tennis shoes, and competitive voices. Heath led them to the left, and this hall stretched longer.

Marcus's arm stiffened around her shoulders. Lee glanced at him, but he shook his head, his mouth a thin, pale line. *Don't say anything.*

She sighed and forced more of his weight onto her shoulders. He didn't resist.

By the time the labyrinth forked again, they trailed Heath by at least twenty feet. He glanced over his shoulder, froze, and loped back to them.

"I'm so sorry. I was in my own head, planning out where to put you, and not paying attention to you at all."

"It's fine," Lee said.

Heath looked Marcus up and down and shook his head. "That isn't true."

Marcus gritted his teeth and glared.

Heath dropped their duffels at his feet and addressed Lee. "Let's trade."

Marcus's stiffness erased any possibility of that. Lee squeezed the hand she held over her shoulders. "Unnecessary."

Heath didn't argue with her, but he didn't resume walking, either. His gaze shifted back to Marcus, piercing and … sad. After a long moment that somehow wasn't invasive or awkward, he stepped toward them.

Marcus stepped back.

"Hey, now." Heath held up his hands. "I'd tell you take it easy, but it's clear neither one of you can do that right now. I'm sorry."

The last thing they needed was an inept attempt at a counseling session. Lee tried to move forward, but the tower of Heath in the center of the hallway wouldn't let them pass without brushing him on one side.

"You've carried burdens too heavy for you," he said quietly to Marcus. "And you've suffered a long time. And that's no word of prophecy, that's my two eyes looking at you."

The glare faded, and Marcus held the man's eyes, searching … hoping? For what?

"We're the hands and feet of Jesus," Heath said. "You know that verse?"

A dim flicker found Marcus's eyes. "The body. Of Christ."

"That's right." Heath held out his open palms. "Brother, let me be His arms for you right now."

Lee waited for Marcus's choice and felt him make it, the slackening in his shoulders, the silent sigh that caved his chest. He took a step toward Heath, and Lee stepped with him and offered his arm, though Heath's height would make this—

The man placed an arm at Marcus's back and stooped to lift him.

"Please." The word burst from her mouth, and Heath waited. "Please be careful. He …"

Marcus jerked a nod. *It's okay, Lee, tell him.*

"There are multiple rib fractures," she said. "And undetermined damage to his left knee."

"Have you been to a doctor? There's a walk-in clinic around the—"

"No," Marcus said.

Heath studied him, then nodded. He scooped Marcus up with a smooth, careful motion, his arm positioned behind Marcus's knees, not under them. "Okay?"

"Thanks." The whisper was almost too quiet to hear.

"What I'm here for. Let's get you two settled in and I'll hear whatever pieces of your story you're ready to tell."

37

Violet hadn't eaten since breakfast, so Austin led her half a mile down the street and they sat at his table at Rosita's. The young Mexican woman who waited on them smirked at Austin when Violet wasn't looking … recognizing him? So he'd been here less than five hours ago. They had good food.

Both of them dug into lunch without a word. Really, what was he supposed to say to her? Ask her to compromise her beliefs so they could …

Have sex? No. Well, yes, of course, he wanted … and she'd wanted it, too. But he wanted more than that. He wanted to find out if they could love each other. If they could last. Based on previous relationships, he had to admit sex wasn't the best way to do that. He'd never told Violet her age wasn't the only factor he was waiting for. Now, he'd probably never get to tell her anything.

Of course, she'd ordered nachos with extra cheese. She pulled out one chip at a time and watched the cheese string apart, thinner and thinner, catching it on her tongue when it tore.

They finished lunch, and Austin threw their trash away, and still they hadn't spoken. The silence was almost content, a scarier silence than awkward or bristling. Content landed too close to resigned.

"Let's walk," he said.

A smile touched her lips. "Okay."

He took her through neighborhoods he'd already vetted, though Kearby seemed the last place a mugger would lurk.

"So tonight." Violet tucked her hair behind her ear. "Where'll you go?"

"Sleep under the stars, I guess. It was nice last night."

"On the ground?" She clasped her hands in front of her, feet fused to the sidewalk.

"Like camping. As you can see, it didn't kill me."

"And are you going to take a shower only after you've found a job and saved up enough for an apartment? Because the lack of shower may affect finding a job."

Austin kept walking, and after a moment, she followed. They passed under an ancient willow tree, branches brushing their arms. One narrow leaf clung to Violet's hair, behind her ear. Austin smiled.

"I walked up to a shelter last night, even went in. Then I walked back out."

Um … where had those words come from? Violet halted again to stare at him. Again.

"I just didn't feel right about it," he said. *And if you'd leave this topic alone now, that would be great.*

"Come back with me. To the church."

"Violet."

"Please."

A shower would be nice. A bed would be nicer. Still charity, though.

The screen door of the nearest house creaked open. Several boys wandered out, probably around the age of Austin's small group at Elysium, seventh or eighth grade. He hurried down the sidewalk, and Violet trotted to match his stride. They didn't need an audience. Or a welcome. For all he knew, Southern kids were as friendly as Southern adults.

"Why won't you sleep at the church?" Violet said.

He sighed and scrubbed a hand through his hair (okay, maybe a shower was in order posthaste). "I'm not entirely sure."

"Was it because of what I said? About leaving me alone?"

"No, though I do want to respect your boundaries."

"I don't own the church, scholar."

His mouth curved. If by some cosmic grace they did stay together for the next ten years or more, he would never be able to predict her use of that nickname. "True, but … Violet, you were upset. You've got a lot to be upset over. I don't mean only me, I mean … your whole life at the moment."

"I've also never had so much to be thankful for."

He'd challenge her to list them, but she would, and the thought of listening to that tasted like old coffee. He let the quiet fill with a group of kids at the closer end of the street, playing basketball with a cockeyed hoop (broken or more challenging?).

"Austin." Her voice trembled. She maintained pace beside him but said nothing else.

"Go on," he said quietly.

"Last night, I had a nightmare."

His muscles tensed. Of course she had.

"I woke up in bed, and I wasn't breathing hard. My heart wasn't even pounding. I don't think I made a single noise. I'm rooming with a girl named Fiona, and I whispered, 'Did I wake you up?' but she didn't say anything."

"Do you want to talk about it?" If she needed to, she should. If she didn't … he'd rather not hear about it.

"It was the guy from the gas station. He—he shot Lee, in my dream." Violet went still, arms wrapped around her middle as if her stomach hurt. "And I had to help her. But she was bleeding so much. All over my hands and the concrete. It was so red."

Austin took one step closer and stopped. *Let me hold you.* But she stepped back.

"I think she died. If I hadn't woke up when I did, I would've seen her die. She was bleeding so much." Violet straightened up and rubbed her arms. "You know how some dreams fade as soon as you wake up?"

Austin nodded.

"This one still hasn't."

"Violet, I—"

She didn't seem to hear him. "I'm not telling you so you get mad at the guy. I'm telling you because … I was lying there in the dark, and my body was totally calm, but my head was so scared. I couldn't sleep. So I imagined … you. Not in the room, just—on the other side of the wall. Like we had two hotel rooms. Like, if I needed help, all I had to do was scream. And then I went to sleep."

Well … good … but what did she want him to say?

She set off down the sidewalk again, shoes slapping. "I'm telling you because I don't want you to think I don't trust you. Or want you around. I don't… I don't know what to do about us, but it's not because I don't trust you. That's all."

Austin grasped her arm, and she swiveled toward him, eyes wide. They stood there in front of yet another old house, under the shade of yet another grandfatherly oak tree, and yes, he wanted to kiss her again.

But he loved her too much to do that.

"I'll come back with you," he said.

Her smile hurt.

"But let's walk awhile first."

"Okay." The smile didn't fade.

A mile later, back on Third Street, as they passed various family-owned businesses and stores, she turned to him. "I want you to do something for me."

He waited.

"I want you to be honest with them. The church."

What kind of ridiculous plan was that? "It would be stupid of them to let me stay if they know everything. I could be a spy, Violet."

"For Michigan? Does that even make any sense?"

Well, no, but … "They're going to see me as a threat."

"No, they won't. Your badge is worthless here. And I'll vouch for you."

"They met you yesterday, babe." Shoot, there it was again. But she'd called him scholar.

Violet didn't flinch at the name this time. "You'll never believe we're safe unless you put us to the test. And you can't go in there and lie to people I want to be my friends. Please, Austin."

Worst case scenario. Let's see now. They could murder him, a revenge killing for the loved ones they'd lost to re-education. The Christians were in force here, unfettered.

You might be paranoid.

Violet was watching him. "You really believe it, don't you? Everything the media says about Christians."

"I believe my training, Violet."

"What if your teachers lied?"

What purpose would that serve?

"Besides, you're armed. They're not."

Maybe.

"So … I trust you, but you don't trust me?" Her voice had softened, no accusation, only … hurt. Awareness of how wide their rift had become.

"I trust you," he said.

"But you think I'm wrong. Not just about Jesus. About the people who follow Him, too."

They walked awhile, not speaking, not touching.

"Violet, if you don't want me to go back with you, I understand."

"I do, though," she said. "Even if you insist on keeping it from them, you have to come back. And we'll prove to you the Constabulary are liars."

38

Several of the fugitives Lee met over the next few hours recognized Violet by description, a few times even her name. Austin must be less noticeable, because no one recalled him at all. Their absence ate a hole in Lee's stomach until a teenage girl mentioned Violet had left around noon to explore the town. When Lee asked if Austin had been with her, the girl said she thought Violet was alone, "… but maybe not, though." Lee's calm was complete when she remembered she and Marcus weren't supposed to be here for another day. Not that she expected a welcoming ceremony, of course.

The rooms down the hall were built into the interior of the structure. No windows other than a narrow pane of glass in each door. They'd probably been used for classrooms before (for some reason, she knew that Protestant churches from before held something called Sunday school). Now each room was furnished with a few folding chairs and various mattresses, cots, or other makeshift sleeping areas. It seemed most of the rooms were literally a place to sleep, too crowded for anything else, yet Heath brought Marcus and Lee to a smaller, unoccupied room with only two mattresses—one a twin, one an air mattress. He gave them a smile and left them alone.

The hallway was a constant bustle, and Lee lost track of names and faces, tired smiles, and sincere handshakes. She needed an hour or two in that garden in the middle of the church, listening to the waterfall and nothing else.

But she didn't shut their door on the wearying noise and the more wearying people, because Marcus sat in a folding chair at the threshold and watched everyone with something like hunger. He didn't speak unless spoken to, and even then his responses were monosyllabic and without a smile. A few people skirted closer to the opposite wall when they passed him. Most greeted him and Lee and made sure they knew where dinner would be served.

How was the church paying to feed all these people? How long did they plan to house strangers like this? And why?

The question slipped out as she was exchanging pleasantries with Sonja, a woman about Lee's age who had brought her three-year-old to socialize with the guests of her church. Or at least it seemed that way, since she wasn't taking part in the organization process, or the cooking that had started somewhere nearby based on the scents of basil and garlic.

"What do you mean?" Sonja said, scooping her child up before he could climb into Marcus's lap. "No, Alex."

"It's okay," Marcus said.

Sonja lifted Alex into the air and then set him down with a whisper in his ear, and while her back was turned, Lee shot a glare at Marcus. *It won't be "okay" if that child displaces one of your ribs.* Marcus glared back.

"I mean, I understand the positive publicity that would result from this degree of outward generosity, but it seems impractical to expect …"

Sonja gaped at Lee as if she'd combined God's name with an obscenity.

"What?" The word faltered. Had Lee said something inappropriate? Marcus watched them, something unnamable in his face.

"Okay." Sonja's voice shook, too. "I'm going to assume you're asking this because you're more familiar with—with 'fellowships' than church. This is not about publicity. It's about providing for our spiritual family."

"Are there no limits to that … ordinance? In the Bible?"

Sonja's cheeks reddened with offense. This time, Lee had definitely misspoken. "It's a command, yes, but it's not about— Lee, it's about loving people, that's all. And no, the Bible doesn't say anywhere, 'Okay, that's enough love, you can stop now.'"

"I see," Lee said.

"Really?"

No. "Yes."

Sonja smiled. "You don't own a Bible, do you?"

"Marcus does."

He straightened in the chair and stared at her as Sonja smiled again. "Oh, good. Read the Epistles, okay? That's the letters to the churches. Toward the end. Start with … let's see. First John. Or James. And come find me sometime. We can chat about what you read."

Lee nodded. Sonja left shortly, though she didn't seem to need escape. She gave them a childlike wave, followed by waving Alex's chubby hand in their direction. Lee lifted her hand in return, and when Sonja and Alex disappeared around the hallway's curve, quiet fell, a soothing blanket. Lee slid down the wall to sit against it, knees bent.

"I should participate in the meal preparation," she said.

Marcus stretched his good leg, then slowly, halfway, his injured one. "You're tired."

"Not very."

"You're tired of people."

Her mouth twitched. "Unlike you."

"Lee, you said I have a Bible."

The words had emerged without thought, a shield against Sonja's prying. Lee frowned at them now. "It's with Violet."

"She kept it? All this time?"

Only four months, but not *only*, not to him or to her. She nodded.

They'd been told a dozen times that "supper" was served at 6:30. She had less than two hours before facing another buzzing roomful of well-meaning extroverts.

Lee pushed to her feet. "How do you feel?"

"Okay."

"Marcus."

He sighed down at the carpet. "Tired."

"Physically."

"Yeah."

She supported him to the twin mattress in the corner, adorned with a rainbow-colored handmade quilt. Were all these things donated?

"You do need to see a doctor," she said as she used the pillows to cushion him from the wall. Lying flat still caused pain to his ribs.

"No."

"We have enough cash left for an office visit, X-rays." And little else.

"No." Fatigue dulled his glare.

She'd force the topic later.

In minutes, he was asleep, fluorescent light above them notwithstanding. He half sprawled, head tilted to one side. Lee sat on the air mattress across the room and opened a book, and her soul exhaled its relief. Quiet. Solitude.

Marcus stirred an hour later, as Lee was turning a page. His groggy blinking did something to her heartbeat. *Enough of that.* He hadn't awakened in a defensive posture. Perhaps that was progress, and post-traumatic stress hadn't affected him very much after all.

"Better?" she said when his eyes remained open.

He nodded against the pillow, which had fallen to the level of his neck. "Good book?"

"I wouldn't have brought it otherwise."

Knock-knock—and without pause, the doorknob rattled and the door swung open. Heath's height rose even taller from Lee's place near the floor.

"Howdy, you two. I have call-to-supper duty tonight, so …" When his gaze included Marcus, he froze. Lee turned.

Marcus was curled up, back pressing to the wall. The pillows had fallen around him. His arms covered his head.

"Is he …?" Heath's voice wobbled.

Lee sprang up and dropped to her knees beside the mattress. "Marcus."

Shallow gasps came faster. Marcus stared at her through his arms, eyes too wide, and tried to speak.

Lee's body clenched, restricting her own breath. She had to bring him back. Quickly. Now. How did he help her, when panic and darkness squeezed her chest? She reached a hand to his shoulder, and he didn't pull away.

Heath moved to stand over them both. Marcus shrank away and clutched his chest.

"Heath," Lee said. Calm. Level voice. Be the nurse. Stop the pain. "I need you out of this room."

"Should I call—"

"No. Just go."

The man hesitated, scrubbed a hand over his hair, and left.

"Marcus." She rubbed his hunched shoulder. "Can you hear me?"

He trembled. His arms came up again, shielding his head.

"I'm here. It's Lee. You're all right."

He clenched his teeth against a moan.

Lee rubbed his forearm, then his back. "Shhhhh."

Time passed, minutes that felt like forever. Marcus's arms lowered, but he remained a tight ball. Lee rambled to him without pausing, a gentle flow of words. He'd taught her this aid for flashbacks simply by using it, discovering it brought her back in half the time.

Maybe it didn't work for him. Or maybe, without her voice, he'd be trapped in a loop, assaulted again and again. But his eyes hadn't blanked. He seemed to be here with her while in this state of … whatever it was.

When he lifted his head, confusion gathered between his eyes. "Lee?"

"I'm here."

"What …?"

"Did you experience a flashback?"

He lowered his forehead to his good knee and continued breathing, long and deep. Another minute slipped away. He sat up again, his face still crinkling. "Lee?"

"Yes."

"Are you okay?"

She sighed and withdrew her hand to her lap. "Of course."

"What happened?"

"Do you remember?"

"We were talking about … your book? And then … it was— I wasn't—" His respiration stuttered.

"Heath entered the room. I believe he triggered a flashback somehow. I'm not sure, but you definitely experienced something … traumatic."

"I was here—with you." He gathered the rainbow quilt into his hands and pressed it to his chest.

"Are you in pain?"

"Like—like—but it's not."

She took his pulse at his wrist. Racing, but strong. "Like what, Marcus?"

He shook his head.

If he couldn't explain, she would piece it together herself. "Do you know where we are right now?"

"Texas. Kearby. In the church with the crosses."

"That's correct. We're safe here."

He buried his face in the quilt, then lowered it, his breathing eased. "Safe."

"Mayweather is not here. The Constabulary aren't here and have no authority to come here."

A shudder seized his body. "I know."

"And no one has attacked you here. No one has harmed you in any way. Yet you felt as if someone was … was kicking and beating you. Is that what happened?"

His face reddened.

"Marcus, I need to know. Please. Just tell me yes, or no. Did your body experience the pain despite at least part of you knowing you were here with me, in safety?"

He nodded, looked down, and then his gaze snapped back to hers. "Heath. He saw?"

"He saw very little. I asked him to leave."

Marcus growled. "Go get him."

Wouldn't he rather have time to himself? "Marcus—"

"Lee, please."

She stepped into the hallway and nearly collided with Heath. He was kneeling to one side of the doorway, broad hands gripping his thighs, head bowed, and eyes closed. He looked up at her and opened his mouth to speak. Moving from Marcus's line of sight, she snapped a finger to her lips, motioned Heath to follow, and set off toward the hall windows.

When she reached them, Lee faced the glass, watched the waterfall on the other side. Someone should plant more flowers. Geraniums in that corner near the benches, a wildflower mix in the center, around the reflecting pool.

"Lee, I—"

"Please don't reveal to him that you heard everything. He would be—" Her throat closed.

"Embarrassed?"

"Ashamed."

"Of what?"

She shut her eyes and curled her hands around the railing that jutted out from the wall. The floor sloped here, not drastically, but any elderly person with a cane would appreciate the additional support as much as she did now.

"Did he deny his faith?"

"No." She spit the word up at him. He assumed all shame was born of guilt, of course, which meant he would never understand Marcus.

"I'm not trying to pry, Lee. I'm trying to help."

"By praying, of course."

"Well …" That she'd taken him aback was betrayed in the drawing out of the word, the extra drawl. "Of course."

"And your prayer reached God and mattered to Him, of course." Be calm. Non-combative. She couldn't.

"Absolutely."

"In your prayerful state, it must have escaped your notice that Marcus continued to experience acute pain brought on by a trigger of post-traumatic stress. He didn't experience any mystical relief because you petitioned God."

"No, he didn't."

Heath approached to stand level with her, one hand on the railing, and looked through the windows at the waterfall. He stayed clear of Lee's space, yet she couldn't appreciate even that.

"Do you have any idea …" His voice bounced quietly back from the glass. "What did I do? Did I just startle him, is that all it takes?"

"I don't know."

He looked down at her, his brow puckered. She shouldn't have said that, but the topic change left her with whiplash. A Christian should lob Bible verses at her about God's unfathomable love and the power of prayer.

And she'd just admitted too much. Suppose he went to the church leadership and told them Lee was not a Christian?

None of that mattered right now, though. He was right: she should be able to identify the trigger. Merely being startled … She scrolled back over Marcus's reactions, everything she could remember, even things that had held no significance at the time. All these dots. She had to connect them.

Heath's voice broke into her analysis. "I'm only asking to avoid making the same mistake again."

She shut him out, drew mental lines between the images. "He's lying at floor level."

"Okay …"

Marcus curled on a filthy floor, hearing the lock, the doorknob, the opening door and knowing who was opening it, what was coming next. She shuddered. "Please don't enter the room that way again. Let me open the door for you and say a few words, give him time to process that you aren't … a threat."

"Of course."

Maybe she'd solved the problem, though it was an affliction in his mind, not his body. Perhaps she wouldn't be useless in helping Marcus battle the trauma. Lee swiveled away from Heath, back toward the room. He followed without words. He let Lee precede him inside.

Marcus sat in the folding chair, facing the door. His face was white as a lab coat. Lee tried not to imagine how he'd made it into the chair.

"Heath," he said, before anyone else could speak. "I want to explain."

"That's entirely up to you." Heath pulled up the other chair and sat across from him, well out of his space but now at eye level. He understood. Probably more than Marcus would want him to.

"I …" Marcus's hands shook, and he clenched them on his knees. "I'm okay. I'm not … not …"

Heath waited, but one thing Lee knew. If Marcus had needed twenty-four hours to tell her Aubrey Weston was dead, he would never be able to tell this stranger what he'd endured at Mayweather's hands.

"It's …" He grasped for a deep breath. "I was …"

"Marcus," she said. "Do you wish me to speak for you?"

The question pulled a blush into his cheeks, but the longer he struggled for words of his own, the deeper the shame would dig into him. He nodded.

Heath's eyes didn't stray from Marcus.

Can't you tell he doesn't want to be stared at right now? Lee cleared her throat, but the man's gaze didn't move. "Heath, until eight days ago, Marcus was a prisoner of the Constabulary."

That drew his attention. His mouth became an O. "Eight days ago?"

"He is recovering from pneumonia and malnourishment, in addition to the injuries I told you about."

"How long?"

Not your business.

Heath leaned forward in his chair. "Marcus, is it okay with you if Lee answers that?"

Marcus held his gaze and nodded.

"One hundred thirty-eight days," Lee said. Anything else Heath could have asked, she couldn't have answered. Her chest, her throat, her body was closing in on itself.

This stranger had no right to know anything. But as if they weren't strangers, Heath reached out and clapped a hand over Marcus's.

"Brother," Heath said, and then his words choked off too. His free hand pinched between his eyes a moment, not a headache but … tears? "Brother, thank God you lived. Thank God He delivered you here. I want you to understand, both of you. The Constabulary cannot touch you in this state. You're free now."

A voice bounded down the hallway from the direction of the smells of spaghetti and garlic bread. "Heath?"

Heath released Marcus's hand, stood up, and poked his head out of the doorway. "Juana, one minute, please."

A curvy Mexican woman popped into sight, gripping the hand of a boy who bounced on his feet until his black hair bounced too.

"Oh, I'm sorry to interrupt," she said with a purely Texan twang. "We'll see y'all at supper."

She tugged at the boy's hand, and he called down the hallway as they left. "Pastor Heath, I want you to sit at our table."

Juana's shushing faded into distance.

Heath turned back to them as if no interruption had taken place. As if the boy hadn't just called him … Why hadn't he introduced himself properly? Was he trying to trick Lee somehow?

That was absurd. He hadn't known until a few minutes ago that she wasn't part of his "family."

"Marcus, you up to supper at a table?" Heath offered his shoulder. When Marcus nodded, the man lifted him to his feet.

Soon they were seated at one of the round folding tables with eight other people. Lee told Marcus she'd bring him a plate and scurried after Heath, who was ambling across the gym.

He smiled when he saw her. "Anything y'all need?"

"I need to speak with you. Immediately, please."

He sobered and led her to a corner. The din of dozens of people masked their conversation. Lee forced out the words.

"You are aware that I don't share …" She gestured around the gym. "This. Your faith and, consequently, this status you all hold as …" She searched for the phrase Sonja had used. "Spiritual family."

He nodded. Waited. Did she have to spell it out?

"However, I'm requesting that you allow me to stay. Marcus is … I traveled here with him, and he is my friend."

"Lee." Heath shook his head. "I don't think you understand church very well."

Her heart pounded. *Please.* "I'm a registered nurse. I cook quite well. I can offer my skills to your organization."

"Lee, listen to me."

She held her breath. Waited for her verdict.

"You are welcome here. There's no keep to earn. Okay?"

"I … I don't understand."

"That's clear." He smiled. "Church is not a club. It's a refuge. And yes, it's a light glowing on a lamp stand, and the light is the Truth. You'll hear Truth preached, quite a bit. But what you do with Truth is your choice."

Her choice. To stay or to leave. "I do not bow to Jesus Christ, and I do not love Him. I doubt He would welcome me here."

"Then you need to get to know Him better."

Lee was still frozen when Heath smiled again and meandered away.

Someone shrieked.

Lee spun toward the sound. A pink shirt, blonde hair, white smile—all blurred and rushed her. She was grabbed in a tight embrace.

"Lee, you're here, you're here!"

Lee's arms circled in return. "Hello, Violet."

39

Violet introduced Austin to all of one person before jumping in place, shrieking, and dashing across the gym, weaving between the foldaway tables. He shrugged at the jock-looking black guy she had introduced as Harrison. "She can be unpredictable."

"She's fine," Harrison said.

Austin cocked his head, and Harrison laughed.

"Man, I'm just giving your girl a compliment."

She's not my ... Screw that. "Okay."

Austin scanned the crowd. Violet was hugging someone, blocking his view. They separated, and ... Lee? They weren't supposed to arrive until tomorrow. A smile tugged his mouth.

"Reunion?" Harrison said.

"We had to separate before the border."

"That's cool, man. Glad she made it."

"Thanks. I'm going to go say hi."

He passed tables, habit noting the sort of people at this gathering, but they defied categorization. All ages, all styles of clothing from distressed jeans to business casual. Mostly whites and Hispanics, plus a random minority of other races. He saw guys who looked tough and guys who didn't, but nobody resembling security. As he passed another table, he glanced at the faces and slowed. Marcus Brenner sat with his profile to Austin, nodding at something said by the man on his left.

Marcus looked … well, not *good*, but better. His spine hunched, but he was upright and focused and less pale. More than that, he looked almost at ease.

He would be. He was among like-minded people.

Austin stepped up behind Violet. "Hi, Lee."

"Hello." Her mouth curved.

"When did you get in?"

"This afternoon. Have you eaten?"

"Just walked in." He gestured to his damp hair. "We were out most of the day, familiarizing ourselves with Kearby, and I wanted to hit the shower before dinner."

"Marcus will be glad to see you." Lee gestured to the table, then hesitated. "I'm glad, as well."

"Marcus?" Violet's thumb rubbed her wrist.

Lee glanced at Violet's hands, then back up to her face. "Is something wrong?"

"N-no. It's great. That he's up and around, I mean. Come on, let's get plates. The garlic bread smells amazing."

They let Lee go first. When she returned to the table with a plate in each hand—one mostly spaghetti, the other mostly salad—Violet tapped Austin's shoulder.

"I can't do it."

"Do what?"

She didn't answer. Austin mounded meatballs onto his plate and spooned marinara sauce over them. Noodles were for sissies—not literally, but they were mostly pointless. He grabbed the salad tongs. Violet piled her plate with spaghetti, finding the cheesiest sections in the center of the warming pan. Her shoulders hunched as if she'd felt a draft.

"Violet, what can't you do?"

"Go over there. I thought he'd be in bed. I can't eat dinner with him like—like he's fine and I'm innocent."

Austin shook his head. "So you'll never talk to him again?"

"Right now I'll give it away. My face, I mean, and he'll ask if I'm okay, and then ..."

"If you leave, they're going to be suspicious."

Her plate teetered on her hand. "You're right."

"Try to relax. He'll be glad to see you. He won't notice anything." Unless he'd already connected the dots. "Do you want to just tell him? Together?"

She shook her head. "I'm keeping this secret until I die."

They found seats at Lee and Marcus's table, and Austin tried to respond to all the greetings while keeping one eye on Marcus. *If he says anything to hurt her, I'll ...* What? Make a scene? No worries, though. When Marcus saw them both, worn crinkles appeared around his eyes, a version of a smile.

Violet was, despite what Austin had told her, the ultimate impetus for Marcus's arrest. Thanks to Austin, Marcus had the pieces to put that together. He wasn't stupid. He should not smile at the sight of her. Or ask about their trip and how they'd been.

Then again, this wasn't the first time Marcus had responded to a situation ... confusingly.

And at least Austin didn't have to hit a guy with broken ribs.

The dinner conversation evolved into travel stories, and Austin's gut knotted around the meatballs. What could they say? That they would've been busted in Illinois, but Austin's Constabulary badge saved the day? That they'd been robbed over the Oklahoma line, and Violet had had a nightmare about it last night?

A convenient thing about most people, though—if they were talking about themselves, they often didn't realize you weren't talking about you. Especially people who were only now able to tell their stories without fear. The voices around the table didn't take turns, pause, ask questions. They poured over and around each other. Everyone listened, yes, but no one thought to prod others into sharing. When forks clanked empty plates, Austin sighed.

Lee had gone more silent than usual, and her mouth crimped every time she slanted a look at Marcus. Austin shifted his attention from the strangers to his companions. There were only tiny giveaways—the pallor and tightness around Marcus's mouth, the way he gripped the edge of the table, hand concealed by his plate. A few minutes later, Lee stood up.

"I'm rather tired," she said. "Marcus, would you walk me back to the rooms?"

Austin sat back in his chair and tried to signal her. *Do you need help with him?*

She gave a slight shake of her head.

Marcus looked up at her. "It's okay."

Lee frowned but waited for him. He looked around at all of them and straightened in his chair.

"I hurt my knee, and it's still … mending. So Lee helps me walk."

He had to know these people had read the aftermath of illness written on his face, on his body. They knew an injured knee was the least of it. Someone would ask. But instead, a tension unnoticeable before now lifted from everyone, and voices chimed together.

"Anything you need?"

"I can help you get back to your room, if you …"

"You should talk to Yvette, there's some first aid supplies …"

Lee spoke over all of them. "Thank you. We will be fine."

Collective disappointment sighed. These people took it seriously, solidarity against persecution or whatever they called it. Brotherhood, family.

Relational conditioning.

For a few seconds after Lee supported Marcus away from the table, silence reigned.

"You came with them, right?" The question came from Becca, a middle-aged brunette who had spoken to Marcus several times as if they were personal acquaintances.

Austin nodded.

"Is he …? I don't know how to ask this."

"He's recovering."

The group seemed to lean forward for more. Austin stood. "Excuse me."

He caught Violet's gaze, tilted an eyebrow. She offered half a smile. "I'll talk to you later."

He nodded and strode away. Hopefully, he could catch Lee alone, once she'd settled Marcus.

He found her in the classroom hallway beside a closed door, propped up by the wall, head tilted back. She sensed him coming and straightened, then relaxed when she saw him.

"How is he?"

"Resting."

"Okay. Good."

She twisted her fingers together, then lowered them back to her sides. "Yes."

"But he's … fine?"

"No."

"I meant relatively."

Lee pushed away from the wall and walked away from him. He ought to let her go, and he would, but first he followed her. She shot a glare over her shoulder and quickened her pace.

"I need to ask you something," Austin said before she could break into a gallop.

She didn't slow. "Perhaps another time."

"Violet wants me to tell them everything."

Lee stopped.

"She isn't objective about them," he said.

"I would agree."

"I told her no. But I was trained on a psychological model that links religious zeal to impulsive violence. I don't know that I'm objective either. I was hoping for a … fair evaluation."

"From me."

"You haven't been indoctrinated by anyone."

Lee started walking again. Maybe she had an actual destination. She navigated the forked hallways back toward the gym and ignored everyone they passed. Her taut shoulders contradicted her blank expression.

He should let her go. But he couldn't.

Lee halted outside the kitchen. From the other side of the swinging door, dishes clattered and people talked and laughed. Before Austin could ask, she gestured to the door. "I came to volunteer for cleanup."

Oh. He should do the same. This aid mission didn't run itself. But …

Lee faced him with her soldier stance, hands behind her back.

"My opinion is based on acquaintanceship with several Christians in my lifetime, mostly through my job, as well as allowing Violet to live with me, as well as over ten years of friendship with Marcus. He has been a Christian less than four years, so I'm able to compare his lifestyles before and after."

Right. That was Austin's point. He nodded.

"My rejection of Christianity is not in any way linked to my interaction with Christians. In most instances, they have treated me with respect and even compassion. They are as safe and stable as anyone else."

"So you would tell them … everything."

"No, I probably wouldn't."

What?

"But not because of fear." Lee pushed the kitchen door open and stepped through it.

Thanks, Lee, so helpful.

40

She did not belong here.

Lee commandeered the sink, and no one tried to argue. Dish duty seemed last on everyone's list, which made it the most appropriate task for her. She let the water scald her hands while their buoyant voices flowed around her. Family talk. A nephew going into medical school, an aspiring painter winning an art contest, a newlywed couple closing on a house—all announcements were met with joy from the others. Lee scrubbed plates and silverware.

They didn't talk to her. She didn't talk to them.

A phone vibrated on the counter, nearest to Lee. No one else heard the buzz. She shut off the water, dried her hands, and picked it up.

"Who does this belong to?"

"Oh, that's Heath's." Juana leaned out the doorway to bellow into the gym. "Heath! You left your phone in here!"

She took it from Lee as it stopped buzzing, and Lee began to wash a ceramic serving dish, stenciled with leaves and caked with cheese.

Heath plowed through the doorway, and Juana handed him his phone. "Thanks. I had it in my hand when it was time to bring out the food trays. Got distracted. Y'all look sudsy and busy."

"The sudsy one is …" Juana gestured. "I'm sorry, I don't know your name."

"Lee."

"Lee volunteered to do the dishes, so of course, we let her."

Heath grinned at them, but his eyes held something else for Lee. Knowledge. She tried not to bristle against it.

"How's your friend?" one of the women said. Oh, right, she'd shared a table with Lee at dinner. Rachel, wasn't it? "His knee okay and … everything?"

Marcus was certainly asleep. He'd collapsed against her as soon as Lee shut the door to their room. She would have intervened sooner at dinner if she'd realized how fast his energy was draining. She pushed away the memory from less than an hour ago—the labored sound of his breathing, the fatigue that weighted his limbs to the bed, his pained whisper. *"Tired."*

"He's fine."

"My husband and I, we'll pray for him," Rachel said. "Whatever's affecting his health, that God will be with him and work out His will."

Crack.

The serving dish lay in the sink, broken in half, her hands still gripping it.

Everyone was still, and then everyone moved. Toward Lee. Gaping.

"Oh, no, Juana, your dish …"

"That was my mom's."

Lee lifted her wet hands and backed away from the sink. "I apologize."

Juana's dark eyes pinned her, welling with tears. "She gave it to me for—"

Lee charged through the group of women without touching anyone. *Let me out.* They did. She collided with the swinging door and emerged into the hallway, empty for the moment. She dried her hands on her jeans as she ran to the closest red-lit exit sign and hit the crash bar. The door opened into a parking lot. Lee stumbled over the cement divider between sidewalk and blacktop. To her right was the street Graham had parked on. She walked around the corner of the building. She sank onto the cement steps where she'd sat with Marcus, mere hours ago. The sun that had warmed their faces dipped to the horizon now, touching the leaves and the grass with a pink glow.

Lee lowered her head to her knees and inhaled composure from the warm evening air.

They would think she'd fled in mortification or remorse. Over broken ceramic.

She pressed her hand to her right ribs, one after the other, lingering at each location of a break in Marcus's body.

"... and work out His will."

She couldn't reside here, couldn't converse with them or even look at them without wanting to scream. She lifted her head from her knees.

Heath stood in front of her.

He might have been looking for her, but the wide unblinking eyes hadn't expected to find her here on the steps.

Unlike socially normal people, Heath didn't mumble an apology and walk away. He stood gazing down at her, took one step forward, and stopped. He squatted down to sit on the curb, a safe two bodies' lengths away. His knees stuck up almost to his chin.

"Juana knows it was only a dish."

"Fine."

"She's not going to hold a grudge over an object, Lee."

"Good."

Heath propped his arms on his knees. "You didn't escape because of that, did you?"

"I wasn't escaping."

He nodded and said nothing. All right, then, they could sit in silence. Lee pretended to watch the shadows of the trees lengthen. Heath seemed competent in nonverbal communication. Eventually, he would get the point.

He stretched out his legs and crossed his ankles. "What was it that angered you? Rachel's asking about Marcus, or what she said about God?"

She glared.

"You're right, I usually get to know someone for a week or two before I pry about their philosophical views."

"I'm not interested in this discussion." Since he wasn't comprehending subtlety.

He didn't answer. Sitting on the curb couldn't be comfortable, but he didn't look inclined to move. He watched a breeze whisper in the tree limbs above him. Formulating his debate, no doubt.

He drew his knees up again. "Are you an atheist, Lee?"

"No."

"What sort of God do you believe in, then?"

"Yours, I suppose. More or less."

That earned her a cocked eyebrow. "Yet you approach church entirely *quid pro quo*, and the mention of God's will makes you break dishes."

Lee gritted her teeth against his easygoing persistence, against the boiling that must not come out.

"Why don't you want to discuss it? Whatever your views, you're not going to offend me."

Oh, really? Lee leaned forward for the first blow. "Your God is a perpetrator of evil and a sadist."

Heath didn't stand up to rail at her irreverence. He didn't wince and walk away. His face remained smooth and accepting. Fine. She'd hardly begun her attack.

"You preach that He is omnipotent and good. Yet you look at someone who has suffered torture for Him and call it His will. You pray, and when you are ignored, call it His will."

Heath crossed his ankles and sat back, hands flat on the concrete, nothing defensive in his pose. Invitation or not, her words were on an automatic trigger now and he deserved every one of them.

"Your blind acceptance of His actions is repulsive."

"So," Heath said before she could continue, "since evil exists, God must be evil."

"It's a logical conclusion."

"No, it isn't."

Lee's neck prickled. She pulled her heels against the base of the cement step.

"It presupposes too much. For example, you don't allow any motivation for God's restraint other than sadism. And with prayer, you don't allow any outcome to be greater, better, than human desire."

Neatly argued, shifting burden of proof from his beliefs to Lee's, matching vocabulary with her. The Texas twang had caused her to underestimate his education. She wouldn't fall into that again.

She had debated this with Marcus for years, and he had never been able to articulate a rebuttal. Not that articulation was his strong suit. But she'd asked the question of other Christians, too—years ago, when they could legally respond—and they utilized platitudes, which signified they couldn't answer any other way. Heath wouldn't be able to either.

He just did, didn't he?

She could refute him, though, shift the burden of proof back.

"Why did God create us, Lee?"

Was he changing the subject? "To observe us. A cosmic theater of sorts. The universe entertains Him."

"And Jesus?"

Lee's jaw tightened. "What of Him?"

"Well, you said you believe in my God. My God is a Trinity."

"Upon Marcus's conversion, I conducted historical research of the first century, focusing on primary source material. I encountered obstacles in categorizing Jesus Christ as merely human. He likely is a form or representation of God."

Another eyebrow arc. "Really."

"Even if your belief system is true, and He paid for sins, it doesn't remove the moral problem with allowing sins in the first place."

"Okay. But it does mean we weren't created for God's entertainment. The theatergoer doesn't get up onstage and join in the drama. And he definitely doesn't pay the bill if the actors go on a rampage and damage the set."

Lee pushed up with her hands and feet to sit one step higher. "Fine. If Jesus Christ is God, then our purpose would be …"

"To have a relationship with God. Jesus makes that possible, and the Bible repeatedly states that God desires a relationship with us. With Adam and Eve, with Israel, with His church."

Adam and Eve? He was shameless, bringing obvious mythology into the discussion. "Are you attempting to distract me from the issue?"

"Not at all."

Heath stood and stretched, but not for a moment did he appear to consider walking away. He brushed his hand against the leaves above him, then sat on the grass easement this time, cross-legged, facing her.

"I'm not going to tell you evil is necessary for good to exist. Some people make that statement, and I don't accept that, because it would mean something was intrinsically wrong, missing, from God's original act of creation that He calls 'good.' But being God, He can use evil's existence for whatever purpose He chooses. And He chooses to use it, in part, to enhance our relationship with Him."

She rolled her eyes. *You see, Heath, that doesn't even merit a verbal response.*

"We can stop talking about this now, if you want."

Did he think she was intimidated? She leaned forward and curled her hands around her ankles. "You cannot make a logical case for that assertion."

"Some things are defined by what they are, some things by what they're not, and some things by both."

Fine. She'd let him tie this noose and hang his argument to death. "Such as?"

"Light is illumination. It's also the absence of darkness. If darkness didn't exist, our human minds couldn't explain light or have any real concept of its existence."

"The same with heat." Help him out. Accelerate the defeat.

"Right. If there's no cold, then what? Heat is just a constant state without degrees, without definition."

"Those are scientific properties." *And you're not as intelligent as you think you are, if this hasn't occurred to you.*

"Well, what about freedom, then? Would you be aware of freedom if no one had ever experienced chains? Would you be aware of compassion if no one had ever behaved cruelly?"

He'd prepared that snare, and she'd stepped into it. Time to regroup. At least he had distracted her. Her intellect worked now, quieting the emotions that twisted her stomach. She held in a relieved sigh.

She didn't have an instant rebuttal for him, though. His debate skills were honed. Defeating him would be more satisfying for that fact. She let him continue.

"God didn't want us to be unaware, Lee. He wanted a relationship with beings that could comprehend their own multifaceted existence. And He gave us free will knowing what that gift would do but also knowing how He would redeem it all. Our depraved choices put His mercy on display, when we accept it."

"I don't agree," she said.

"Don't agree with what? That God wanted us to be aware? Or that evil enhances our awareness of good?"

Both. But … no, if God hadn't wanted Lee to be self-aware, then she wouldn't be. *Violet said that. Something like it.*

Heath leaned forward, onto his knees. "Can you consider that what I've described to you might be reality?"

Possibly. After all … "It's convenient for God, isn't it? A way to justify anything He does to us."

"So you believe God has to justify Himself to you?"

He was putting words in her mouth. *Not entirely. Your statement does imply that.* She gritted her teeth.

"Because now we have a different conversation. If God has to justify Himself to you, then why bother calling Him 'God'?"

"I simply want Him to make sense." Too much rancor in her voice. Dial down. Intellect, not emotion.

"No, Lee. That's not what you want."

"Excuse me?"

"Everything I just said to you did make sense, or you would have called me out and knocked my argument flat."

Her stomach knotted. She lined up their two views. God as the Viewer of the cosmic play, jeering and throwing rubbish, preferring the human carnage. Or God as the … well, Father … wanting communion with people who chose to commune with Him because they preferred it to estrangement, because they comprehended estrangement.

"I'm going to push the boundaries a little bit here and tell you what I think you want."

Heath, be quiet.

"You want God to subject Himself to your will. You've decided that what happened to Marcus isn't just wrong—it's a wrong perpetrated by God Himself. And you won't forgive Him for it."

Nausea welled in her throat. "Marcus should have been spared."

"He was."

She pressed a hand to her stomach. Battled the flood of everything she had done in the last week, fending off Marcus's fever and his exhaustion and his pain. Fending off his death.

"I'm not saying he didn't suffer, isn't still suffering. I'm saying he's alive. He's healing, he's safe, he's free here."

The gentle voice stabbed her head, turned her stomach.

"I don't know how you and Marcus got here, but you can't convince me God had no hand in it."

The agent shaking Marcus's bad knee … and Marcus fast asleep.

"He should have …"

"Done more? What would be enough for you?"

Violet's question.

"Would you be willing to submit to Him if Marcus had never experienced any pain in his whole life? What about the rest of the world, they don't matter to you?"

I'm a nurse, Heath. They all matter to me.

"Lee. Look at me."

She wouldn't. She shut her eyes.

He waited.

This was absurd. She wasn't a child. She opened her eyes and tried to glare and probably failed, because her stomach still wanted to turn itself inside out.

"Talk to God," Heath said. "Tell Him all of this."

She had to clear her throat, but then her voice was level. "He's aware of my thought processes."

"Not to inform Him."

"For what purpose, then?"

"I can't answer that one. Just tell Him." He stood up and smiled at her. Then he turned and walked back into the church.

Lee pressed her hands to her mouth and closed her eyes.

Something touched her back.

She jolted to her feet, jumped off the step, and turned. She reached back to brush a hand over her shoulders. Nothing there. Perhaps it hadn't been a tactile sensation so much as … She shivered. *You want me to speak about these things to You?*

"Then I will not," she whispered.

41

"Not because of fear."

Austin let Lee's words propel him forward, into the glassed-in conference room. Identifying the organization's leadership had been impossible. No one used titles. Eventually, he'd asked someone random to point out a staff member ("you mean a church member? Sara is"), and he'd asked the church member to point out someone in leadership. She had pursed her lips, ticked options silently on her fingers, and then said, "I'm pretty sure Walt is here right now. As long as we're housing y'all, we're constantly rotating, but I think I saw him less than an hour ago."

So strangers didn't have the run of the building. The church was being subtle about it, but they recognized the need for supervision. That showed more sense than Austin had been giving them credit for. Probably more sense than he'd seen displayed at Elysium, which taught that people were too inherently sinless to rob you or harm your children.

When he stepped into the conference room, a man with a fringe of white hair and beard stood up from the long table. He offered a smile more cautious than welcoming. Good for him.

"Sara said you have information, and you asked to speak with an elder."

"You make decisions for the church?" Austin didn't let himself shift on his feet.

"I and others, yes. A board, elected by the members."

Good enough. Austin nodded.

"Walton Cantrell." He stepped forward and held out his hand.

Austin shook it firmly. *See, I'm not a kid.* "Austin Delvecchio. Sir, I don't want you to discover this later and feel deceived. Actually, if I don't tell you, you *will* have been deceived."

Walton didn't prod. He also didn't reassure Austin that his sins were between him and God, and no one needed to tell anyone anything. This man seemed to be a sensible leader. Still, Austin's mouth was dry. He cleared his throat against the silence, dug his wallet from his back pocket and held it out, open.

Walton backed up a step, stared from the badge to Austin's face and back again.

"Michigan Constabulary. I'm an agent. I have no authority here, obviously, but back home, this is who I ..." Am? Was? Would he ever have a word to finish that sentence?

"What are you doing here?" Walton's voice was carefully level.

"I don't know if you've met Violet DuBay, but I came with her and—"

"Violet? Does she know what you are?"

Something tightened in Austin's face, in his gut. "She pushed me to tell you. She said you wouldn't turn me out."

There it lay between them, exposed, both of them knowing the test for what it was, tasting the flavor of manipulation. *Don't let me do it, Walton. Prove you're smarter than that.*

By turning him out? Was that what he wanted?

"I believe Violet mentioned more than one traveling companion," Walton said.

So the girl had shared her biography with everyone here. "There are four of us."

"I'll be honest. You seem to be trying to do the same. I don't understand how Christians accepted traveling with a Constabulary agent. Even once you'd left Michigan, you could have turned them in to any state at any time."

And why he hadn't was one of the things he'd sort out when he got to Australia. "They've known for the entire trip. How it happened is … a long, unpleasant story. But I have no intention of causing trouble here. I can't legally, anyway."

Walton eyed him, crossed the room, and turned back around. "Are you armed?"

"Not right now."

The pistol nestled under his left arm, snug, safe, concealed by the loose-fitting shirt he'd shrugged over a crew-neck tee, left unbuttoned. Violet's eyes would grow sad if she knew about the lie, but he wasn't walking a plank even for her.

Best case scenario, Walton was armed and would try to put him down. Simple solution, final answers. He'd have a case to cite when he told Violet not to trust these people. He'd have a reason to walk away from Christians and their incomprehensible belief system. Maybe even a reason to go home, stop Jason somehow, and get back to work.

On the minus side, he might have to shoot somebody's grandfather.

And lose his girl.

Walton studied him a moment, nodded, folded his arms. "I respect your decision to come forward."

Part of Austin wanted to sigh his relief, and part of him wanted to smack the wall. "I assume you don't want me to stay the night."

"You're not asking to join our membership. You're asking for food and shelter."

"Actually, I'm informing you of the fact you've had a Constabulary agent in your church for a few hours, and he might be back around occasionally to visit his friends. With your permission."

"You have no money, son." Walton's eyes smiled, though his mouth remained tense.

How could he …? Austin huffed. "Violet."

"You're welcome to stay tonight. Long term, I'm not sure what we'll decide. There is, of course, freedom here to put your past behind you and have it kept private. There's also the fact that you represent—not saying you still are, but you represent—a vivid, real threat to many folks here. Seems they shouldn't be kept in the dark about it, find out by accident later … what have you. But I guess we'll deal with all that another day."

Austin stopped his hand halfway to mussing his hair. "So you can make the call to give me a bed tonight."

"Make the call?"

"It's not something that needs a vote?"

Walton chuckled. "Jesus wouldn't turn you out on the street because of your past. None of my fellow elders would expect me to either."

How odd.

"I assume your service weapon is with your other belongings."

The lie itched now. He nodded.

"And you'll respect our property and leave it there."

"Of course."

"I don't feel the need to force this issue, son, because your gun isn't the only one on the premises."

The man lifted his suit jacket. A silver handle jutted from a leather holster at his hip.

"It isn't common knowledge, but you're somewhat of an uncommon stranger."

These people were sensible, after all. *But he didn't pull on you, even thinking you were unarmed.*

"Thank you, sir." For several things.

"You're welcome, Austin."

42

She couldn't remember all their names. Faces blurred in front of her as the travelers, gathered in the youth lounge, looked up at her. Some of them sprawled on faux leather sofas with wide cushioned arms. Several played foosball in a far corner.

"Come on in, join the party," someone said.

Lee searched for a familiar face, someone she could ask. There, by the coffee machines—Juana of the broken dish. Lee steeled her nerve and crossed to Juana.

"Hi, Lee." Her smile looked ready to bolt for cover.

"Marcus isn't in our room. I thought he might be here, but ..." But he had been exhausted less than two hours ago.

"Oh, right. Will took him outside or something."

Will? "I don't understand."

"Hey, Will!" Juana beckoned to a slim ponytailed redhead who looked to be in his twenties. "Where's Marcus?"

"At the park."

They must have a friend named Marcus. Lee kept her tone level. "I'm speaking of a new arrival, a fugitive. Brown hair and eyes ..." *Five-foot-eleven, muscular, broad shoulders ...* She cleared her throat. "He was injured recently. He's ... thin."

Will nodded. "Yup. Marcus Brenner."

He was waiting for her confirmation. "Yes."

"He said he wanted to be outside for a little while, so I got one of the wheelchairs from the closet, and then he asked if there was a park somewhere. It's not even a ten-minute walk, so I took him over there and gave him my cell number in case he needed anything, and for whenever he's ready to come back."

The room spun, but a deep breath steadied it. "Marcus shouldn't be outdoors at this time of day."

"He told me he got sick awhile back. But he said he's okay now."

Of course he did. Lee clenched her teeth.

"Are you Lee?"

"I am."

"Yeah, he said you might come looking for him."

"If he wanted to tour the park, why didn't he text me?"

"Well …" Will shrugged. "He said you'd been traveling a few days, close quarters and stuff. And you could both use a break."

True, under normal circumstances. "What direction is the park?"

Juana was moving away from the conversation. Before Will could answer, Lee turned to her. "Thank you for your help."

"No problem."

"And I apologize for damaging your property."

Juana blinked, then gave a small smile. "I know you didn't mean to."

Intention was irrelevant. The dish was broken. Lee tried not to stare at her. "I … thank you."

Before the moment could become more awkward for either one of them, Juana gave a quick nod and walked away.

A few minutes later, Lee slipped on her ivory jacket, pocketed her phone, and set out. Will's directions were easily followed, and soon she strode up the dirt path to enter the public park. Dusk would fall soon. She had to get Marcus back to the church.

She ignored the playground and processed the rest of her options. Will wouldn't have taken him far from the entrance. Picnic tables sat at random in a small clearing, and she walked from one end to the other, but he wasn't there. Her chest began to tighten. She texted him. *I'm at the park. Where are you?*

She sat on a bench and waited. No response.

Anything could have happened to him.

She headed for the nature path. Marcus would have been drawn to the canopy of trees over the wood-chip walkway.

The park must not close at dusk, because this path was already lit on both sides with small globe lanterns, hanging by chains from three-foot shepherd's hooks. Should she call out? Lee fast-walked, peering ahead.

A wheelchair stood in the grass, several feet to the left of the path. Empty.

Lee ran.

His voice reached her as she neared. "And for the Bible. I didn't think Violet would still have it. And for the food tonight. There was so much."

Where was he?

There. Lee froze.

Marcus lay a few feet from the wheelchair, his right arm under his ribs, his face toward the ground, his left arm keeping him raised mere inches above the grass. His good knee bent slightly. His other knee held none of his weight.

"And for the water. And the ice cubes. And the beds. And the blankets. And for the windows in the church. For the light. God—" His voice broke. "Oh, God, all the light everywhere."

A quake began in Lee's feet, spread up her legs.

"I—I think that's everything from today, Jesus." Marcus coughed, and his arm tightened against his side. "Thank You for it."

She marched off the path, and her feet made barely a swish in the trimmed grass. He gave no sign of hearing her. Lee stopped a few feet away, relaxed her shoulders and clenched her hands.

"Get up," she said.

Marcus jolted, pushed up on his good knee. "Lee."

"The ground is cooling. You'll become chilled." Her voice sounded digital and dead.

He leveraged up from the ground and knelt with all his weight on one knee. "I'm staying here."

"You completed your list of gratitude. You're ill. You need to come with me."

"No."

"Fine."

She wasn't going back to the church. She would take the last of their money, walk to a hotel, and go to bed. He could shiver out here all night in his devotion to God, and in the morning he would shiver with fever, and Violet and Heath and everyone else would pray for God's will, and when Marcus was dead in the ground they would speak of heaven and God's will. She walked back to the path and followed it out of the trees. A cricket's chirp silenced to her right as she passed it.

She reached the edge of the path and stopped. Behind her, many yards distant, a slow crunching of wood chips came not from footsteps but rolling wheels. The sound stopped often, then restarted.

She turned back and met him past midway. He panted, arms and body straining.

"Have you thanked God for the wheelchair?"

Marcus stared up at her, the waning light throwing a shadow over half his face. "What?"

"For the phlegm that clogged your lungs and the pain every time you had to cough it up? For the boot that kicked your ribs until they broke? After all, how could you comprehend being rescued from Mayweather unless he first beat you nearly to death?"

A muscle jumped in his jaw. "Don't do this."

"I'm only calling on you to be consistent. Bow your face to the ground and thank God for the Holocaust, Marcus. Thank God for every time a child has been molested. Thank God that I was attacked and raped in a parking garage."

He closed his eyes. "Lee."

Deep in her chest, something pricked. But if she tried to find it, identify it, control would be lost. "Do you want to pace while you try to form a response? Stand up and pace. If God isn't cruel, He won't let your knee give out."

Marcus gripped the arms of the wheelchair and leaned forward. "Stop."

Heat poured through her body. She felt nothing, because logic had regained the upper hand. Marcus wouldn't be able to refute her words.

"This isn't about me," Marcus said.

"Clearly, it is."

"This is you. And God. Just like always." His eyes burned into her, steady, unflinching.

"No. We're discussing your determination to thank a God that left you to be—"

"He did not leave me." Marcus pushed halfway out of the chair, both feet on the path.

"You were—"

"No. You listen to me."

His gaze held hers, and the prick became a pang. The heat, the words, sputtered in her chest.

"God was there. Every minute. With me."

"And prevented nothing."

Marcus slammed a fist against the arm of the chair. "No. Hate God on your own. Spit in His face every day for the rest of your life. But don't you use me for your new excuse."

Use him? Her pulse throbbed. "I know you. And I know God should have spared you."

"You don't know anything about it. Anything. You weren't there."

He pushed the rest of the way to his feet. He swayed, then steadied. He stared down at her from his full height, the first time he'd stood over her since … before. His shoulders hunched, the shirt hung on his frame, yet his physical presence wasn't diminished.

The heat inside Lee, fueling the words, sputtered a final time and went out. "I would never use you."

"Then stop throwing pill bottles and looking at me like I'm dying."

"You were."

"Stop blaming God for the things people choose."

Lee's insides hollowed. Nothing left.

His body folded down into the wheelchair. "Will said he'd come get me."

She couldn't move.

"You can go," he said, as if his first dismissal hadn't been clear.

She nodded. She set off away from him, toward the exit. When she reached the gate outside, sporadic traffic sounds whirring past the tree line, she veered left into the woods.

The trees grew denser here, untrimmed. No lanterns, no wood chips. Fireflies winked around her, some near, most distant. In her hollowness, Marcus's words ricocheted and resounded. His grip on his God had been strengthened. It didn't make sense.

And how could such a rift grow between them that he would permit a stranger to see his weakness before he let her help him?

You attacked him.

The prone reverence. The sacrifice of pain. The halting, verbal exposure of his heart.

She had charged roughshod over all of it and then mocked it, her blood boiling so high she couldn't see Marcus at all and didn't care to. Lee sank to her knees among the old wood and green leaves. Her stomach balled up.

"Why?" she whispered.

A firefly winked beside her hand. The leaves high over her head whispered back. She shivered. The park was growing colder. She should have left Marcus her jacket, at least to cover his chest. But she hadn't thought of that, either.

"Was it emotion?" She gripped her shoulders with the opposite hands. "He said I'm angry."

Was she angry?

A roaring in her ears and a wash of red over her vision rocked her forward. "I wound him. Always him, the deepest."

Perhaps the dark confinement had taught him not only to hold more tightly to his God but also to hold less tightly to her. Perhaps she had, minutes ago, ended ten years of friendship without seeing it. And she could not blame him. She could only blame herself.

"Stop blaming God for the things people choose."

"I won't," she whispered. "I'll blame You endlessly. I'll hold You responsible."

For all the sins of the world.

"Yes." She pushed to her feet and leaned her head back. "You stand by. You do nothing."

Except walk onto the stage and pay for the damages.

"It does not absolve You."

No, Lee, it absolves you.

Her shoulders prickled. That was only a thought of her own mind. Nothing more. But a shiver was racing along her spine. She backed against a tree.

"You …"

It was not God Who wounded Marcus just now. Her own blind rage had done that. But consistently, logically, she could not accept the guilt of one action without accepting …

All of it. She ducked her head. If God was not responsible for the sins of the world … if she could not hold court over God and morally judge Him … and the image of that flashed in her head with such clear foolishness: she, Lee Vaughn, hitting a gavel and shouting out a sentence and still calling Him God, still claiming His omnipotence though He stood before her acquiescent to her ruling.

She pushed away from the tree. "You should have …"

The words died in her throat. She could not make decrees that bound Him.

So His decrees bound her.

Lee locked her knees. Drowning. Guilty. And God, everywhere, inescapable, pure authority like white fire.

Her knees gave out. Her arms covered her head. *I see You. And I can't bear it.* Lee huddled but couldn't be small enough. He saw her, too. She shook, hands tight against her sick stomach.

"Talk to God."

I can't, Heath.

But something else prodded her, too. *Speak.*

"I am guilty. Of too many things."

It wasn't enough. She choked. She curled up until her forehead touched the grass. She held her barren belly.

"I killed my daughter."

Tears.

"She thrashed and stopped. She died inside me because I chose her death."

The tears fell into the grass. She lifted herself a few inches from the ground, and more tears fell onto her knees.

Her stomach settled as the tears drained out of her. She sat up and leaned against the tree. Bark pressed into her spine. Around her, fireflies danced, crickets resumed their music, and a chilling wind gusted like a long-pent breath, then died back down.

"If …" She strained for a deep breath. "If I asked for absolution … would You give it to me?"

Of course, Marcus and Violet and Heath—everyone—would tell her to ask. Would tell her she'd never be denied. But none of them knew the selfishness that curled in the deepest pit of her. None of them knew that her hand had willingly signed for her baby's death. None of them knew how she'd railed at God, when she spoke to Him at all, over the last twelve years. And for the last four months.

"I don't see how You could possibly pardon me at this juncture."

Lee strained to hear, to sense, but nothing prodded inside her. The fire of Him had receded. Was that her answer?

"It's only reasonable, I see that." But a desolate pain wormed into her chest. "I suppose this ends our … encounter."

For a moment, she couldn't fill her lungs. Her eyes burned. For her own condemnation? She hardly deserved tears. She forced the deep breath and pushed to her feet. She would return to the church. To Marcus. If he would allow it.

43

Violet didn't ask much, only a quick "Well?"

Austin wanted to commend her restraint. Not blurting his life story to this group of people—definite progress for her. He flashed a thumbs-up, and she smiled.

About a dozen sojourners had gathered in a lounge off the gym, walls painted the clashing colors of toffee and mustard, to chat or play foosball or blackjack. The leather couches were set up around rustic wooden tables, exuding a coffee-shop aura. One was spread with an oversized checkerboard. On the other sat, no kidding, two leather-bound books. Gilded words on each spine claimed, *Holy Bible.*

"I wonder how old those are," Violet had whispered when she first noticed them. "The one's kind of worn out, but the other one looks newer than mine. Marcus's. Whosever."

She had inherited Marcus's Bible? They needed a long talk involving full faith disclosure. Though Violet wouldn't guess that, given his nonresponse to the topic so far.

And anyway, why do you care?

Because he was her protection.

Except he watched her introduce herself to people of all ages, guys and girls, warming them with her smile, with the care in her eyes, and … really, the protection detail was obsolete now.

He joined a game of foosball instead of thinking about that.

Half an hour later, his phone buzzed in his pocket.

"Score!" yelled his teammate, whose name he hadn't bothered to ask. "Good reflexes, man."

"Yup." Austin spun the goalie rod. "I'm out."

"We've got to finish crushing these guys."

Really? It was foosball. "Might be back."

But this was probably Esther, so he might be an hour. She still owed him a catching-up, and Esther didn't abbreviate stories. He hurried to accept the call before it went to voicemail. He wandered toward the lounge doors. Too much noise in here. "Hey, middle sis."

"Austin?"

"Livvy? You'd better not let Esther catch you on—"

Her breathing shuddered.

Austin's feet froze in the middle of the room. His pulse jumped into overdrive. "Liv, what's wrong?"

"D-D-Daddy said—" She sobbed.

"Livvy." His hands were shaking already. Adrenaline overload. Just from hearing Olivia say that word. "What did he do?"

"It was an accident."

"Olivia! What did he do?"

Quiet crying.

Hand on his arm. He jolted and spun, ready for defense. Violet's eyes widened. The lounge had hushed. The foosball game had stopped. Austin fought to process both, the people around him and the people on the other end of the phone call—far away, helpless. The effort curled his free hand into a fist.

He gulped in a breath. The ugly walls seemed to be shrinking while Olivia cried.

"Baby, put Esther on the phone."

"Esther …" Another sob.

Austin couldn't get his breath. Violet took his hand and pulled him to the door, and his legs followed her while he fought images he couldn't yet know were true. He had to have the facts, not his imagination.

Violet pushed him to a corner, near the swinging doors. More privacy. No one would hear him now unless they stood right here, and he'd see them coming.

"Your sisters?" she whispered.

Somehow, he nodded.

"I'll be over there," Violet whispered and pointed at the couches. "I'm going to pray."

Right, because in the course of their journey, he'd told her things. She knew what could have happened. Well, she could pray if she wanted to. In case it would help. He shut his eyes and took stock of his body while Olivia's weeping pushed his heartbeat higher. Dry mouth, shaking hands, hot face. *Get a grip, man.*

"Olivia, I need you to talk. Say something."

"Esther's going to the h-hospital, but it was an accident."

He was going to be sick. "Why is she going to the hospital?"

"Daddy—"

The phone fell. Olivia shrieked. A low, chugging breath came over the line, and Austin cringed against the wall like a seven-year-old who couldn't move fast enough to avoid—

"Hello, son."

"What's going on over there, Vince?"

Dad gave a chuckle, and Austin fought back the hyperventilating. "Did you know you've been calling me that since you were about nine years old?"

The year I decided not to be your son anymore. "What's going on?"

"Girl fell and hurt her arm."

Arm. Not head, not spine, not internal organs—Austin drew in a bit more air. "And how did that happen? The falling, I mean."

"Who do you think you are, anyway, Mr. Big Con-Cop Man? Questioning how I raise my girls."

"Vince, you tell me what happened or I swear I'll—"

"You'll what? Grab a flight home to beat on your old man? Oh yeah, I know you're out of the state, kid. The girls let it slip."

"Is that why you finally decided to beat them into shape? Because I can't drive over and shoot you in the face?"

"Mr. Big and Brave, Mr. I've Got a Gun, Mr. Only People I Can Arrest Are Religious Fanatics. News for you, boy, I ain't religious."

Austin strangled his phone and pressed his free hand into the wall, flat, palm sweating on the mustard-colored paint. If he let the fingers curl, he'd start beating holes in the drywall. "Yes, I will grab a flight. And I'll decide on the way whether I'm going to plant a Bible in your house and arrest you, or whether I'm going to pin my badge to my chest and walk in and shoot you, and report that you assaulted a Constabulary officer. See, Vince, I have so many options."

The pause might be rattled, a little, anyway. But then Dad's chugging laugh dug into Austin's head. "Sure, come on over. I'll be ready for you."

Stop antagonizing. Stop meeting him there. Or Dad would hang the phone up and run the kitchen faucet over it. Or just throw it into a wall. Austin breathed, keeping it silent.

"Vince, you need to let Olivia talk to me."

"Oh, I need to, huh?"

His face pulled into a grimace. "May I speak with Olivia, please?"

A few bumping noises were followed by Olivia's sniffling. "Hi."

"Livvy, he's standing right next to you, isn't he?"

"Uh-huh."

Austin kept his eyes closed and lowered his head to his arm, his hand still glued to the wall as if he could push it over. "Okay, here's what I want you to do. If you think—not if you're sure, but if you *think* he had anything to do with this, I want you to say, 'We're perfectly fine.' And if you know he didn't, one-hundred percent, say, 'We're all clear.'"

Her breath shook. "We're all clear."

"Did you see what happened?"

"Uh-huh."

"You sound scared, Livvy. Are you?"

"Because—because Esther was screaming. Because the bone popped out of her skin."

Nausea welled up. Tough Esther, or trying hard to be, cradling her arm and bleeding. "Did she fall?"

"Off the garage roof."

"Why was she up there?"

Silence.

"Liv, why was Esther on the roof?"

A shriek, a scuffle. "Daddy, wait—"

The call ended.

He redialed. The phone rang five times before picking up. "It's Esther D, hey, don't leave a message 'cause I don't listen to them, but when I—"

He ended the call. Opened his eyes, drew his arm back to hurl the phone, and went still.

A middle-aged woman stood about ten feet from him. Short, brunette, Capri jeans and a purple T-shirt. Staring. She'd had dinner at their table tonight, the one who seemed to have met Marcus before. Behind her, Violet sat alone on a couch apart from the group, head bowed, hands folded on her lap. Most of the others still talked amongst themselves, but one or two were glancing from her to Austin, trying to figure out what had caught her attention.

He probably looked like a freaked-out wuss in front of all these people. He pocketed his phone and cursed his trembling hands.

"Was that your family?" the woman said.

Austin nodded.

Violet glanced up, saw he was off the phone, and darted over. "Are they okay?"

"Esther broke her arm."

Violet clenched her hands. "Oh, no."

"Liv said it wasn't … what I thought." But his left wrist gave a phantom ache halfway to his elbow. His hadn't been a—what were they called, compound fracture?—but a broken bone was a broken bone.

"Austin." Violet came closer but didn't touch him, and that observation ached too. "Are *you* okay?"

"I … I have to go home."

He hadn't known until now. But yes. He had to get them out of that house once and for all, and if Mom wouldn't help him, he'd do it himself.

"Austin."

"I have to."

"That might not be a bad idea."

Both he and Violet jolted at the voice over her shoulder. The woman was still standing here, listening to their every word.

"Um, Becca," Violet said, "this is kind of private."

Becca shrugged, her focus on Austin. "Not if he's really a con-cop."

The regionalism and lack of twang said she was at least from the Midwest. Maybe Michigan. Austin nodded. Nothing else to do.

"Were you going to tell anyone?" Becca shifted her weight back on her heels.

"I did."

"Good, then it's public knowledge." She marched over to the group at the couches, two of whom had started a checkers game. "Listen up, people. This is important."

Violet barreled after her. "Wait."

The foosball guys wandered over from the game table. The blackjack players abandoned their cards. Becca had garnered the whole room's attention.

"You can't do this." Violet's voice caught on the threat of tears.

Sure, she could. Should, in fact. But Austin wouldn't let her. He sidestepped around Becca and faced them all. A moment hung while they watched them, mostly confused faces, a few gathering suspicion, caution. In a minute, they'd all look like that. Best case scenario.

Worst … He'd be fleeing.

"In Michigan, last year, I earned my Bachelor's degree in sociology and minored in philosophy. I don't know how the system works, but the Constabulary—"

Quiet intakes of breath. Collective leaning back. Confusion morphing to more hostile expressions. Was he watching a mob form, before they knew what they were about to become?

"—at least in Michigan, they recruit students who have the academic background they want. And they recruited me."

He waited for … well, anything. But the moment wore on while they all sat, frozen.

Violet moved to his side and hooked both her arms around one of his, as if the group might rise up and drag him off somewhere. "We wouldn't have made it here without Austin. He's not part of the Constabulary anymore."

"Is that true?" asked an older man. "You … quit? Can you quit the Stab?"

"As far as I know, you can." Austin sighed. "I didn't, though. Not officially."

"It doesn't matter." Violet turned to him. "You left, and you'll never go back to your old job."

Would he? Another sigh bled from him. He pushed a hand through his hair, and if none of the rest of them understood his silence, Violet did. Her gaze dropped to the floor.

"The point is, I have no jurisdiction here. I'm not a threat to you."

"That's not the point," Becca said.

He couldn't deal with this now. His phone was still and silent against his thigh. Esther had possibly made it to the hospital by now. She'd need surgery to put the bone back. What if they couldn't fix it? And Olivia, terrified by the scream and the blood. Had they called an ambulance, or had Mom driven Esther and left Livvy home with …?

"Maybe he's like the apostle Paul," a girl said. Then to Austin, "Are you a Christian now?"

"No."

Becca folded her arms. "There's no way Marcus Brenner traveled here with a con-cop. You obviously lied to him, like you were going to lie to all of us."

"Marcus was sick, he didn't know where he was half the time." Violet's thumb was setting a new record for speed-rubbing against her wrist. "And if Austin hadn't helped rescue him, the con-cops would've killed him. That should mean something, especially to you."

So this woman had been part of Marcus's resistance movement. Austin didn't have the energy to care. But these people were his jury, weighing it all, and he should care about that, at least. He pulled out his phone and stared at it, but calling again would be pointless. Dad had decided Olivia had talked long enough.

It didn't mean he'd broken Esther's arm. He was being Vince Delvecchio, not letting Olivia talk to Austin for one reason: she wanted to.

It also didn't mean he hadn't broken Esther's arm. Olivia's denial wasn't enough.

"Excuse me." He left the crowd and, this time, pushed through the swinging doors to the solitude of the hallway. They could announce his sentence later.

He kept walking, found an exit, paced up and down the parking lot in the dark. Moths fluttered around the floodlights. Crickets serenaded. Austin dialed the last number he wanted to call.

"Hello."

"I'll make this quick." He sank onto some cement steps. How many entrances did this building have, anyway?

"Austin? Is that you, son?"

So his number wasn't even recognized. Well, whatever. "Do you have Esther with you?"

"She's going into surgery as soon as they have a room for her." His mother sighed. "I guess Olivia called you."

"Did he do this?"

"You know how he throws things when he's mad."

"Oh, I definitely know about that."

"Austin, please."

He rubbed a palm over his face. "You're right. Let's stay focused. Did he or did he not break my sister's arm?"

"Of course not. He's never raised a hand to us."

Austin nodded, though she couldn't see him. If he was thinking straight, he could admit the unlikelihood of Dad physically harming the girls. "So, he throws things, and Esther fell off the garage roof, and you're going to tell me how they're related."

"That child. You don't need to be burdened with all our—"

"Focus, Mom. And tell me."

"Esther's been moodier than usual, more sensitive. I'm sure she's just dealing with hormonal changes and such. But Vince seems to get to her more lately. He went off about something, and she'd left her pottery wheel on the coffee table."

And he'd broken whatever Esther had been working on, if not the wheel itself. "So she went up to the roof?"

"We've had some contractors working on the house, and they left a ladder out. I think she wanted to have some time to herself, that's all."

At this point, Austin could say a dozen different things. *She didn't want time to herself. She wanted to escape a father that breaks the things she cares about.*

Maybe one day it will be her bones, Mom. Or yours. But Mom would scoff at that. Only Austin's bones had ever cracked at Dad's hands.

I want you to leave him. For the girls' sake. That, too, would earn only an annoyed sigh.

"Mom?"

She must be expecting one of those things, because she sighed. "He didn't touch her. This was an accident."

"I believe you." What was he trying to say? What words had the last week loosed in him that now pushed to come out? "Has he ever talked to you about it? The … anger, I mean."

"Why would he do that?"

Shut up, Austin. You're accomplishing nothing. "It's just, there's this girl I … but if … then I don't ever want to have kids. A boy."

"Are you asking if having a temper is hereditary?" She laughed.

Austin bent forward on the steps. "I guess not. Listen, I want to talk to Esther. As soon as she's awake."

"She'll be loopy, but I'll let her know, and she can call you if she feels like it."

"Thanks."

He hung up and lowered his forehead to his knees. His limbs felt heavier than the typical crash from an adrenaline buzz. Maybe his father's voice, his father's low breathing directly in his ear had spiked his stress response more than usual.

So Dad wasn't broadening targets. Still, Esther was old enough now not only to feel it, the hurt and heaviness of living in that house, but also to know she felt it. Austin had to get her and Livvy out. He wouldn't let them go through this—their hearts pounding out of control, the hot tingling in their hands, the wondering how someone had set them off this time. His sisters would never have to fight a piece of Dad inside them. Not if he could help it.

He stood, and his legs quivered only a little. He had to tell Violet. He had to find a way to get home.

And Jason?

He'd have to be very, very careful.

44

Lee trudged up the church steps and peered through the glass door. She tried to open it. Locked. To be expected after dark, yet certainly a sign. She should go. But she had to—not apologize, that word was too formal. Too perfunctory. She had to express her remorse.

It won't matter.

She couldn't leave without trying to mend the wounds caused by her own words and actions. She tugged at the door. No one came.

He made it quite clear he wants you to leave him alone.

But not forever. Not Marcus. Her hand was steady as she pulled out her phone, typed a text to Violet, and didn't send it.

From the other side of the building, the main entrance, a car was running. Voices drifted closer. Lee sent her text. She couldn't converse civilly with anyone right now, not until she spoke to Marcus and heard, saw, his response.

As a long-haired silhouette jogged toward her down the backlit hall, the strangers—a family of four—rounded the corner of the building and spotted her.

"Hello?" The man hurried toward her. "We were told this is the shelter of Kearby."

"It is," Lee said.

He gestured to a woman, midfifties like him, and two teen boys. "We're here from Nevada. We didn't think we'd make it."

Violet opened the door before the man could elaborate. "Lee! Where've you been?"

"These are new refugees," she said. "A member of the church should be informed."

Violet glanced past her, and her eyes lit. "Hi. Come on in. I'll go get somebody for you."

They straggled inside, tired eyes and rumpled clothes and smiles.

"I'm Benjamin Schneider," the man said, "and this is my wife, Hannah, and our two boys."

"Lee."

"Good to know you."

In the next few minutes, Benjamin speed-talked through an entire story of their road trip trials—a flat tire and a Good Samaritan who stopped to help but then asked too many questions. Lee would have tuned him out on her best social day. This wasn't.

When Benjamin brought the story around to its moral—gratitude to God for bringing them through every obstacle—Lee waited for the heat of anger, the cutting words that would stun him into silence. Perhaps she was too tired for them. She tried to analyze further, but her thoughts seemed to have weight, too much to lift. She might never have been so tired in her life as she was right now.

After concluding his story, Benjamin tilted his head at her. "So where are you from, Lee? Let me guess, Minnesota?"

"Michigan."

"And you came for refuge?"

"Yes."

Benjamin's wife smiled. Did she speak? At all?

"We nearly had to split up," Benjamin said. "Prayed we'd be able to find each other again, if separating proved necessary, but we made it over together in the end."

In merciful rescue, Violet approached with Austin and an elderly bearded man. Violet and the stranger were immersed in comfortable chatter. She might as well have lived in this town, participated in this church, all her life. How did she manage such true warmth? Perhaps some people were born with an inviting fire inside, and some with a heart of sharp icicles.

Or perhaps Lee had chosen this, too.

Violet reached Lee's side with a grin. "Everybody, this is Austin and Walt."

The bearded man beside her extended his hand to Lee. "Walton Cantrell."

"Lee Vaughn."

"A pleasure, Lee." He turned to the Schneiders and exchanged names and handshakes. "Y'all have excellent timing. With newly arrived folks, we like to give you a quick education on what to expect here—'here' being our church as well as our new country. You can ask questions, too. There's a group gathering in one of our conference rooms right now, if you'll follow me."

No gathering, not now. Lee watched them start to walk away, Violet nearly bouncing on her feet. Benjamin had already begun a conversation with Walton when Austin looked back and stopped.

"Lee?"

"I'll join you later."

Violet said something to Walton, and the others disappeared around a corner while she jogged back down the hall. She focused not on Lee but on Austin.

"Did you talk to Lee?"

Austin sighed. "Violet."

"You need to let her talk you out of this."

"No one's going to talk me out of it."

Perhaps Lee should care, but at the moment … "Before we go to any meeting, I'd like to check on Marcus."

Violet's frown smoothed. "I did, about half an hour ago, because he seemed really worn out when Will brought him back. He's sleeping, and his breathing sounded good."

Sleeping easily. Waking him to unburden herself would be selfish. *Go ahead, then. It would be in character.* She shut her eyes.

"Lee? You okay?"

"Fine."

She focused on these two people, these … companions. Austin's hair was ruffled from the finger-raking habit she'd mostly observed when he'd been driving too long. The knitting between his eyes might be a headache. Violet's frowning, wrist-rubbing worry was directed all at him.

"What's happened?" Lee said.

As Austin began the story, Violet moved to stand at his side and curled her hand around his forearm. Her thumb rubbed a slow rhythm below the crook of his elbow. He clearly left out details, but Lee didn't need them.

"You cannot go back," she said.

"I have to. My sisters—"

"Mayweather aside, you have no legal guardianship. They're minors. They can't live with you simply because they want to, especially the younger one, not without some sort of evidence of abuse. You just stated your father hasn't physically harmed them."

He pulled in a harsh breath.

Violet's other hand latched onto his wrist. "That makes sense. Your mom would have to file charges or something. Right, Lee?"

"Correct."

"See? You can't go back there and kidnap them from your mom's house."

"Esther would go," he said through his teeth.

"You have no means to support two children, Austin." And Lee couldn't assist with that yet, not with her accounts frozen by Constabulary order. "Realistically, you won't succeed in this if you try to do it now."

He pulled away from Violet and paced to the visitors' desk, stacked with paper programs and more Bibles than Lee had ever seen in one place, much less on one surface. He rubbed a hand over his hair and ducked his head.

"It's all gone," he said quietly. "The great job. The money I saved. Getting ready to support them if I had to. None of it means anything here, the degree and the training and ..."

His hand pressed flat against the desk. He sighed.

"Austin?" Violet didn't move toward him.

"Never mind. Let's go to this meeting. We need all the information we can get."

"I know where it is," Violet said.

Lee followed them with nothing else to do, nowhere else to go.

The conference room was full. She never should have bothered to hope for a small meeting. She followed Austin and Violet into the room and found a place to stand against the wall, half her view blocked by the Schneider family who had stopped only feet ahead of her. In the space between their bodies, she glimpsed about a dozen more people seated at the table or in chairs dragged from other rooms. A floodlight shone from the parking lot outside the north wall's vertical windows. All attention was glued to Walton, who stood at the head of the room facing them, a whiteboard at his back bearing a rainbow of children's signatures and a game of hangman. The answer was *Galadriel* and the hanged man had all his limbs. Lee stepped to one side to view the room better.

Marcus was seated at the table, his back to her.

She stationed herself behind his chair. "Marcus?"

He glanced back and did not smile, not even with his eyes.

"I thought you were sleeping." It came out as an observation, calm and secure. The tension eased in her shoulders.

"Will came and got me."

No doubt with instructions from Marcus not to let him miss anything. Around them, other conversations were hushing. Lee allowed theirs to do the same. Marcus's hand curved around the table edge, but he seemed steady. The moment his arm trembled, she would …

Would what? Try to force him to bed? No. She had to stop … looking at him as if he were dying.

Violet stood to her left, their arms just brushing in the crowded space. Better Violet's arm than anyone else's.

"Welcome, all." Walt's feet were planted apart. "To this church and this country. To freedom."

He said the words as if he'd said them many times, but sincerity rang in them. Several people around the table nodded acknowledgement. Walt spoke for about ten minutes, explaining the available programs at the church and how they were structured, including an email network of available jobs in Kearby and the surrounding cities. They even had an email list for those in need of transportation—carpools and cars for sale. Arriving here without a vehicle must not be so extraordinary.

So much support, none of it driven by a desire for publicity. People were fueling this—not an organization but individuals who cared.

"A final thing," Walt said after going over meal schedules and other miscellany. "The most important thing. In the last two months, there's been a new threat ascertained to some of you. Not all of you. The Constabulary isn't legally present here, but they are present."

Marcus's knuckles went white against the pebbled beige tabletop.

"Working in the open isn't an option for them, since they have no jurisdiction. None of you are going to be arrested walking down the street. Most of you don't have to worry about this at all, but we've discovered that certain state Constabularies have sent agents with specific targets—namely resistance workers who had influence back home."

A chill slithered up Lee's spine. If Michigan came after anyone …

"Why?" Violet's voice broke. "Why can't they just let everyone go?"

Marcus's shoulders pulled back into a line of tension that had to cost his ribs. Lee's hand moved to touch his shoulder, then fell to her side. Not now.

"What we've figured is that there's too much resistance, more than we know. They need to send a message, and high-profile people, any of y'all who were making a difference before you had to run …" Walt folded his arms, further rounding his shoulders. "You could be a target, and as a church body we request that information from you. For our sakes as well as yours."

Silence soaked into the room. Across the table from Marcus, a woman pushed her chair back and stood. Rebecca. About ten years older than Lee, brown hair, brown eyes, feminine curves. She'd eaten at their table tonight. Marcus had called her Becca, didn't have to tell Lee this was Becca Roddy from the Ohio resistance.

"Are you asking for a head count now?" Becca said.

Walt's mustache twitched. "Or later, if you'd like some anonymity with the congregation at large."

"Doesn't bother me." She smiled and waved. "Hi, I'm Becca, and I distributed Bibles illegally."

Laughter wafted throughout the room. Becca's glance rested a moment too long on Marcus, then moved on. Violet shifted from one foot to another, and Lee waited too. He'd speak, raise his hand, force himself to his feet. Something. He trusted these people. He'd already shown that. But he was still.

Benjamin Schneider broke the quiet. "There's no way they have legal grounds to do what you're saying. You think they'd actually publicize it, coming here and taking people back? And the media would go along with it?"

Multiple people around the room pinned him with hard looks. *Of course they would.*

A lanky blond man sat a few chairs from Marcus. He flattened his palm against the table and half stood. "Will you want Becca"—he nodded at her—"and anyone else to talk to someone, a Texas cop or a criminal lawyer or someone? Is that required?"

"No." The word snapped from several people.

Distrust of law enforcement wasn't logical in this new place, yet it coiled in Lee's gut as well. At the very least, they had to be cautious.

"No," Walt said. "Nothing is required of you—not even coming forward. We won't make you fill out a questionnaire or anything of that sort. Your safety is your business. But we can offer help if you think you need it."

Help? What would that entail?

"Does local law enforcement know what's going on?" Austin said. "Do you know if these agents have *carte blanche* at the federal level?"

"Yes and yes." For a moment, Walt and Austin seemed to measure each other. Then Walt shrugged. "We're not able to confirm that last one, but it seems to be the case given their presence here at all."

Austin nodded.

The blond man sat back and drummed his fingers, and a pang passed through Lee. Sam's famous pondering pose. She hadn't let herself think of him before. Couldn't now, either. In front of her, Marcus was a stone. Perhaps he was collecting words, would identify himself any minute, but … no. The tension in him wasn't easing.

The conversation moved on. Wrapped up. Walton twitched a smile and said, "That's all, folks," but no one left.

Marcus might need their protection. If only his pride stood in the way, Lee would enlist Austin and Violet to help her combat it. Many people knew him, in Michigan and in Ohio, though no one knew the entirety of his work. The miles upon miles he'd driven, transporting fugitives to safety. The Macomb County network map he held in his head—half a dozen safe houses he'd recruited, every deck and shed that word of mouth had turned into an overnight hiding place until he could reach frightened people and take them to better concealment, to food and a bed.

The exhaustion, the constant stress, burdens too heavy that he'd carried anyway. Heath had seen it. Still, the Constabulary knew more about Marcus than anyone in this church knew. Lee's teeth gritted on that fact.

She gripped the back of Marcus's chair. She needed to understand this silence, but she might have forfeited the right to ask.

She looked away from the line of his shoulders, the cowlick at his neck, and her gaze found Austin. He had faded into the corner and now spoke quietly with Walton. The man's beefy hand gripped Austin's shoulder, and a frown creased his face. Arguing? No. Austin's words were easily read on his lips. "Yes, sir."

A gentle hand squeezed her arm. "You okay?"

She nodded without looking at Violet.

"You seem … I don't know."

"I'm fine."

Walton crossed the room halfway and raised his arms, and the few conversations faded. "We all need to get some sleep. Let's adjourn the same way we opened."

With prayer. Lee didn't let herself leave, but couldn't they do this independently?

The prayer circulated throughout the room, beginning with Walton, continuing in what seemed a spontaneous fashion—not only the words, but also who spoke and who didn't. People spoke to God about every detail—explaining the situation as if He didn't already know, then asking for guidance. Asking for safety, especially for Becca Roddy. Praising God for bringing them all together. Trusting His will no matter the danger or the outcome.

If He had entered the human drama not to wreak havoc but to redeem … then perhaps their trust wasn't unfounded.

The praying voices wrapped around Lee and constricted, shortening her breath. She gripped Marcus's chair and watched the group, their closed eyes, bowed heads, some hands linked and some lifted, open. Across from her, Austin watched them, too, and frowned. Beside her, Violet's hands were folded under her chin, like a figurine Lee had once seen of a kneeling child.

Walton ended the prayer after a long silence. "Father, we offer up all these prayers in the name of Your Son, Jesus. Amen."

Heads lifted. Hands lowered. People stirred.

"Could we close," someone said, "with a hymn?"

This brought out a few smiles. A woman blocked from Lee's view called out, "Something to give praise."

"I know the one." Benjamin grinned, and then his baritone filled the room.

"All creatures of our God and King, lift up your voice and with us sing, alleluia! Alleluia!"

Voices joined in, first following the melody, then breaking into harmonies. About half the people only listened, perhaps not knowing the song, but the spirit of it enfolded the whole room.

"Thou burning sun with golden beam, Thou silver moon with softer gleam, O praise Him! O praise Him! Alleluia!"

The images soaked into Lee. Lovely. Stirring, somehow. As the alleluias resounded on, Marcus shifted in the chair to find her gaze, but when she thought he would speak to her, he turned to Violet instead. To someone with whom he could share this.

"A song for God," he said.

"It sounds old," Violet whispered. "It's beautiful."

Lee closed her eyes and let beauty buoy her, though the song, the praise, did not belong to her.

"Let all things their Creator bless, and worship Him in humbleness … Alleluia! Alleluia!"

So this was required for worship—humility. That made sense.

"Praise, praise the Father, praise the Son, and praise the Spirit, Three in One! O praise Him! O praise Him! Alleluia!"

The blended voices believed these words. God was to be trusted, praised, not resented, certainly not mocked. But for these people, for Marcus and Violet, there was more. Devotion. And …

The song ended, and in the quiet, a young female voice began a new one.

"I love You, Lord, and I lift my voice …"

Yes, that. Lee stood in the midst of their love and tried not to let herself ache.

45

Esther and Olivia had been texting him a lot in the last twelve hours, mostly pictures of Esther's cast decorated with neon markers and some juvenile stickers he teased her about. He'd woken up multiple times in the night to the vibration of his phone, hiding the light so as not to wake the other guys in the room. Not that a buzzing, lit phone would rouse Will. The guy had slept through Tommy's snoring and the *thud* when Harrison dropped his Bible. The thing was massive, too heavy for the skinny table that needed a few additional screws.

Four guys in a little classroom, sleeping on mattresses. Strangers. Christians. Austin hadn't slept much, even when the girls weren't texting him.

When morning dawned, he found Violet with hair wound up in a towel. He pulled her outside, down the street, to Rosita's.

"Look at my face," Violet said when she realized their destination.

"Looks clean to me."

"Exactly. Scrubbed down, mascara free. And then there's the towel around my head. Pretty sure there's a sign on the door about this. Shoes and shirt required, dripping hair strictly forbidden."

Austin took a silent breath and a risk and wrapped his arm around—okay, not her waist, her shoulders. For today. Still had to earn a lot back. *But I will.* Violet stiffened only for a moment. Surprise, not objection. She leaned into his arm as they walked.

"I don't really care about my makeup," she said.

"I figured."

"Are you leaving?"

They ambled up the walkway to the outdoor tables. He pulled out a metal chair and motioned her to sit, then took the one across from her. "Not yet. Lee's right. I can't do anything without … well, money, at least."

Violet rubbed her wrist.

"I … I want to talk to you," he said, as if that weren't obvious, the way he'd dragged her to this restaurant when the church was serving breakfast in the gym. (Did those people ever run out of food?)

She lifted her eyes and met his and waited. His heart started to hammer, not too much adrenaline, not stress or anger. Something less familiar. *Admit it, you're nervous.*

"Uh." He cleared his throat. "I didn't get a chance to tell you some things, after the meeting last night. First … I'm not going back to the Constabulary, and it's not because of the threat from Jason."

A tiny smile curved her lips. "I was hoping."

"They're violating the sovereignty of Texas as a country after the government said they *wouldn't* violate that. And I just … it's just …"

"Messed up."

He leaned back in his chair, and a sigh poured out of him. "The second thing—"

"Good morning." The smirking Mexican girl stood at his shoulder, though today she smiled. "Burritos?"

He fisted a hand at her timing, then loosened it. Stress. A lot of stress. He wasn't really mad. "Two boring American ones for me, the one with the sausage."

"And for you?" The girl turned her smile on Violet.

"Um, do you have kind of an omelet in a burrito? I like tomatoes … and, um …"

"Let me bring you a menu."

The girl disappeared into the restaurant and whisked back to their table in less time than Austin needed to form his next sentence. She offered a single laminated sheet to Violet.

"Take your time. I'll be back in a few minutes."

Those two statements were not conducive to each other. *Focus, man.*

Violet flipped the menu over—"Oh, lunch stuff, gross, it's barely nine o'clock"—and flipped it back. After less than thirty seconds, she set it aside, and the girl popped back into view. Watching, of course.

"What can I get you?"

"The one with eggs and salsa and cheese, please."

"To drink?"

Violet shrugged. "Orange juice, I guess."

"Coffee," Austin said.

"Coming right up." She took the menu and vanished again.

"She's kind of like a genie." Violet giggled.

"Um."

Her smile melted. "And you were saying the Constabulary is messed up."

"Actually, we'd moved on to the second item, which is … um …" His face heated. The hammer of his heart kicked up a notch. Nerves versus stress response? Or they were teaming up. Great.

Violet leaned forward and folded her arms on the table. "Go ahead."

"I think it's possible that … well, you already know this, but I think there's possibly something … wrong with me. The way I lose it over things. Or over nothing. I'm going to do some research on it, but I think it might be possible that I …"

He shut his eyes. His chest burned, but he had to get this out. Violet had to know, deserved to know.

"I might need to talk to someone. A … um, a counselor."

"And you're embarrassed about it?"

He opened his eyes. "It's really not something you want to admit to your …"

Her lips parted on a whispered syllable. "Oh."

"That's the third—well, the third and fourth thing."

Her mouth curved. "These sound like thousand-dollar things coming up."

"What was the last one?"

"Eight hundred and fifty."

Their server materialized at Violet's shoulder with a tray, two plates, a glass of orange juice and a mug of coffee. She set their plates and the juice in front of them, set the mug to the left of Austin's plate, and chirped something cheerful that Violet smiled at but Austin didn't fully hear. Because the next item *was* worth at least a grand.

Violet used her fork to take her first bite. She closed her eyes and leaned her head back. "Mmm. Salsa."

"But not chive and onion."

"Right."

He cleared his throat. Stared at his food for a moment, but no way he could take a bite until he said everything. "Violet, this whole … star-crossed thing of ours."

She laughed around a sip of juice. "Seriously?"

"You know what I'm talking about."

She set her glass down. "Uh-huh. Austin, I …"

"I'm not asking you to date me."

Red suffused her cheeks. "Oh. Well, I—that's cool, I—"

"No, listen, babe. I'm not asking you to date me today. You'd have to say no, which would make me feel like crap, and I'd deserve it for asking you to choose."

"There's no choice," she whispered.

"I know that." And for some reason, the knowledge didn't make him want to throw things. "So … look. I want us to … I just …"

"You kind of like me." Her smile held no flirting, no playfulness, only an unsure pleasure.

Kind of? She had no idea who she was. How priceless. How beautiful. Austin reached for the hand holding her fork and ran his finger over her knuckles.

"Austin …"

"I know." He left his hand stretched toward her, but rested it on the table. "So that's item three."

"Okay," she whispered.

"Four is …" The one he didn't want to say. The one she'd wrap her hopes around. But in light of item three, she deserved to hear item four. "It's this … religion thing."

Her eyes widened. Her shoulders lifted with a long breath. "Yeah?"

"I'm going to investigate. That's all, Violet. I don't want you to start believing I'll turn into one of you, because it's probably never going to happen."

She blinked hard, stared at her plate. He'd known the words would pierce her, but that didn't lessen the sting in his own chest. A slow nod, and then she took a bite of her food, as if she'd arrived at some resolution.

"What?" he said.

"You're not lying anymore. Or hiding." She took another bite, and she smiled. "I'm proud of you, scholar."

Warmth filled him. Not the conclusion he'd expected from her. His stomach rumbled. He gobbled down half a burrito and half his coffee while Violet picked at her salsa concoction despite insisting it was delicious. Austin had been so hyper-focused on his list, maybe he'd missed the source of her stress. Maybe he should ask, but the quiet between them was easy right now, comfortable, and they both could use a few minutes of safety after the last twenty-four hours. The last couple days, week, months …

He gulped his coffee and set it down. "If Christians are right about things … It would matter. Quite a lot."

"It does. I'm praying for you."

If none of it was true, who cared? If all of it was true, he should thank her. "I guess I'm not opposed to it. As if I could stop you."

She grinned. "As if."

When their food was gone, Austin disposed of their trash and held up a finger. "Give me one minute?"

Violet shrugged. "We've got all day, I guess."

There it was again, the uneasy shift of her gaze, the pointing of her toe into the ground. Austin pushed it away and went into the restaurant. Their server bounced up to him.

"How was everything?"

"Good. Um, is Rosita an actual person or just the name on the sign?"

"She's my mama."

"Could I talk to her?"

"One moment." The girl disappeared through the swinging door to the kitchen. In a minute or two, a portly woman came out and frowned at Austin.

"There is problem?" Unlike her daughter's, Rosita's accent was thick.

"No, no. I, um, noticed the sign in the window." He pointed. *Help Wanted.*

"This is for cook."

"Do you have to have prior experience?"

Rosita propped her hands on her apron-tied hips. "I train maybe, if I like you. What were you before?"

His stomach tightened. He never thought these words would gall him. "I worked for the Constabulary. I'm trying to … um, start over."

Rosita stared at him for a not-so-small eternity. "How old?"

"Twenty-two."

"Can you cook?"

"I can learn anything. And I already make a decent pizza sauce."

Her mouth twitched, but he wasn't supposed to see it. He maintained his expression.

Rosita's arms crossed over her bosom. "I train you one day. If you learn, I keep training you. Yes?"

"Yes. Good. Thank you very much."

Austin exited a few minutes later with the application he had to bring back tomorrow morning at seven.

"What's that?" Violet motioned to the single sheet of paper.

"I think I just got a job in Kearby, Texas."

46

If anyone asked, Lee would say she enjoyed flowers and wished a closer look. She should be unobserved, though. Everyone had gathered in the gym for breakfast. In the cavelike acoustics, voices had echoed, seemingly multiplying the two dozen people. The bagels hadn't looked appealing. No one noticed Lee leave.

She cracked open the glass door to the waterfall garden and slipped inside. The quiet cascade and the mixed scent of flowers enveloped her. High overhead, the domed ceiling was made of glass. Sunlight beamed down on the plants, sparkled on the pool and the waterfall's slight spray. Lee walked the circular stone path, probably less than ten feet around, then sat on a rock alongside the pool. She stretched her feet toward the water but didn't allow her shoes to get wet.

This. Solitude. Rest.

To her right, someone had arranged four potted chrysanthemums on stair-stepped plant stands. She leaned in. No other flower smelled like a mum. One could find them blindfolded in a roomful of blossoms. Like her resilient geranium. Someone should acquire more plant stands to balance these, for the other side of the pool, and alternate the mums with geraniums. Every flower arrangement ought to have at least one. She cupped her hand around a rust-red mum, and thin, smooth petals brushed her palm.

Beauty. Like the chorusing voices last night. Her grappling with it had begun while lying on the air mattress, while Marcus slept across the room.

"I don't understand You." She caressed the mum's petals. "Humanity could survive and even accept the role You wish to play in their lives without this."

What did she hope to accomplish by addressing Him?

"The only purpose of poetry and melody, and this, color and scent and texture … The only purpose seems to be … enjoyment."

Lee stood. This was absurd. The God of all things had no desire to hear the puzzled ramblings of a woman who was damned. She crossed the garden to the door, gripped the handle, but what awaited her out there? She'd come here to breathe for a while, hoped the garden would ease the sense of heaviness that hadn't lifted since last night in the park.

Perhaps this weight was not meant to be lifted.

She turned away from the door and went back to the garden. She sank to her knees beside the pool, not in reverence but unable to bear up under the weight.

"Did You give us these things for our enjoyment? Are You a God of … gifts?" Lee gripped her knees. "Jesus Christ, if there is any chance to— I don't know if … if I can continue like this."

The water continued to rush and tumble. The flowers blazed in the sun. Lee's fingers dug into the grass along the path, deep into the soil, holding on.

Look up.

She hadn't sensed the watchful presence on the other side of the glass. He was on his feet today with the aid of a cane, perhaps from the donor of the wheelchairs. He held it with both hands, centered in front of him, leaning heavily. Their eyes met through the window, and Marcus didn't turn away.

She shook her head. She couldn't speak to him. But he moved toward the door, one step at a time, and used his entire body to push it open. Lee rose and hurried to hold it for him.

His breathing labored, but he was steady on his feet. "Thanks."

She couldn't even nod.

Marcus trekked from the door to one of the benches, braced and lowered himself, wincing as he bent his injured knee just enough to sit. His gaze took in the waterfall and the pool, the grass and stone, the flowers.

"It's a good place," he said quietly.

Lee managed a single nod.

"I'll leave you alone if you want. But when you left, you didn't look okay."

"I …" Her heart hammered. The weight shifted from her shoulders onto her chest, starting an ache. "I wasn't able to tell you last night, but I—I regret my words in the park. My ridicule."

He rubbed his neck, sighed, but didn't break eye contact. "It's not like I don't know what you think."

"No, Marcus. You're right, I was angry. Emotional. I may even have wanted to wound you, though I don't understand why I—why you're the person I choose to attack. I don't—I don't—"

"Lee."

Her name in the shelter of his voice, the voice she'd once known she would never hear again. Lee raised her hands to hide her face.

"Oh." Marcus pushed to his feet to stand beside her. "Hey. Lee. It's okay."

"It isn't."

"I mean—I forgive you."

Not those words. She shook her head. *Please don't.*

The waterfall filled the silence while she tried to regain her calm. Level breathing, blinking until her eyes ceased to burn. She had to live with what she'd done. Marcus couldn't erase it. She had to live with everything she'd ever done.

"What is it?"

She shook her head. Didn't he understand? Why wouldn't he go?

"It's time to talk," he said.

He wouldn't go because he was Marcus. She lowered her hands but kept her eyes closed, tried not to let her voice shake. "I'm simply facing … my future existence."

"What?"

"Before God."

He cleared his throat. "Tell me. What you mean."

"I—I have been made aware that He does not bend to my standards. Yet I have not bent to His. There is a—a large discrepancy between His requirements and my actions."

His warm arm encompassed her shoulders. Her feet were moving, her body guided to a bench, and her shoulder pushed down until she sat. The words she'd spoken filled the garden, squeezed into every space, created a pressure she could hardly stand.

"I don't meet God's standard, either," Marcus said.

"No, Marcus. I've hated Him. I know—I believe I know—Who He is now, and still I want to hate Him. It was easier. Numbing."

Why was she saying these things? Marcus couldn't help her. He would only be wounded when he realized she was so far beyond assistance.

"You're not numb now."

"I can't get it back."

"Good."

She shut her eyes against the sting. "I know. I deserve to feel it."

The quiet lasted so long, she thought he would struggle to his feet and leave her. Instead, he whispered. "Feel what?"

Lee shook her head, though he was ignoring that communication so far.

"Lee. What do you feel?"

She couldn't avoid it while he forced the issue. But she couldn't endure it, either. "It's like drowning."

And not drowning in a movie or a novel, going to sleep amid floating bubbles. This felt like a true, endless drowning, the evidence of which she'd seen on victims, brought to the emergency room past saving. Water filling her, weighing her down, squeezing out her air and preventing her from drawing in more. Struggle. Pain. The knowledge of impending death.

"Lee."

"It's terrifying," she whispered. "He is terrifying."

"Did you talk to Him?"

"Yes."

His breath caught.

"I have acknowledged my … violations."

"You know the rest. We've talked about it."

Over and over, for years. Yes, she knew. "I can't."

"Why not?"

"I don't deserve to."

Marcus shifted on the bench to face her, ablaze, the way she'd seen him only a few times in his life, only since he'd come back. "Lee.

If you deserved the gift, where's the glory in giving it? If you know now Who God is, you know He wants glory. Deserves glory."

The gift. Like harmony, like poetry, like blossoms and the sound of water. But greater than these. Necessary. Costly.

"I don't know how to want Him," she said. "I don't know how to feel anything toward Him that isn't … vile."

"Okay." Marcus gripped the inside of his knee. "Ask Him for help."

"Help to want His gifts? No one has to ask for this. I'm not …"

Words crumbled to dust inside her. She huddled on the bench and caved forward, arms wrapped around her body. His hand settled below her neck, where he'd left a handprint of bathwater on a too recent night, ravaged by fever.

"Lee," he said. "Ask."

She covered her face, though she couldn't hide. She trembled. She flailed inside against the current of her hate and her selfishness and her pride and her daughter's blood. On her own, she would indeed drown. Deserved to. Wanted to.

"God," she said. "Jesus Christ."

She waited for the weight to crush her, but her chest rose and fell with breath. Another gift.

"I am requesting … if You will give me … I am requesting absolution. Based on Your sacrifice of blood in payment for the—the blood I have shed and the—the numerous wrongs I have—"

I can't. Please, if You will. She doubled over, all the way to her knees, and a shudder gripped her. Marcus's hand stayed in place, firm and warm, not leaving her.

"Please forgive me." Every word came with a fight for breath. "Please help me."

Shaking. Spent. But air filled her lungs. She was pulled out, away from the flood of herself. She felt no love, no joy, no warmth like Violet's, but a quiet relief. And inside her, there was a glimpse. Radiance. His blood washing her baby's from her hands, washing all her grimy soul until she emerged naked and spotless. *Thank You.* Inadequate, which was the point. The way of His glory. *I almost understand.*

Lee pressed a hand to her chest. She no longer ached. *In time, will I love? Will You help me to love?* Slowly, she sat up. At some point, the hand had lifted from her back. She turned.

Marcus was weeping. Head in his hands. Lips pressed tight to keep his silence.

She set a hand on his arm, and a quiet sob broke from him. He rocked forward. His tears fell on her hand.

"Marcus."

"Lee." He covered her hand with his. "Lee. Oh, God, Your gifts."

EPILOGUE

Return the Bible. Say as little as possible. Keep the secret.

Violet repeated her checklist as she searched for Marcus. Juana finally pointed her outside. Sure enough, Marcus sat with his back to an oak tree, next to the parking lot, one knee bent. The tree's late-afternoon shadow sprawled across the sun-washed grass.

Around his mostly straightened knee, Marcus had wrapped one of those rice-filled heating pads, its flannel material patterned with red and blue birds. He'd shaved since Violet last saw him, and his face without the beard looked thinner but more like himself. He seemed to be watching nonexistent traffic pass and leaves fall and … well, there wasn't a whole lot else to watch. He looked intent on it, though.

Maybe she shouldn't walk up to him without a warning. "Hey."

He jolted, then turned his head. As their eyes met, his smiled, worn crinkles showing around the edges. "Hi."

He'd be a good brother. If only she hadn't ruined it. The part of her the Bible called her "old man" wished Austin had never told her. If she didn't know, she could have been Marcus's little sister without any dishonesty.

"I won't bug you," she said. "I just came to bring you this."

She held out the Bible. Marcus took it in both hands and looked down at the cover. His thumb caressed the worn leather at the spine's edge.

He gave a long coming-home kind of sigh. "Thanks."

"I, um, I highlighted. With pink. And I wrote in it. I think I started around Luke—and Acts and Romans. I wrote a lot in Romans."

Marcus opened the book, found Romans, and began to turn the pages. Heat rushed into her cheeks. The pink highlighter and green pen—good grief, ink was everywhere. She hadn't realized at the time how much color she was spilling, all over. She just kept reading things she didn't want to forget.

"I'll get you a new one, if you want. There's a bookstore in the church that sells them, and I'm going to get a job as soon as I can, and—"

"It's okay." Marcus looked up at her. This time the smile that started in his eyes reached his mouth.

She hadn't seen his mouth smile since he'd come back to them. She sank down next to him, and the grass tickled her ankles. "I thought it would be over. When we got here."

"Over?"

"If Walt's right, there's danger here, too."

"Not for you."

"Only because I'm not worth anything." Was it the old man who felt the relief of that?

Marcus glared at her. "Don't."

"Well, I don't mean—"

"I know Lee would call you her friend. And I know you've been showing her love. Showing her Jesus." His voice caught on the Name.

Violet crossed her ankles in front of her. "I try to."

"Well. It isn't worthless."

It would be wonderful if he was right, but four months had taught her the difficulty of witnessing to Lee. Maybe they were too different, their personalities. Maybe the gap between them existed because Violet had never in eighteen years hated herself and, for some reason, Lee lived with self-hatred every day. These days, praying was all Violet could do.

The side door of the church opened, and Juana marched out, an apron over her T-shirt and jeans, a plate in her hands. Marcus gave a small sigh.

"I see you found him." Juana squatted down in front of him. "Surprise."

"Juana, I had lunch."

"Three hours ago."

"I'm barely hungry."

"Barely counts. Come on. Protein and carbs." She held out the plate of potato salad, baked beans, and a grilled burger with cheese and relish oozing from under the bun.

Marcus took it and set it over the Bible in his lap. "Thanks."

She grinned and disappeared back into the church.

"I think Lee put her up to this food-every-three-hours thing." He picked up the burger and took a bite. He chewed as if he were thinking hard about it.

Dear Jesus, I didn't need another reminder that he's hurt and weak.

She wouldn't be able to keep the secret forever. Look how that had gone with Khloe. Sometime, the truth would slip out of her, or maybe out of Austin—he'd already done that once.

Being disowned might hurt less if she did it now. And Marcus deserved honesty.

"Are you okay?" he said.

She glanced down. Her thumb was rubbing phantom charms on a phantom bracelet. Would she ever break the habit? Her wrist no longer felt naked, but every once in a while she caught herself rubbing her wrist as if the bracelet still hung there.

"Violet."

She tried to bury the tears, but they surged into her eyes. "Marcus, the con-cops didn't figure it out. That you were leading the resistance."

For a moment, he looked like a statue. Then he set the plate aside, in the grass.

She pushed the words out before he could ask questions, interrupt, kill her nerve. She tried not to tremble. "Austin told me. Clay gave you up to them. I know in heaven I'll be your sister in Christ, but I know this means I can't be, here on earth. I didn't want you to know, but I had to tell you."

Marcus's hands curled on the cover of the Bible. "Clay thought they had his daughter. He thought he was making a trade."

The shuddering inside her went still. "You … know?"

"Yeah."

"Did Austin tell you?"

He shook his head. His hands tightened to fists.

"You …" She shouldn't keep pushing, but he'd treated her like a sister anyway. She had to know. "When did you find out?"

Marcus drew in a breath, too sharp, like the sound Lee made before her panic attacks. *The whole time. He's always known.* Locked in the dark, he'd known who put him there.

Her tears overflowed. "How can you not hate me?"

"You didn't want it to happen."

"Do you hate Clay, then?"

Marcus looked away. "I don't think so."

He probably thought she couldn't understand. Well, she couldn't, not what had happened to him. But some days, she thought she might hate her mother. It was so hard to tell. She didn't hate her every day, for sure. And when she'd only half woke from the worst of her dreams, thinking Lee was gone, in hell, she'd hated the robber with the gun. Even when reality cleared, she'd had to pray to stop hating him.

"Does this mean …" She swiped at her tears. "I can still be your sister?"

"Violet." He said it on a sigh, as if she'd been completely ridiculous to think otherwise.

"Oh."

Marcus let her cry a little more, and then she sat against the tree with him, and their outstretched legs made a right angle from the trunk. He finished eating the burger, then put the plate down without touching the potato salad or the beans.

"Marcus."

"Hm." He was beginning to sound sleepy.

"I was part of what happened. It's … inside me. Even though God forgave me, and you forgave me."

Cars passed on a main road out of sight, and a bird sang in the tree limbs above them. Maybe Marcus had fallen asleep. After a while, he pulled the heating pad from his knee and began to massage it. He didn't speak for another minute, until he leaned against the tree with a strained sigh.

"Last winter, I watched a man get arrested. An old man, preaching in a store parking lot. The agent told me to go back in the store. And I did."

"You couldn't have stopped it, though," Violet said. It wasn't the same.

"Probably not. But I let the agent think there was only one Christian standing there. I listened to the customers cheering while the agent put handcuffs on the guy. I didn't say anything. And that's just one thing inside me, and … compared to a lot of things, it's … well, small."

"I have more too," Violet whispered.

"Well. There are things inside everybody. Even after God forgives us. I don't know if they're supposed to be gone or not. I know for God, they are. But for me, there's still … a stain of them."

"Do you know what Lee's inner things are?"

The quiet stretched out like their shadows, until he said, "Some of them."

Those were what Violet had to pray for. And Austin's, too. That he'd left his sisters at home—that was one thing he felt the stain of inside. She needed to learn more. The more she knew, the better she could pray. And … well, he was Austin. Everything about him was worth knowing.

"Lee's going to talk to you soon, I think. After she … well, she would call it processing."

A bird of hope soared in Violet's chest. Maybe Lee was processing the Bible and would talk to Violet about it. Marcus's tone didn't leave room to ask, so Violet said, "I'll wait."

"Thanks."

She leaned her head against the bark and let herself remember a night she'd huddled against a tree at least the size of this one, having run from a half-lit country store. A night she'd hidden and waited for the ruining of lives. She'd never be so stupid again. So young.

Minutes passed. Marcus's chin dipped toward his chest. Violet should go, let him sleep here in the sun if he wanted to. She drew her knees up to stand.

His hand jerked, struck the paper plate. Potato salad and beans spilled over the grass. A breath shuddered into him.

"Hey," Violet said. He didn't look at her.

He probably wanted her to leave him, but she couldn't yet. She wrapped her arms around her knees and watched from the corner of her eye while he pulled in another breath. Should she say more or stay quiet?

"I keep doing that," Marcus said. So flat, the voice didn't sound like his. His hands curled, pulled into his lap.

She scooted away from the tree to face him and sat cross-legged. She waited.

"Falling asleep." Still flat, but now he glared at his hands.

Violet reached back to yesterday, a conversation with Lee about what to expect. "It's called convalescing."

His glare cooled as his forehead crinkled.

"You know, getting better. You heal while you sleep."

He shook his head. Opened and closed his fists a few times, old scars stretching over his left knuckles, new sharpness to his wrist bones.

"Marcus?"

He met her eyes, unblinking. Before he'd dozed off, he'd been having a real conversation with her, words falling as easily as they ever did from Marcus. Now he seemed lost. Violet propped her elbows on her knees, her chin in her hands, and held his gaze.

"I can promise you this—Juana won't be offended if she comes outside and finds you sleeping. And neither will anybody else."

Another head shake, and distance rose behind his eyes. He blinked and it was gone, his focus on her again. He was her brother, safe and steadfast, but there was more to him now, more in his head, and she had to remember that for as long as he needed her to.

"You've got to stop that," he said.

"Um ..."

"Trusting."

"Trusting Juana?" He wasn't making sense. Violet tucked her hands under her thighs and leaned closer, as if a few inches could help her understand.

"All of them."

"Marcus." She didn't try to smooth the tremble from her voice. "You ate spaghetti and meatballs with them last night. You slept here, and you were safe."

"I didn't know then."

"Know what?"

"Constabulary. Here."

"They're still our family. We can trust them."

"No."

He couldn't mean it. Violet folded her arms over her chest but kept her eyes locked on his. She waited for him to take it back, qualify it somehow.

He didn't.

"This is why you didn't tell them who you are."

No denial. No response at all. In the fusion of their gazes, something passed between them—an acknowledgment that she wasn't going anywhere. But what could she say? If he refused to trust people who'd done nothing to him, then he didn't trust an ex-spy who'd gotten him arrested, whether she'd meant to do it or not.

He sat watching her, silent and still. A crease formed between his eyes. Lee would know what he was thinking. Violet couldn't begin to guess. She huddled closer to the tree, threw out a prayer, and imagined it floating up through the branches above them, into the cloudless Texas sky. *Jesus, help me help him.*

Talk? Sit quietly with him? What was she supposed to do? A long sigh poured out of her, and Marcus cocked his head. Questioning.

"It's just …" She shook her head. "I think you're wrong about them. But how am I supposed to convince you when I'm not any better than they are?"

In fact, she was worse. Her stomach panged. Maybe she should go.

"No," he said. "You're you."

"Yeah." *Just me.*

"I mean …"

She wrapped her arms around her knees and waited for him to explain. His eyes wanted to tell her something, but the words seemed trapped in his head. Certainty shrouded Violet. Deep down, Marcus was hurt more than anyone knew.

"Marcus?" She made her voice as gentle as she could. "Do you mean … you do trust me?"

Slowly, he nodded.

ACKNOWLEDGMENTS

Now it's April, and I've been a published author for seven months. Should it be real by now? It isn't. Except in moments like this one—trying to count all the people who deserve my gratitude along this beautiful road.

To *Found and Lost*'s advance reviewers who continue to offer time and enthusiasm and thoughtful reviews: Andrea, Corrina, Emily, Hannah, Jess, Jocelyn, Megan, and Melodie. And to everyone who told me they couldn't wait for Book Three.

To my author-friendly coworkers who don't roll their eyes when I am too excited not to share publishing news, and who are still reading and letting me know what they think of this story.

To Jordyn Redwood, author and ER nurse, for the medical consult on Marcus, especially the treatment of pneumonia and the prioritizing of physical injuries and neglect. And for putting me in touch with Tim.

To Tim Bernacki, PT, owner of Front Range Therapies Castle Rock in Colorado, for the medical consult on Marcus, especially details on MCL injury and rib displacement and anxiety pain. And for responding when I had even more questions.

To Jocelyn Floyd, for the new prologue, for friendship, and … are you still telling me to try meteors? I do think that has recently happened.

To Jess Keller, for frankness and friendship, for story feedback, and for psychological dissection of Jason Mayweather.

To Melodie Lange, for liking this book the most and approving of the romantic progress, and for friendship without masks.

To Andrea Taft, for the best bracelet ever, for being the first to call this one the most "intimate" book so far (I needed that word to see it clearly), and for constant friendship.

To Charity Tinnin, CPF (Critique Partner Forever), for wanting to protect Marcus from the world, for knowing what needed fixing in the last act, and for listening to me always.

To agent extraordinaire Jessica Kirkland, for forthright story feedback, industry savvy, determination on my behalf, and mutual trust.

To Nick Lee, for a third cover design that is the most beautiful yet.

To editor Jon Woodhams, for seeing everything and, in the process, teaching me how to write cleaner.

To the David C Cook team, especially Michelle Webb for answered questions and Renada Thompson for being constantly available and knowledgeable and gracious.

To my siblings Joshua, Emily, Andrew, and Emma, for being the lovely people you are. And special thanks to Emily for being a first reader of Haven Seekers, for plot feedback and melodrama alerts.

To my parents Bill and Patti, for everything I've already said. And for being proud of me.

To my Lord and God and Savior, for keeping Your hand on me and for every good gift You have showered on me lately. For making me a little creator within Your immense creation. Let my stories and my life sing glory to You.